PRAISE FOR CALCULATED

"A high-stakes YA tale of betrayal, revenge, and numbers... An enjoyable thriller with an intriguing, relatable protagonist."

— Kirkus Reviews

This delightful book will hook readers from the first page and have them longing for more."

— School Library Journal

"I can't think of a word good enough to describe this book. Masterful? Gripping? Addictive? Powerful? Perfect? Calculated is all of these things, and yet the words don't feel big enough, or strong enough, to encompass all that is contained within these pages. It is a thrill ride from start to finish, with so many twists and turns, you wonder how it could ever be wrapped up, only to have your mind blown at the end and your heart aching for the next chapter. Don't let another minute go by without reading this book."

— Chelsea Bobulski, author of
THE WOOD and *REMEMBER ME*

"Calculated is an intelligent thrill ride! In Jo Rivers, author Nova McBee has given readers a heroine who is mathematically gifted beyond what most can imagine, and somehow immensely relatable, even as her greatest skills are exploited by international criminals. Sleek and sophisticated, with dark secrets at every turn, Calculated is impossible to put down."

– Shannon Dittemore, author of
WINTER, WHITE AND WICKED

"In this gripping thriller, McBee balances high-stakes, page-turning action with a powerful exploration of revenge, justice, forgiveness, and love, as well as an inspiring heroine readers won't soon forget."
– Kimberly Gabriel, award-winning author of
EVERY STOLEN BREATH

"An intense and wonderfully complex thriller that kept me on the edge of my seat and turning pages!"
– Jessica Day George, NYT bestselling author of
SILVER IN THE BLOOD

"A cunning story of strategy destined to keep readers chasing resolution from Seattle to Shanghai."
– Jennifer Jenkins, author of the *NAMELESS* series and
TEEN WRITER'S GUIDE

"Fast-paced and suspenseful. A thrilling debut!"
– Stephanie Morrill, author of *WITHIN THESE LINES*

"Calculated is smart with plenty of page-turning action, and a brave heroine who is deeply relatable. The timely subject matter is heart-wrenching even as it inspires us to use our gifts to make a difference in the world. Twisty and original, this story will keep readers guessing and hoping to its pulse-pounding end!"
– Lorie Langdon, bestselling author of
DOON and *OLIVIA TWIST*

"Calculated is a fast-paced and thrilling story that will keep you reading long into the night. Its twists and turns will take you from Shanghai's glittering high rises to underground prisons and the plights faced by the characters who feel achingly real. An action-packed adventure with heart."
– Judy Lin, author of the forthcoming
A MAGIC STEEPED IN POISON

CALCULATED

CALCULATED

NOVA MCBEE

 WISE WOLF BOOKS LAS VEGAS

WISE WOLF
BOOKS

CALCULATED. Copyright © 2021 by Nova McBee. All rights reserved.
For information, address Wolfpack Publishing,
5130 S. Fort Apache Road 215-380 Las Vegas, NV 89148

wisewolfbooks.com

Cover design by Cherie Chapman

Paperback ISBN 978-1-953944-50-4
eBook ISBN 978-1-953944-00-9
LCCN 2020947844

First Edition: February 2021

For Bethany Zhu
&
For the Chengdu Crew—
and an era that impacted our lives forever

*"They say believing in infinity will ruin you;
make you long for impossible things;
a limitless world; even love that lasts forever.*

*If anyone asks what happened to me,
tell them I believed."*

— *JO RIVERS*

PROLOGUE

THE PRATT, SHANGHAI, CHINA

I planned to start by telling you my name, but that won't work. I've had too many. I don't know who I am, much less which name suits a girl like me. So I'll start by telling you what they call me. Double-Eight. Like the digits. *88.*

I live in China—no, living implies choice. I *exist* in China and my existence depends on my gift.

I don't believe in luck, but that's what people say I have. Of course, all they see is my ability to make millions of dollars at the drop of a hat, not the constant bombardment of numbers that rule my inner world.

I've learned to live with my gift, even maneuver in it, but if someone had told me how my life would turn out, I'd have opted for the fate of a sewer rat instead.

My mother, whose hands are clean of anything that has happened to me over the past two years, told me I had this rare gift for a reason. I remember her eyes shining brightly, gazing down at me. "You could change the world with your mind, Little Seagull." If only she knew what my mathematical genius was being used for. The shock might cause her to jump right out of her grave.

But she'd die twice if she knew what Dad and Mara had done. It almost makes me laugh—a girl who can predict almost everything around her, except the betrayal of her own family.

It's completely logical that I missed it. I loved them and love cannot be calculated or measured in numbers. It requires trust, which acts on unseen forces, not sound theory. It takes risks and sometimes we lose. In my opinion, it's easier to stay away from things like love.

People who don't see the world through a screen of equations often say love happens by chance. But accidents are a joke in my world of numbers. There's no such thing as coincidence. I'd be a fool to say my ending up here was left to chance.

But numbers, no matter how you calculate them, can never answer the question we all ask at some point, the one burning craters in my heart: *Why?*

Red—the only reason I'm not some *fengzi* rocking back and forth in a corner—says that each one of us is given a destiny. That the choice to walk in that destiny is also ours. He says I can go down in history.

But at seventeen years old, I have no future to speak of, let alone history to make. "So what do you do," I asked Red, "if your destiny doesn't turn out as you once thought it would?"

Red gazed at me with his dark piercing eyes and said, "That part, *qin ai de,* is up to you."

ONE
PAST: JOSEPHINE

ALKI BEACH, SEATTLE, WASHINGTON

My dad is going to kill me. I went and did the very thing he asked me not to do. It wasn't as if I planned it. I didn't wake up thinking, *Today I will defy my father.* Not at all, he's the best dad in the world—even if he did fire me without an explanation from his company three days before graduation, on the anniversary of Mom's death. Hopefully, he'd take my news as well as I took his.

I twisted the stem of a white lily between the pads of my fingers as I stared out into *my* ocean waiting for him to return. As always, my calculations keep me company.

A girl in green Nikes ran down the beach. From the footprints in the sand, I could tell that her stride is 4 feet, 8 inches, which means she was roughly 5'7" and over-striding by 3 inches. At her current stride, she would reach Alki Point Lighthouse in 15 minutes, 48 seconds. If she shortened her stride, she'd run faster and arrive 1 minute and 12 seconds sooner. But she wouldn't think about this, because she isn't me. She isn't a mental calculator. Numbers don't invade every aspect of her life and odds are she isn't fifteen years old and graduating with a PhD in Mathematical Economics.

Thirty-eight waves had rolled in during the six minutes and thirty-two seconds since dad left to buy ice cream—my compensation. *Why* he fired me, I had yet to discover.

Dad stepped out of the corner shop with two double-decker cones in his hands. Mint chocolate chip for me, peanut butter chocolate for him. Our usual.

The light at the crossing was red. He stood there, dressed in a suit, patiently waiting to cross. His hair, the color of dry driftwood, was loose and wispy. Since Mom died, he didn't comb or style it as nicely as he used to. He saw me and waved with his pinkie.

The light ticked down from forty-five seconds. Numbers streamed through my mind. At a speed of 1.5 miles an hour, with 89 steps to go, it would take less than 35 seconds for him to cross after the light turns green.

Green.

A seagull shrieked overhead. A familiar bitter-sweet sting pinched my stomach. Looking up, I followed the bird's descent into the salty waves below—seagulls always remind me of Mom.

Like me, Mom loved the Pacific Ocean. As often as we could, we took Dad's boat out and released a lily on the water to remember her. It was where we could still feel her.

After months, I'd finally trained myself to focus on good memories whenever Mom came to mind. Lily, my youngest sister, named after the flower Mom loved, had almost bounced back to normal but Mara, my older sister, had gotten worse.

When mom was alive, Mara was my best friend, my biggest fan. After mom died, she believed I was born to ruin her life. She claimed that because of my gift Dad did everything for me, placing her and Lily on the back burner.

It wasn't true, of course. But if you calculated the time and money Dad put into me—and I did—Mara's argument appeared valid. But what was I supposed to do about it? Stop being a genius? Yeah right. I already calculated the chances of that happening, and while it was possible for prodigies to lose their gift when they got older, it was also highly unlikely.

Dad plunked down beside me and handed me the ice cream cone. A troubled expression was wedged between his furrowed brows like a man caught outside during a storm.

"Here you go, *Little Seagull*."

I stiffened at the sound of the old nickname that Mom gave me. If I met his gaze, I might lose it and our talk would become a cryfest. I released a long breath and accepted the ice cream. "Thanks."

Dad bit off the top of his and said, "All right, I gave you my news, your turn. Spill it."

I licked at my ice cream, torturously slow. "Dad, before you explode with all the reasons I shouldn't do this, hear me out. I know you didn't want me to start working right after graduation, but I can't sit around doing nothing. Especially with Mara breathing down my neck every day. So, I've accepted a job…" And then I dropped the bomb…"with Prodigy Stealth Solution…in China."

He froze, looking icier than the ice cream in our hands. "Jo. How could you?" His face was visibly hurt. "You know how I feel about PSS," he grumbled in his serious tone. "They shouldn't be hiring kids. It's not right. It's dangerous. If anyone finds out what you can do…"

"PSS doesn't just hire kids. They hire *prodigies*, no matter how old," I said, more whiny than I intended. "It just happens that most of us are young."

PSS was a private think tank out-sourcing company, which drew on solutions from prodigies like me to solve all kinds of economic, agricultural, and political world problems. They operated secretly, to avoid drawing attention to the prodigies they employed. When they sought me out during my first year at Stanley, my family and I had to sign a confidentiality agreement just to learn more about them. Despite my father's outspoken dislike, I'd always been interested in the work PSS did. They did real things to help people.

Just like every other prodigious kid I knew, I'd always been expected to do something great. Most of us were shoe-ins for high paying jobs in very boring companies. Some were content with that, but not me. I wanted to know *why* I was born with this gift. Was it for the greater good or could I just use it to eat, drink, and be merry? Did it even matter?

I wanted what Mom said to be true, that I had this gift for a reason. But numbers could not prove it. So, working with PSS made sense while I figured out what I wanted to do with my life.

"How long is the job?" Dad asked in his get-to-business tone.

"Three to six weeks, max. There's an economic issue—stock related, they think—in the China Asia Bank. If it's not solved it could cause serious trouble for the markets around the world."

"They have economists for that."

"Not like me." I didn't have to remind him that the European Union used my theory to solve the last two economic crashes before Asia Bank stepped in to stabilize the world economy with the Chinese Yuan. "PSS thinks I might be the only one who can fix it." I paused, reexamining my strategy. Dad didn't care about the stock market or bank issues. He cared about me. I sighed. "Dad, no one is going to discover anything. I promised you I'd never tell anyone what I can do."

After my mom died, the house was as happy as a graveyard. Even Tails our cat walked around groaning for Mom. So I joined Dad at the office. It was there that I realized my untapped potential. In less than a year, Dad's company made more money than he'd or I'd ever imagined. So we made even more. It was thrilling for a while. But money wasn't as joyful as everyone thought; it couldn't bring back someone you loved. Eventually my gift frightened him. He worried I'd be taken advantage of. He made me promise that under no circumstances was I to tell anyone what I did there, not even my sisters.

"I know, sweetie. I'm sorry. I trust you." He pinched the bridge of his nose. "I just don't trust others and that scares me."

A month before graduation the phone had started ringing and it hadn't stopped—job offers, everything from professorships to government to private enterprise. My dad told everyone the same thing. *She's fifteen. Call back in a few years.*

But he was coming around. "Dad, PSS is not dangerous. It's a bunch of geeks getting together to do math. And no one knows about this job. PSS is totally confidential. I'll be escorted there and taken care of the whole time." I grabbed him by the chin and turned his face to look at me. "Come on. I want to be useful. Mom would have wanted me to go."

He sighed, staring at the waves crawling up the sand. Dad had met Mom in China. They'd both worked there in their youth. Dad said he stuck out like a sore thumb while Mom had nearly blended in. Dad had a strict Northern European background, but Mom was a mix of everything. I took after her. My hair was dark, a shade of brown that matched neither of my parents. My eyes were an undecided hazel. And I had one of those faces where, at the right angle, I could be from anywhere. It was the chameleon effect, which I quite liked.

A cold drip fell on my leg. I paused to inhale a mouthful of ice cream and secure the edges of the cone. Brain freeze ensued for the next fifteen seconds before I said, "There's another reason I want to do this. Mara. She needs a break from me...even if it's just for a little while."

His eyebrows furrowed. "Will you two ever act like sisters again? It's hard on Lily and on me. Your mom would've hated this division."

Mentioning mom was like pouring vinegar on an already open wound. But of course, he was right.

"So let's look at this trip as my way to keep this family together. You get alone time with Mara and Lily. Mara gets space and, you get to handle all the stress of the office by yourself. Seriously, Dad, bad business move firing me like that." I bumped him with my shoulder.

He let out a small, nervous laugh. "Fine. Go to China. But no matter what, don't tell anyone what else you can do."

"Deal."

He grew quiet and found my free hand. "I love you, Jo. You're worth more than millions of dollars. Remember that, ok?"

My heart melted just like the ice cream we were *not* eating. "Thanks, Dad," I said. "Now, can you tell me why you fired me?"

He crunched a bite of his cone. "It's complicated, sweetie."

"Dad, I am considered a genius." A sly grin plastered to my face. "Maybe I could help?"

He frowned. "I don't want you to worry about it, Jo. Everything will be fine," he said, an anxious look in his eyes. "How about this—after you return from China, we'll sail up the coast, as family, then I'll tell you everything."

He's lying, like many people do to cover up concerns, but I trusted him. He'd tell me soon enough. "You got it, Dad."

He looked at me with a strange smile, the one he

gives Lily when she'd soon grow out of something, like playing with dolls.

"You're growing up so fast, Jo. In just a few days, you'll walk away with a PhD. I can't hold on to you forever." His eyes welled up with tears.

My chest swelled. This was the most emotion I'd seen from him in months. "Dad, don't worry about me. I'm going to be fine. I know it."

TWO
PRESENT: DOUBLE-EIGHT

∞

THE PRATT, SHANGHAI, CHINA

In one week, there will be a kidnapping. Yours.

Red's last words pool in my mind. That was twenty-one days ago. When he promised the word "freedom" to me, he had never sounded so sure. And now Red—the light in my dark world—is gone. Dead. Zero odds of him returning, no matter what I factor into the equation.

My cabbage soup is cold, and the strong vinegar smell is making me sick, but I swallow the last few bites. In the Pratt, only fools turn down food. I push the empty bowl and chopsticks away just as Guard San's gravelly voice calls my name, an urgency in his voice not usually present.

"Double-Eight! Quick!"

What does Guard San want now? King's dirty investments, which he needs me to manipulate, have been finished for the day.

My body jolts towards the door of my cell, where the digits "88" are etched on the wall among a barrage of other mathematical notations.

I take a piece of chalk and strike a diagonal line across four straight ones and sigh. It's been 700 days since I've seen my ocean. Measured its waves. Calculated the tide. Smelled its salt.

700 days of betrayal.

Right now, that number means nothing compared to the abyss multiplying in my heart. Red deserved to die in peace, in his own home, with his own family. Not with me, on a worthless metal-framed bed in the Pratt.

I move mechanically as my mind drowns in a world where the name *Double-Eight* no longer exists.

Before Red died, he gave me a new name. Just once, I'd like to hear it spoken out loud. Maybe then I'd believe, like Red did, that I really could start over. Where I'd use my gift for something great, rather than ruining people's lives.

But as long as I'm imprisoned in these ancient rat-infested barracks, that will never happen.

A small chess piece rests in my jacket pocket. I take it out and rub my thumb over it. The pawn is small, the wooden carvings completely rubbed smooth. I put it back and button my pocket, wondering why it's so important. Something, call it a gut feeling, tells me my fate is tied to this old pawn.

"Double-Eight!" Guard San comes down the darkened hall just as I'm swinging open the iron bars. He's one of the main guards who supervise the Pratt. On the outside, Guard San is big, rough, and tiny scars mark his face. He is like a pit bull in a dogfight, but he's really not the hardened criminal people think he is. I gained his trust a year ago when I found him melted in a corner, babbling uncontrollably about a gambling debt, and losing his family. That one word—family—compelled me to help him.

He knew I'd been taken because of some gift with numbers, but he never knew how it worked and he still doesn't. It'd be like trying to explain Newton's Law of Universal Gravitation to a five-year-old. So, without explanation, I told him what he should do to save his family. Apparently, my advice worked, because after that, my cell was never locked, he started slipping fattier chunks of meat into my soup and the harassment from other inmates stopped.

Now, the lines in his ever-present scowl are deeper, like he's frowning, nervous. Did King, the boss of this clandestine operation, return in a bad mood and start wreaking havoc on everyone in his path?

"This way. Quick, before they—" His head snaps around at the sound of running feet. Two large men, judging by the heavy footfalls pounding down the tunnels.

"Who? What's going on?" I ask.

"Quiet," he says.

It doesn't take a genius to realize something's wrong. But I trust Guard San. He's kept his promise to protect me under King's order that I not be hurt. I'm far too valuable to King to be damaged.

Guard San's large hand holds my arm and leads me down a corridor where burning incense tries unsuccessfully to cover the scent of the latrine.

My chest constricts as I pass the room Red once

occupied. The simple bed is still covered with his raw wool mattress and thin cotton blanket. The cement walls are still marked with Chinese characters written in white chalk. His first words that dark night asking me to trust him still echo in my head, with my last words to him, begging him not to leave me.

Before the memory feasts at the barren table of my heart, I turn away and begin to calculate as I walk: cigarette butts littering the floor—nineteen. The number of seconds until we pass the fighting rooms—thirty-nine. The height and width of the tunnels—eight feet by ten. I also note San's pace is thirty percent faster than usual.

Finally, we reach a hallway I've only seen a few times. There's an exit up ahead to the right—one they never use.

I feel safe until we arrive at the crossroads in the tunnels, where the footsteps materialize into two tall men in dark suits and stop Guard San in his tracks.

Guard San spits out a curse and tightens his grip as the two men lead us to the left instead of right. He looks down at me, eyes full of remorse before he barks out, "King's office," like a command, loud enough for the whole Pratt to hear. It's not his usual voice.

My feet stick to the floor. *King's office?*

Negative numbers begin pulsing in my mind. I'm dizzy with probabilities. King's office is the end of the road. Prisoners are taken there when they have ceased to have purpose or function.

I look up at San, my eyes wide with disbelief. "Why? What have I done?"

His sad eyes tell me there's nothing he can do. He must obey orders.

Judging by the bend in the dank crossroads, there are seventeen feet until we reach the door. My mind breaks them down into inches, then millimeters, the size of my feet and how long it will take if I drag my feet instead of walk. I need time to think.

King must have discovered Red's plan to get me out and now he has to kill me. Someone learned the truth of who I am. Or a third possibility, much worse than anything else, *Madame learned I'm still alive...*

Maybe King's office is for the best. A final freedom—my true way home. I could forget the last two and a half years. Forget Madame, who took everything from me, then threw me like a bone with the meat gnawed off to King. I could close my eyes and maybe I'd find peace, silence. My family's voices wouldn't bleed in my ears anymore.

But somewhere, deep in my heart, Red's words are louder than my own. His song of redemption tugs at me, urging me to fight, to lift my head, to grab hold of my destiny—to walk in it. The destiny I thought I came here to find.

We reach the door, which is flanked by two men in suits. I've rarely seen Guard San show any emotion, but I swear his eyes fill with tears. His strong hand squeezes my arm gently, the same hand that handed me the key to my own cell and gave me authority in the Pratt. With one squeeze, San is telling me goodbye.

Because he knows, like I do, that those who enter King's office rarely come back out.

One of the men at the door shoves me inside, a billow of cigarette smoke swirling out. Behind the smoke are two men. Neither of them is King.

The room is small with only one desk and three wooden chairs, covered with old cloth cushions. The floor has a smoother kind of cement than the tunnels and there are no windows. A dull bulb dangles from a thin wire and shines enough light to make out two faces and the dust gathering in the corners.

An overweight man sits behind the desk, sipping a clear liquid out of a glass the size of his small finger. He wipes sweat off his bald head with a napkin. The Buddha belly, hanging over his belt, does not fool me. I've seen him in action before. He's trained to take down a charging ox if he has to: Bo Gong.

The bottle behind him is glass, decorated with a golden emblem shaped like a dragon devouring a lion. It's very expensive, used for special occasions. Not the typical white liquor seen in the Pratt and by the look on his red face, it's strong too. I'm not sure I want to know the reason for this celebration.

Bo Gong nods to me. I dip my head in automatic response.

I haven't seen Bo Gong since the first year I was brought here. He's always stumbling in to someone else's private business and making money off their life spinning into utter chaos. In my case, I can either thank him or hate him. He's the reason I "work" for King instead of residing at the bottom of the Yangtze River, as Madame paid him to do. As soon as I understood King would spare me if I produced great sums of money, I succumbed to life in the Pratt.

The other man wears an expensive suit cut close to his long, thin frame. One single *moli* flower, or jasmine, hangs from his lapel. I've never seen him before and he's not smoking or drinking. His face isn't hard and unforgiving like the other men I've seen come and go from this place. No, this man is nervous. He's a fish in the wrong pond, but he's taking a good, long look at me too.

"Double-Eight, the Pratt's lucky girl," Bo Gong says, "How've you been?"

I huff a laugh so thick with sarcasm I might choke. "Living the dream, obviously. The Pratt's so lovely this time of year."

The Pratt is what King, or *Wang*, in Chinese, calls his *Palace*. The property once harbored the old port buildings, which are mostly vacant now. Underneath the Pratt lies a valuable secret—endless, ancient tunnels stretching up to two miles. It's also a convenient place to hide the criminals—and occasionally unlucky people like Red and me—that he blackmails into working for him. Life in the Pratt was simple, work for King or risk your own life or the life of someone you love.

Bo Gong laughs as smoke seeps from his mouth. "You've grown up, I see. You finally speak."

My feet rub against the dank, gray cement oozing with bitter cold. "What brings you back?"

"The escape you have been planning."

My smile fades, but Bo Gong's grows wider.

"While you have been doing that," he continues, "we have been planning your death."

The word *death* falls on me like a ton of bricks.

My ocean. My vow. Red.

Jiche! King knows. How did I fool myself into believing that I could have a new life after everything that has happened? I scoff, shake my head. Red almost had me convinced.

Of all the times I calculated my own death, it never went down like this. Is dying well the only thing left to do? I look at the men in front of me, but fear doesn't plague me like I thought it would, instead confusion spreads like a disease. The calculator inside me produces positive numbers, swirling like a tornado around Bo Gong.

Bo's completely relaxed and tipsy, pouring another drink, a smirk on his face. The man next to him looks terrified, clutching the edge of his suit jacket. For men about to carry out a death sentence, they should be a bit more vigilant. But then again, nothing King does is predictable.

The thumping in my heart explodes to my limbs. I have experienced adrenaline before, but this time it's different. It's calculated. My odds are good. If I act now, I can survive. I must. For Red.

Something snaps within me. All of Red's faith, his love, his lunacy comes alive in me—I take hold of his words: that I'm a new person, commander of my own destiny.

Without further thought, a scream rips out of my throat as I lunge through the air. Like a cat in a room with two dogs, I become someone I don't even know. Fierce. Bold.

The years of people pushing me into a corner are over; I won't go without a fight.

THREE
PRESENT: DOUBLE-EIGHT
∞

THE PRATT, SHANGHAI, CHINA

A chair crashes to the floor. My fist flies wildly into the thin man's nose and blood begins to flow. I scratch and grab at anything I can but before I know it, Bo Gong has hold of both my shoulders. He drags me off the man with as little effort as it would take to remove a toddler. He secures both my arms and legs in his, throwing my face to the ground until I stop struggling. Bo Gong's laugh rings in my ears.

"Good show," he says. "It'll be more believable this way. But, lucky girl, this is the last man you want to hurt."

I'm panting, looking at the man I hit in the face. "What are you talking about?" I snap.

With one hand, the thin man pinches his nose while he holds his head back. His other hand wipes away the blood.

Bo Gong releases me, stands, and pulls the chair

out for me. "Sit. This isn't the way we are going to do things."

At first, I hesitate. "What? You're going to torture me first?" I spit some blood on the floor. I think my tongue is bleeding. I must have bitten it when Bo Gong threw me down. I'm sure, too, that my eye is swelling.

"Ha," he grunts. "Just sit, would you?"

"Please, please," the hurt man insists as he stands up. There is a gash on the bridge of his nose. The blood has run down onto his suit and tie. They might be ruined for good.

The man glances at Bo Gong as if to ask whether it's safe to sit down next to me. Bo Gong smiles like he is enjoying whatever is happening here. The man sits.

Crap. A moment ago, this man was my death sentence and now by the look on Bo Gong's face it's more likely that he's my ticket out. What has the Pratt turned me into?

"My name is Chan Huang Long," he says quickly. He's still pinching his nose. He sounds nasally and ridiculous, but I'm stuck on his name. I've heard it before. Everybody knows this man.

"Why are *you* here?" I ask, calculating the odds of one of the richest men in Asia coming to me. He couldn't possibly need my *services.*

"I know it's unusual to have a meeting like this," he says, his voice straining to sound calm. "No one likes talking about death, especially one's own."

"I've died twice already," I say. "This time shouldn't be too hard."

We size each other up in silence. Apparently, Chan has never been *below* King's palace. He tries to hide his disgust at my appearance, without success. My clothes are faded and dirty and reeked of mildew, smoke, and sweat. King's men wouldn't even notice. Everything reeks in the Pratt.

He is also sweating and more nervous than I would expect from such a powerful man.

"You don't work with King, do you?" I ask.

King plays the role of an Import-Export businessman perfectly but anyone really looking at him could see something is off kilter. Half of King's meetings take place at night in the vacant Pratt buildings. He has an incessant nervous twitch, looking to the right and then the left, over his shoulder. His entourage looks like they've been plucked from the International Most Wanted list. He's rich, though he only allows a few private clients to come to the port, and his *cargo* is never seen. Few people have any idea what King specializes in, either that, or they don't dare ask.

I know the truth. He's a gangster, a lackey for Madame, her second in command in one of the largest criminal rings in the world. She chose him because of his connections to the Shanghai International Port. His smuggling, gambling, embezzling, and brothels, which he runs for Madame, are spread across Shanghai, China, and the rest of Asia.

"No. I have come for you." He takes the handkerchief passed by Bo Gong to clean the blood from his face. "To bargain for your freedom."

Did Chan Huang Long just say *freedom* or did I imagine it? Does he know who I am?

Red. He came through—but with Chan Huang Long? Red had his secrets, but hiding his acquaintance with the richest man in Asia? Something's not right. Chan wants something from me. They all want *something.* But this time, I want something too.

"Kidnapping won't work," Bo Gong jumps in. "Death got you in here, death will get you out."

The billionaire looks up at Bo Gong. "Can I talk to her alone for a moment?"

Bo Gong nods calmly. "I'll see to the arrangements." Then he eases out of the room.

I nearly choke. Chan *is* rich—because his money is talking very loudly right now. Meeting me must have cost a pretty coin and buying Bo Gong far more. But asking to see me alone can only mean one thing. A deal within a deal. The rich always have their own agenda.

Chan folds his hands on the wooden table and takes another long look in my direction. His eyes make me sad, like I'm staring into a painting of only blues and grays. There's fear there too, I suppose from the Pratt itself. Wickedness hangs in the air like a tangible mist. Even after years, it still makes my skin crawl.

"How long have you lived in China?" he asks.

"You call this living? Ha!" I say.

He grunts. "American?"

I'm silent, calculating. Men in the Pratt have forgotten which country I'm from. Even I've forgotten. Besides, I'm not sure how much I want to say. Apparently, my fluent Mandarin doesn't mask my *laowai* face. Red obviously told him about me, but I'll keep him guessing.

"How old are you?" He tries a new question. "The guard told me you have been here for over a year, which means whatever education you had is outdated."

"Nice observation," I say, my face hard. "What did you expect to find in the Pratt?"

"Someone older. You look like a kid."

I laugh. "What do you want?"

"Red told me about your special *talent*," he says bluntly.

My face tingles as I shake my head. "He'd never tell you that."

"I wouldn't be here if he hadn't."

Red knew me better than anyone, knew what I wanted. Playing genie for another power monger isn't it.

"I'm not looking for a job," I say.

"Don't you want to get *home?*"

The word *home* pricks at me like it's a gift wrapped in thorns, or a beautiful glass full of poison. He says the word like it's bait. But I'm not that thirsty or that stupid. He'll have to offer me something better than that.

"I won't do for you what I'm forced to do for King, not even for freedom."

"This is a real job. I will pay you, *well*."

Huh. If Chan was anything like King, this conversation would be over. But he is bargaining, which means calling his bluff will be easier than I thought. I've got to play this guy just right if I'm going to come out on top.

"Not interested," I say, stalling. "I've had my fair share of dirty money."

"Not all men with money are dishonest," he says, his eyes squinting.

"What about you, Mr. Chan?"

"That's not fair. I'm my only witness. Unless you count Red, who set this up." His eyes keep steady on

mine. "Business is business, however. I'll pay the 20 million to get you out, plus five million to fix my company."

"Pocket change," I smirk. "I can make that in
an hour."

"How? Red didn't tell me that part."

"I bet you'd like to know. Most crooks do. Although they're not smart enough to understand it even
if I tried to explain." I expect him to stand and leave
the room, taking my ticket out of here with him. I'm
about to recall my bluff, but he sits there calmly even
though I'm sure I've offended him.

He watches me. I inwardly groan at my own bad
attitude. I'm treating this man like King. Where is the
girl I once was? I used to want to help people. I was
never so hard-boiled.

Chan takes out his wallet. I assume to offer me more
money, but instead he shows me a picture of a woman.
"Let her be my witness that I do not cheat on women
or in business."

"Who's that?"

"My wife." His eyes flick toward the flower in
his lapel.

"I'd like to hear that from her own lips," I snap,
doubtful after what I've seen in the Pratt.

"She's dead." His voice drops an octave like the
frown on his face. I don't miss the emotion he tries to
hide. "But my love for her is not. My business was built
from the ground up. I worked hard. Fought hard."

"Then how did you get here?" I say.

"I don't deal with criminals if that is what you
are implying. Red made the arrangement knowing
Bo Gong would help, for the right price. I am not

breaking any laws, considering this place isn't even supposed to exist."

So, he knows what the Pratt is. "What's your connection to Red?" I ask.

He drops his eyes. "He was a dying man I made a promise to."

He's lying. There's more, but he doesn't want to tell me.

Chan hardens as I suspect he does in a business meeting. "Look, girl. I came here because I was told *you* are honest. You obviously need my help and it turns out I need yours."

I'm about to say something smart when I see it. Chan Huang Long is desperate. There's something wrong. Regardless of what he's not telling me, we're not dealing with small matters on either of our sides. The stakes are high. His billions and my freedom.

"What's the problem?" I ask.

"I'll show you everything when you are out." Chan's fidgeting again. He glances at his watch. He does not want to be here any longer than he has to be. "I made arrangements. Tomorrow you will be free. Ten percent of everything you make for me will be yours. I'll provide a house for you."

In the year Red took me under his wing, not once did he betray me by telling anyone my secrets. Nor did he do anything without a purpose. If Red sent Chan, it's my safest bet. Right now, all I need is to get out of here and make a lot of money. And Chan's handing it to me on a platter. It may not be the destiny my mom had in mind, but it's a start.

I just need a bit more.

"Forty percent," I say. "After I solve your problem, I'm gone."

"Never," he says. "No one in my company will possess nearly half. Twenty. Besides, I am only taking the word of an old man. I haven't seen what you can do. And I am paying your way out of here."

"Ask King why I'm here. Or Bo Gong. They know what I can do. And you want—no—you *need* what I can give you. Forty or no deal." My arms fold across my chest. He doesn't have my motivation. I want my life back.

His hands shake, a nervous twitch of his forefinger rubbing over his thumbnail. It's clear I have the upper hand though I still don't understand why.

"Look," he says, his fingers fiddling with the flower, "something terrible will happen if…"

I stop him. "Look around us, Mr. Chan," I say, leaning over the desk, getting in his face. "Do you think I don't know about terrible?"

The billionaire looks disturbed and I don't even tell him the worst part.

"Forty." I hold his gaze. He could be somewhat honest, but my gut tells me not to budge.

He turns his head and cracks his neck. He's sweating more than before, but his will is breaking—something, I suspect, that does not happen easily.

"Okay," he relents, touching the tissue on his nose. "Only until the problem's solved, then it is over."

We shake hands.

Chan pulls back and rubs a finger over the swollen, now purple part of his nose. A brief stillness follows as everything sinks in. He has just signed over a large portion of his company's profits to me, while I'm trying to comprehend freedom and a life outside these walls.

Everything Madame started 700 days ago could come to an end. The thought buzzes across my mind like a wasp ready to sting. I could finally stop her. Fulfill the vow I made to Red. To right the wrongs. To start over.

"So," I say, breaking the silence after thirty-three seconds. "How will you get me out?"

FOUR
PAST: JOSEPHINE
∞

**UNIVERSITY OF WASHINGTON,
SEATTLE, WASHINGTON**

When I was five years old, Mom invented a game to play whenever the numbers overwhelmed me. We called it Seagulls. It started one day when I was watching the birds on the beach. I really wanted to fly. Mathematically, I knew why birds could fly and I could not. But as a child, knowing the odds of everything you could and could not do severely dampened normal playtime. The odds were clear. No matter how hard or fast I flapped my arms, or how light I was, or how windy of a day, or how long I practiced, I'd no sooner fly than the bench I sat on.

I buried my face into my mom's chest and cried. "It's impossible, Mom."

She lifted my chin, her eyes blazing into mine. "Forget the odds, Jo. Numbers will never define you or what you can do," she said. "Close your eyes. Just imagine you can fly. See? We're seagulls right now."

I squeezed my eyes shut, blocking out the numbers as best as I could. I let the salty wind rush over my face, arms, and legs. Soon I felt it, clouds were under me, along with waves and sand. There were no numbers there to stop me. I was in the air, soaring. Free.

I wish I could tell Mom that I still played that game from time to time. That I played it now in a stadium of a thousand faces locked onto the stage for one reason. Me. A fifteen-year-old girl prodigy earning her PhD.

After sitting for twenty-eight minutes and five seconds, it was my turn to speak. I brushed my long brown hair over my shoulder and stood.

I picked up my gown and crossed the stage as Dean Storr announced, "Josephine Rivers."

The purple and gold mortarboard sat upon my head a bit unnaturally. My classmates, beside me, fit the part, but I did not. They'd earned this degree over many years of hard work. Me? Less than a year. But then again, they weren't writing algorithms at age seven.

Harvard was the first to explain my acute aptitude to estimate hundreds of variables and probabilities among things going on around me. Unlike other math prodigies they'd studied, where solving equations seemed merely to tickle their world, the mathematical lens through which I saw *defined* my world. Apparently, that made me a hot commodity, which was why my decision to secretly work for Prodigy Stealth Solutions was a big deal.

It wasn't for them; it was for me and Mom.

My father's words about being confident reminded me to straighten my back, raise my chin, and ignore the *woots* in the audience. A line of sweat trailed down my back. I pulled a handwritten paper out of my pocket and spoke into the mic.

After my speech and more applause, I focused on Dean Storr as he distinguished me from my fellow classmates.

"Our youngest graduate in over one hundred years...because of her contributions, our understanding of fields such as differential equations, economics, and computer simulations have increased significantly..."

As Dean Storr spoke, a woman who stood off to the side of the stage caught my attention. I had seen her once before. She was stunning. Impeccably dressed. Her hair was a striking dark red and her lipstick matched it perfectly.

She was at my interview for the Stanley Department. She shouldn't have been there. She wasn't a professor or a judge. By mistake, she had slipped in and here she was again.

For a brief second, we locked eyes. Negative calculations link the distance between us.

If people saw the world through my eyes, they'd see that odds were calculated, that numbers slid our days together like puzzle pieces—which meant, if I had seen her twice already, the odds were I'd see her again. The unease knotting in my stomach told me I wasn't sure I'd like that.

After the ceremony, I was ushered into an elegant room. My eyes darted from the recently polished hardwood floors to the six bookshelves lining the walls, to the glow of the crystal chandelier twenty-two feet above me and finally to the boy every girl in our economics class referred to as '*Surfer Sam*' because of his perfect tan, wavy blond hair and eyes that knock you down like waves in an ocean.

Samuel Davis stood with the older graduates who were mingling around tables draped with white linen holding cheese and fruit and wine that I was too young to legally drink.

A familiar voice hissed in my ear. "You should be celebrating. Not pining for *Surfer Sam*." Britta, another prodigy from PSS came up to hug me. "Anyway, don't you have a thing with that math-boy from your blog?"

"Britta," I say, happy to see her. "Thanks for coming. *FYI*, I shut down that blog a long time ago. Besides, I never even knew that boy's real name or saw his face. Sam is smart, gorgeous and in front of me."

"Your brain might be an adult's but all Sam sees is that we're still not even old enough to drive. Come on," Britta said, tugging my arm.

Unfortunately, she was right. I'd calculated Sam's movements and mannerisms. It was safe to assume that he didn't daydream about me the way I did about him—a fact I wish I didn't know. At least once in my life I wanted to sit next to a boy and wonder if he'd grab my hand, without numbers foretelling the possibilities. I wanted to live in the moment and believe I could actually change the possibilities around me.

We walked over to another table designated for non-alcoholic beverages and ladled some pink punch into a glass. It was sweet like strawberries and lemonade. Soon a group of graduates gathered around me.

"So, tell us, what will Jo Rivers do with her life?" they asked.

Ugh. I dreaded these questions. Was it so hard to believe that a genius didn't know what she wanted to do with her life? With my eyes, I begged Britta for help, but she shrugged her shoulders, mouthed '*sorry*', and darted off to greet another friend from our department.

I smiled at the crowd. "I'm weighing possibilities right now," I answered. Obviously, I didn't mention Prodigy Stealth Solutions. Only my family was allowed to know. "My dad says I need to take some time off. Travel maybe." Not exactly a lie.

A boy from the university newspaper approached me. "So how does it feel to be a math prodigy?"

After getting asked this on average 20 times a quarter, I still didn't know how to answer. How did I explain that numbers were tattooed on my brain, like books on a shelf, forever there at my disposal?

"Don't know how it feels *not* to be one."

We jumped into small talk. Within the span of three minutes this guy said "like" a total of 26 times, made four grammatical mistakes and cursed twice. But who's counting?

A girl from the Physics department cut in. "Is it true you memorize numbers the first time you see them?"

Yes, and more, I thought. It was hard to explain that with each new theory, dimension, or phone number, my library increases. I might come across as proud, or nerdy—or worse, boring. So I didn't try. Instead, I just shrugged it off.

"We all have gifts," I said, generously. I thought

of Dad's knack for good ideas, Lily's brilliance on the piano, Mara's knack for sailing. Mom used to say it wasn't which gift you had, but how you used it.

Above the chatter, a familiar voice squealed, "There she is! Jo!"

"Excuse me," I said, sneaking out of the circle that had formed around me. "My family's arrived."

A bouquet of sandy brown curls bounced toward me. Lily wore a blue satin dress and mom's pearl necklace. Beside her my father, looking weary, smiled proudly, and held two thumbs up.

Surprisingly, Mara came too. Instead of wearing her usual smug expression, tonight she looked different... she was as pale as a ghost.

"Congrats, Jo." Lily linked arms with me. "That was so cool back there, watching you on stage. Your speech was beautiful. I want to remember it *forever.*"

"Thanks, Lily." I kissed her forehead. "One day I'll watch you up on stage, too. Just keep practicing that piano, ok?" I took out the folded piece of white lined paper with my messy handwriting and handed it to Lily. "Here, my speech," I said, winking. "Keep it *forever.*"

She pressed the paper against her chest and beamed. "I will," she said.

If anyone would take those words to heart, it was her.

My father hugged me. "You make a father very proud, Jo. I wish your mother were here to see you."

A pang stabbed my chest—once, twice, three times. She should have been here. She believed in me more than anyone. He grunted, like he shouldn't have mentioned her.

"Thanks, Dad." I inhaled the woodsy scent of cologne and rested my head on his chest. His silk tie was soft on my cheek.

A voice, dripping with artificial sweetness, pulled me back. "Congratulations, Josephine. Marvelous ceremony. Even though we were sitting for a really long time." Mara shot me an evil glance that said, *if you say it, I'll kill you.*

What she meant was if I translated her "really long time" statement into an exact answer of 43 minutes and 11 seconds. That was the annoying difference between me and *normal* people. In my world, there was no "really long time". I knew exactly how long everything lasted. Mara hated when I corrected her *time*, but how could I not when she and others played the 'be back in five minutes' card and didn't return for twenty?

My father went to get some refreshments. Lily followed him. Mara stayed back, pursing her lips, arms folded across her chest.

"I'm glad you came, Mara," I said, hoping an effort of kindness would appease her for an hour.

"Sure, you are," she scoffed. "Well, I heard about your trip. Lucky you. The first one—as always—who gets the dream."

It didn't surprise me that even on my graduation day Mara couldn't shackle her jealousy. I refused to let her sour this evening like she had the past year of my life, but the sting of her words hurt deeper than she knew.

We used to be so close. When we were young, she never cared that I was smarter than her, she only cared that we were sisters. I adored her, the way now Lily adored me. I'd do anything to get our relationship back.

I turned away, fighting tears, and bumped into Dad.

"What's wrong, Jo?" he asked, reading my face.

"Nothing," Mara answered for me, faking a sniffle. "We're just emotional about Josephine leaving tomorrow."

"Right," I said, eyes to the ground. Why was I protecting her? Mara needed correcting on a regular basis. But I couldn't bring myself to do it because Dad's hope that we'd act like sisters pooled in his eyes. My promise to him did too. Besides, Mara was my sister. I loved her. "While I'm gone, all that's mine is yours, Mara."

"Aw, you'd do that for me?" Her voice was sarcastic.

I stared her right in the eye, already willing that with distance our relationship could heal. "I'd do anything for you, Mara."

Her eyes glistened before she smirked, and my father wrapped his arms around us both.

"It's about time you acted like sisters," he said. He raised a glass of sparkling wine. "And now my turn. To my daughter and her bright future."

The number of glasses chinking registered as we toasted each other. Then one by one, students, professors and other notable faculty came to congratulate me. My family dropped into the background.

Behind them all, Mara stood there looking lost. I hope she knew that what I said was true. I'd do anything for her, for them. Now that Mom was gone, it was up to me to keep this family together.

Too bad numbers couldn't help me with that.

FIVE
PRESENT: DOUBLE-EIGHT
∞

THE PRATT, SHANGHAI, CHINA

Bo Gong walks into the room as my question to Chan about how they plan to get me out of the Pratt is barely out of my mouth. "Early tomorrow morning my personal guard will discover your dead body in your cell."

"Why tomorrow?" I ask.

"Before dawn fewer people will be watching. King never comes in the morning."

"How will I die?"

"Suicide by poison. King gave you an ultimatum. You chose death. We will tell him Red slipped you poison before he died—out of mercy. After we dragged you into his office today, no one will question the story. Especially with your cute little scuffle."

I don't like the idea of death being the only way to solve a problem and I don't want people in the Pratt to think I'm a coward. Not after all I've done to prove myself and gain their respect. Some even consider me an *ally* now. It must be done another way.

"No. Tonight. Now," I say. "Tell them I fought back—until the end."

"What?"

"Now, or nothing," I say. "Tell King whatever you want but leave me with my honor."

Bo Gong considers the idea. Honor is something all men try to protect, criminal or not. "We do have blood on the floor thanks to your friendly greeting to Chan. It could work. But you'll have to leave with me. Not Chan."

Bo Gong pulls out a gun, opens the barrel and removes the bullets. He fumbles in his desk and pulls out what look like more bullets, only bigger and reloads the gun. I'm not familiar with guns and I don't like them. I'm not sure what he's doing. But my eyes widen—what does a real gun have to do with my 'fighting until the end' idea? Does he need to show people a body?

"Blanks," Bo Gong says, answering the question on my face. "I can't shoot a real bullet in here. We will need it to be loud enough for several prisoners to hear it. Guard San is near the door. He will be the first to tell people. He knows nothing of our plan. Poor soul, you have bewitched him into thinking you're a saint."

"What do you think of me?" I ask.

"You're not who Madame said you were. Old Red trusted you. That counts for something." His eyes linger on me. "Whoever you are, you've earned another death and resurrection. Lucky you."

"Why are you doing this?" I ask him. In this world, double-crossing is to be expected. No one trusts anyone.

"Because tonight I'm dead as well," he says smiling.

"At least that is what the police report will say."

He leans forward, like he is about to share a secret. I lean in, hungry for it.

"I am getting out," he confesses. The dim light accentuates the wrinkles around his strained and tired eyes. "For good. By tomorrow morning I will be a citizen of Brisbane, Australia. My family and I will be long gone with the last large bundle of cash I need to complete the deal, thanks to him." He indicates Chan. "The only person getting double-crossed is King."

My chest swells. The plan is better than I thought. A penny turned over. Bo Gong is getting out of crime. Like Red says, it's better for a person's heart to change before the law changes it for them. Now I understand why the bottle of expensive liquor is here. Bo Gong sees me eye it and pours a shot for each of us.

"Here's to freedom. If you are ever in Australia, look me up—if you can find me. *Ganbei!*" He raises his glass, then throws his head back and downs the shot. I take the small glass in my hand. Why not? No one has ever offered me a drink before. I copy Bo Gong, shooting fast, in one fell swoop. The clear liquid ignites a trail of fire down my throat until it sets off a flaming bomb in my stomach. I cough, gag. *Ugh.* Why do they like this stuff?

Chan pops up from his chair. "So, tonight it is." He fidgets with his finger again. "Should I stay in the room, uh, for the, you know?"

"No. Leave now." Bo Gong scribbles down an address and hands it to Chan. "Meet here. One hour."

Chan nods and stands up, obedient and ready to be done with this.

Before he leaves, I catch his arm. "Sorry about your nose."

He shakes a hand in the air, as if to wave it away. "Forget it," he says, then he looks at me. "Red never told me your name."

I look at Chan before I open my mouth. Without a doubt, everything Red talked about starts now. *Pure gold does not fear the fire.* "My name is Phoenix."

Chan leaves King's office, closing the door behind him and a gunshot rings out. Double-Eight is dead. My new life begins now.

SIX
PRESENT: PHOENIX

∞

FRENCH CONCESSION, SHANGHAI, CHINA

Even after a shower at the small spa where we meet up
with Chan, I still feel dirty when the door swings open
to my new house. My black eye doesn't match the designer interior of the house, either. Shiny marble floors,
spotless white leather couches, and golden-framed
mirrors reflect the glow of chandeliers. I shrink and
hesitate to cross the threshold.

"Please, please." Mr. Chan waves me forward with
his practiced courtesy. "Enter, enter."

I slip my shoes off at the door, as custom requires.
The marble is smooth and cold against my bare feet,
making the house feel colder than it is. I grasp at the
thin black jacket I'm wearing.

Mr. Chan opens a cupboard holding white slippers
like I have seen in nice hotels, setting a pair before me.
I slip them on and compare Madame's hotel, where
removing shoes was also an expected civility, to the

Pratt, where if you took your shoes off there was no guarantee you'd get them back.

"We have always used this villa for important visitors," Mr. Chan says leading me further into the room. "As I promised, it is yours while you work for me. Rent free." He walks across the room, pointing out antiques and paintings and, of course, their prices.

Great. Feeling at home here will be as easy as relaxing in a dentist's chair. It's like walking through a photo in a Chinese *Vogue* magazine. Tall acrylic-painted vases and hand-painted scrolls decorate the front room. Silk carpets lay under ornate wooden furniture that is in mint condition even though it was most likely crafted a hundred years before communism ruled China.

"The whole property belongs to me," Chan says referring to the entire city block, formerly the Swiss Consulate, located in one of Shanghai's wealthiest areas, the French Concession.

When we pulled up at the front gate, it felt like we had left China and were entering Buckingham Palace. The gate alone must cost as much as the property. There were two rustic French villas on the estate, one very large and rusty pink, with white shutters and a large porch. The other, where we are now, was the larger one's twin, though much smaller. The two houses were separated by a very large manicured garden but connected with a path.

I stare out the window at blooming jasmine plants and young bamboo shoots in wonder. Am I really out of the Pratt? Nothing feels real. Certainly not this beauty around me.

At the back of the property sits a wooden dome

of sorts. Chan catches me eyeing it out the window. "What's that?"

"It's a pool house, small but clean. Use it whenever you like," he says. "We have twenty-four surveillance cameras around the gate. No one comes on your side of the property unless invited. Except the dog, occasionally." He continues explaining everything in the house—it has recently been remodeled, and there is a small cellar that contains tea that has been aging for more than twenty years, and on and on.

I stop listening because the pool reminds me of dangerous hands. I shudder like I do every time water comes to mind. I won't be swimming any time soon, or ever again.

"We are just across the path, if you need anything."

"We?" My whole body tenses. "You said your wife was dead."

"My son," Mr. Chan answers like it's a well-known fact that all of Shanghai is aware of but me. My muscles relax. "You will meet him tomorrow. He's interning for me now when he shows up." He grumbles the last part. "It's a program set up by his school. He's good with numbers like you. Now please excuse me. I will grab something in the back office, then leave you to rest."

He walks off, leaving me alone in a small castle, lost but curious.

Chan indicated the bedrooms were down the hall. I stop, take in all the dimensions of the rooms, and listen. No sound comes from the hall, so I wander in that direction to check them out.

A fragrance stops me in my tracks. It's subtle, but

sweet and fresh, a scent I know, making my heart swell nostalgically.

The scent becomes stronger as I turn the corner into the master bedroom. I stop by the door. A bedside table lamp is on and there's a vase of flowers next to it. *White lilies.* My mother's favorite. The last gift I set on the water for my mom before I was ripped away from my life.

I set my bag down and lean over the petals. This is my room. The smell intoxicates me, like she's here with me, like a sign that everything will be okay. A slight grin pushes my cheeks up.

Only I can't decide how they got here. Certainly, placing a vase of lilies in my room was not Mr. Chan's idea. I'd bet my life on it. Mr. Chan is all business. But maybe he has a maid or a secretary to think of these things for him.

Before I can sit down on the bed, Mr. Chan's voice calls from the front room. Following the hallway, I find him standing at the door with a briefcase he didn't have when we arrived.

"I am sorry we couldn't get new clothes for you tonight," he says hurriedly. "I'll have my secretary send for some in the morning."

"No, thanks." I'm done with other people buying my clothes. "I'll get my own."

"As you wish," he says. "Do you need anything else?" I shake my head. He opens the door. "See you tomorrow."

Seriously? One measly night to sort out my new life before I start work tomorrow? I sigh. Good thing I'm as eager to make money as he is now. While I've been waiting to get my life back, Madame's life has gone on long enough without justice.

"Goodnight, Mr. Chan." I close the door.

Even after locking all three deadbolts I still don't feel safe. There are more than 50 miles between the Pratt and here, but the enemies I've come to know aren't scared by distance, and locks don't stop them.

A faint buzz of traffic hums outside, an even fainter buzz of lights inside, but mostly, my new house is silent. The Pratt was never quiet. I wonder if I can adjust. Sadly, the Pratt had become some kind of twisted comfortable. At least there I was surrounded. Here I'm alone, without a clue what to do.

My body groans for rest, but my mind is too wound up to sleep, so I decide to look around outside to get a numerical calculation of my new home.

Back through the kitchen, behind the breakfast nook is a sliding glass door. It's unlocked. Does Chan always forget to lock the doors? I slide it open and a cool breeze rushes over me. The lights of the city sparkle in the distance.

I stare out at the garden full of manicured plants and trees. It's beautiful. My mother would have loved this place, her hands in the dirt, gardening. My sisters playing hide and seek back here. For a split second, I picture my dad mowing the lawn and how fresh cut grass smells. *Stop, Phoenix. You're only hurting yourself. Let them go.*

My throat tightens. Suddenly I don't want to be here.

Why couldn't Chan live in a luxurious high-rise apartment instead of a *house* with a *yard* and a *fence*? It's too close to the kind of house I grew up in. The thought pricks at me as I step on to the grass and it won't stop, the same way blackberry thorns catch on your clothes.

Calculations take over as I survey the yard. The beauty around me morphs into a series of equations, graphs, functions, and algorithms, measuring, mapping, and calculating every space and movement around me.

The yard becomes a blueprint of numbers. First, I note the square area of the yard then break down each section, measuring the distance from point A to point B. The grassy area, four lawn chairs and one table, to the patio—one hundred feet away. Next the tennis court to the basketball hoop—forty feet. The wooden dome, with another patio with two large green plants, four flowers in pots, and one small palm tree. Every tree now has a number. This is what people can't see in my brain.

It's like a radio always playing music in the background. An internal GPS navigating my every move, with no option to turn it off. My mind calculates a room's dimensions when I walk into it. Actions—the swing of an arm, standing or sitting. I don't simply see faces, but symmetry. A sunset is not merely pretty oranges and pinks on a horizon but a web of axis, rotations, and time zones. Don't even get me started on stargazing.

A branch snaps under me and I come to an abrupt stop. There's a light on inside the wooden dome.

Mr. Chan didn't come out here. He said no one would come over to this side. But two small torch-like lanterns encased in glass are burning brighter and a human shadow moves around inside.

Turns out I'm not alone here after all.

My mind jumps into hyper speed and numbers fly like sparks.

Within seconds I've configured three escape routes and three possible ways to defend myself with plant pots and gardening tools, but the numbers insist the shadow inside isn't threatening. It just moseys about slowly, unconcerned with me outside. I push the door open without a sound.

The room smells sweet again. More potted flowers are in the corner on a small table. Orchids.

The pool is steaming. Humidity wraps around me like a sticky blanket, even still, a shiver rushes over me at the sight of the water.

Bent down beside the pool a young man is working. He's wearing gray linen pants and no shirt. I don't blame him. It's like a sauna in here. His back and arms are lean, but strong and sculpted.

The boy, engrossed in his work, doesn't notice my arrival so I observe him quietly. He's older than me, but not by much—maybe 18? He can't be Chan's son because he's working on the pool. He must be a servant on the estate. Except why would a worker be on call so late?

The boy moves around, adding chemicals to the pool, pulling out different tools, and fidgeting with different valves on what looks like a water heater. He's light on his feet and his movements are controlled, precise. I recognize those movements. In the Pratt, men gambled on mahjong, cards and *fighting*. Game-fights, they called them. I've seen too many of those matches not to notice—there's an 83% chance this boy can fight.

After a minute, he packs up his tools. He takes a tee-shirt hanging on the side of a wicker chair and pulls it on. I back up, expecting him to leave, but he heads to the orchids. His fingers glide over their petals so delicately, so obviously delighting in them, that the numbers around him change. The lilies in my room come to mind.

Once he's finished, he turns and jumps at the sight of my could-be-but-not-quite Chinese face.

"Who are you? How did you get in here?" he says in clear, nearly flawless English. His voice is low, calm, and confident. "This is private property."

"I live here," I say in English. It sounds ridiculous to say since it's my first night here, but I'd rather twist the truth than give information to a stranger. "If you are done with your work you can go." My chest tightens. Why is the pool boy speaking to me in English? Why am I responding in English?

We stand there, eyeing each other until he lets out a laugh.

"You can't be my father's new employee." He takes a good look at me from head to toe, staring at my bruised eye and not-so-nice clothes. "She's not coming until tomorrow."

My chest releases a deep breath. He is Chan's son. "Change of plan and yes, I am her." The sound of my stuttering voice in English makes me feel small, young again.

"Huh," he says, still staring. "I was expecting glasses and gray hair, not..." he gets a funny grin on his face. "You."

Heat charges like an army to my cheeks as I meet

his eyes. I switch back to Mandarin, where I'm more confident, where Phoenix speaks. "*Chan yijing huijia le,*" I say. "He told me I was alone."

"Sorry if I scared you on your first night here. I'm Kai." He responds in English, disregarding my ploy to speak his language. "The repair guy was busy, so I fixed the water heater, changed the light bulbs, checked the gas. You know, just wasting my time on blue-collar work. My father hates it when I do menial labor." He smirks, but behind the jest, his stare is intense. He's gauging me. Few people have looked at me as deeply as he does now.

He's not what I expect from Mr. Chan's son. I'm tempted to distrust him even though I have learned that pigeonholing somebody can be deadly.

There's no trace of his father in the curves of his face. Most of his features must come from his mother, yet I feel as if I have seen him somewhere before. His dark eyes are big and round and soft. His strong jaw line complements his broad shoulders. Black hair falls into his eyes, messy. Numbers zip up and down his face pinpointing all of the imperfect symmetry and flaws, and yet his face is mesmerizing, and the way he stands there staring at me, so at ease with himself, makes me think he knows it.

"I should go." I head for the door.

"No, I'll go," he says, following me. "After I wash my hands and grab my things in the cottage, I'm gone. Won't come again unless called. Promise."

"It's fine. Uh, thanks for fixing the pool," I ramble, trying to smooth things over. It wasn't his fault. He didn't know I'd come tonight. But I do want him gone.

He turns out the lights and leads me through the garden and back through the small cottage's sliding glass door.

Inside, he turns to me. "What's your name?"

"My name is—is—" His stare lingers on me. It's distracting because his face...I've seen him, or the symmetry of his face before. Either way, I should respond, not stare. "Phoenix."

He walks closer, *too close,* stretching out his hand. "Nice to meet you, *Phoenix,*" he says in a low hum. "If you're new to the city, I can show you around or something..."

His hand, big and warm wraps around my small, cold one, igniting a small shock. The memory of him without his shirt returns.

I blush, quickly taking my hand away. "I've lived here for a while, but thanks."

Inside, he sets his tools on the counter and washes his hands at the sink. He's so familiar with the surroundings that are now supposed to be mine, it makes me uncomfortable, like I'm invading his space. Doesn't matter. I'll be out of here as quickly as I can anyway. Soon I'll find a place of my own.

"Groceries are already stocked," he says, drying his hands and motioning with his head towards the fridge. "I lived in America for a year during high school. Even though you speak Mandarin like a local, you still must like bread, milk, cheese, and butter – just like every other foreigner I know. There are also eggs and fruit."

As he lists the foods, my mind jumps to the Pratt. I'd fall asleep dreaming about bread and cheese and milk. Younger Chinese have started to eat these things, but they're not common outside of big cities and certainly not a household item in the Pratt. It took months to adjust to *soy milk*, and steamed *mantou*, and *rice porridge.*

When I realized how utterly impossible it was to be free, relinquishing the desire for the food I grew up on was one of the hardest things I'd had to do. Now here they are, a few feet away, but to take them so easily seems dangerous. Would Phoenix eat them?

"I prefer Chinese cuisine," I tell him dismissively.

His face mirrors mine and frowns slightly. He's put off by my haughty tone. "Fine," he says. "We can do more shopping tomorrow."

Ugh. I've been ungrateful. Rule number one: The Chinese always give "face" to another person, no matter what gift is presented to them. It could be dog food and you'd tell them it's your favorite.

"On the other hand," I say as an attempt to flip the situation, "it's been one year and ninety-seven days since I've eaten any of those things, except eggs."

"Wow." He stops to look at me as if I told a joke. "That's precise."

Too precise. Not sure how that slipped out. "What I mean is," I say, swallowing back embarrassment, "that I look forward to eating them. Thank you." My voice sounds rehearsed, but the corner of Kai's lip curves upwards anyway. I've managed to salvage the situation.

He doesn't continue talking about food and I'm glad. He doesn't need to know any more than his father has already told him. And I certainly don't need to make friends. I don't want any ties to this place. I want to forget it entirely when I leave.

As he walks toward the door, I calculate his route—the

length of space from the sink to the door and the angle he must turn if he goes around the table. Two routes he could take. If my prediction is right, he'll intentionally choose the way closest to me. If I do not move back at least one inch, our bodies will collide at the hips. The thought of him touching me again makes me squirm.

I step back, changing the variable in the room. He scoots past me without contact. I follow to let him out, reopening the three locks.

Before he steps out onto the small three-step porch, I stop him, curious to know if my predictions were right. "Who should I thank for the flowers in my room?"

The smile on his lips gives me my answer. "I heard somewhere that most girls, no matter how old, like flowers," he replies mischievously.

"Most," I reply because he's flirting and it's the right answer. "Thanks."

A flutter of warmth, like sunshine, shoots through me. It's a strange feeling, that warmth. It's connected to hot summer nights and a few distant memories of boys who used to smile at me. I instantly shut it down. That feeling wasn't always bad, but I don't like it. It's just another thing to figure out in my new life—that is, if I ever learn to trust someone again.

Our conversation appears to be over until Kai surprises me. "But you're not like most girls, are you?"

Twice, my cheeks have turned red without permission. The grin hanging on Kai's face tells me he's happy to have succeeded in making me blush. Again.

"What makes you say that?" I ask, pretending I'm not flattered and simultaneously alarmed.

"My father doesn't hire just anyone."

"I guess we'll find out." My hand drops down to my wrist, where I fiddle with my ragged hair band, not sure what to say. "Nice to meet you, Kai."

"Goodnight, Phoenix."

I close the door, head back to the master bedroom and collapse on the bed. The scent of lilies intertwines with thoughts of my mother and Red.

An ache starts in my heart and moves to my arms, but there's nothing to fill the void.

As sleep arrests me, I fight desperately to believe that I'm free now, but I know better. Freedom isn't just a physical thing.

Eventually I fall asleep and just like that, I'm on Madame's boat, *Secrets*, again. Another nightmare. The water turns crimson, the same color as Madame's lipstick, then she appears with a thousand ghosts.

I jolt awake in the middle of the night, sweating, panting, wondering where I am. I pull my knees up to my chest and soothe myself with a soft whisper. *You're ok. You're at Chan Huang Long's. She doesn't know you're alive.*

What's wrong with me? I promised Red I'd start fresh. Reclaim my gift to help people. To make the wrongs right. To end this.

But how can I ever live or love or trust knowing she's out there? Her face, her voice, what she does—*is doing*—will always haunt me. Another pair of dark eyes—warm, kind, and questioning my resolve, haunt me too. *What will you do about it?*

Stop her.

A new life is not possible in a world where Madame roams free.

SEVEN
PAST: JOSEPHINE
∞

PIER 51, SEATTLE, WASHINGTON

It's no wonder Seattle is nicknamed the Emerald City—especially in June. Miles of green hills and blue water surrounded all my favorite spots: The Space Needle, Gas Works Park and Seattle's Piers, where we were headed. Usually the piers are full of commercial and private boats and tourists eating fish and chips and drinking cappuccinos, but not today. The piers feel empty. There is hardly a seagull scavenging on the boardwalk.

Dad pulls over at the curb where Mrs. Zhang and Prodigy Stealth Solutions commercial boat will take me to a private airport up in Everett. A young, dark-haired man stands waiting with a sign that reads, **"Josephine Rivers."**

"Here we are," Dad says, getting out of the car to get my luggage from the trunk.

"Ms. Rivers? Mrs. Zhang is waiting for you." The

poor boy looks like he hasn't slept in a week. His face is pale and dark circles line his eyes. I want to ask if he got in a train wreck last night, but I don't know him well enough to joke like that. He probably just stayed out too late.

I nod. "Yep, that's me."

My family stands close around me. "I'll miss you," Lily says, squeezing my arm.

"I'll be back before you know it, Lilypad." I kiss her forehead.

"Call us when you arrive, sweetie." Dad hugs me goodbye again for the sixth time this morning. Lily joins in.

Mara peers down at me. For the first time in over a year, she embraces me. When she pulls back something flickers in her eyes that I don't recognize.

"Goodbye, Jo. Have fun."

"Thanks. Goodbye, Mara." I turn to the boy, who takes my luggage so I can adjust my backpack.

"Follow me."

We head down Pier 51. I'm familiar with this area. My dad's boat is docked here. Numbers bounce off the piers with conflicting equations.

Up ahead, when we should have gone left to the commercial harbor, the PSS representative takes a right. Equations—with negative outcomes—flutter in my gut like a bout of nausea.

Without thinking, my mind analyzes the boy. I calculate his shaking hands. His uneven stride. His alertness. The charts in my mind mirror that of a polygraph test—a man under distress, though I can't determine *why*. Maybe he's feeling sick?

We walk through rows of boats. The water shimmers with rainbow tints of gasoline. Gray clouds swirl in the sky. A ferry whistles in the distance.

"Excuse me," I ask. "Where are we going?"

"Almost there."

He doesn't look me in the eye. He has peered over his shoulder seven times in the last two minutes, checked his watch twice and glanced at my new backpack repeatedly.

"PSS wanted you to have the nicest boat there was," he adds.

More negative numbers. Predictions. He's lying. I should stop, run back the way we came. But I don't understand why I have these feelings.

The sick feeling deepens in my stomach as we walk out onto the harbor's docks towards the yachts.

We stop beside a fifty-foot schooner. *Secrets* is painted in red on the starboard. I log the boat's dimensions—numbers that forever will be tattooed in my brain—but I can't account for the negative numbers. I feel like an architect in front a building, breaking down the designs. Instead of seeing how it was built, I see how to tear it down. I am suddenly dizzy. *Why is this happening?*

We step onto the beautifully furnished boat. The door locks behind me. The boy takes my luggage, backpack, and jacket, with my cell phone in the pocket.

"Ah, here she is, Ms. M herself." Then the boy leaves.

A woman, who is not Mrs. Zhang, walks into the room followed by several tall men. The temperature of my blood drops a few degrees. Up close, she looks about the same age my mom would have been, early forties. She is just as stunning as the first time I saw her. Dark red hair, matching lipstick, pale face, and eyes as gray as winter.

"Josephine Rivers," she says. "We meet at last."

Secrets, the schooner, departs immediately heading north into the Puget Sound. The red-haired woman pulls out the chair across from her and motions for me to sit. Her hair ripples down her shoulders like flowing water. I wonder if it is real or not.

My inner calculator estimates the cost of the gold she is wearing—necklace, earrings, rings—gold shoes even—a minimum of 45,000 dollars. She is petite, slender, one inch shorter than I am. Her face is unnaturally white, her expression powerful, like she has the ability to cast a spell if I stare long enough into her icy eyes.

"Um. Where's Mrs. Zhang?" I ask.

"Working. Please sit," she says with a strange accent. The table is laid with platters of luxurious meats, cheeses, and fruit, on eight plates with exactly eight pieces of food on each. "Eat, please."

The spike in numbers happens so fast I barely recognize it. I began multiplying and dividing almost too quickly to comprehend, like my calculations have been shot with adrenaline, like the day my mom died. I am dizzy with predictions, possibilities. I tap my leg, like a nervous tick.

"Thanks," I say, and a lump rises in my throat. *Dad.* I reach for my phone, but it is in my jacket, which the boy has taken. Now he is gone too.

That terrible feeling in my gut is back. I fold and unfold my napkin and notice the pounding in my chest. *Breathe Jo. Nothing is wrong.*

"My name is Maxima, or Ms. M," the woman says, her voice calm and sweet. "I've wanted to meet you for a very long time."

A very long time. Why didn't people at least make an effort to be precise? For example, she saw me three years, twenty-one days ago at the Stanley Interview and yesterday in the stadium. How long had it really been?

"You were at my graduation," I say, watching for a reaction. I stall, trying to read her mannerisms but the woman sits as still as a dead fish. She doesn't outwardly process her thoughts through movement, like most people—a nervous tick, a twitch of an eye. I can't read her as I can others. "I hadn't realized you worked for Prodigy Stealth Solutions."

"Ah, yes. PSS has always been an interest of mine. I keep up on the progress of all the prodigies." She grinned. "But your interview at Stanley impressed me the most. You're not like the others. When I saw your uncanny ability to calculate, I knew we were destined to work together. Thanks to your sister, that's possible."

"*My sister?*" I ask. "Don't you mean PSS?"

"We'll get to PSS later. For now, let's talk about your father." Her tone was warm, friendly—like this wasn't the creepiest conversation I'd ever had. "He hasn't told you, has he?"

I shake my head, confused. "Told me what?" Then it hit me. The reason he fired me. He'd promised to tell me when I returned from China—is this connected?

The woman picks up a newspaper and hands it to

me. "He's under investigation. Being audited by the IRS and his board." Ms. M looked at her fingernails. "Take a look."

The article was dated a week before graduation. *Jeffery Joseph Rivers, CEO of iVision linked to insider trading.*

"Insider trading. That's preposterous. He's never done anything illegal in his life."

"The Securities Exchange Commission disagrees," says Ms. M. "How else do you explain his track record? He could lose everything. Even go to prison."

I sink deeper into my chair. This is all my fault. I had showed my father where to invest. I understood how it would appear as "insider information" since we'd invested a lot very quickly and never made a losing investment. Even as I advised him, I never knew for sure if it would work or not. They were just theories, predictions in my head, a game. I wanted to see if I could win. I never dreamed it would get him in trouble.

"He can't go to prison for something he hasn't done." I was vaguely aware that this conversation shouldn't be happening with some lady I didn't even know. I should have been talking with my dad. "Why isn't he defending himself?"

She leaned in. "He's either guilty or he's protecting someone."

"I can't go to China yet. I need to help my dad," I say. "I need to go back."

"I'm afraid it's too late for that."

"But I can prove his innocence." My mouth is dry.

"Oh?" Her finger taps against her lip. "Please explain."

"I, uh—" My father had made me promise never to tell anyone this information, but I had to help him. I couldn't let him go to prison. "It's not my dad. It's me. I know which investments will succeed. They're patterns, predictions. I *calculate* them."

"Each one?" Her eyes narrowed.

"Yes." My voice cracked. "Can we help my dad now?"

She sighed. "I already have." She spoke in another language to a six-foot blond man and stood up. Three more men entered the room.

Numbers attack me like arrows, but I can't dodge them fast enough to understand what's going on.

"You're not PSS, are you?" I ask, dread like a stone in my stomach.

"PSS is expecting you tomorrow," Ms. M says coldly. "Unfortunately, you won't show up."

"Who are you? Why are you doing this?" I ask.

She snaps her fingers and the boy comes around the corner flipping through my passport.

"You'll soon find out."

I dart to the door of the boat. We are still close to shore. I can jump if I have to. Just as I reach the edge, the tall blond guy steps toward me with something in his hand. A calculation forms right before mist is sprayed in my face. It smells funny, like oranges and bleach. Red circles form around my peripheral view, then yellow. I feel it. I have 3 seconds.

3. The numbers fade as colors take over, but not before I understand one thing.

2. I can't calculate myself out of this.

1. This was an—

Black.

∞

Click!

A noise startles me and I'm shaken from a deep sleep. My eyes open to gray walls. The woman, Maxima, with red hair is there, standing over me. I blink, eyes stinging. I sit up slowly. My hair is draped over my chest. That's when I notice it isn't brown anymore. It's red. Just like hers.

"Good morning, *Octavia*," she says in a sickly-sweet voice, confusing me. "Welcome to China. Let's begin, shall we?"

EIGHT
PRESENT: PHOENIX
∞

FRENCH CONCESSION, SHANGHAI, CHINA

Bright light streams in through the window at Chan's cottage, waking me with warmth on my face. My hand rises to touch the sun on my cheek. When I was a child, my mother would open my curtains each morning. "Lean into the sun," she'd say. "It wants a kiss good morning."

The memory makes me wince. *Why am I thinking about her?* I blame it on the flowers.

A dog barking outside startles me from my mood. Leaning over to the windowsill, I peek outside. Kai is there with disheveled hair in gray sweats playing a game of tug-of-war with a black lab. The dog play-growls, his tail going crazy with delight. Kai growls back, a smile on his face.

A slight pinch of jealousy rises in me seeing his joy. A carefree boy playing with his dog. Kai bends down, changing the angle of his foot. Calculating his height, weight, the position of his body toward the dog, I predict the dog's next yank will pull him to the ground in 3.2 seconds. If I yelled a warning now, he might not bite the dust, but I don't interfere. Why would I? He won't get hurt. It will just—*oops.* There he goes. Kai gets up, laughing. A laugh escapes my lips too before trailing away in the silent room.

I head for the shower. It's already well past nine. I'm not sure when Chan will come to get me but I'm anxious to have resources at my fingertips and a safe cover to learn Madame's whereabouts.

When I walk into the master bathroom thoughts of Madame vanish. The free-standing porcelain tub is all I see. I groan with happiness. A long hot bath is overdue.

As the tub fills with water, my fingers run over the Egyptian cotton towels. I find a collection of soaps in a drawer, holding them up to my nose one by one: lemon, lavender, and mint. There is a shelf stocked with lotions and infused bath salts. I wastefully shake three large handfuls of purple bath salts from a glass bottle into the water. As they dissolve, the scent of lavender fills the steamy air. I'm not sure if it's the freshness or the clean water but hope dares to rise. I step into the bath, afraid to cling to that feeling and afraid to let it go.

Soaking in the bath is divine. I close my eyes for 22 minutes and let the hot water and scented crystals resurrect a fact I may have forgotten—I'm a girl with soft skin and the need to feel beautiful, without being scared.

My eyes open on the dingy hairband around my wrist and I'm brought back to reality. The hairband is a reminder of why I never wear my hair up. I remove the elastic black band from my wrist and move to toss it in the trash. But my hand involuntarily reaches to the back of my neck instead. Despite the heat, chills race over me.

Beauty is so easily scarred. I slip the hair tie back around my wrist and drain the tub.

When I'm finished blow-drying my hair, I stare at the clothes on the bed. They're the same as yesterday. Even though the spa washed them, I cringe at slipping into clothes permanently stained with the Pratt. But I have no other options, so I put them on and make a note to buy new clothes right after my first day in the office.

At 10:00 o'clock there's a knock on the door. Chan's son appears in place of Mr. Chan. A split second of warmth circles my chest. As I walk out, I decide to act cheerful, but my smile drops abruptly.

"We will be in touch this afternoon, Mr. Shu," he says into the phone. Kai holds his finger up in the air until I back up a step.

This is the boy I expected Mr. Chan's son to be. Gone is the carefree boy playing with his dog and the shirtless workman repairing the pool. He's wearing a suit, like my father used to wear—expensive, tailored, new. Kai is my age but now he looks as stiff as a mannequin, just like Chan. His hair does not fall in his face like last night but is neatly parted to one side, so firmly held in place by product that not even an atomic bomb could loosen it. His shoes are expensive and highly polished, possibly this morning. My father says shoes say a lot about a man and the combination of his wardrobe added to his hairstyle, I'd wager Kai is nothing but a self-centered rich kid.

"Yes, of course, anything for our favorite client," he flatters whoever is on the phone. "Right away. Have a great day. You deserve it."

Ugh. If I have to talk like that to Chan's clients, I won't last a day.

He ends the phone call with a dozen thankyous and good wishes, then turns to me. An irritated look is on his face. "Good morning."

To my surprise, he extends a silver cup with a white lid to me. "You like coffee? I made you some."

I take it because he made it for me and it reminds me of my dad, not because I like coffee. "Thanks."

"Ready to go?" He steps away from the door, using his hand to indicate the way to the garage. "We're already late."

"Yes." I take the key to the house and the chess pawn, but nothing else. I don't have any other possessions, besides the hairband around my wrist.

In the garage there are three different motorcycles and an SUV. A loud beep sounds and the automatic locks on the black Range Rover slide open.

On the drive to Chan's office, I sip my coffee, wishing there were at least one drop of milk in it. We pass a billboard advertising a Chinese kung fu movie. The men on the board are shirtless, holding swords and crouched in a fighting stance, muscles rippling. It sparks the question I've been meaning to ask Kai.

"What kind of martial arts do you practice?" I ask, cutting through the awkward layer of silence.

"Did my father tell you?" he asks, surprised.

"It's obvious by the way you walk and move." I

look at him. "I've known many men who can fight, unfortunately."

"Unfortunately?" he repeats.

The drunken brawls over gambling in the Pratt, game-fights, guards extracting information come easily to mind. Even my own scars sting. "Yes. Unfortunately."

"Okay. Since you asked, I'm a student of traditional kung fu," he says seriously, "which is not *fighting*. It's not meant to harm, but to protect." He takes a drink of his coffee as we pause at a red light. His hands are gentle as they grip the cup. "My father said you had great talents, but he didn't mention your keen observation skills. That's an important part of kung fu, to know your environment and the people in it. I'm impressed."

"What else did your father say about me?" I say, harsher than I intended. Chan promised he wouldn't share anything about where I came from with anyone, but did that include his son? How many details did Chan tell him—found with criminals, smelled of garbage, makes millions miraculously? That I broke his nose?

"He said you don't like talking about yourself," Kai says, matching my tone and presses down on the gas pedal.

Apparently, Chan mentioned our ride into Shanghai. Chan had tried chatting, asking very normal questions, which I politely refused to answer but he kept asking. Finally, I erupted, warning him never again to ask about my life. We didn't speak after that until we arrived at the house. I sure know how to make a good impression.

Likewise, now, the car is silent again.

We zip through the city. My mind buzzes with counting heights of buildings, scooters, cars, speeds, horns honking, but while numbers scroll and log, my mind is stuck on Chan. Asking about my past doesn't mean he doesn't know about Madame. Red could have told him or even Bo Gong. I suspect Chan's told Kai more than he's letting on.

I could ask questions, too. *How does Chan know Red? Why was Red in the Pratt?* As we break for a red light, I decide to drop it. It's better that we don't ask any more questions of each other, so I don't have to talk about myself and get off track. I have one purpose right now—one I've waited a long time to fulfill. I must stay focused.

We're now in Pudong—Lujiazui, the financial district and pulse of the city. We pull up in front of 126 floors of wealth and power. A new and improved Shanghai Tower dominates the city's skyline with its shiny-windowed presence, as if proclaiming money is the real leader of the land. It was one of the landmarks I could see from Madame's hotel. I always wondered if I'd ever see it in person one day.

Kai motions to a guard at the building to come over. "He will let you in," he says to me.

"Good morning, *Chan Gongzi.*" The guard greets him respectfully, talking for several minutes, asking about his father, and complimenting his suit, then throws in a few flowery words, usually reserved for near royalty—or in this case—billionaires.

"This is Ms. Phoenix, my father's new assistant," Kai says. "You'll let her in from now on without question. We'll have her security card by the end of the day."

The man, who looks just a bit older than Kai, opens my door, acknowledging me with a bow of the head. His clean-cut, black hair and alert dark eyes catch me right away. We are also the same height.

"Yes, sir." The guard dips his head, but I don't miss the cocky smile on his face.

"Phoenix, I'll meet you in the lobby." Kai disappears down the driveway under the building and I'm left with the guard, whose mannerisms—posture and use of language—have my calculations spinning.

The guard is out of place. He's confident, hyper aware of everyone around him. He speaks perfect standard Mandarin, including a very high level of Chinese idioms. He's educated or from the upper class. So why is he working as a doorman? The question itches in my brain. In my world of numbers everything counts for something, even a doorman.

Before we part ways, I turn to him. "What's your name?"

He gives me a strange look, as if I shouldn't be associating with him because of my social status but I know better. A handful of friends are worth more than a pocket full of cash. "I am Yu Tai," he says.

The lobby is impressive, like entering a five-star hotel. A bubbling fountain pours rose scented water over white marble statues. Black leather couches line the windows to my left. A large round carpet—possibly from the Ming Dynasty—has a red symbol woven into the middle of it and lies under a modern chandelier that glows softly. To the right are the elevators and veering hallways.

An elevator lights up and opens. Kai walks out with a girl, slender and well dressed. Her hair is twisted into a playful roll on top of her head. Her earrings flash and dangle against her cheeks. Pretty, if you like the flashy look. They exchange words too quiet for me to understand. Business or personal, I can't guess. But from the way the girl continues to touch Kai's arm, she either likes him or is just the flirty type. A moment later she wiggles her fingers in goodbye and leaves, turning heads all the way to the main door.

Kai spots me and heads in my direction.

As he moves forward, I calculate an embarrassing collision about to occur. In less than five seconds a man barking into a cell phone will bump into a woman holding an open tea canister who is walking backwards while waving to a man at the door. If Kai keeps moving at his current pace, the woman, in effort not to fall will latch on to Kai and there's a 81% chance she'll spill her tea on him. For the other two, there's no chance to avoid it. It's an action already in motion. As Newton's second law requires, there's no impulse to stop it but Kai has a chance because he's looking at me.

I stick my hand out, palm forward, a universal symbol for "stop" and hope Kai pauses at my weak command.

Like a soldier attuned to warning signs, he stops in mid-step, looking confused. Then right before him, the woman falls, tea is spilled, and the man lands on his back. No one is hurt, just embarrassed. Maids rush over to clean up the mess. It's no one's fault. Just carelessness.

"How did you know that would happen?" Kai asks, walking up to me.

I shrug. "I've always been a bit jumpy."

I move quickly towards the elevator, but Kai hangs back, his eyes fixed on me. The expression on Kai's face reminds me of another boy—the one boy who saw past the facade, the one boy I used to think could save me—Rafael. He used to give me that same look. The one that says "jumpy" has nothing to do with it.

NINE
PRESENT: PHOENIX
∞

SHANGHAI TOWER, SHANGHAI, CHINA

Upstairs, people hurry between offices, busy with what they think are important tasks. Phones ring. Computers light up. It's not the Pratt or Madame's expos. It's a real office, like my dad's, where people work for an honest living at jobs they have chosen—kind of like I wanted to do for Prodigy Stealth Solution when they hired me a long time ago.

For a moment, there's a prick in my conscience. If I bring my plans for Madame into this environment, I could endanger innocent people and myself all over again, but the weight of my vow wins out. I promised Red I'd use my gift for good. If stopping her isn't a good use of my time, I don't know what is.

As we maneuver down halls, people greet Kai respectfully and look me over with open curiosity. I ignore their stares, whether they're directed at my clothes or my young, *laowai* face and look around—

sizing up dimensions, spaces, people, prices—the new place refreshes me, like reading a new book. I realize I'm gawking—real wood floors, more leather couches, crystal vases with real flowers. The desks, floors, and windows literally shine. I forgot things could be this clean, this normal.

"Here we are." Kai drops me off at his father's corner office. I'm even more impressed. Everything in the room is *fengshui* and perfectly symmetrical. It's shaped like a circle. Half of the room is one long window, curved smoothly around the building in one long sheet of glass. The view follows every bend and stretch from downtown, along the famous Waitan on the river.

On the other half of the room water trickles down a granite wall. Plants and *moli* flowers, are everywhere. Why *moli,* I wonder? Peasants sell this flower on the street. It's far from common in a place like this. Then there's an oak desk, a long leather couch, a bookshelf with small plaques on it and a marble chess set. Very few personal items.

Mr. Chan sits at his desk in a classic tailored suit, a fresh *moli* flower in his lapel. I take the chair opposite of him, set my coffee down on a small jade coaster and cross my legs.

"Welcome, Phoenix," he says shooting me a courtesy glance. His nose is bandaged and there's a slight bruise under his left eye. It appears he's still a bit upset with me. "Sleep well?" he asks indifferently. He's counting out money as he speaks.

"Well enough."

A large fistful of red bills with Chairman Mao's

face on it goes into an envelope, then into my hands. "You will need money to live. This will be deducted from the first transaction."

My first paycheck. The calculated width of the pile of cash puts it roughly around 20,000 yuan. Too many variables to be more precise, but it's enough money to start. I shove the envelope in my pocket.

"Kai told me you met each other on the grounds. I apologize that he disturbed you last night," he says stiffly. "He usually isn't at home. He is quite busy with his internship, and his girlfriend or should I say, soon-to be-fiancée."

Kai is nearly engaged? I wouldn't have guessed it by his manner last night. A numerical analytic summary usually detects small actions displaying attachment, but I hadn't. Not like it matters. "It's fine," I say.

"Next time he tries to fix something, ask him to leave and call me. He needs to focus on his school internship, which means working at my company. After all, it will be his one day," he says wryly and clears his throat. "Shall we?"

"Sir, before we begin," I say, bringing up my fist. The small chess piece, scratched and faded with time, is cradled inside. I don't know why it's so significant. Nor could I have guessed it'd be Chan Huang Long I'd be giving it to. Regardless, my orders were to pass it on and trust that this trinket would accomplish its purpose.

"Yes?" The look in his eyes is contrived.

Suddenly, I know this isn't the moment. I tuck it back into my pocket.

"Um—" I spot the trash beside his desk and lift my

cup towards him. "My coffee's finished," I say lamely.

Chan takes my cup and places it in the trash bin. "Was that all?"

I clear my throat. "No."

There's something else I need to make clear to Chan. If Madame were to find out I'm alive, she'd suspect me in every investment to cross her desk, even from Chan's corporation. I've got to take precautions. "Outside of this office you speak only Chinese to me. I'm not American. I don't speak English, got that? Everything about me is private. You'll provide a translator for me in every meeting that requires English. Tell Kai to do the same."

He swallows hard. He's still skeptical about working with me. He's not convinced of my honesty. Especially now that I've asked him to lie. He finally nods. "Done. Can we begin?"

I nod eagerly. The anticipation of this moment bursts like a shaken soda can. *Madame's reign would end soon.* To my surprise, I'm not hyper or anxious, I'm cool and calm, like a hunter preparing his snares.

Then King's mantra whenever he went into a business meeting—words I never thought I would say—come out of my mouth. "Money time." The irony makes me laugh.

"Phoenix, please, this is serious," Chan says as I stifle the laugh. "My company is in a financial mess. If you can fix the problem as you claim—"

That's right. I almost forgot Chan's company had a problem at all.

"If?" I stop him, eyes steady, "No offense, Mr. Chan, but *when* I fix your financial mess is more like it."

"You're very confident for one so young. I'm only trusting Red's judgment now. I haven't seen anything you can do for myself," he says again.

"If there is one thing I can do, it's make money. I'm actually excited to work for you, *an honest man*, but like you, I haven't seen that for myself."

Eagerness to use my gift in an honest business also wells up inside me. But Chan is a pawn in my game, I remind myself. I'll solve his problem, pay him back, and put an end to Madame. Then I'll take my hard-earned money and go back to Seattle and try to piece together a new life. The sooner I leave this life behind, the better.

"Just show me the files so we can get started," I say. A file lies open on his desk, displaying a stack of papers. "Are these the documents?"

"No," he says. "These are standard reports, mainly from this quarter's gains and losses." A slight panic comes over him. "You can *read* Chinese, can't you?"

Without replying, I pick the files up and look them over.

After a few minutes Chan stacks a foot-high pile of papers in front of me. Oh boy. This is going to be a long day.

He stands and motions for me to follow. I trail behind him, still holding the financial report in my hand. He escorts me to a private office with an oval table.

"For you." It is set up with a notepad and pens, a cell phone, a transportation card, a printer, and a computer. *A computer!* And to my dismay, there's also a black leather love seat next to a small window reminding me of Madame and King. I wrinkle my nose.

Logical or not, I will always be wary of people who own black leather.

He sets the tall stack of files on the desk. "You can work here. No one will interrupt you. All right, that should be everything you need." He sighs, then he turns the computer monitor towards me and enters a code for guest users.

"First familiarize yourself with my corporation. I also expect you to attend the investments meetings every Monday and Wednesday morning until we discover what the problem is."

"Can you sum up the problem, so I have an idea what I'm looking for?"

He takes a deep breath. "I have reason to believe that my company will go bankrupt by the end of the year if I don't do something," he says, glancing nervously around the room as if the walls had ears. "I'm not usually superstitious but the same day Bo Gong found me on Red's behalf, this hit my desk from the accounting department. See the numbers?" Chan breathes deep.

He hands me what looks like normal financial reports. I glance over the income and cash flow statements and balance sheets. Everything appears in order until something tiny pops out at me. The pages are spotted with numbers dropping from *eight* percent to *four*, or *eighty* to *forty*...it's not that often, but it's present on each report.

I raise my eyebrows in disbelief. I thought Chan—a highly experienced financial guru—would be a bit more logical. Chinese assign value and belief to many numbers—eight, for example, represents wealth and prosperity, while the number four represents death. Mega corporations like Chan's do not simply go bankrupt after a bum deal or a few sour investments, but he seems to believe that according to Chinese numerology, it will.

"Any real *proof?*" I ask, perhaps a bit condescendingly.

"My company's cash flow numbers are dropping like flies in summer. Something's not right but I can't locate the source of the problem. My accountant can't find anything wrong, either. I should be making money like everyone else in this economic climate. There's a glitch, a mistake somewhere. I want you to find it and fix it before I lose everything. That last financial report was some kind of sign."

"Ok. So your numbers are dropping," I say. "I'll find the problem. Must be related to the stocks."

"I admit, it sounds trivial, a usual business occurrence but I've never seen anything like this, especially after the Asia Bank initiative. Have you heard of it?"

I stop, frozen in the past. Before Madame, I was hired to help Asia Bank. Apparently, everything was solved without me.

I don't say any of this. Instead I say, "Of course. Anyone alive knows that Asia Bank initiated a world stabilization with the Chinese yuan."

"Fine. You say you can make money, so prove it to me. Get the numbers back up and meanwhile solve the other side of the riddle—figure out where these losses are coming from. Please begin as soon as possible." The same look of desperation returns to his face. "Let me find the investment folder." While Chan digs through a filing cabinet for several minutes, I scan the reports.

When he looks up, I close the quarterly report and set it in front of him. "For starters, you should fire whoever does your bookkeeping. Too many slips in there."

"What are you talking about?" he asks.

"Take the Jiangsu Auto Factory—you are losing 20% a year by paying out injury insurance. Right now, you have them operating ten-hour working shifts, but the report clearly states, all the accidents happen in the last two hours. It's a classic Ford dilemma. Reduce it to an eight-hour workday. You'll have fewer accidents and higher production."

He looks at me with disbelieving eyes.

"Secondly," I go on, "you need to sell the Ji Fu chain store. It's doing well now but the quarterly numbers tell me that it won't last."

"That is one of our highest profiting ventures!" Chan says strongly.

"If you don't believe me, track it on paper. In six months, you'll be sorry you didn't listen." He's fidgeting. A sign of his nerves? Or is it just the effect I have on him? "And something's wrong in your C-Suite. Several thousand a week is missing with no reason. Someone's using company money for personal investment."

"This took my accountant weeks to prepare. You expect me to believe you saw all of that in a matter of minutes?" His face is red.

Oh, he dislikes me, or he's just like other people and doesn't know what to make of me. One thing I know for certain, if he wasn't desperate, I wouldn't be free right now.

"That's why you hired me, right? Just trying to help," I say, pulling over the other files.

He stares at me like I'm a magician who has just pulled a rabbit out of a hat. He's not sure if the rabbit is a fake or I am and by the look on his face, he's still searching for the hole in the hat. "Hmm, I will look into it," he mumbles and leaves the room.

After he leaves, I push the folder away and draw the computer close. I'll figure out his company's petty problem later. I've got more important things to do, like stopping Madame.

I've made plans like this before—433 times to be exact. Even shared them with Red, but he said I could do better. *"Orphans dream of vindication,"* he'd whisper. *"Sons and daughters dream of destiny."*

Red believed in my destiny; in the history I could make. But as long as Madame is out there—ruining our world, I can't do anything. Not until she is stopped. For good.

Online, my fingers type the name Maxima Moreau into the search. An advertisement for an upcoming expo in Shanghai immediately appears on the screen. There she is front and center. Turns out, I won't have to wait very long after all.

My body turns cold as I click on her picture, staring into her icy eyes.

"I failed to expose you once," I whisper to her picture. "But I've had time to think about how to play your game and I've done more than just plan. I've *calculated.*"

TEN
PAST: OCTAVIA
∞

GOLDEN ANGEL HOTEL, SHANGHAI, CHINA

The hard click of Madame's heels coming down the hall sounded like a hammer nailing a coffin shut. My insides twisted like a slithering brood of snakes at the thought of seeing her. It had been ten days and I still didn't know where I was or why I was here or when I could go home or why she called me Octavia.

The last thing I remembered before waking up was being on her boat. She sprayed me with that mist. It smelled of oranges and bleach. My numbers vanished right before I blacked out and woke up in a luxurious hotel room filled with expensive gifts and clothes.

The door opened. The woman named Maxima, or Madame, snapped her fingers. "Come with me."

I rose, trembling and red-eyed. Never have I felt more like an animal, ripped from its natural habitat, now caged, and expected to perform. She hadn't answered my questions. She hadn't responded to my pleas.

Her icy hand slipped the bracelets around my wrists—restraints, like an electric dog collar—just like she did yesterday. My brain calculated our path as we went—hallways, stairwells, elevators, distances, and dimensions until we came to the same place where she set before me another pile of documents: lists of investments similar to the ones I picked for my dad's company.

"Please, I need to call my dad," I begged. No response.

"At least let me call PSS," I tried. "They're counting on me. I was hired to help solve a critical economic problem. So much could go wrong if I don't help them." Nothing.

"Who are you, please?" I asked.

She repeated what she told me each day, "I'll tell you everything soon. For now, no questions, only obedience."

Trembling, I did everything she asked, not really knowing what it was I was working on. I just wanted to please her so I could call my Dad. The atmosphere weighed on me—her coldness, the equations, the secret nature of the investments.

I did this, day after day. Fancy food and drink were given to me, but the only thing she said was, "If you want to live, Octavia, no questions. Only obedience."

At the end of day eleven, we passed a new door. Escape was the only word bulleting through my mind. The cold metal of the restraints was there but I was past feeling it. I couldn't think straight anymore. My odds were less than one percent but the urge to flee overtook my need for safety. I bolted for the door and ran with all my might.

I flew into the stairwell until an electric current shot through me overriding my control. I collapsed, a cold electric seizure taking over my senses.

A hard yank pulled me back. Two men shoved my face to the floor. Madame's grip tightened on my neck. There was a click, the smell of gas, then smoke. Something was burning.

Moments later, a loud scream ripped apart the room. It took me eighteen seconds to realize it was me screaming. Fire etched a straight line across the back of my neck. Burning flesh was the smell in my nose. My flesh.

The pain was so great my body started fluttering. I was going into shock. I was going to die. She was burning a hole right through me. She lifted the fire and her lips were on my ear.

"It was mercy that I took you. Your father was accused of insider trading. You did that. You got him arrested but I solved his problem. With your disappearance, he got pity. He could blame it all on you. Do you think he will come to look for you? No. He's concerned with himself. And your foolish sister is the one who told me all about your PSS trip, so I knew exactly where to meet you," Madame said, her voice fierce and shaky.

Mara told her about PSS? *It couldn't be true...she didn't know what she was doing...* My heart, like my flesh, was now burning, scalding, blistering. All I felt was more pain.

"Don't you see? They never loved you. They loved only themselves. You deserve more. You should be grateful I took you away from them. I'll give you everything you will ever need to succeed. You could not live a greater life."

"My family loves me," I choked out, tears streaming down my face.

The flame came down again on my neck. I lost consciousness as the fire seared my skin, but before I passed out, her next words seared into my mind.

"I don't want to hurt you, Octavia. So I promise I'll only do this once—so you know who I am and who you are. And so I know where to cut later if you ever disobey me again."

Infinity was a beautiful concept, but any MIT professor would tell you that believing in it would ruin you. I used to think real love was infinite, that it would continue no matter what happened. What a fool I was.

My hand traveled over the back of my neck. Goosebumps sprouted as I touched the protruding five-inch long scar. Even after 39 days, seven hours and thirty-eight minutes, it was still sore to the touch—though I'd never confess that to Madame.

I pulled my legs up to my chest and wrapped my sweater tight around them, but it made no difference—the black leather couch was still cold to the touch. Since my flesh stopped burning, everything had iced over. To me, everything in China was cold.

So far, I'd earned Madame what I was sure was 187 million dollars of dirty money. Problem was, I had no clue who she was or what she did with it. On paper, she was a lady called Maxima Moreau, a successful international businesswoman, trading high quality textiles and silks in China and around the world through her company *M's Textiles*. She traveled a lot and always attended the four most important textile expos in the world—Shanghai, London, New York, and Milan.

I could have used my math gift to dig up the truth, but I was too afraid. If she found out that I knew her secrets, she'd kill me. Each day I struggled with guilt and shame because I knew what I was doing for her was wrong, yet, I did it anyway. I cried 101 hours and spent 39 days in unending calculations only to realize escape was impossible.

A knock on the door made me leap to my feet. Madame stood in the doorway, a newspaper in her hand.

"Octavia, I wanted you to see this. Your father's company is nearly bankrupt, and he blames you for ruining him."

Tears slipped from my eyes without permission. I hated to cry in front of her, like I was giving her a victory, but I couldn't stop. Then, she walked over and touched me, the briefest squeeze of her arm around my shoulders.

Maybe it was meant to be a hug? It felt more like someone jammed up against me in an elevator and leapt out as soon as the door opened. I jumped back, too.

Her face unmistakably twisted with pain. A glimmer of something passed across her eyes that made her look like a different woman. She was like a child, frightened and needy, as if she were the one who had heard the bad news.

That expression, that glimmer of a different Celia, mixed pity in with my hate. Until a second later when she snapped out of it.

"Forget those traitors. I'm your family now. No one will hurt you under my watch. *We're the same, Octavia. Powerful. And I'll make you more powerful yet.*"

She left, wobbly on her spiked heels, and spent the rest of the day in her office. The room shrank that day or maybe she grew taller—either way, I felt like a speck of dust could crush me if her words hadn't already.

The only thing in my life that I could trust not to lie was numbers. And they showed that Madame wasn't *always* watching me. Which meant escape was not impossible. After days of being completely alone, or the deranged dinners I was forced to have with Madame, my borderline insanity had produced lots of calculating, starting with the door to my room.

It was securely locked with an electronic keypad. This type of keypad had 100,000 possible permutations. Most people would call it a combination lock but technically that was incorrect. In a combination, the order of the numbers didn't matter. Only in a permutation did the numbers need to be in a particular order, like the keypad on my door. *They are counting tools.* Extremely helpful to a math genius. They helped me determine the total number of possible outcomes and which ones were likely to be successful.

So I counted them out, one by one. And finally, I cracked the code on my door.

A cacophony of horns honking, cymbals clashing, people shouting and fireworks snapping outside reminded me it was the eve of Chinese Spring Festival—8 months, 2 days, 15 hours after I'd arrived. They were celebrating the year of the snake. *Go figure.* If I looked outside, there might be boats on the river, lanterns sent up into the night sky, and a dragon parading down the road.

I didn't look. I'd seen too many snakes since I came here. Besides, there was too much smog to see anything clearly.

I glanced up at the gold clock hanging on the wall. It was almost time. I slipped off the couch.

I went to the door and entered 81818, a bit agitated. I was still upset it took me a lot longer than it should have to crack this code, but I hadn't planned on Maxima choosing something so simple. It was like hiding out in the open; so obvious that no one would realize it was there. My mental calculator friends at PSS would have laughed at me if they knew.

The door opened to a hallway with brown carpet and cream walls with pictures of angels riding swans.

My bracelets, I learned, were only triggered beyond the hotel perimeter, and I rigged the video security in my room—*my cell*—with a glitch, which meant I could roam the hotel, unseen, for an hour. My almost daily slipping out had gone unnoticed for 6 weeks now but I had to be careful. If Madame, or Maxima, or whatever her name was, knew I cracked the code on my door, the scar on my neck would be the least of my problems.

I slipped out and continued what I had done for the past six weeks—I calculated. I studied. I saw things. I'd nearly memorized the first sixteen floors of the hotel. I had another sixteen to go.

The hotel was exceptional. Maxima and I lived on the top floor—the penthouse suite. Gold curtains. Golden-sheeted bed, plush and king-size. There was a bathroom in the corner next to a large armchair. The TV sat on a polished desk, and a plaque on my door read, *Octavia*.

"Octavia." A lump rose in my throat as I read *my name*. I even answered to it now. I wished I could tell someone the truth of who I was.

I shivered as I snuck into the stairwell, went down two flights of stairs, and entered an identical hallway. I looked back to make sure no one followed me.

As I passed the emergency door, I cringed. There was a very small chance I could get out of the hotel down the fire escape if I found a way to remove these bracelets. But the scar on my neck stopped me. Madame promised never to hurt me again. She even looked like she regretted it, but for months I couldn't wear my hair down. I glanced at the hairband on my wrist—the last piece of evidence belonging to a girl named Josephine. Now, I wore my hair down to hide my scar. Only when my odds were high enough would I try to escape again.

As I slipped in and out of the hallways, I considered outside networks I could hack into. I needed to find an anonymous way back into Maxima's accounts. Recently, while working for Madame, a file had appeared on the screen suddenly and then vanished before I could hack it. It was undoubtedly a floating file. Basically, a hidden file designed to float within the network's cyber-sphere, making it hard to pin down. Floating files usually stored very confidential information. I knew this because PSS used these file types to store much of their sensitive job details.

There had to be clues or evidence in it, proof to expose her. Maybe there was information I could use to escape. Courage stirred within me. But finding a floating file again would take work, especially with Madame tracking everything I did on her phone.

I finished my rounds and headed back to the suite, another day gone with no safe way to hack into Madame's accounts.

Madame was an anomaly. I still couldn't figure her out. She kidnapped me, forced me to work for her, then personally threatened death to anyone who touched me. Her obsession with me was bizarre. I'd calculated 32 options as to why. The money I made for her wasn't one of them.

Back at my office, I deactivated the lock. I slipped inside, eased the door handle back into place so that it would not click. I was overly cautious but getting caught defying Madame was scary enough that caution was critical.

I exhaled and turned towards my desk. My body involuntary jumped back against the door in a violent jerk.

Someone was sitting on my black leather couch. "Caught you."

ELEVEN
PAST: OCTAVIA
∞

GOLDEN ANGEL HOTEL, SHANGHAI, CHINA

Two dark eyes examined me from head to foot, as a wicked grin slid across his face. "Someone has been very naughty."

I froze in place trying to calm my heart and think up an excuse for being out of my room. My mind was totally blank.

"Found a way out, did you?" His finger traced the contours of my fifteen-year-old body in the air. "What will you give me for keeping this little secret, hmm?"

I shuddered with disgust. It was Lev, Madame's sleazy husband, who cheated on her every chance he got, despite Madame's boasts of his loyalty. If there was anyone I despised almost as much as Madame, it was him.

Lev was dressed in a finely-tailored suit. He was European, like Maxima, some French mix, six-foot, 180 pounds. His face was red, most likely from alcohol.

Hopefully, he was too drunk to remember this.

I was grateful Madame forbade anyone to touch me. She was adamant that I belonged to her and no one else.

Lev was early to pick me up for dinner. He rose from the couch and stepped toward me, a fire in his eyes. "Where were you, Octavia?" Lev asked, moving closer to me. "Won't you tell Lev? I'll keep it a secret for just one kiss. Maybe we can share secrets." He laughed the way he did when other women were around. I caught a whiff of his cologne, mixed with the scent of alcohol. *Sick.*

"Wait!" I commanded but my voice sounded too fragile to be demanding. Madame couldn't know I was out of the room. God only knew what she'd do to me.

Blackmail was my only defense. I was terrible at threats, so I worked out the words cautiously, hiding my trembling fingers behind my back.

"We do share secrets, Lev.*"* I whispered. "What will Maxima think of your guests last time she was in Milan? You keep my secret, I'll keep yours."

His face flattened. He had been caught too.

"Dinner is ready," he said through clenched teeth. "After you, *Cherie.*"

I turned and punched in the code, 81818, and stepped out into the hallway before Lev could touch me.

He let the door shut with a *thunk* and took a few rapid steps to catch up to me. Lev slid his arm around my waist and grabbed my hip. Fear swept over me in a cold shiver. Every equation around Lev was negative. He was dangerous.

His breath was hot on my ear. "Always so tense, Octavia," he said. Apparently, our last conversation had gone in one ear and out the other. "You really do need to loosen up."

"Your *wife* is waiting," I said, wrestling myself away. I held back tears on the brim of my eyes. I felt completely powerless. I walked faster, towards Maxima, *my protector.*

I had to tell her about Lev. Only I didn't know how, or what kind of reaction it would cause. If Madame had one weak spot, it was him.

Her belief in his loyalty proved how delusional she really was. She was brilliant, but she overlooked the simple logic that anything built on a lie would one day crumble. That day couldn't come soon enough.

My lie, that I liked her, would also collapse the moment I found a way out. The lie was not meant to last. It was meant to aid me. After two months, I learned that begging and tears wouldn't help me escape. The only thing that worked was a charade reciprocating what she wanted, my loyalty, my respect, even my love.

The lie worked.

Now, in her mind, I was not her captive but finally her protégé, her dear Octavia.

"Do you know why I call you Octavia?" she finally said one day. I shook my head. "It means 'the eighth'. There are seven in my operation, me included. I promised myself the eighth would be my successor. All this will be yours. You will inherit my wealth, my empire. Only you can do it."

I was one of the only people allowed to call her Celia—another name—and live in her suite. Her obsession with me must have been rooted in someone from her past—I reminded her of someone. A sister, her mother, a friend, but she'd never let on whom.

As I tried to work out who she really was and why, I answered her questions, no matter how off the wall. At first, I'd been too afraid to speak, too confused, but I didn't refuse her anymore. Each day I worked up enough courage to talk with her. In part, it was because of my mom's game, Seagulls. I imagined I liked her, which was as impossible as me flying. But I was not a seagull anymore. I was a vulture and I was circling.

Lev distanced himself from me before we entered the private dining room. I remembered my plan—*make her trust you, Jo. Find out who this woman really is.*

Lev leaned down, and kissed Maxima. "Bon soirée, ma chérie," he said to her. "I brought Octavia, as you requested."

"Merci, amour." She returned his kiss. How could she appear so normal?

"Lev, darling," she said, her gold necklace sparkling, "I need to talk to Octavia alone tonight. I'll meet you later."

"Bien sur, my love." He winked at me as he walked away.

Their relationship must have been a lot like Madame's and mine. A contract of sorts—Maxima proposed a death threat unless we complied with her will and we gave in while concealing how much we despised her. Lev must know that she'd most likely kill him if he ever decided to leave her and therefore found his freedom in other girls and the money she threw at him. For a moment, I understood his deceit.

"Happy New Year, Octavia."

"Happy New Year, Celia." My eyes darted to the newspaper folded by her dinner plate. It was probably for me. When I first arrived, I pleaded and bargained to be in touch with my family. Newspaper articles were all I got.

She flashed her icy grin then held out an article from the *Seattle Times*. "An interview with your father."

"What did he say?" I considered taking the paper but decided against it. If I looked at it, I might cry. Like the last article Celia had shared—there had been a funeral for me back in Seattle. I was officially dead.

"His business has nearly dissolved," she said. "He's very upset about the loss. On the bright side, he's glad your death bought a lot of sympathy and your sisters are doing better than ever. No one left to be jealous of. Let's be honest, Lily would have hated you as Mara did sooner or later."

At first, I didn't believe what she said about Mara or Dad. She lied to everyone as far as I could tell. But after months of nothing from my father, no sign of help, and the articles, the truth became blurry. I had started to believe a part of what she said was true. *Your father loved you for what you could do, nothing more.*

My nights were still an emotional game of tug of war. Love and hate, hope and despair, desperate to hold them and anguish that they hadn't looked for me. I couldn't deny a bitter root grew in my heart, crowding out the love I once had for them.

It would have been easier just to forget them forever. But no matter how hard I tried I hadn't come close. The nights I pushed them out were the darkest nights of all.

"Thanks for the update but I really don't care anymore," I lied.

Celia looked pleased. "On a brighter note, Rome worked out after all."

I'm stunned. The numbers didn't check out. There was no way for her to get on board that project so late. "How did you—?"

"Darling, I'm always one step ahead. Please eat." She motioned to the table.

The meal was hot. There was no ceremony in this room. No prayers or speeches, not even a *bon appétit*, just eating. I picked up my chopsticks and surveyed the banquet. Steaming plates with meats, fish, vegetables, and sauces all neatly-placed onto beautiful serving plates. I picked at some chunks of chicken in red sauce. Tasted like sweet and sour.

"Octavia," Celia said, sipping a glass of wine, "I hope you like your new appearance."

"Very much, Celia," I said. I was blonde this month. Last month I was a redhead, like her.

"And your winter wardrobe?" Her eyes stared hard, unflinching.

"Love it."

I dressed a lot like Madame. Expensive leathers, wools, silks. Madame filled my closets with the finest clothes, and she changed my appearance often—hair color, contacts.

"Didn't I tell you that if you do as I say you'll never want for anything?"

Anything except my own life. "Yes, Celia."

"I've arranged another gift for you. The private pool," she said. "You can swim in the morning before work for one hour, alone. Would you like that?"

"Excuse me?" I nearly choked on the chicken. Eighteen days ago, Celia asked me to tell her my greatest fear. Being kidnapped didn't seem like a response she'd like, so I told her that although swimming is my ultimate pastime, death by drowning would be it. She nodded attentively. I assumed she'd been marking it in some wicked part of her memory, ready to pull it out later. I never expected this.

As she waited for my response, that glimmer appeared in her eyes again. Something fragile—as if I refused, she'd break apart. Or was it the look of a workaholic mother, who threw money at her child, desperate to buy love? Whatever it was, she wanted me to accept her gift.

I was too afraid to say no, and unlike her other gifts, this one I really wanted. I'd missed any form of exercise, and swimming reminded me of home, a piece of who I was.

I snapped up a fried shrimp dripping of lemongrass and garlic. "I would love that. Thank you."

After I said yes, the glimmer vanished. It never lasted long enough for me to understand it. Celia seemed calmer now. I wondered if it was a good time to tell her that Lev was in my room.

I swallowed a bite of sticky rice and formed sentences in my head. *"Lev cheats on you." "He's been coming on to me."* But the words were imprisoned in my throat, kind of like I was in this hotel, because if I spoke up, Lev would too.

"You're quiet," Celia said. "What's bothering you?"

Was she asking me outright? I *felt* like it was the

time to tell her, but my calculations produced odds of a mixed outcome. Feelings weren't always mathematically logical. Could mine be trusted?

I tapped my leg. Fear muddled up the numbers, and my moment of courage dissolved. I couldn't tell her yet.

"I feel apprehensive about you leaving tomorrow," I said instead, which was true. Shivers traveled down my legs at the thought of her being gone. She was my captor, but she was also my protector.

Celia put down her spoon. "My dear Octavia," she said in an unpracticed voice. It took a moment, but she stretched out a hand to touch my shoulder in some odd attempt to console me.

The touch was brief, and she recoiled before I could reject it.

"I'll only be gone a few days," Celia said.

A few. Didn't anyone try to be exact? Last time she said that, it was ten.

"All right," I said. I focused on the soup I'd just ladled into my bowl. It smelled fishy and had long skinny strands of seaweed in it. I used my spoon to swirl them around. "What did you want to talk about?"

"I'm promoting you." She pulled out her cell phone and punched in a code. "I want you to follow through with Gao's assignments. I sent him to *King.*"

My spoon dropped from my hand, clanging against the small white bowl.

King? I gulped hard. According to rumors, meeting the grim reaper was better than meeting King.

Madame didn't miss a beat. She continued gently spooning her soup as if Gao, her employee, would find another job someday. But Gao couldn't work again if he wasn't breathing.

Did I want Gao's position? Did I even have a choice? One slip and I'd be fish food. Or maybe not. Everyone knew Celia had a heart of stone…except with me. Even Lev saw how she looked at me. Promoting me was her way of trusting me.

"Octavia?" she asked. "Did you hear me?"

"I want the position. I'll do whatever you ask," I said, playing up the charade. I couldn't stop now. No, *especially* now. Taking Gao's position meant access to information. I was ready to learn what was happening here and ready to do something about it.

TWELVE
PAST: OCTAVIA
∞

GOLDEN ANGEL HOTEL, SHANGHAI, CHINA

Celia left at dawn.

My first morning at the pool was glorious. It was empty except for Guard Ma, who escorted me. I dove into the wet warmth heading for the bottom of the pool. I glided over it, touching my fingers on the bottom. I used my feet to push up to the surface, then did it all over again until my one hour was up.

I finished my crawl stroke and pulled myself up on the edge of the pool. My eyes opened to two fleshy, hairy blurs. Feet.

My head tilted up to Lev in swimming trunks. It was seven o'clock. He usually slept in, but here he was, disgusting and wide-awake, with a rabid look in his eyes.

"Nice suit. Is it new?" Lev asked, stifling a yawn.

"No." I made a beeline for the lounge.

"Leaving so soon? I thought we could swim together

for a while," Lev said following me.

"Sorry, my time's up." Guard Ma came at my wave.

"Have it your way." Lev dove into the pool, and I hurried back to the office.

Although Internet was limited and there was no phone access, I used her personal computer to work on Celia's investments. I was right about having more access to her files in my new position, but her computer was linked to her phone, so I had to be careful. She tracked everything I did.

Since she was on a six-hour flight and she'd never trust open networks, theoretically I could get in and out and erase all my history before she got online again. This was the chance I'd waited for.

It took 83 minutes to break simple security pro-tocols—three times longer than usual. It was new technology—stuff I'd never even seen at PSS.

Finally, I broke into her documents. At first glance it was just housekeeping, travel expenses—nothing to prove a lick of who she was or what she did.

But as I dug further, I noticed an arbitrary game folder. Madame is not the game type. I clicked on it and noticed a ghost folder encrypted into it. After a hassle of unlocking it, a file marked X appeared. Bingo. The floating file!

I clicked on it as there was a knock on the door.

The door opened and Lev walked in. I sighed with relief. He wasn't at all tech-savvy. In this moment, it was an attribute I liked.

"I waited for you at breakfast," he said, pouting like a spoiled boy. "I hate eating alone."

My stomach knotted up. Even his voice oozed creepiness. Although mathematically evolution did not have a sound theory, there was a high possibility that Lev actually did evolve from slime. "Wait for Celia."

"She won't come home until Saturday. That's two days," he whined. "Dinner later?"

"Can't. Too much work to do," I said, tilting the computer screen away from his eyes. Two more files left. "You know Celia's really picky about getting things done."

He cocked his head. "Her work never takes you this long." Numbers swarmed like angry bees. He couldn't care less about Celia's work, which meant he'd been watching much closer than I thought. Suddenly, I was alarmed.

"After dinner drink?" he pleaded. "Come on, I need comfort when she goes away."

"Sorry, Lev. Can't. I didn't sleep well last night."

He paused, defeated. "Fine. If you sleep badly again, come and find me. I sing lullabies," he whispered. Thankfully, he left and I jumped into latching on and breaking into the floating file.

After fifteen minutes I still couldn't crack the wall. I wished I had my mental calculator friends. What did they used to say? Start with what you know about the person.

The first thing that came to mind was Celia's obsession with gold. Where was she flying to today? Italy. My mind spun with four hundred and sixteen possibilities until it merged gold and Latin. After looking up the translation, I tried a sequencing code with letter affiliation for *aurum* or "gold" in Latin.

Transmuting the alphabet affiliation, *a-u-r-u-m* became -120232013- then decoding it once more, it became, 1-20-23-20-13—and finally I cracked it. Not difficult at all, just had to know the person.

Inside there were two folders. One folder was entitled with a number, but it was empty when I opened it. The number on the file looked like a phone number with a +61 international code. I memorized every country code when I was five. +61 was Australia.

Strange. Her containers never went to Australia, and there were no expos there. Equations buzzed in the back of my mind. The questions piled up, but I couldn't investigate the phone number until tomorrow. Instead, I memorized it and moved on. Right now, I had to focus.

The second folder appeared empty too, but I knew better. Its visibility was locked with a serene code.

A serene code was like a pill bottle with a childproof safety cap. You just had to be one step ahead of the child to open it. This, I could do.

As I unlocked the files, my mouth gaped open. I clutched at my stomach, fighting the urge to be sick. Celia's empire was beyond anything I could have imagined. Her collaboration extended to every remote corner of the earth, with a who's who of the world's most-wanted lists. I finally knew who she was.

She was the queen of hell on earth.

The next morning, I headed to the pool, wishing the filthiness I felt for my part in Madame's horrors could wash off in the chlorine. I had finally learned exactly what she smuggled. Her *cargo* could be in this hotel.

The United Nations report that I had read in the file played like a broken record in my head: "*International Criminal Mastermind, Madame, who has evaded arrest for more than 20 years, has officially grossed more than $1 billion on hidden smuggling-trade routes, with sophisticated operations that overlap with criminal gangs who traffic in arms, drugs, prostitution and trafficking.*"

Smuggler.

Trafficker.

Mastermind.

The puzzle pieces of all her investments finally fit together, showing me a clear picture. Operating as *M's Textiles,* Madame successfully hid her most precious imports in plain sight. With each new expo, she publicly displayed her new "line" for each season. Her products were rare, expensive, and symmetrically perfect. Some clients saw exotic textiles draped over girls, other customers saw exotic girls draped with textiles.

Human lives. My life.

The file contained confidential police reports full of other pictures too: women with blonde hair, blue eyes. Pitch black hair, green eyes, glasses. Brown hair and pink lipstick. The differences were striking, but all of them were *her.* All of them were Madame.

And of course, *gold* was encoded into everything that she did. Names. Cities. Airlines. She really was obsessed.

Last night, when it hit me that Madame used my genius to finance her malicious operations, things got dark. The last candle in my world was snuffed out because I knew these crimes were on my head too.

A nauseating guilt churning inside me soon morphed into pure rage. It took everything in me not to scream bloody murder—not to want her dead, her ashes burning for a thousand years in hell—but death would be too easy. Any mercy I had for her vanished. Even now, I trembled with adrenaline so violent, so bent on her demise that I thought it might be possible my intent alone could slay her.

I dove into a focused and furious lap swim to think and solidify today's plan.

First, I'd transmit the rest of the information about Madame and my captivity into cyber space using Arrow-Mail, a handy PSS invention. Surprisingly, the link worked yesterday.

Arrow-Mail was an intelligent spam, only invisible and much more precise. It only hit your tagged targets and was able to penetrate security systems. Arrow-Mail was never open to the public and those at Stanley who knew about it were sworn to secrecy. I was pretty sure they'd forgive my violation of it. I just hoped whatever authority received it, believed it.

The only glitch was that Arrow-Mail couldn't deliver big files. It was one mega-bite at a time. In my case, my tagged targets were the police, Interpol, FBI, and CIA, so I had to send the most relevant information first. To be safe, I uploaded all three files but only sent one small file last night. I'd send the other two bigger files today. Too much fiddling with a system would cause alarm.

Celia was coming home tonight. And by now some

authority would have received my first bit of information. If they followed the trail, it would lead to Madame, and to me. Which authority would it be, I wondered? FBI? Interpol? CIA? Had they already started tracking her?

In the locker room, I'd just covered myself with the robe that Madame gave me when Lev entered, wasted drunk. Every muscle in me tensed.

"Morning, servant girl." The smell of *baijiu* was strong on his breath. His eyes were glazed over, and it looked like he hadn't slept all night. Calculations graphed out three exits, two possible weapons, and a hundred ways that seemed to shout *flee*. I backed up. He moved closer. "Swim?"

"Sorry, Lev," I tried to say with a steady voice. "I'm not the *prince* of the castle. I have to work." I looked around for the guard.

"You think of me as a prince?" He tugged at the belt on my robe, and it came loose. I backed away, but he came even closer. Too close. His snakelike breath was on my neck. "What if the prince has fallen in love with the slave girl?"

I froze in place, calculations firing like crazy. I needed to leave, fast. "Guard Ma!" I shouted out. But Ma didn't come.

"He's occupied." Lev took my hand. "Follow me."

"No. Go away, Lev!" He still had a hold of my robe. I pushed him in the chest, but he yanked on my sleeve. To get away, I let the robe slip off my body and into his hands. Crap. Now I was in my bathing suit, exposed. I ran toward the door, but he followed.

"Don't torture me anymore, Octavia," he whispered.

"Don't let Celia stop us from the love we deserve. You're always alone. So am I. If she has her way, we'll be alone forever."

"No, Lev. Celia loves you. I won't betray her." I calculated his next move and blocked his hand.

"But I have something of yours. If you want it back, you'll do as I say." *Something of mine?* What was he talking about?

But I couldn't ask because he was too close. Too volatile. Too hungry. I had to say something to make him stop. My legs were shaking. "You shouldn't do this. If she learns of your behavior…"

"You're threatening me?" His voice became angry. On the table there was a small wooden tissue box. My hand grappled for it, hoping he wouldn't notice.

"Reminding you that you have it all," I choked out. "I'm just a slave."

"I could free you. We could escape together," he said, voice soft again.

"No." I threw the wooden box at him as hard as I could then darted for the door.

Still in my bathing suit, I ran as fast as I could to my room, leaving my robe hanging in Lev's hands. The last thing I heard was Lev's threatening voice.

"You'll regret that!"

The door was ajar when I reached my room. Someone had been here. Lev must have come looking for me. I scrambled the code and double locked it. There was no way he could get in.

Safe inside, I dropped to the floor—crying, disgusted—processing what happened or rather, what almost happened. "You're okay, Jo," I repeated to myself. "Nothing happened. You're alright."

Shivers. I needed clothes—on my body—shielding me. I fumbled for a minute in the wardrobe. My hands felt numb and shaky. Whatever I grabbed, it was gray and thick. Gray jeans, black sweater, and a dark gray leather jacket. I zipped the jacket up to my neck. I pulled on my boots that stretched to my knees. I wanted to be hidden by many layers.

Even after I was fully dressed, I found the corner of the room that was most concealed behind my bed and slid down into the tight space, trying to sink into oblivion, trying to think through this. It was time I told Madame everything.

I pulled on my jacket zipper, but it was already all the way up. No pool for me ever again. After six minutes I went over to my desk. The computer was missing!

Lev's voice in my ear was crystal clear now. *"I have something of yours..."*

Without it there were no more files to send. My chance at freedom was gone. My opportunity to expose her was lost.

I called for Guard Ma, but there was no answer. I called another guard. Nothing. I could risk getting it back, but there was no telling what Lev would do.

I dropped to my knees. A soundless scream dropped from my lips and onto the floor. It was too late. Madame was nearly home.

THIRTEEN
PAST: OCTAVIA
∞

GOLDEN ANGEL HOTEL, SHANGHAI, CHINA

There were hundreds of abnormalities on the wall in my room. Dings. Discolored areas. I knew—I'd re-counted them for four hours until a guard signaled on the intercom.

"Madame just pulled in," he informed me. "We're taking her luggage in now. She's coming to see you."

What was I going to say?

I had to choose my words carefully. Lev was her anchor. If I informed her of how deep his betrayal went, she just might crack. If I didn't things would only get worse. Why didn't I tell her about the other women earlier? It would have been easier, more believable. But in some sick twisted way, she trusted me, loved me. I anchored my chances on the fact she promised she wouldn't hurt me again. But what if she saw the files I opened on her computer?

By dinner there was still no sign of Madame. I began

to think things would be okay. Maybe she knew about Lev. Maybe she'd been dealing with him. Maybe our lives would be rid of that nasty eel.

I sank down on the black leather couch. Just as I closed my eyes and relaxed, screams came from the hall followed by pounding on my door.

Less than a 15% chance that something good would come from that.

The keypad clicked open.

Celia was at the door. Her eyes were wild, like a soulless beast—void of warmth, like the first time I met her. My robe hung from her fist.

She threw it in my face and screamed.

Lev lied. About everything.

For five incoherent minutes Madame repeated his fabricated stories; namely, that for months, I'd flirted with him and pursued him secretly.

"I trusted you, Octavia, with everything I owned." The sting of betrayal was in her eyes. "I chose you. You were the one. I should have known better."

Celia wanted to hurt me, but her hand held back even now. "How could you?" she snapped. I'd never seen her hesitate to punish people. She never *talked it out.* But was that what she was doing with me now? Maybe she'd listen. I searched for that glimmer of humanity as I talked.

"Celia," I said. "I swear I'd never do this to you. Lev betrays you with all kinds of girls when you're not here. I should have told you earlier. I didn't know how. I never thought he would come on to me because you warned everyone to leave me alone."

Her face twitched with doubt. If she were any other human, I would have wagered on the odds of her believing me. But after I factored in her insanity...

A stagnant three seconds later her icy mask went back up. "How dare you accuse Lev to save your own skin." The minute it came out, she twitched again.

"Celia. Trust me. I know you genuinely love Lev. But he doesn't love you." As I spoke, the glimmer of a young girl flickered in her eyes. No matter how wicked she was, she was still a woman who wanted a loyal mate. I got bolder. "You don't deserve to be treated like that. Send him away. I'll stay with you."

She shook her head. "I tried to protect you, Octavia. Tried to save you. I wanted to give you everything. But I realize there's no going back."

She called out for Guard Ma. His footsteps picked up speed down the hall.

"Celia," I said, trembling. "Lev will hurt you again. But I'm helping you, remember?"

"I don't need you anymore. Because of you my income will triple for the next decade," she said coldly and laughed. "It's funny, the timing of this. Considering the fate of your family." Her lips twisted and puckered.

"What are you talking about?" She pulled out an article.

Before she crushed it in her palm, I caught the headline and date. *Boating accident in Seattle leaves family of three dead.*

"I told you we would pull it off. You can finally join your traitor family."

I dropped to the floor. A ringing—no—blaring pierces my ears. I was dizzy-sick as the headline ripped holes in my brain, cut down my chest and into my stomach. *They're dead?*

"What will you do with me?" I cried.

"I've thought about that all afternoon." She sounded normal again, like at so many of our meals together. Guard Ma arrived at the door. Celia's smile almost looks warm. "I want you to suffer your greatest fear, darling. I know just the person to arrange your long date under water. Ma, take her to the Port Lands. Give her to King."

FOURTEEN
PRESENT: PHOENIX

SHANGHAI TOWER, SHANGHAI, CHINA

My first day in Chan's company is half over. I've completed three days of work, but my mind feels as if it's been only a minute. I'm jittery, wired like I had ten cups of coffee, yet I force myself to take it slowly. I don't need to rush. I need to put all my chess pieces into place.

Chan didn't look surprised when I requested lunch in my office, but he was alarmed when I told him his company's glitch had not been found yet. I failed to mention I hadn't researched it at all. Could it really be that bad?

After lunch, I jump back on Chan's computer, thankful to finally have non-traceable, censor-free devices at my disposal.

The first thing I do is type into the search engine that random Australian phone number I found in Madame's odd empty file. A nursing home website appears. Summer Set Nursing Home. The main office is in Brisbane with branches all over Australia, normal finances. Nothing significant about it.

I'm perplexed. Why would Madame keep the number for an Australian nursing home in a secret floating file? Is it for herself? Someone she knows? Is she hiding money in their system? I knew a boy who could do that at PSS. Or it could be a red herring. I'll look into it later. For now, I've got to think.

Next, I pull up the files that I hid in Arrow Mail's database. Thankfully, they were easily recovered.

I shake my head as I review her worldwide streams of information, distribution, and cooperation. There are seven leaders all over the world but it's no wonder Shanghai is her favorite city. It holds the busiest container port in the world. Her cargo can go in and out without getting noticed, not to mention King and all her loyal men inside customs and at the port. Her business, like the Shanghai Port, is a small empire.

There are three ways to enter her domain. The Port. The Shipping Company. Her Textile Company.

I start with Golden Global Shipping, which is also a dirty operation, run by one of the seven leaders in her web of crime, Haddock, an American businessman. I used to be able to work on her shipping accounts online—not knowing what her cargo was—but now my old access codes are denied.

If I can get in, I could reroute her shipments carrying to ports where the authorities can receive them. Shut down her trafficking avenues. Expose her. *Ruin her.*

My body hardens as I remember that I lived with her, ate at her table, all the while she pillaged the world, and then there were the expos...

This coming Expo in Shanghai will be her last.

The authorities wonder why she hasn't been caught, but to me, it's obvious. It's like she doesn't exist. There is no proof of her smuggling. No trace of her tainted money. First of all, she uses a highly advanced form of crypto-currency. Second, her accounts are woven into a complicated web of routing numbers. It's like her money just disappears. If I want to be in control of her empire and expose her, there's no way around it—I need a way to trace her accounts.

As I review old expo records left in the file, numbers stick out like sore thumbs. M's Textiles has two types of buyers and for certain buyers she encoded the transfer routing number with what looks like a spin code.

Spin codes? How is she smart enough to do that? Who taught her to do that? I thought only PSS knew about spin codes. Essentially, spin codes are numerical passwords that open a back door. It's simple: You enter the routing number, the spin code scrambles, decoding a password, and opening a route to a new path.

I click on one of them to test my theory. It begins to scramble the routing number then stops.

Expired.

I click on another. Expired.

So that's it. Celia uses a spin code to make her transfers, which makes it untraceable to banks or authorities, then she eliminates the middle-man account. Fool proof.

Very few people are able to trace a spin code because the numbers scramble so fast. Fortunately, I could, if I had a chance to see it. And if I get an active spin code, it can act as a chain-entry into all her accounts, gaining access to all her money.

But when and where do buyers get the routing number?

They could get it from King, but a more logical answer is that Celia makes the buyer do the deal at the expo. An illegal operation in an open legal environment: once the deal is done, the routing number expires. Celia is always ahead of the game.

So that means...theoretically, the buyer gets a guaranteed glimpse of the routing number. Madame knows no average buyer or even the police could trace a routing number with a spin code—it scrambles for mere seconds...but a buyer like me could. I could memorize it as it scrambles. It's the only guaranteed way to get what I want.

I push away from the computer, fingers frozen.

All along I've been thinking like Octavia—who only had a computer in a locked room, or as Double-Eight locked in the Pratt. But as Phoenix, I can go anywhere, even to an expo. *I could become a buyer. Gain access to her accounts. Get proof. Ruin her.*

An expo advertisement flashes on the screen, catching my attention. I take it in. There's even a picture of Maxima Moreau's stunning face, red striking hair, with lipstick to match.

Fingers shaking, I close my eyes. My heart rate raises by 30% and a dizzy spell hits as the revelation slaps me straight in the face. I'd always imagined doing everything from behind the scenes. If I become a buyer that means I'll have to enter a building where she is and do what I never wanted to do again: I'll have to meet Madame face to face.

At the end of the day, I prepare three investments to pitch to Chan—all Madame-related that will eventually help me control her empire. They're not in Chan's regular investment portfolio, but maybe he won't guess why I've really chosen them. I'll have to wow him with numbers if I want him to agree.

A knock on the door startles me and I automatically close the computer. Chan peeks his head through the door, eyes hopeful. "Anything significant?" he asks. It's only been two hours since our last conversation.

My face pales. "Not yet, sir. It'll take some time to get through the files."

"Naturally." He clears his throat. "Tomorrow, perhaps."

"Here." I hand him a report. "A few profitable investments for you to consider."

"*Xie Xie.*" He hands me a bag with several boxes inside. "A gift from the company." I peek inside. Clothing. Shoes. A coat. Didn't I tell him I wanted to do my own shopping?

Kai walks in. His tie is off now, and his collar is open. His hair, to my surprise is out of place like he has been wrestling all day.

"Kai will drive you home."

On the drive home, Kai makes small talk about the only thing we have in common—his father's company. He's polite, but emotionless. It's obvious he's only there because his father wants him to be. For a second, I think about asking Kai what he wants to do with his life, but reconsider. Instead, I change the subject and ask him about Yu Tai, the doorman at Chan's company. The way he *doesn't* act like a doorman is still like an itch in my brain. I want to learn more.

"Who? You know his name?" He's surprised. "Sorry. I don't know anything about him. He's just the doorman."

"So, not worth knowing, huh?" I snap. In the Pratt, recognizing *clever* can be a life-saving skill. It bothers me that people can be written off so easily.

"I didn't say that," he says. "It's just that we have nothing to talk about. We're different, that's all."

"The sun and moon are different too," I say staring out the window, "but they both bring light into the world."

Kai whips his head in my direction, heat in his stare. "Where'd you learn that saying?"

His reaction startles me. A lump gathers in my stomach but I keep a straight face. I'm not fool enough to pin Red as its author. "It must be some old saying I picked up living here in China. Why?"

"I've never heard anyone say that except my mother," he says, wrinkling his brow. He shrugs it off. "You must be right. China has hundreds of old idioms. Anyway, we're home."

I should shake it off too, but I can't. A lingering feeling tells me his mother learned that saying from the same person I did.

When we pull in through the gate sixteen minutes later, I thank Kai and rush into the villa. My head clouds with equations of danger. Meeting Madame face to face is too risky. She'll recognize me.

Inside the villa, everything is foreign except the scent

of lilies and the familiar stitch of Madame throbbing
in my side. I maneuver to the bedroom and lock the
door. My eyes close and my knees hit the floor beside
the window. Outside the last hint of light fades as
Madame shows up like a black hole. There's no other
way to take her down. Come what may, I will have to
become a buyer.

Red's voice echoes in the far corners of my mind.
Destiny brought you here...

Fine. Did it also bring me here to make me suffer?
To kill me trying to bring justice? What would Red
want me to do?

I made a vow to Red to make the wrong things
right—to stop King, to bring down Madame, to use my
gift for good. Red was a man of faith. He believed in
what he couldn't see. What if his lofty ideals of destiny
and justice aren't real but just myths from old poems?
What if he believed too much in what I could do?

What's real is the thorn in my side, twisting and
burning and screaming to be removed. And in six
weeks, I will remove it. Even if it means I join Red.

Streetlamps turn on, and my eyes turn from the light.
Before I fall asleep, I make sure to close the curtains.

When ten o'clock the next morning comes, I open the
door and Kai is there. Woodsy-scented cologne floods
my senses. It's a smell that men should have, I think.
Like they have been hard at work in the mountains,
surrounded by fresh air and stone and forest. Only the
boy before me looks like he has never left the city in

his life. Black suit and tie pressed and ready to devour dollar signs for lunch.

"*Zao shang hao*, Kai," I greet him good morning.

Kai stops short. His eyes trail from my eyes all the way to my heels. My cheeks flush. The dress and shoes Mr. Chan bought for me are far too fancy for my style, but my old clothes were forming adhesive ties to my skin, so it was an easy choice.

"Nice dress."

"*Xie Xie*," I thank him, embarrassed. I make a mental note to go shopping later. We stand there silent for three beats until Kai seems to interpret my discomfort and opens the door, leading the way to the garage.

On the car ride, Kai tells me how his father taught him to trade stocks at age eleven and how everything he has done since then has been to prepare him to work at China Generation. The annoyance in his voice is not hard to detect—he obviously wants to do something else with his life. But he's far from a typical eighteen-year-old boy. I'm certainly not an expert, but I remember boys this age playing video games and pushing girls into the pool; Kai likes martial arts and motorcycles. I guess that counts. If I'm honest, for a non-prodigy, his understanding of the stock market is really attractive.

I catch myself calculating even small things that I usually dismiss—his jawline, the small neck muscles leading into his shoulders. He looks so familiar. The same question returns from that night in the pool house. *Who is Kai's mother? How does Red know Chan? Why doesn't Kai know about Red? What does Kai want for his own life?* He catches me staring.

"*Kan shenme?*"

"Sorry. You just remind me of someone, only I don't know who."

"Interesting. Most people just see my dad. Or his *money*." Kai sighs.

A twinge of empathy tightens in my chest. I know exactly how he feels. People back home always saw my father or my gift. I wondered if they ever just saw me.

"It's definitely not your father I see," I assure him.

"Well then, I hope it's someone you like." He flashes me a half smile.

We lock eyes for an instant. My insides swirl with positive numbers. It's definitely someone I like. But I don't tell Kai that and I don't keep staring.

At the office, Chan knocks on my door immediately after I arrive.

"Phoenix," he says approaching my desk. "The investments you made yesterday checked out. They'll do nicely for spring quarter. So I'd like you to focus only on my company now. What's urgent is the anomaly in my financial reports."

That's the last thing on earth I want to do but I made a deal. It's most likely something small and simple, a mere stock problem. I'll fix it, then move on with my plans. It shouldn't take more than a day.

"All right, Mr. Chan," I say. "I'll find it."

After he closes the door, I take a long deep breath and flip open the first folder.

The first hour is rather boring. I go over the company's financial history from its beginning until the present. Chan is a classic Chinese Warren Buffet. He has stocks, owns more than a few multi-million-dollar corporations, invests in whatever he wants.

Next, I sift through the latest bank statements. There's nothing unusual except a one-time personal wire transfer of 20 million to a bank with a country code of *(+61)*. A click goes off in my brain. Australia. Like a pinball machine, my brain shoots through thirty-seven connections I have to Australia, including that number for the nursing home. Chan's wire transfer, however, is designated to a Bob Lee, which could only be one person. I laugh out loud. Bo Gong didn't make it too hard for me to find him.

Further down, there's a column of payments recording Chan's gifts to charity and holiday bonuses for his low-income employees. I wouldn't have guessed he was so generous. Apart from this, everything is business as usual until I come to financial reports from the last six months and the numbers shift. I follow the declining numbers and a pattern jumps out at me—one I studied back in basic economics.

A few files later, I recognize the same pattern in businesses that are similar to Chan's–some of the strongest businesses in Asia, all connected to one bank. Asia Bank.

Prodigy Stealth Solution hired me to solve a problem at Asia Bank. Could this be related? It'd been months since I thought about Asia bank and PSS. What if the problem was never solved and now it's far beyond control?

Hoping I'm wrong, I devise an equation to predict future income and losses.

Maybe it's another recession, like the one in 2008 or 2017? 2022? If so, that would be easy to fix. But the pattern is different than the normal economic cycles of failure and growth. In fact, it's almost identical to a pattern seen in history, only it's incomplete, like a tree with a thousand branches but the picture only shows a few small twigs.

That's where my gift comes in. While no experts or prodigy friends could predict the real outcome from this pattern—*I can.*

I don't feel well. A horrible coldness courses down my chest and into my stomach, my arms, my fingers. I drop my head low, holding my face in my hands. Chan was right. His company will be bankrupt by the end of the year. But his company is not the problem.

The stakes are much higher. My fingers, now cold, start tapping on the desk as mathematical models form in my head, calculating the repercussions this will have in China, in America, and onto the rest of the world. Not to mention on me.

I request lunch in my office again and keep digging. I search for anything that might sway the numbers. Chan arrives at the end of the day. "Phoenix, did you find anything?"

I consider telling him, but I can't yet. This is not something you share casually over a cup of tea. Then again, there's no perfect setting to share news this bad. Still, I can't say anything to Chan, or anyone, until I'm absolutely sure. I can't rely on theoretical mathematical predictions. I need proof. I need a solution.

"Sir, I want to finish this first," I say without lifting my head, hoping the worry on my face doesn't show. "I'll get a cab."

He nods. "I will have the executive restaurant send

you dinner." He closes the door and I continue working. Only when my stomach growls do I realize it is far past dinnertime.

Before I eat, I compare everything: numbers, theories, banks. I compare American economic history to the history of modern-day China, until there's no doubt left in my mind that the glitch in Chan's company is a far bigger problem than I bargained for.

I bite the knuckle of my thumb, cursing the odds. Why does disaster always find me? I don't want to focus on this. I don't have time to solve this. I have one goal—take Madame's empire down, then start my life over.

I rest my elbows on the desk and exhale loudly. Twelve minutes, eleven seconds pass as I stare at the wall. A picture of Seattle comes to mind—slipping once again out of reach. It's not just a plane ride across the ocean anymore. It's across a sea of a billion numbers, mouths, bodies, buildings, economies, nations, and dreams.

What kind of life would I have there if I returned? Could I really start over again near my ocean? Before this morning, home felt so close. But now...

The clock reads four in the morning. After a dozen cups of tea, cold water, and a small amount of pinching, my body shuts down. The couch by the window looks more comfortable than the chair I'm sitting in, but I've avoided it because it looks like a black hole trying to suck me back into the Pratt.

After several minutes of cringing, I lie on the couch and give into my exhaustion.

This office may be nicer than Madame's or King's,

but the news is just as bad. I wish I could dismiss what I found as just a theory. But I can't. Because if I'm right, a global economic crash will hit before the end of the year and it looks as impossible to stop as an avalanche. If there was any hope to stop it—any solution to be found—it would take someone like me to find it. But that would mean delaying my plans to stop Madame, and that is something I cannot do.

FIFTEEN
PAST: DOUBLE-EIGHT
∞

THE PRATT, SHANGHAI, CHINA

My last memory would be of King's hands. Rough, hard, wicked. Hands that had killed before. Hands that would kill me now. Hands that kept me under water—60 seconds, 70, 80...

My throat capsized under the most wretched hands on the planet. In less than ten seconds water would flood my lungs and I would drown. Important dates—Lily's birthday, my parent's anniversary, the day I learned to swim—bubbled up as I fought to hold on.

Pain, like firecrackers, pinched me as blood vessels popped in my face, but it was nothing to the burning pain in my lungs—water had entered.

Gasp! King pulled me out. "Why were you so special to Madame? What did you do for her? Why did she send you to me?"

I heard the questions. I was willing to answer but my head spun, and I couldn't stop coughing.

My head went back under water before I caught my breath—30, 40, 50...

My mom floated in the water beside me. Lack of oxygen was making me hallucinate. Her eyes told me to fight. To hold on another minute. To answer King.

I was yanked out by the throat. I crumbled to my knees, convulsing. There was an 85% chance contusions on my larynx would interfere with my ability to speak. Water spilled out of my lungs. I heaved, and choked, and spit, still half-drowning, still contending to breathe, still calculating if death beat the odds over a life with King.

He backhanded me across the face. Pain mixed with numbers splitting apart my world in which there were two options: I wanted to die. I didn't want to die.

"Last chance to tell me everything, little girl," he growled. "Or your next date with water will be your last."

Tapping. All I could do with the numbers spinning possibilities in my head was tap. My leg. The ground. My lip. I tapped, but I managed to force out a hoarse, choked whisper.

"Money. I make her lots of money." As much as I could through a damaged throat, I told him everything he wanted to know.

When I was done, he rubbed his hands together like he'd found his golden lamp with a genie inside. As greed took possession of King, Madame's command to kill me became void. I'd entered a new dragon's lair now and his mountain of gold was already piling up.

"I'm going to keep you, lucky girl, to test your *powers.*" A cruel smile spread across his face. After another initiation of sixty seconds underwater, I entered his *employment.*

Thirty-eight days later...

The Pratt's tunnels were dark, musty, and cold. The smell of cigarettes, sweat, and mildew caught in my nose. I covered my face with my sleeve as we walked.

We came to the end of the corridor and passed a different guard station. This section of the tunnel contained two rooms apart from the rest. One of the cells was empty; the other was mine. Each time I entered the room, it hit me like a death sentence. The clank of the lock behind me was loud and heavy. It was so absolute, like a tombstone being laid over my grave.

I could speak again, but I couldn't breathe here.

My clothes, the same leather jacket, gray jeans, and sweater I wore the day I left Madame's, had been dry for thirty-eight days, but I was still chilled to the bone. Terror had permanently moved into my body. I'd become jumpy.

Besides the tremor in my hands, I didn't feel anything anymore. I was numb. As soon as I understood King would spare me if I produced great sums of money, I sold my soul. Working under a threat, like everyone else who worked for King.

A pain in my stomach urged me to eat, but I had no desire for food. I'd tried playing Seagulls here, but it didn't work. Rarely seeing the sky might have had something to do with it.

My eyes were so bloodshot I lost vision. I fell on my metal cot and pulled the thin blanket over my bony frame. The darkness folded around me. Not even numbers could occupy my mind. I had calculated everything in this room, these halls, four hundred and sixty-three times already. My mind already slept. I slipped into oblivion, hoping that against all odds, I'd stay there.

After a couple hours of cold, fitful sleep, I woke to two eyes staring at me through the bars of the neighboring cell. I jerked backwards to escape them. They didn't feel like eyes but arms reaching out to me—to help or hurt me, I didn't know. I was scared, but when I looked again, the man's eyes drew me in. They were not dark and cavernous like Celia's. Not wicked and devouring like King's. Maybe I was delusional and half dreaming, but his whole being glowed like a candle in the night. He was still, gauging me, as if a keen sixth sense was at work. I wondered what he saw.

He stood slowly and opened the door to his cell. For a fifth of a second, I questioned how it was unlocked but quickly calculated an 84% chance of him speaking. I was weak, but I swung my legs over the side of my bed and sat up, clutching at my blanket. His face contorted. He was in pain at what he saw. That answered my question—I must have looked even worse than I felt.

He approached my cell door and gripped the bars. "You can trust me." It was all he said, in a low, nearly perfect English accent, before he returned to his metal-framed cot to lie down.

Then I knew I'd dreamed him, because it sounded too good to be true. I didn't know if I could trust anyone, ever again.

In the morning, Guard San returned and placed a bowl of watery rice before me.

"Who's that?" I asked, pointing across the hall.

He glanced over his shoulder. "Crazy *Hong*?"

"Is he a prisoner or an associate?" I asked. "His cell's unlocked."

Guard San didn't answer or give me an extra glance before he walked away laughing. I grabbed my bowl and choked down each bite.

For the next three days, the old man walked in and out of his unlocked cell, always throwing a look my way. He watched me too, especially when Guard San fetched me on the occasional afternoon to work for King.

On the fourth day, the old man came over to me, holding a small white bowl. To my surprise he offered it to me.

"Rice porridge?" He sat on the ground next to my cell, his hands holding the bowl between the bars. "I'm Hong Rui. You can call me Red."

I looked at the bowl because I was starving. To my disappointment, it was full of what they'd served me the last three days. Watery, mushy rice soup. *Xifan*, is what they called it. No flavor, lukewarm, texture like baby food. There was a stringy green vegetable on top, slimy like seaweed and a pungent smell, like it had been pickled. Last night it made me nauseous. My lips puckered and my nose turned up at the smell. He saw the look on my face. I didn't mean to look ungrateful or disgusted, but I couldn't stomach the food. I felt sick just looking at it.

"A person who is full refuses honey," he said in

a low voice, moving the bowl to his lips, "but even bitter food tastes sweet to the hungry." Then he slurped down his soupy porridge and walked away.

His analogy was clear right away, but it had the opposite effect on me. Honey came to my mind instead, then butter and warm toast. My stomach growled. I remembered how hungry I really was and cursed myself the rest of the day for refusing an opportunity to fill it with more food.

The next day he came again. I retreated to the back of the cell. He squatted, flat-footed, by the edge of my cell. "Why are you here?"

I didn't answer. King forbade me to give any such details to anyone here for fear that Madame would learn he kept me alive. Besides, I found it strange that this old man spoke to me because no one else in this underground prison would.

When I didn't respond, he took a piece of white chalk from his dirty pocket and scribbled a string of symbols on the floor. I supposed he was writing something, but Chinese characters all looked the same to me—that was, until I looked closer.

As his hand wrote from top to bottom, left to right, a pattern in the strokes emerged. I began to decipher different strokes on the left of each pictogram. Whether I liked it or not, my mind assigned numbers to the different parts of the characters. I leaned in closer to continue my observation. A certain pleasure surged within me. *Stimulation.* The language was a puzzle. I had the first variable in the unknown equation. *I was learning.*

The man Red noticed me watching and stopped. He stood. With those intense eyes he stared me square in the face again, reaching. "Do you read?"

I remained silent.

"Is my English coming out in German?" He feigned a test of his ears.

I shook my head.

"Ah ha, you do understand," he said. "They have etched two 8's onto your cell. Do you know what 88 signifies in China?"

I shook my head again.

"A sign of great prosperity. Perhaps the luckiest number in China. Is that what you are? Lucky?"

I knew it. King was mocking me with my new designation. Most likely this old man was too. Didn't Guard San call him crazy?

"I don't believe in luck," I said, in a whisper.

"Interesting."

"Why are you talking to me?" I asked, a slight crack in my voice. "No one else talks to me."

"No one else respects you."

"Why not?" I squeaked. I was nothing but a cornered mouse.

"First, you belong to King. Second, you are not one of us. You're a *laowai*. An outsider. You know nothing about our ways, cannot speak our language. Why should we waste time with you? Especially in the Pratt. Here, you earn respect."

"Then what do you want from me?"

"Nothing," he said. "What do you want from me?"

The question threw me off. I shivered with fear wondering what he could mean. Before I processed a proper response, I snapped back, "Nothing."

After one last glance from his intense eyes, he dipped

his head and left. That was twice now that I watched him go and cursed myself. Why did I shoo away the first person who talked to me, who gave me information, who asked me what I wanted? Wasn't it obvious I wanted to go home? Of course, it was. That could not be what he was asking.

So what *was* he asking? A web of possibilities spun in my brain. Did I want something from him? If so, what was it?

SIXTEEN
PAST: DOUBLE-EIGHT

∞

THE PRATT, SHANGHAI, CHINA

After my blindfold was removed, I looked around. The Port Lands looked like a cemetery for derelict buildings, old rusty boats, a rundown lighthouse that King used as a watchtower. There were signs of what used to be docks but now they were a string of broken wood. The sea was close, but I couldn't see it. A line of trees, a small tributary, and an ugly warehouse blocked the view.

I breathed deep. The air here smelled of chemicals and coal, smothering the scent of salt, but at least it was better than the air I breathed down below in the tunnels of the Pratt.

I shivered as I descended the steps of Building Seven following Guard San underground. No one could believe that under this wasteland were hidden such a complex framework of old tunnels. Judging by the decay in the walls, I'd bet if they did some optical dating down here, they'd be more than just old; they'd be ancient.

I resigned myself to the dank air and followed San after another day spent embezzling for my master. Down the aisles, we passed different crooks living in King's odd mix of private prison and criminal safe house.

In the first group of cells, a handful of Chinese men set their cards down to look up at me. I was one of only a few females in the Pratt, so it didn't matter that my body was still young and undeveloped. As I passed the men's cells, their eyes followed and feasted on the few curves I had. One of the men asked the guards, "When will she grow up so she can give us a real show?" I shuddered with disgust and pulled my jacket tighter.

Red's words echoed in my mind. *No one respects you. Here you earn it.* I saw now what he was talking about. In the States I was often mistaken for being much older because of the way I talked, or the things I talked about. These men saw only flesh and bone, and I remembered how young I really was.

Further down there was another area holding a few Russians and Azerbaijanis gambling over a game-fight. They set their faces against the bars to see who was coming. They were relieved it wasn't King and resumed their match of sweat and blood.

When I arrived at the hall of my cell, the man named Red was speaking to one of the guards. It wasn't Mandarin Chinese, or what they called *common speech*. It was a dialect. It was the third time I'd heard him switch in and out of a different language, not including English. How many languages did he know? Why was he here? How much did he know about this place?

Red noticed my return and said goodbye to the guard. His gaze lingered on me before he walked over. His face and ears had dark spots, most likely the result of frostbite. His teeth were stained, and his body looked like it could fall apart if exposed to daylight. He must have had a miserable existence here. Although, I had to admit his eyes were bright and untroubled.

He pulled a small box from his pocket. The box unfolded and became a small chessboard. He arranged the pieces. "Play a game?"

I glanced at the chessboard. He really was crazy. The last thing I wanted to do was get cozy and play games or gamble like everyone else did in here, even if he wasn't creepy like the other inmates. I thought there was something different about him, but maybe he was just an old man, driven mad by being locked up in a rat hole.

"No, thanks," I said, disappointed.

"I can teach you if you want."

For some reason, that annoyed me. King knew I was smart but no one else did, and I was sick of looking like a pathetic little kitten who got pushed around. "I know how to play," I said, arrogantly. "In fact, chess is too easy for me."

"Too easy?" he said, rubbing his chin. "Ah ha."

"It's a game of numbers and odds," I said. "Predicting countermoves. *Too easy.*"

"Ah ha, you *are* special," he said, "but you forget that every game is different, because every king and queen have a different weakness and every pawn has a different strength. What if I am good at countermoves too?"

"I'm not interested."

His eyes were just a slit open, but that small slice pierced me. "Ah ha. Then what are you interested in—*gold?*" he said in a long, drawn-out hum, as if he was pondering something. "King keeps you in a private cell. Protects you. To him, you are *gold*. Which kind would you say? There's all kinds of gold here."

The mention of gold reminded me of Celia and I completely snapped. "Stop talking about gold! *I hate gold!*" I screamed. Another greedy lunatic obsessed with gold. "I hate money. And I hate people who want it. You're just like the rest of them. You asked me what I want?" I raised my voice, my anger filling the eight-by-five-square-foot cell. "I want out of this godforsaken place and I want you to leave me alone!"

I was on my feet, retreating to the corner of my cell, fighting back tears, waiting for him to leave. I wanted to isolate myself as I did at Madame's. I glanced over my shoulder. I expected him to spit some dirty remark and leave, but he stayed there, face calm, no vengeful response to my red-faced blow out. He set his chess pieces down, cleaned them up very mechanically, without an ounce of anger. It made me feel worse.

He stood and set his face against the bars of my cell. We locked eyes. "You fear your circumstances more than you fear yourself. Pure gold does not fear the fire—it endures it. In the end, it will shine brighter than the sun, and the sun cannot be caged."

Then he walked back to his cell.

For three weeks his words burned into my head. *Pure gold does not fear the fire…More than you fear your-*

*self...*What had he meant?

His cell was right next to mine, but we hadn't spoken to each other since that day. Partly because King took me out of the Pratt for transactions, then had me working on several investments in another cell next to where the laundry was done.

When I next saw Red, he was writing on the walls with chalk. As I watched, my mind processed the language. I could recognize over one hundred symbols now. I wanted to ask him what they all meant, but I didn't. Instead I avoided his stare because I sensed he was doing it for me.

Pure gold, he'd said. *All kinds of gold here.* He may have been crazy, but he knew something about this place I didn't, and for unknown reasons he was willing to share it with me. Numbers spun in my mind and an idea wove together about what I really wanted.

King was in Shenzhen, crossing the border into Hong Kong with the forty thousand I made for him on Tuesday. I had a week off from wondering what atrocities he was planning. It was a good time to talk to Red.

If I admitted it, speaking to another human may have been my first motivation. Besides the few words of English I'd spoken to King, which didn't count because it was either yes or no or quoting a number, I hadn't spoken to anyone. Red was the only person who spoke English well enough to have a real conversation.

He saw my wave and came over.

"Um," I attempted an apology. "Last time—"

"Forgotten," he said.

I nodded and gathered up enough courage to ask

a question. "How do you know what all the other inmates are saying?"

"I speak many different dialects," he said. "And English, like you plainly hear."

"How did you learn them?" I asked.

"A good ear and a few years," he said. "I am a teacher."

"You mean *were?*" I motioned to the bars.

"Am. Bars cannot change who you are." He started writing again.

"What are you writing?"

"Classical Chinese poetry. It talks about how even a small flower has purpose in our great world." He set his chalk aside. "What is your purpose?"

I glanced at the three walls and the bars in front of me. "I don't have one."

"Impossible," he said. "We all do, if we are willing to find it."

"Maybe I'd know if I could get back to America."

"Ah, *Meiguo.* Beautiful country," he said. "But are you so sure you have no purpose here?"

"No disrespect but I'd leave today if I could and never come back."

He frowned. A pang hit my gut. He didn't do anything to me.

The lines of his mouth softened. "Ah ha. China and America are very different. So are the sun and moon, but both bring light into the world. Perhaps you will see it in time. For now, what do you want?"

"I want you to teach me," I said. "I want the respect you talked about. To speak Chinese, dialects, poetry, understand conversations in the Pratt."

His face remained unchanged. "Why?"

"Before I came here, all I ever wanted was purpose. But that was taken from me. Now the only thing I want is my life back," I said. I didn't explain that I'd need allies and *language* to get out of here. I held my tongue about Maxima, the root of my pain—and how I'd stop at nothing to cut her down. But Red wasn't blind; he saw anger burning in my eyes like flames.

He scratched his head, gauging his decision. A solemn smile came over his lips. "When do you want to start?"

"Now."

He squinted. I could barely see if his eyes were open. "*Hao.*"

He grabbed a white piece of chalk. "First lesson. My name is Red, but you will call me Grandfather."

I scoffed. "Why? You're not my grandfather." I looked at the holes in his jacket and his black woven shoes that were falling apart.

"Culture and language are not separate from one another." His eyes fixated on me. "If you cannot do this, you will speak but you will never understand."

In my world, the word *grandfather* was an intimate name connected to birthdays, football games, and family—but now, family was connected to a knife ripping up my insides. Logically, however, it made sense for language study and I wanted to learn. "Fine," I said, reluctantly. "I still don't get it."

"You do not know how to respect your elders," he said. "I am old enough to be your grandfather. So you must treat me with respect and honor. If you call me Red, I become your equal and you dishonor me.

I allow it because you are not Chinese. Only when you can say this can we start our lessons. Now, do you understand?"

"Yes." I swallowed. By the look on his face, he wanted me to prove it. The word was lodged in my throat. Red waited.

My eyes locked on to some divot in the cement, as if something in the crack pulled me into it. "Yes, Grandfather," I finally choked out.

"I, in return, will call you granddaughter," he said, "and in here, you will be like my own family. I will teach you everything I know, and I will love you like my own flesh and blood."

My neck snapped up, catching his fatherly gaze. *Love?* I hadn't heard that word for months from anyone. I'd forgotten that word existed; lied about the need it encompassed, the weight it carried, the power it possessed. I told myself love wasn't real, when really, I was desperate for it.

Instantly, I wanted my mom, to hear her voice. For her to pull me close and tell me she loved me. The word consumed me as it ricocheted in my mind.

Love. Love. Love. To love. *To be* loved.

Infinity raced in my calculations. One path with two loops forever chasing each other without end. A limitless world. As it spun, my heart was on fire and frozen like ice. I was shot dead and resurrected. I was hungry, thirsty, brave, and frantic; like the tide coming in and out, I had no control. Love was supposed to be infinite. Love was made to last. So why was I alone?

Hot tears burned trails down my cheeks as I reached out. For my mom. For my dad. For anyone.

But they were all gone. I had lost everyone I loved and Red saw it in my eyes.

He bent down beside me. His old hand, warm and light, rested on my shoulder through the bars.

"Yes, granddaughter. Love. We are created for it. To become one with it. Without it, we die. A lesson more powerful than them all," he said. "Come now, let's start."

SEVENTEEN
PRESENT: PHOENIX

∞

SHANGHAI TOWER, SHANGHAI, CHINA

My eyes blink open at the light sneaking through the window. I check the clock. Not yet six. The bad news sits on my desk like a meteor streaming towards earth. Sadly, experts will see the pattern but not understand how colossal it will be until it is too late. Hopefully, Chan's bout of superstition will be enough to convince him.

I walk to the bathroom. The large mirror haunts me as I watch a girl wash the tears off her face. It's not Phoenix staring back at me. It's some girl I don't know, asking if there is anyone out there who can love her for who she is. Not the money. Not the gift. Not even her face. Who could love the girl, for whoever she really is?

Whoever I am.

Josephine. Octavia. Double 8. Mila. Phoenix. An American. *Laowai.*

After the 74 steps back to my office, I'm driven to print off an old article about myself as a child. I want to see the girl I used to be. To remember what it felt like to be her. When I pull the paper off the printer, it's hot and crisp. But I can't read it. Can't even look at it. Instead I shove it in my drawer.

I stand and walk to the window. My fingertips touch the glass, as I stare at the city. The red sun battles for its throne in the hazy eastern sky. The streets and squares of Shanghai's financial district enjoy their last few minutes of rest before they're crawling with millions of people.

The skyline towers with the tallest buildings in the world. I find myself admiring the Oriental Pearl Tower, the icon of Shanghai. In my sleep-deprived state, it looks like a pillar of bubbles, glowing purple and blue. It reminds me of riding the elevator up the Space Needle in Seattle with my parents and sisters when I was a little girl.

The Waitan is also magical at this hour. With my eyes, I float down the Huangpu River to the historical boardwalk where hundred-year-old buildings line the west bank of the river. The different architectural styles—Gothic, Baroque, Romanesque, Classical and Renaissance mesh with modern day China. Did they imagine a hundred years ago that Shanghai, a small fishing town, would become a major global contender?

Beyond the river, past the banks, penetrating the vast circuit of thousands of apartment complexes, commercial centers, and hotels, are more than 40 million people, sleeping, showering, eating, working, laughing, and crying. Warmth stirs in me. Even after everything that has happened, I still want that. A family. Home. Love.

My eyes sting as the memory of Red's love rushes over me. He'd care about each and every one of the people in those buildings. He'd help Chan. He'd stop the criminals. He wouldn't think about revenge—but a way to act. He'd focus on destiny. His impact on one life—the life of an innocent girl who once believed she could do something that mattered.

A light blinks on in a building across the street. Through the window, I watch a Chinese woman brush back the hair of a small girl. Afterwards, she leans down to hug her. My chest swells. It's worth it, I think, those small moments in which love wins. It's a small slice of hope, but I cling to it.

I'm suddenly very self-aware, like Red is in the room. My plans of revenge shrink in significance as I count human life popping up on the streets. *Pure gold does not fear the fire.*

These faces are more than numbers and statistics. They've got dreams and purposes and a billion ways to fulfill them. The city looks wondrous under the coming dawn. A childlike desire to go exploring rises in me. If I had come here with PSS for that month, with nothing harder than a few math problems to solve, would I have liked it?

Because of Red, the answer is yes. He stripped off what Madame and King had tainted to reveal layers of depth and beauty. I won't let them steal that from me.

The city is awake now. Buses crammed with people zip through the streets. Metro exits flood with people, hands holding briefcases and canisters of tea. Students tromp across the square, shoulders slumped under heavy backpacks. Couples hold hands and kiss as they part ways for the next eight hours, which means... people will arrive soon.

I sit and bend my head from side to side trying to work out a tight muscle in my neck. In each twist I debate where to start with Chan.

Before eight o'clock Mr. Chan comes to the door. When he sees my face, he stops dead in his tracks.

"Did you stay the night here?" he asks, glancing from my hair to my strung-out face.

"Regrettably." I hold my eyes shut for five long seconds, both easing the burning sensation and wondering where to begin.

Chan picks up on my cues. He ushers me into his office and asks me to sit at the desk beside him.

"I was right, wasn't I?" he says. "My company is failing."

"If only that was the problem, then we'd be okay," I say. "Brace yourself. It's much worse than you think."

Chan rubs his forehead, like a headache is coming on strong. He buzzes the intercom on the phone. "*Hong cha*, very strong, please." After he orders his black tea, he faces me. "Tell me everything."

I bite my lip. How do I find words to explain this?

"Please don't keep me waiting. How bad is it?" Chan asks nervously.

I don't want to tell him. I'm tired of fixing people's problems. Tired of doing what others want. Tired of doing everything for everyone else while my own life drifts farther away. Chan stares at me, getting ever-redder in the face, cursing under his breath for finding such an oddball. But I'm stuck somewhere between dreams and reality, obedience and rebellion. Like a kid who knows what is right but doesn't care anymore.

"Well?" he says. "Did you find a solution?"

It drives me crazy that Chan doesn't even know what the problem is and all he wants to know is if I can fix it. Little does he know that I am probably the only one who can even identify it, let alone fix it.

I'm about to rip into him when I have a thought. *PSS believed in me. They thought I was the only one who could fix it.*

Only, that isn't entirely true. I can't fix this. Not alone.

Red once said that even without Madame or PSS, I might have ended up here all the same. *Why?* I'd asked. *We often end up where we're needed,* he'd say.

Is this what he was talking about? *No coincidence.* Right? The thought strikes like a hammer on molten iron. All night I'd been scrutinizing the problem, how impossible it was to fix alone, how I'd have to give up my plans to focus on it. But what if I'm not alone?

"Phoenix?"

"Wait." I snatch the pen on the desk, grab a notepad and scribble equations down madly.

My mind reels with possibilities as numerous as the stars—which makes narrowing it down about as easy as bringing world peace. Numbers fire faster than neurons, finally a solution knits itself together. With Chan's resources coupled with my gift, it could work.

Chan mutters something, but I tune him out. I don't even notice the secretary has brought Chan's black tea until I see it steaming in front of him.

I study the new formula. It's daunting. Theoretically, there's only a small chance of success because of who sits in front of me. Nine minutes of silence and calculating pass. When I look up, Mr. Chan has loosened his tie and taken off his blazer. Sweat beads on his forehead. He's fuming. I've made him wait. *Again.*

"You were right," I say, shaking my head. I open the file on the desk. "There's a lot at stake." Chan is wide-eyed and lingering between panicked and annoyed. "The average eye can't see it. But you, Chan, you're the one who needed to see it."

Red said this moment would come. A chance to right my wrongs. To use my gift for good. Is this how I fulfill my vow to Red? A knot tightens in my stomach. What about stopping Madame? King? What about justice?

"I can't fix the problem, sir," I say. Dread discolors him, and his eyes drop to the floor. "But you can."

"You haven't told me what is wrong."

"I stumbled onto an economic phenomenon," I say. "A cycle of sorts."

"Such as?"

"Last century the world was knocked on its back for more than ten years by the very same economic pattern. It affected the world economy for 40 years following the crash. Since that time, our world has been riddled with smaller economic crashes, but we haven't experienced anything as extreme. Until now."

He stares at me, a restrained fear in his eyes. "Do you mean the Great Depression of the 1930s in America?"

"You got it," I say. He nods, still silent. "If my predictions are right, another Economic Cycle of Failure will hit China before the year is up. It'll be a massive depression, bigger than America's. If China crashes, everyone else will too. But you can stop this. Prevent the same chaos from striking the world. You could stop widespread poverty. The dissolution of business and industry. Migration. Starvation. Desperation. Even war."

"War?" He laughs. "I should have guessed you were as crazy as Red. This is ridiculous. Like talking to a lunatic."

"What happened directly after the Great Depression?" I ask him seriously. He doesn't answer, so I do. "World War II! This is the same pattern. Inflation. Debt. Only this time it will hit China first and the *renminbi* that leads the banking system of the world will plummet. People out of jobs. Homes. Widespread bankruptcy. A hundred years ago globalization was just beginning, but now there's no disconnecting us. If China falls, we all fall."

Using my notes, I dive into more explanations of stock markets and China's role in world economy. He still stares blankly at me.

"Impossible," he mutters, "the last crash was hard, people lost jobs, there was struggle, a bit of unrest, overall, nothing catastrophic happened. Certainly not war. Depressions come and go. Prosperity always returns." He shakes his head in disbelief. His steadies himself, his left hand against the window.

"The Great Depression blew the industrial world to bits—shanty towns popped up in prosperous areas, babies died on the side of the road, crime rose everywhere, families split apart, countries divided and dictators rose with authoritarian ideals—Hitler, Stalin, Mussolini!" I catch my breath. "If the crash from a hundred years ago can do that, what will it do today?"

Mr. Chan rubs his temples. He may be the type who doesn't like to even acknowledge that poverty exists, let alone an economic crash, which creates more poverty.

"Look," I say, trying to keep my head, "I don't want it to be true either, but after calculating 236 different scenarios, the results are the same, unless you change the course of the future."

"What are you talking about?"

"Puzzle pieces. It's not a coincidence that I'm in your office," I say, taking a deep breath. "Because of you we discovered the upcoming crash just in time to act. You have a net worth of over 100 billion US dollars, which means you of all people can do something about this, and with my equations, it can succeed. You can make history, Mr. Chan."

I pause to let that revelation soak in. For almost two years I had no control over my life, yet I end up in Chan Huang Long's office at just the right time to discover the coming crash, like I was always meant to be here, to help *him*. The odds of me going from Seattle to Madame to the Pratt to land in this office are greater than a monkey finding a needle in a billion haystacks.

Suddenly, I understand. Destiny, or whatever I've been looking for, isn't about history or the future. It's about the choices I make *right now.*

But I'm going to have to spell it out for Chan because he's got a game face on—one I'm sure he uses at every big deal. Clearly, no one pulls the wool over Chan Huang Long's eyes.

For the next hour I explain the intricacies of how this phenomenon will affect the world financial system, everything from governments to banking to private enterprise.

"See, Chan. Too much has been invested under false pretense. Governments have flooded their stock markets beyond recovery. Have your connections check it out." I slide my research and numbers over to him. The math, he gets. It's the outrageous prediction behind it that he's still mulling over. "Don't tell anyone how serious this is yet or about me."

Chan lets out a heavy sigh. "Assuming you're right," he says, sliding his hands along on his upper thighs, "what will it mean for my company?"

Is he starting to believe me?

"Your company is easily saved," I answer. "We could even double your money, but you must act now."

"How long do we have?" he asks, confused.

"Six weeks, eight at the most. The crash could last several years. I've created a way to hold back the flood—but you'll have to initiate my plan in less than 6 weeks if you want it to work."

"Me initiate your plan? What do you mean *me*?" He sits up now, on the edge of his seat. "What exactly are you suggesting, Phoenix?"

I drop the bomb on Chan. "Your money, sir. You will have to part with it."

Chan's hand strikes the desk. The thump sends a pen flying to the ground. But I see it coming, so I don't even flinch. He's on the verge of either sweating to death or erupting from the gut up.

"You are crazy," he says, slapping both hands on the table. "You have only brought me bad luck since you arrived. Down 20 million. A broken nose. Now you propose I give all my money away? Never!"

Chan pulls the blue pocket square from his jacket draped over his chair and dabs his nose, his face still crimson with irritation. "Let the banks—the World Bank—solve this!"

"Banks won't be able to help—not without you. Let me explain," I say. "In the simplest of terms, I've created a bailout plan where we flood the monetary system with an exorbitant amount of cash—and I mean *a lot* of cash—for the first year of the crash. Theoretically, the disaster will be significantly less damaging. We can do it—if I work with you to make more money."

Chan's face is hard, but since he is quiet, I continue. "Here's how it will work. With one half of your money, we focus on sustaining currency, stock market, and banks. With the other half, we offer a super bond to major corporations and businesses to stay afloat." Chan's eyebrows stitch together in thought. "You'll have to buy Asia Bank for central bank distribution, and then you'll—"

"No." He stares at me long and hard. At first, I think I see a spark of compassion flash across his face, but it vanishes. "No." He shakes his head, all business again. "I appreciate your spirit, but I need to protect my interests. We made a deal. Focus on rebuilding my company. If the crash ever comes, I'll take the proper precautions." He crosses his arms against his chest, like he has closed a deal, then looks up at me and gives me a long hard stare, eyes unblinking, decided. "Everything my company makes from your counsel will profit you at forty percent—until my numbers are up again. You can do what you want with your money, but I will do as I think best for mine."

"In theory, everything you invest will come back to you ten-fold."

"No."

My cheeks flush crimson as I stare back at him. For a moment I see King's face. Greed looks the same on everyone, I think. I'm a fool. I really thought if Red picked Chan there'd be a good ending to the story, that some kind of destiny was wrapped up in this relationship. Red was wrong. Or I'm wrong. Either way, for Chan, it's plain what he's about—his interests. His money. His life. Singular. It takes everything in me to hold back from a total blow out.

"You won't do anything?" I ask again.

"Other people's businesses are not my responsibility." He drops his gaze, focused on something he's pulling out of his wallet. The picture of his wife?

"Businesses?" I say. "I'm talking about people, families, children! You wouldn't help them if you could?"

He turns away, looking out the window as if our whole conversation is over. "Don't expect me to be a saint like Red, giving up everything. Look where it got him!" His voice is just above a whisper, masking anger or sadness, I can't tell. "I am not interested in saving the world," he says.

"You're right. You're not like Red at all," I tell him. I walk over to where he's standing because I won't let him not look at me. "You can't leave a legacy if you live only for yourself."

Chan is beyond angry. His hands tighten into fists, and his face comes inches from mine. "Did Red tell you what happened? Did he tell you why he was in that cell?"

This silences me. Because I don't know. I'm not even sure how they know each other.

He moves towards the window, breathing slowly and deeply, trying to regain his composure. "I didn't think so," he spits out like venom. "Let's get one thing clear. I do not need your counsel on how to live my life any more than I needed Red's, nor do I need you to tell me how to spend my money. You do your part. I will do mine. We made a deal. This conversation is over."

"Fine," I say, my eyes fixed on him.

I think about walking out for good. Never coming back. Mr. Chan doesn't own me. Even if I did make a deal, I'm free to leave. Right now, I need air, or I might suffocate.

"Here. Your first step to doubling your billions," I say as I slam down a piece of paper I prepared earlier. "Do this by the end of the week and your company will be on track. I'll be waiting for my forty percent. Goodbye."

"Where are you going?" he says loudly. "You can't walk out of here. There's more work to do. We had a deal!"

There's a knock on the door. Kai comes in.

"Do it yourself." I slam the chair back under the desk.

I remember the pawn in my pocket and dig it out. Chan is about to say something when I bring up my fist and unfold my fingers. The small chess piece, scratched and faded with time, sits in my palm.

"For you. I assume you know where it came from." I slam it on the table.

Mr. Chan swallows hard as he stares at it. His face contorts, as if I had just handed him a funeral slip.

"What's going on here?" Kai asks. His father doesn't answer.

Kai's blocking the door. I push against his shoulder to get him to move. "Ask your father."

EIGHTEEN
PRESENT: PHOENIX
∞

SHANGHAI TOWER, SHANGHAI, CHINA

Outside, the dizziness spreads from my head to the rest of my body. Alternating waves of numbers and Chan's words crash in my mind. The lack of sleep isn't helping. My eyes burn, but I don't want to go back to Chan's villa.

A taxi pulls up to the curb just as Kai exits the building. He spots me and waves his hands. "Phoenix! Wait!" he yells, but I have already hopped inside the cab and the driver pulls out.

"Do you want me to stop?" the driver asks as he sees Kai running on the sidewalk.

"No." I stare straight ahead as if I can't hear or see him. "Take me to the nearest mall."

I pull out Chan's envelope—Chairman Mao's solemn face stares back at me from the red bills. I shove a few thousand into my pockets and secure the envelope inside my jacket liner.

As we weave through the city streets, guilt plagues me as I think of Kai. Why would he come after me? Does he want to convince me his father is right? That I'm a lunatic for heralding the next financial crash? Whatever the reason, a part of me wants to believe that he ran out just for me. That someone cares. But it's a silly thought. Exhaustion must be taking over.

The driver compliments me on my Chinese and treats me to an unwanted lesson on our surroundings. Three minutes later, he brakes at a red light near Shanghai's People's Square and asks, "Do you want to go north to the most famous shopping street, Nanjing Lu? Or south to Huai Hai Street?" He lists three more places of interest. Seattle cab drivers were never this eager to please.

My head aches. I can't take his questions right now, so I tell him I'll get out and walk but I give him a tip for being so helpful.

I stop at the corner of the People's Square, staring, calculating. The city roars around me. I can't help the web of numbers spinning my past together. Within it, my mother's birthdate, my father's cell number, my best friend's address. They're all there, lurking.

Instead of bee-lining it to the mall, I head for the illuminated fountains and find a seat. The square's angles swallow me. It's funny how public places can be one of the best places to hide.

Pedestrians are bundled up in warm clothes, carrying shopping bags, enjoying themselves. Laughter and smiles. A mega-size screen perched on one of the corner buildings broadcasts New Year's activities.

This is "normal" life. Hundreds of people walk

around, happily sipping on tea, unaware of dark corners where the wicked strike deals, economic crashes loom, and stolen children cry out to be found. I scoot back on the bench and cross my arms over my chest. It's not them I'm mad at.

Anger grips me as I think of Chan. I'm barely given a night of freedom before I'm confronted with another terrible situation and a man who could do something about it but won't because he's as stubborn and self-serving as the rest of them. Now I have another choice before me. What will I do about it?

I've planned to use my earnings to strike at Madame. But in light of this new information, I'm confused. I know what Red would want. But I don't know if I can.

A sudden thought buzzes across my mind. While King's people often do their exchanges in the dark, in alleys and shadows of night, Madame prefers to work in broad daylight at an expo or in squares like this one.

A group of young girls pass me, giggling. Rosy cheeks and big brown eyes. Did King or Madame take girls like these? Did they deceive them into believing there was a man who would love them, a job that awaited them, only to walk into their merciless jaws?

I search girls' faces in the square like a trained dog, an instinct I can't stop. Each time a girl passes, my eyes dart to her wrist or her ear searching for that small X claiming ownership to Madame. I follow 137 girls with my eyes, growing more delusional, before a cold wind cuts across the square, and I shiver. It reminds me I'm wearing this ridiculous red dress. I've got to move.

A blast of heat from the ceiling fan warms me with my first step into the mall. Straight ahead, escalators lead up four levels and down two. Bright lights, music, and people come at me from every angle. More equations hit me, but I'm so tired, I can't filter them like Red taught me. They clutter my mind and I get stuck in slow motion.

The chatter of people shopping is as loud as the commotion outside. The mall should feel like a palace after navigating the Pratt cells, but despite the tall ceilings, and large walkways, I feel like it's closing in on me.

I'm suddenly anxious again, examining every face. A girl spins by me, her hair up in a ponytail. I swear a small X is tattooed behind her earlobe, but then it flashes silver. It's just an earring.

A man on his cell phone bumps into me. My body tenses as his hand squeezes my arm. I yank hard, freeing me from his grip but quickly understand he had just wanted to steady me. He apologizes several times and skitters off.

Get a grip, Phoenix.

A couple strolls down the mall in front of me. The man, roughly mid-thirties, argues with a girl in a pink sweater and bright lipstick. Judging by her looks, she's around my age. The dispute heats up. She raises her voice at him. The man yanks her arm towards the door, but she jerks back. Several people glance over at them, but they keep walking, as if it's no big deal.

What I see is quite different. The man mutters a word, and she stops fighting. She's upset, her eyes petitioning the crowd until they land on mine.

It's the same look as those girls in the file. As mine. *Desperate.* I order my feet to run after them, to save her, but my body won't obey. Numbers compute that I'm wrong, but my heart won't listen. I call for help, but my voice is lost, like in a dream—nothing comes out.

I'm destined to help her. I promised Red I would help them. Why can't I move?

Powerless, I watch as she slips from my fingers. With each step, images of girls taken from their families slice me apart.

My head twists back and forth as I check behind me for King, or Madame. I know they'll be here any moment. People stare and point at me, or maybe they're just talking amongst themselves. People pull out their cell phones. Are they calling Madame? The police? Everything is jumbled in my brain. Noises crash down on me, multiplying my equations.

The world is too big. There are too many numbers. I can't solve anything. I'm only one person.

A loud *smack* shakes me sober.

The girl's right-hand flies through the air, slapping him across the face. I expect the man to rip into her mercilessly. But he shrinks, pleading with her not to leave, apologizing pathetically. Soon they're embracing. Kissing.

It's a silly relationship dispute—she's not them, or me. Not taken.

My mind's cracking. Operating on two hours sleep has caught up to me. I need to move, to think.

What I need is Red. But he's no longer an option. So I drag up his voice in my head. *Three things in life are certain,* he used to say. *Purpose. Change. Death.*

Death I've avoided, so far. Purpose will be determined. But change, I can do. *I'm Phoenix now*, I tell myself. She could use a little change.

The skylight above me has darkened. I stand up, clear of mind, determined. A new plan, calculated. I know what to do. I know where to go. I will not stop until I get what I want.

The mall is closing. As I ride the escalator, I gaze into the adjacent mirror. I'm stunned by my new look. The little girl I knew from Seattle, the one with nut-brown hair, is gone. My cheeks are defined, and my lips are full. My eyes look older than seventeen, as if I'd lived nine lives already. My body is still thin, but I didn't realize how shapely I've become.

The salon darkened my hair to a rich espresso, along with my newly shaped eyebrows. My wavy hair is now bone straight and layered nicely around my face. The stylist added makeup, which I haven't really ever worn before. With the dark eyeliner, eye shadow, and mascara, I noticed how truly light my eyes were—and bought dark brown contacts. Now, I'm totally unrecognizable. If I hardly recognize myself, how will Madame?

Over my shoulder and in my hands hang bags of new clothes, both fancy and casual. Shoes. Boots. Jackets. Dresses. Even a bathing suit. The bags weigh on my arms. I look forward to setting them down.

Outside, a taxi sits in the pick-up area. I open the door and get in.

"Urumqi Street, French Quarter," I say as I lift my bags into the cab.

The taxi weaves through the city. Even if I can find

a way to help any of Madame's X girls, I have nowhere for them to stay. Chan's house is not safe—it's too high profile. Everyone knows Chan and Kai, and soon they'll know me.

I need somewhere to operate. Somewhere to hide. Somewhere to take the girls. What I need is a safe house. But where will I find one?

When I arrive at the villa, the dog is barking and thoughts of safe houses drift away. All I can think of now is Red as I walk up to the gate fumbling with all my bags.

"Who are you?" The guard's voice asks from inside the gate.

"Phoenix," I say.

"Oh?" He glances at my new appearance, surely wondering if I looked this way the last time I saw him. I don't explain. "Do you need some help?"

"Thanks, I can make it," I tell him, even though I can't deny my arms are tired, along with the rest of me.

"Chan's son told me I should watch for you tonight," Lei says. "To call him when you arrived."

There's another voice behind him. "That's right, I did," it says.

Then without another word, Kai shoves his phone into his pocket and lifts the bags from my hands.

The guard locks the gate behind us and wishes us a goodnight. I rush to hide my embarrassment from ignoring Kai earlier. Kai follows with all the bags.

"Thanks," I say as we reach the garden where the path splits directions—one to my door and one to his.

"Shopping, huh?" We take the path up to the guesthouse door. "So that's what women do when they get upset." He smiles to let me know he's joking, then takes in my new hair and makeup, cocks his head. "I didn't think it was you until you spoke."

I don't have the energy to explain that my changing appearance is synonymous with staying alive. "You look different too," I say. "Were you on your way out?"

He's not dressed in his suit anymore, but he's still too dressed up to be on a casual errand. He wears navy slacks with a light blue button-up shirt under a brown leather jacket. His leather motorcycle boots, a bit beat up but still well taken care of, match his belt and watch. Not nearly as crisp as this morning, but still a bit stiff. Despite that, I can't deny he is very handsome. There is something so calming about his face, his voice, like I've known him for years. But we have never met until a few days ago.

"Yes, I'm meeting someone, but I have time to help you," he says as we reach the porch. "Look, I'm sorry if my father upset you. He's not usually like that with people."

This morning Kai was cold and distant, unlike the night I met him, unlike now. I don't know which is the true Kai, or if I even care.

"Did he tell you? About the recession?" I ask.

"Yes." Kai is silent, pensive. His eyes lock on mine.

"He can do something about it."

"He doesn't know what to believe." It looks like he's going to say something more, but then he decides not to.

This upsets me, so I deliberately break away and stare downward, concentrating on the stupid brown welcome mat. I'd rather say nothing than lecture two people today. Besides, I don't want to hear any more excuses. While I fumble for my keys, we are both quiet, lost in thought, holding back what we really want to say. It seems to contradict both of our personalities.

Once the door swings open, I grope for the light switch with my left hand but can't find it.

"On the right," Kai says patiently.

I move my hand and find it immediately. "Thanks," I say, removing my boots and finding the white house slippers.

Kai sets down my shopping bags in the entry room then stands there as if he is waiting to be invited in, but I don't want him here. He told me he's meeting a friend and even though I've worked with people who live, breathe, and eat lies, I still expect people to do what they say. Besides, I'm about to drop dead from exhaustion.

"Do you think my claims are crazy too?" I ask him before I close the door.

"Not exactly," he responds. "But another great depression? That experts can't detect? That theoretically my father can prevent?"

"I'm not lying."

"I didn't say you were. I guess I need time to let it soak in."

"Sure," I say just to get him to leave. Really, I don't care to discuss it anymore. "Well, I don't want to delay your meeting."

"Don't worry, she's always late," he says, eyes lock onto mine.

She. The girl from the office? His girlfriend? "Thanks for your help, Kai. See you tomorrow."

"You'll come to work for us after all?" he asks, surprised.

"I made a deal, didn't I?"

He smirks. "You sure gave my father a scare when you ran out," he says. "He thought he'd lost you."

"Yeah, well, the news didn't scare him badly enough, so I thought I would."

Kai laughs. "You may just be the equal he never had. No one really stands up to him like that."

Equal? I've never thought of myself as a real contender before. The thought lightens my mood. It feels good to know Chan is scared of losing me and would have let me go as an equal player, or at least, an employee. The thought is...freeing.

"Do me a favor next time," he says. "If something like that happens between you and him, come to me first before you run out. I can help."

I shake my head and smile to acknowledge his kind words, but really, I think Kai's offer is ridiculous. He knows nothing about me, and his interests are entirely tied up with Mr. Chan's. A pat on the shoulder won't go very far in an economic spiral.

"Ride in the morning?" he asks.

"I'll take the metro."

"Phoenix, we live at the same address and work at the same place," he says casually, "it's no trouble."

"Okay. Thanks," I say. Anything else might arouse suspicion. I lean my head on the side of the door, closing it slowly. He gets the point.

"Goodnight." And he is gone.

Fatigue crashes over me. I head down the hallway, leaving all the packages at the door except one. Before I sleep, there is one thing I need to do. Change. I slip into new sweats, then fold my old clothes up and breathe in their musty smell of wet dirt, cold cement, and green tea for the last time.

Heading to the kitchen, I snatch some matches from the drawers and a bottle of oil and sneak out the back door. Chan's house looks dark. Kai has left. No one will bother me. I head to the back of the pool house patio.

There's an empty tin bucket by the watering can in the garden. I throw my clothes into the bucket, add a bit of peanut oil from the kitchen, then strike a match.

A fire starts slowly at first then gradually grows. The night is windy and the smoke changes direction as it curls out of the bucket. My clothes blacken and shrink as the heat takes them. "Goodbye, Double-Eight," I whisper.

The clothes burn away along with all the cold nights I prayed, asking God *why* with no answer. The nightmares, where my arms reached out to hold my father, rise with the smoke. My love and rage for Mara burns in the heat. Lily's piano music cackles in the flames.

The clothes can't fight the fire. They shrivel. They're only material. Soon they are ash, burned pure, without smell or stain. The ash rises and drifts in the night sky, dissipating with each twist of wind.

"Red. I know you're safe now." I look up into the heavens. "I'm still here. I won't give up. You were right. The fire can't destroy me. I'm going to do what we talked about. And I do it for you."

NINETEEN
PAST: DOUBLE-EIGHT
∞

THE PRATT, SHANGHAI, CHINA

I could breathe again.

For 47 days I met with Red each night and learned more than I bargained for. I was taking back control of my gift and it felt good. One day I'd shove it in King's and Madame's faces.

The Chinese language was made for me and my gift. I had mastered 2376 more Chinese characters this month, an average pace of 100 new characters a day. While before Chinese looked like hieroglyphics on steroids, they were now clear, complex, and logical strokes of math. I learned it twice as fast than I had other languages, and 50% faster than an average person—especially their numbering system. It was far more logical than Roman numerals. I could do everything for King in a third less time, which granted wasn't that long for me, but it was faster all the same. My brain was meant to think like this.

Chinese were obsessed with numbers and their meanings too. Take my name for example, 88. The number 8 is "Ba," which sounds like "Fa," which means good fortune. Eight was the luckiest number in China, associated with prosperity, success, and social status. People and businesses would pay good money to have the right numbers, especially the number 8, in phone numbers, flight numbers, and license plates. The Chinese world of philosophy and superstition was inextricably entwined with math.

Red entered, his whiskers curved up with his grin. "*Tu fei meng jin,*" he said, quoting one of China's many idioms. "Your Chinese has soared to high places."

For the first time in the Pratt, pride welled in my own chest. "You have a talent for learning," he said. "Soon you will know all the dialects I do. How is it you can learn so fast? What is it that you do for King?"

He slipped an inch-thick mat through the bars of my cell onto the floor. I sat with legs crossed. "I make a lot of money because of a gift I have with numbers."

"A prodigy?"

"Yes, Grandfather," I said. "I bridge math. I bring two or more math disciplines together to solve something very complex. But I'm different. Numbers aren't just something on a page, but a filter through which I see and judge everything."

"How so?"

"It's like a screen of partial differential equations, except ten times faster and greater." His face went blank. "Never mind the term. For example," I said, "take a ball falling through the air. To determine its velocity, you must consider both gravity and air resistance. I look at ball size, weight, and material. Then I determine the ball's acceleration, the velocity as a function of time—I can calculate these things in seconds."

His face went blanker still.

"Try this," I said. "I see things before they happen because I calculate the possibilities of them happening before they happen."

He nodded silently for a minute. "Let's stick to me teaching you Chinese." We both laugh.

"Can I ask you a question?" I asked.

"You may," he replied.

"Why do they call you Crazy Red?" I asked. "Guard San says you've changed into some poetic mystic man since you arrived, but I know that's not why."

"Ah ha, perhaps it's because I believe bad people can change?"

I sighed, growing impatient.

Finally, he relented. "I was given a favor that I haven't cashed in."

"What kind of favor?"

"I'm blackmailed to stay. King wants money. I know someone who has it."

"You mean, someone who could pay your way out of here?"

"Yes. But it's not that simple."

"Why don't you try?"

"It's not time yet," he said. "I must c*hi ku.*"

"Eat bitterness?" I said. "Isn't eight years of bitterness enough?"

"Ah ha, don't forget that after much bitterness everything tastes like honey," he spouted off a riddle as usual, though if I wasn't mistaken, a sour grin hung on his face. He stood.

"Can't you tell me what got you here in the first place?" I whined. It was the third time this week I'd asked him without receiving a straight answer.

"I'm making all the wrongs right," he said sadly, once again avoiding the real answer. "Come, we have lots of work to do."

Up top, I watched King hop into a sleek black car and drive away. He didn't live among his *subjects*, but he would be back tomorrow to swindle all he could from others' mistakes. Madame was not the only one who used his services.

King was too resourceful to throw out another man's trash without searching the pockets. He liked information, so he never just "took care of business" without learning something useful so he could have the upper hand. King called it his "tax".

Besides an occasional date with my head under water, King left me alone as long as the money kept rolling in. Although I was silent most the time, I paid attention and calculated, especially when we were out of the Pratt. Even though I was blindfolded, I recorded the distances and directions we drove, which way we turned, how many miles, feet, minutes. A map developed in my head.

I could have walked from the Pratt to the Port blindfolded by now, but I would really have liked to map my way to the warehouse. All of King's and Madame's records were there. I'd been there once, in a whirlwind of activity before and after, so I wouldn't be able to map my return.

On another occasion, King forgot to blindfold me right away. I saw a sign, a name of a town, Song Valley. Later that day, I asked Red about it and his eyes darkened. I could tell he didn't want to talk about it, so I dropped it.

In the Pratt, however, I was not blindfolded, and things happened here—like last night—that took days to forget.

King had drunk too much. I sat watching, as he spilled secrets he shouldn't have to Madame's buyer.

"Our shipping containers sent upriver never get checked," he boasted with a raspy laugh. "My men often sample the *cargo* before it leaves."

After discovering those hidden files of Madame's, I knew that cargo meant girls and I almost threw up.

The two men's graphic terms clawed at my mind until it bled me dry. Tears wet my face. A condemning voice sliced up the last of my integrity. "*You helped them commit these crimes.*"

I will end this, I vowed. I'd gain the guards' trust, turn everyone against King. I'd sneak up to the warehouse, light it on fire. I'd rescue the girls. I'd send those buyers to their own abyss.

And King—the unknowing fool—revealed that his records of shipments, schedules for new shipments, and buyer information, even the names of dirty custom officers who worked for Madame, were stored at the warehouse. To destroy Madame and King, I'd need that information.

Having a plan to destroy them didn't erase the turmoil of guilt festering within me. My only consolation was in meeting Red. Day by day, I opened up to him about my pain. I even told him about Mara and my family.

A violent cough across the way shook me from my daze. Red was back, and we'd start our class. I sat up and strutted over to his cell.

"What are we learning tonight, Grandfather?" I lowered my eyes in respect to him as I sat on the floor beside his cot.

"We will start with poetry," he said. "Your local dialects and slang are good, but your classical Chinese is behind. Later you'll review geography, economy, and history."

"Yes, Grandfather." I grabbed a piece of chalk and wrote the classic poem in Chinese that Red insisted I start each lesson with. I read it as I slid the chalk down the wall.

"*White sun leans on the mountain then vanishes. Yellow river flows into the sea. If your eyes desire to see a thousand miles, go up one more floor,*" I finished.

"Again, this time in perfect Beijing accent," he commanded.

"Grandfather," I said, "why must I always rehearse the same poem?"

"This poem is famous. Everyone knows this poem by Wang Zhi Huan," he said. "My teaching would be nothing if I did not teach you this."

Reluctantly, I repeated the poem again—enunciating those extra *errrs* that Beijing people add to the end of their words—all the while thinking about King, and all the money I made him. I still wasn't sure where it all went.

"Red?" I said when I finished, "when we first met you told me that King has 'all kinds of gold' but actually, there's no account for him personally, which means he must have a stash. Am I right? Is that what you were referring to?"

The way Red breathed deeply, contemplating his response I knew he knew. But he ignored me. "Focus, Granddaughter. Wielding your numbers is more important."

"Yeah, yeah," I said, not letting him drop it. "You know where his stash is. I know you do. If we find a way to take it, we could be free and hurt King where it counts. Come on," I whined. "Tell me where it is."

"No. You can't understand what I want you to learn. Justice is what you should pursue—making the wrongs right—but you seek revenge. You won't balance the equation that way."

My eyes shifted to the part of the wall marked 105—the number of days I'd sat in my cell. "He kills, he steals, he destroys. Why is it wrong that I wish him to die?"

"He will die. As you and I both will one day. You see, three things are certain in this life. Purpose. Change. Death. But death refuses us an option to change. We must make that choice while we are living. So must King."

"Who will defend my cause if I don't?"

"Fool," he said. "That's an orphan thinking!"

"I am an orphan!" I shouted back. "My parents are dead! I've been kidnapped, and I'm nothing more than a slave!"

"That's not who you were created to be!" he retorted.

"I don't care anymore! I want justice! Those girls need justice!"

"Orphans dream of vindication. Sons and daughters dream of destiny," he whispered. "You are not ready. You have not understood my teachings. I will not speak of King's stash again."

It was Tuesday. Another day of me racking up profitable investments for King went by. King's depravity was like radiation. I couldn't shake the nuclear feeling crawling down my spine.

But even though I kept my eyes down, my ears were always open. I was rewarded with another piece of information: according to King, half of the X girls were distributed into the Shanghai system of what Madame calls "the lower five"— high-end hotels, massage parlors, hole-in-the-wall venues, and personal buyers. More info stored at the warehouse.

Evening came. After a meal of tofu soup, Red brought up my gift.

"You don't use your gift to your advantage."

"What do you mean?" I asked, slurping up my soup.

"For being a genius, you're pretty slow," he said, poking me with a smile. "Your gift is for much more than making money. It's a key to unlock your destiny. You say you can see what will happen in advance?"

"In theory."

"So then, you can move faster than everyone," he said. "Get what you need, learn who to trust, become your destiny—it has brought you here and you must ask why. History depends on it."

All of Red's talk about destiny was pointless. I'd never be able to do anything as long as I was in the Pratt.

"Betrayal brought me here, Grandfather," I reminded him.

"Perhaps. But destiny or not, you are here nonetheless," Red said. "Now focus on the numbers."

"It's hard. Sometimes they clutter my mind," I admitted. "They project multiple possibilities. I don't always know which outcome I should pursue. I see all the outcomes, but I can't choose."

"You're still acting as if these numbers are separate from you. Wield them. Harness them. Become one with them. Let them guide you, teach you what is already inside. Then you will know where to help, which answer to choose."

"How do I know what's inside of me?"

"Let the numbers teach you, like your game Seagulls," he said. "You are full of destiny. You dream and hope to make things right, to see the X girls freed, King and Madame stopped. Each time you see an equation, react to its answer. Make sure all you do matches who you are in your heart. This is the key. If you can't find the answer here"—he tapped his heart—"you won't find it anywhere."

"I'm afraid."

"Of what?"

"Here," I said, also tapping my heart. "Grandfather, I'm losing who I am. I feel it. I don't want to trust anyone, only you. You're right to say I want more than just justice. I want them to suffer like we have. I want them to rot in the Pratt for years, eating mush, their fingers turning blue, reliving the moment when everything was taken from them."

"Revenge is not justice. Their time will come. But first, promise me that you will find your destiny."

"What destiny, Grandfather? Why do you keep saying that? I don't know what I'm destined to do!"

"Have you understood nothing? Destiny is not what you do. Destiny is who you are. Everything flows from who you are, then folds into everything you do." Red was angry and solemn, and calm all at the same time. "Destiny gives, saves, *loves*. Destiny creates legends and history. Do you think history just happens? No. History isn't made. It's calculated."

"Then why do I have this gift?"

"Listen to yourself!" His face was hard set on mine. "Wasn't it you who told me there is no coincidence? That day by day you see each circumstance constructed?"

I nodded.

"So, stand up straight and stop your sulking! You can affect this world with who you are and what's been given to you. It starts here, now. Don't wait. Use your gift to become who you are." He calmed down, but his intensity grew like a fire and it started to blaze within me too. "You have the ability to make very large decisions in a moment because you see the future unfolding before anyone else can. Therefore, you can also make small decisions. Use your gift to win people over. Show them there's a better way. Friends are worth more than money. Do you trust me?"

"Of course."

"Then do as I say and trust others too. Or you will never have the blessing you desire," Red said.

When it was time for me to work for King, a younger guard instead of Guard San came to fetch me. I bowed my head to Red and made my way through the tunnels, head full of thoughts. *Who was I? What was my destiny?*

The guard dropped me off at Guard San's office, but no one was there. The younger guard told me to wait. Five minutes passed and no one came around. I poked my head around the corner. Guard San's chair was still empty.

"Guard San?" I looked further down the hall. I came upon him crumpled in a corner, head gripped in his hands. He had never been kind to me. I wanted to walk away, but something urged me to turn back.

"What happened?" I asked him. He didn't look up. He mumbled something about losing his family if he didn't pay another large debt.

There was a jolt in my chest. I understood what to do, or rather, what I wanted to do. *Were my numbers and my heart aligning? Were they showing me who I was?* A thumping started in my chest. I was nervous.

I took a small step towards him and whispered, "I can help you."

Guard San looked up and scowled. "Why would you?"

One more step, and I reached out my hand. "Because I can."

If Red were right, this small decision would not only affect my relationships in the Pratt but my future.

TWENTY
PAST: DOUBLE-EIGHT
∞

THE PRATT, SHANGHAI, CHINA

I focused on the dull fluorescent lights buzzing overhead in the dark corridors. I pretended the hum was the sound of cicadas and imagined myself lying outdoors on a hot summer night because tonight I ate meat. It wasn't much, but it was meat all the same, compliments of Guard San. It was also the ninth night in a row he didn't lock my cell.

As I lay on my back, hands under my head, I reflected on my last week stepping out with my gift. A suggestion to the prisoner with the hurt leg, tipping others on the game-fights, wowing them at a card game. I was acknowledged as I passed them now, and occasionally joined in their gossip.

The Pratt was changing. I was gaining respect. Red said if I kept it up, I'd run the Pratt. What he meant is I could be free.

I got up and trailed the tunnels, numerically mapping

out the twists and turns as Red taught me. A hundred years ago foreign businessmen named this area the Port Lands. The Chinese locals mispronounced it, deeming it, the Pratt Lands, eventually reducing it to the Pratt.

Shanghai's ports were located on the Yangtze River delta. Over time, as mud and sand built up along the delta, the shoreline moved south to where the main ports were now.

Red wasn't clear on who discovered the underground tunnels first, or how the facility was kept secret from the authorities, but the shift in the shoreline had at some point revealed the underground tunnels, some nearly two miles long. Red suspected they were part of an ancient local folk legend from the Song Dynasty, which claimed that an estranged emperor's son had built underground caverns to store his treasures arriving on ships from across the seas. The legend was written off as false because historians and archeologists never found any evidence of the tunnels or the treasure. Yet here we were, held captive in a warren of tunnels clearly as old as dirt. King cared nothing for history, only the secrecy it provided. Song Valley must have once been connected to these tunnels.

Which reminded me of King's warehouse. I assumed it was by King's house in Song Valley, but it must have been closer to the Port, closer to the tunnels. A map derived in my head. Finally, I could clearly see its location.

Down the hall, Red's ragged cough preceded his voice. "Granddaughter, is that you?" Apart from the quiver, his voice soothed me as I arrived.

"Yes," I responded loud enough for Red to hear.

"Are you coming?" His voice was soft, weak. His cough had gotten worse since winter.

Guard San mumbled something about fetching me around dinner to tip him off on his mahjong game, then shooed me in Red's direction.

"Just one minute, Grandfather."

I entered my cell. The wall, wet with moisture, had two characters written on it. *Pure gold.* Under that, a sticky substance like sap dripped from a crack. On the floor, an apple core decayed. I forgot it was there. Now small black bugs crawled all over it.

My hour above ground had been warm. Now the sunless chill of the Pratt cut through me, reminding me of months of shivering in my bones. I reached for my leather jacket, the only coat I had. The leather was faded and worn, but there were no holes. Thank God I was wearing it when I was plucked from Madame's.

The cell next door was open. Red lay on his cot, wrapped up tight in his blanket. Why had he never tried to run? Of course, there was nowhere to go. The gates of the Pratt were locked so heavily and the tunnels so vast, that you would die trying to find a way out. And people had. Red said his time would come. Until then, he didn't cash in on that one favor.

As I entered, Red brushed his thinning gray hair off his forehead, obviously trying to hide the pain and tiredness he felt. He coughed all the time now. His body seemed to age a year each day. But his kindness, a quality hard to find in the Pratt, radiated brightly.

"It's time for your studies," he said and sat up. I took off my jacket and rested it over his shoulders.

A normal student back in America might turn their nose up at a man who made them study every waking moment they were not busy. But these lessons were life to me—not only the academic ones but also Red's sayings, which taught me more than any teacher at Stanley.

"I'm ready." I dove into classical Chinese and history for the next hour, as Red asked me to retell portions of the history of the Tang and Ming dynasties.

After we finished, Red told me to close my eyes. I knew what he was asking me to do. I drew in a deep breath and released it.

"Rays of sunlight paint my face orange and red," I began. "The salty, green scent of the ocean mingles with the crescendo of waves. I walk forward. The water is cold. Each wave rolls in, bubbling, fresh, the sand between my toes feels—" I stopped. My hands folded over my forehead through my hair. "I can't do this anymore. Pretending won't get me there. It's a stupid game."

"It's your game," he said, referring to Seagulls, "and it's your home. I don't want you to forget."

"My home is gone, Grandfather. I can never go home again."

"Let's reenact the funeral. Last time you couldn't finish. Close your eyes."

"I can't do it. I've tried," I said, regretting I ever told Red about the game Seagulls. Visualizing going home was one thing but performing a mock funeral for my family was another. "All I see is Mara's face the day she dropped me off. I can't speak the kind words you want me to."

"You must resolve this if you are ever to be free.

Now try again. Go back to them. Bury your family in peace and finish this."

"They are already dead!"

"But you are something worse. You lie at the bottom of a sea of bitterness while there is still life above the surface," he said. "There is a way back, if you will learn to swim."

"Grandfather," I cried, not in defiance, but pain. The thought of them needled at my heart. I wanted to speak to them, to let them go like Red said; but I couldn't help thinking my chance was gone. I'd never see them again. I threw my head into my hands, holding back the sting behind my eyes. "They are dead."

"There now," he said. "Your pain is not without love. And love is always stronger than pain. Do not let them go in this way. Bury them in peace and forgiveness, and in peace and forgiveness you will be reborn."

I lifted my head.

"Now," he said. "Are you ready to try again?"

"Yes."

My head fell on his shoulder. One by one, hot tears streaked my cold cheeks as I tried, as Red instructed me, to go back to a happy memory. Soon I was there, with Mara on the beach, laughing, and I began to speak to her.

After three months, everyone knew my name in the Pratt. Well, not my name. Some called me Double-8, others called me *laowai,* but they all knew who I was and respected me. The blonde highlights that Madame gave me were long gone, faded into beach wood brown. They had forgotten any traces of my white face and a time in which I couldn't speak Chinese fluently, or even multiple dialects. More importantly, I knew who they were.

No one knew the truth of who I was, except King and Red. Being respected felt good, but the guilt of helping King weighed on me daily, especially since I knew he handled the girls for Madame. I'd give anything to pay back all the wrongs I'd helped create. Red was convinced I'd get that chance.

"Start from the top," Red said as he marked the walls up with chalk.

My eyes zoned out. Usually I'd obey Red. But today I couldn't. I had just watched King walk away with 100,000 Euro after three bribes, two blackmails, one bloody fight and any number of broken laws.

"I have too much on my mind."

"What is it, Granddaughter?"

"Money. I *hate* it," I said nearly spitting the word. "I wish I was born an idiot. Then I wouldn't be here. My sister wouldn't have ever hated me. My father would have loved me for who I was. I wouldn't have helped smugglers traffic people all over the world. I would have lived and died a nobody, but I'd have been happy. I'd have been innocent."

Red leaned back. "If you eat honey—"

"I don't want to hear another idiom, Grandfather," I said, cutting him off.

"This is no idiom. I am trying to teach you something." He tried to sit up again but was too weak. I pulled him up. "Money is neither good nor evil. It's neutral. Money can feed the hungry or it can oppress them. People are good or evil, generous or greedy. Money tempts everyone, but each must conquer it. Does generosity start here?" He shoved his hand in his pocket. "Or here?" He tapped his heart. "Right. If it is absent in your heart, it is absent in your pocket, no matter how much you have."

"Who can conquer it? Look at Madame. King. Even my own family."

"All men must choose. How do I use what's been given to me?" he said. "If you trust in money, your world will fall. Money cannot love nor is it loyal. It comes and goes without our asking. Economies rise and fall. Look at history."

"King and Madame don't care about things like that."

"Ah, but they are forgetting one thing: If you steal honey, one day you will get stung."

I laughed, shaking my head. "You love honey," I said, the corner of my mouth turning up.

He patted his stomach, giving me a wink before continuing. "Madame and King have chosen to use their life and wealth for evil. This is not living. They have lost the path to true blessing."

"Which path is that?"

"The path of Love. To live by love is to walk on a path with higher rules than of this earth. There, you will always prosper." He pulled the blanket over his chest. "Many things are like love. The more you give away, the more you receive. And no matter how many times you uproot love, it always grows back. It is infinite."

Infinity.

I refused to argue with him. I always wanted to believe in infinity, in love that lasts forever. Problem is people always get in the way. They're imperfect and imperfection cannot loop forever. So I simply said, "I don't get it."

"Most people don't. There are things in this universe that we cannot understand outright. They're built on paradoxes far beyond our thinking, but if we learn to live by their rules, we never fail. *Test it.*"

I went back to my cell and thought about his challenge. I thought about how infinity could keep going even if the imperfect equations around it should cause it to stop. After 37 minutes I came to a conclusion. I was so excited I had to share it with Red even though he was asleep.

"Grandfather," I whispered, gently tapping his shoulder. "Wake up. I want to tell you something."

"Yes?" he mumbled, shifting slightly. It triggered a violent coughing fit.

His face disfigured with pain. A moan escaped his lips, barely audible, then he rolled onto his side and slipped back into sleep.

A tear slipped down my cheek. I couldn't remember why I had bothered Red now. I didn't even care. Only one thought ran through my mind, the one thing I cared about. Red—I was losing him.

"Happy birthday," Red said handing me a steaming bowl. "Noodles. They symbolize long life."

I give him a sideways glance. "You could've told

me that a bit sooner," I joke. "I would've eaten a few extra bowls." I thank him and try to ignore that Red can barely lift his bowl to his mouth. Apart from my hungry slurping, we eat in silence.

Eventually Red pushes his bowl aside. "I have already taught you all I know. Now I want to give you a gift."

"Yeah, what is it, Grandfather?" I poked him gently in the arm. We didn't have a thing in the Pratt. Red said we gave of our minds. These gifts were better than new clothes or shoes, although I could definitely use some new boots.

"Don't tell me you're saving your noodles for me," I joke. "You need to eat. You're too thin."

"Haha." He laughed. "No, no." He took a piece of chalk. His frail hand drew a picture on the wall. From the outline, it looked like some kind of bird. "This gift is much more important than food." His hands traced the wings, the beak, the eyes. Was he implying I could fly? Like my game Seagulls? Metaphorically soaring into my dreams?

I was better at guessing Red's hidden codes in his riddles but this one was different. It wasn't a seagull, as I assumed he'd draw. This bird had a slender body with narrow curved wings like a hawk's, a streaming tail and head feathers that looked like a small crown. Red was telling me something different. The bird was coming out from the ground. Then I saw it. It was rising from the ashes.

"It's a phoenix," I said.

"Yes. My gift is a new name for you. You are *Phoenix* now," he said. "It is your time to rise. From the ashes into your destiny. When you are out, use this name until you find it."

When I was out. He had very high hopes. Was he trying to cheer me up on my birthday? But I liked the name. Besides, everything Red did symbolized something, so if he wanted me to be called Phoenix, I'd do it.

"Thank you, Grandfather, for your gift," I said. His smile lasted a second before a frown crossed his face.

"What is it?"

"You will suffer to hear what I must say next," he said quietly.

"Don't tell me, then," I said. "I've suffered too much."

"What have I taught you, dear girl?" He coughed. "Come closer."

I obeyed because he was the closest thing I had to family. Around this time of night, I usually bid him goodnight and let him sleep. Tonight, he was so weak he couldn't get into bed alone. I helped him in, picking his legs up, covering him with the blanket. The Pratt had drained all life from him. I grabbed hold of his hand.

"What have I taught you?"

"Pure gold does not fear the fire," I said, repeating one of Red's many lessons.

"Good. Remember what is inside of you. Suffering cannot burn it away. The more fire, the more pure you will become. I believe in you. Now, listen to me."

My head rested on his frail chest. I braced myself for the bad news. His weak hands folded over my hair.

"I'm dying," Red said. "You have known for a long time."

It was no secret, but nonetheless his words were like needles in my heart. Each time the idea of Red leaving me came to mind, I pushed it away.

"Look at me."

My head lifted. I searched his watery eyes. He was sad but not about dying. Red didn't fear death. We had talked about it a hundred times. That wasn't the news he was trying to tell me. My mind calculated. When I deduced what he wanted to say, I gasped for air.

I never calculated this possibility into our planning. I believed he'd never do it. But he was. That was why he was sad.

"You're cashing in your one favor, aren't you?" It made sense. He wanted to see his family before he died, to make right whatever went wrong.

"Yes."

The needles in my heart now pricked my entire body, like I'd fallen into frigid water. Tears started falling. I was losing the only good thing I'd had in the last year. I would be alone.

"For you," he said.

"What?" I whimpered.

"In one week, there will be a kidnapping. Yours," he said. "An old friend will come for you." He reached into the pocket of the jacket hanging at the edge of his bed, taking out a chess piece. A pawn. He put it in my hand. "When you are out, give him this. It will make him remember."

"Grandfather, no. You can't do this. You deserve to see your family. You deserve to get out." Gripping his sleeve, I clamped down so tightly I feared I'd crush his fragile arm. "Don't ask me to leave you. You're the only family I have."

"Don't cry, daughter." His eyes wandered off. "What have I taught you?" He coughed again, violently.

"Grandfather, please." I couldn't fight the stinging in my eyes and throat.

"Promise me you will use your gift for good," he muttered. "Remember, we all have a destiny. It's our choice whether or not to walk in it. Those who do, go down in history."

"Grandfather," I begged, frightened at how resolute his voice sounds. "What about your purpose? What about making your wrongs right?"

"All these years I stayed here. I believed it was for King. I was wrong. It was for you." His hand slipped away from mine. "Take King's stash. You will need it to undo the evil that has been done."

"How can I? You never told me where he hides it."

"You know where it is."

I didn't. He never told me, but in that moment I couldn't have cared less.

"Grandfather, listen to me. You're going to get well. I'll ask Guard San for more medicine. You'll see."

"What have I taught you?" he mumbled, his eyes on mine.

My mind raced through hours and days and months of lessons. How could I have summed up everything this man taught me? How much he had given me? I was crying now, not just a whimper but sobbing.

"I taught you to trust me," he said. "You'll leave me. But you won't be alone. You'll have another family one day." He wiped the tears from my cheek. "You taught me something as well, you know. Something you need to remember."

"I didn't teach you anything." The thought was so preposterous. I was a terrified, angry girl when Red befriended me.

"Wrong. You taught me to believe that I can beat the odds, and I did. I never had a daughter." His voice was barely a whisper now. "Destiny gave me you. Seven days from now...you will beat the odds too. My family...sister..." He wasn't making sense. These were the hallucinations of a dying man, nothing more. Except he had never given me false hope before. This man didn't lie. I forgot about the kidnapping and squeezed his hand.

"I'll take you with me."

He was slipping away from me. His movements grew still. I clung to his frail arm, stroking the wrinkled skin barely holding on to his bones. He used all his strength to focus on me.

"No, bury me in peace and love. I will always be with you," he said, eyes closed. "Goodbye, daughter." He found my hand.

"Goodbye? Bury you? Don't talk like that." But he didn't respond. "Grandfather?" His hand slipped, loose and lifeless, from my grip. I checked his mouth. He wasn't breathing. "No, Grandfather, don't leave me!" I shook him. "Wake up, Grandfather!" I pinched his wrist. No pulse. Then I realized he had told me goodbye but I never got to tell him what I should have said each and every day.

"Thank you for everything," I cried into his chest. "Thank you. Thank you. Thank you." He couldn't hear me, but I kept telling him until sobs overtook my ability to speak.

It was dark.

After 92 minutes it was time to go. My face was inches from his. My light in the darkness had gone out. I forced myself to stand.

Red lay on his small cot, fingers still clutching on the worn wool blanket. I took one last look and memorized how he looked. Calm and quiet, even now, his eyebrows were raised as if in a pleasant thought. He had gone from one world to the next, where the Pratt didn't exist, where there was no cold, no pain, no hunger, no screams stalking the darkness.

The world did not deserve this man. So many people could have benefitted from his brilliance, his kindness. He was forced to live out his days in this small cell when he deserved a castle—not King.

I closed the bars behind me, and the realization hit—I'd never see Red again. Tears spilled down my face all over again. Back in my cell, I collapsed to the floor with my head on my folded arms across my bed. I cried all night and into the morning. I gave into it, to the pain of losing Red, the hurt of never being rescued by my family, the confusion, the fear. I let it all drain out for over ten hours.

Morning came. I sat up, ran my sleeve across my eyes and face. I unfolded myself and stood in my cell. A new plan swelled and solidified. I set my face to it like stone and resolve rose in me like a consuming flood. Madame would not be the only one to suffer from my hand.

King. Will. Pay.

TWENTY-ONE
PRESENT: PHOENIX
∞

FRENCH CONCESSION, SHANGHAI, CHINA

Breakfast is a nightmare. Scrambled eggs, toast with butter and jam. Americans eat this. I ate this growing up. How long did I dream of eating something like this while I was in the Pratt? Now the taste in my mouth is foreign. The toast is dry, the jam too sweet. But that's not really why I hate it. It's because with each bite I see my father across the table from me, hear my sisters in the kitchen before school, and feel my mother kissing my forehead.

I shove the plate away before tears come to my eyes. How many years will it take to stop thinking about them? To stop seeing them in everything, even in eggs? Josephine's family is dead—she has already mourned for them. I'm not going back to that grief. Ever.

There are more important things to think about. I think I've found a way to solve the economic crisis and stop Madame at the same time. Two birds, one stone.

The doorbell rings. Ten o' clock again. Kai. Does he always go into work this late?

"Morning." He greets me in English like usual, then does a double-take, checking every part of me. His expression changes.

For a second, I feel like the girls in the Pratt, unsure of themselves.

"What?" I ask a little too brusquely.

"You look completely different *again*," he says surprised.

I'm covered from head to foot: dark slacks, gray blouse, a blue scarf, and a black leather jacket lined in merino wool. Black boots peek out from under my trousers, new and stiff; even I feel a bit rigid in them. A complete change from the girly dress I wore yesterday, different makeup. I straighten up, make sure my hair is down my back, and try to act like everything is normal.

"Get used to it."

"Don't get me wrong," he says softly as he holds the door for me. "You look *hen mei.*" He shyly looks away after his compliment. I just barely notice his cheeks turning pink. So. The billionaire playboy can blush.

"Thanks," I say, softly this time.

We walk to the garage and hop into his Range Rover in silence. There's no coffee for me today, and apart from two more brief looks, he's as reserved as the day before. I ignore it.

Outside, the city is masked in gray pollution. This makes me angry. Once I calculated that if people like Madame contributed .01% of what they earn, the pollution problem could be solved within five years. But she'd burn her money before letting a penny of it slip into another's hands.

I don't notice how bad traffic is until a loud horn blares for an ear-piercing three seconds, waking the dead.

"*Tai nao huo le!*" Kai says, slipping into Chinese, slightly irritated.

I stay silent. The gridlock of cars ahead doesn't bother me. I'm riding in a comfortable, clean car. Master of my own life. Traffic is the least of my worries.

"Let's take the back roads." Kai makes a U-turn.

He pulls into a small alley. The roads become narrow as we dodge behind the big buildings into an older neighborhood. "I know these roads well. My father owns a factory here."

"A factory?" I ask, perking up. "I didn't read about a factory in his reports."

"Probably because it's been empty for more than ten years," he says.

"No plans for it?"

"Not that I know of."

"How big is it?" I ask, an idea rising. The area around us is not a flashy part of town. Not a lot of people. Very quiet.

"Three stories," he says, maneuvering through the tight streets. "It was built at a time when employees lived at the factory where they worked. It's old, needs fixing up."

"Can you take me to see it?" I ask.

Kai brakes for a red light. "Why?" I don't respond. Thankfully, the red light turns green. He accelerates slowly. "We're already late. Normal people work at 8:30."

"Screw work. You hate the office, right? And your father can wait another hour for his millions," I say, my hand on the door handle, ready to get out of the car at the next stop just to spite Chan. I refuse to let him or anyone else control me, not when I can give him Shanghai on a silver platter.

Kai looks at me again, contemplating his father's reaction, but a glimmer in his eye tells me this is not the first time he'd be playing hooky from work.

"Okay, if you promise not to run off again, *pretending* not to see me." So. He knew I ignored him in the cab. He drives on, eyes forward. On his lips, he cracks a playful smile.

"Deal," I say. Kai may be watching me closer than he lets on. Little does he know that I'm watching him even closer.

Kai parks the car in an alley locked in between brick buildings. "Typical old Chinese neighborhood," he says.

Plants in large pots line the streets, greening up the dull red bricks. People cook on the sidewalk. The smell of garlic whirls. Laundry hangs from the windows. Bundles of chives, links of sausages, celery, and pumpkins perch on window ledges locked in by iron bars.

The area is full of old factories. It's a nice change from the skyscrapers downtown. Migrant workers chatter in groups on the corners. It's reminiscent of a China I read about in books.

Kai steers me around a corner and looks up at a sign, 'China Generation'.

"Here we are."

As far as I can tell, a wall surrounds the whole premises of 5000 square feet, with three old cameras, most likely not functioning, on posts. Spikes of broken glass cover the top of the cement wall-gate, a common form of home security a few decades ago.

"The gate controls have no power at the moment. No one has been here in at least a year. We will have to use the back gate."

As we walk around the block, I notice that each factory on the street has a tall metal gate. Outer gates frightened me when I first arrived in China. I'd felt caged. As I walk past them now, I'm reminded that gates have another purpose – keeping unwanted things out.

Kai leads the way. I hound him with questions about the rooms; the security; what kinds of products were produced here.

"Why are you so curious about this place?" he asks.

"I like old buildings," I say, which is true. I have come to see their value in hiding the obvious.

We arrive at a small metal door within the large gate frame. It's locked. Kai steps up on an empty bucket, lifts the top off a prong in the gate, and pulls out a rusted key.

"This is where my father's first company started," Kai explains.

We enter an overgrown courtyard behind the factory. The space is completely private and enclosed. The building is dirty, but there's no visible damage.

I'm not disappointed when I see the inside either. It's in good condition despite a thick layer of brown dust.

Apparently, Chan has always had good taste. The

windows are all intact and double paned, unlike most old Chinese factories. The floor is not cement but hardwood, another nice touch. The front room is vaulted, and there are fans scattered across the ceiling in a star formation.

A waiting room, with a sink and storage cupboards, is in the corner by the entrance—perfect for medical supplies, I think. Kai notices a broken cupboard. "Feel free to look around," he says. "I'm going to fix this." I watch for a moment as he tinkers with the hinges before I head upstairs.

The bedrooms are roomy and fit several beds; the bathrooms and kitchens function, and the lounges are spacious enough to create a comfortable living space. It's exactly what I need.

When I come downstairs Kai is dusting off his pants.

"How's the cupboard?" I ask.

"Good as new."

"Your father asked me to tell him if I saw you tinkering again."

"Please don't. He might fire me." He folds his hands as if in prayer, feigning remorse, then throws them down. "On second thought, please tell him."

A small laugh bubbles out of me, almost a giggle. I'm surprised. I haven't heard myself laugh since Red. I can't deny sharing a joke with someone feels nice.

Our tour ends, and Kai leads me out.

Walking down the alley, Kai talks about the factory. "The only drawback is it's not close to the metro."

"Not too far," I say, without thinking. "Just 1126.8 meters from the last metro entrance. Less than a mile."

He cocks his eyebrow. He's about to comment when

a car tears down the street. Instinctively, Kai grabs my arm and pulls me toward the side. I grab on to him, too.

Judging by the speed, and the potholes in the road, the car will swerve right towards an old garbage can. They will hit it.

"That'll be a mess," I comment automatically.

Seconds later the car jolts into the can and trash spills over onto the street.

"How did you...?"

I've let my guard down, twice. *What's wrong with me?* I only do this with people who are safe.

He's staring at me—four seconds. My hand is still on his arm. Even under his suit I can feel how solid it is. His hair is as stiff as an accountant's, but his eyes are so gentle and kind. I don't answer.

"You're an intriguing girl, Phoenix."

"Just jumpy, remember?" Embarrassed, I walk faster.

Almost to his Rover, I ask, "Why hasn't your father sold the factory?"

"You may not believe this, but he's sentimental. It reminds him of my mom. They had their last conversation there before she died. After that, he moved locations, but he never had the heart to sell it." Kai's gait slows.

I swallow hard, daring to ask a question that is inappropriate in Chinese culture. "How did she die?"

"I don't know. My dad never told me." He shrugs it off.

Kai doesn't know how his own mom died? Then I can rule out a natural or death by illness. She was young to begin with, but Chan not talking about it, hiding it from his son, plus his association with Red indicates something darker. If I could bet money, I'd say her death was not an accident either.

I say nothing of the sort but continue our conversation about the factory. "For the right offer, I bet he'd give it up."

"With the crash coming, he just may. Why do you care?"

"None of your business." It comes out snappy, rude even. I don't like it when people pry. I don't want Kai asking so many questions.

"Sorry," he says, "I was just curious."

After his apology I feel bad. Kai's been kind to me these past few days, even skipping work to show me the factory, but I don't trust him or Chan to know my plans, especially now that I've found my safe house.

The next week slides by quietly. When I don't hammer Chan about the soon-to-be burning economy, he can be agreeable. Not pressing me when I advise him, treating me like a real employee, even greeting me when I arrive. Maybe I was too hard on him? Even other employees have been kinder to me. It's not so bad here.

My proposal for another investment is nearly finished when arguing next door in Chan's office steals my attention. I creep over and crack my door.

"You would destroy the legacy I built for you? All my work to become dust?" I've never heard Chan's voice so angry.

"No, Father, that's not it. I just think…" Kai's voice

becomes too quiet to understand.

"Do what you want, Kai!" Chan says, his voice still loud as ever. "But stay away from that girl! She's trouble. She doesn't belong here. When this is over, we will send her on her way. Out of our lives forever!"

My stomach knots like I've just been punched. *That girl* could only be one person. There's no mystery about what Chan really thinks of me. Not surprising I suppose, but I'd hoped Chan would see what Red saw. See who I really am. In the Pratt everyone says they don't care what other people think, but that's a lie. A residue of feelings remain. People harden. Walls go up. For me, putting walls up is easy. Breaking them down is another story.

I sneak back into my office and close the door. "I'm not here for Chan, or Kai," I breathe over my computer in a sharp whisper. I've got bigger things to worry about...like my new plan.

Chan, who has the resources to prevent the disaster, won't do anything—which means securing an unthinkable amount of money is up to me. I review my calculations. They're daunting, like a giant blocking the way of a child. It's a long shot given the timing of the impending crash, but this time I won't feel guilty for not trying to help. First, taking my cut from Chan's investments, I'll do what I do best: invest. I'll generate more money to sustain the currency, banks and stock market, and prepare a super bond.

Second, in my pursuit of the impossible, I'll need to find some filthy rich donors. Fortunately, *filthy* people aren't hard for me to find and it'll bring me nothing but pleasure to rob them blind.

On Friday, I stand at the bottom of the Shanghai Tower looking up at the 126 floors with high hopes of hearing good news from Chan about the factory since I made him an offer last week. Doorman Yu Tai stands at attention, watching me.

"Nice day, isn't it, *Yu Shifu*?" I say in Chinese.

"Beautiful, like you, Ms. Phoenix." He opens the door.

"Excuse me, Yu *Shifu*, do you work anywhere else?" I ask.

"I moonlight as a driver," he says, whipping out his card. I receive it with two hands, as custom. A private driver? Again, not what I was expecting.

I head towards the elevator, pondering. Yu Tai's life is none of my business. I don't need to solve another mystery at the moment. Only I can't pretend it doesn't matter. If I could only find out w*ho* gave him the job here, then I'd feel better.

I reach floor 79, which bustles with busyness. I put Yu Tai out of mind. For now, I have to work.

Noon rolls around. I'm eager to get Chan's go-ahead on the factory, but he's nowhere to be found. I wander over to Kai's office to ask him about his father's whereabouts, but Kai is gone too.

I take the elevator up to the executive restaurant.

When I enter, Kai is at a table, laughing. He's in his stiff business attire as always, but his posture is relaxed, and his dark hair isn't cemented back with hair gel but hangs loose down to his strong jawline. For a moment, happiness at seeing him stirs in me and I *want* to talk with him.

Sweet, delicate laughter follows Kai's. I think it's

mine until I register the young woman sitting across from him. The one from my first day of work. Is this the girl his dad was talking about?

She's draped in pearls hanging down to her mini skirt. Her hair is pulled up in a cute roll. I finger the hairband around my wrist, wishing I could put my hair up too, then I sneak backwards trying to slip out unnoticed.

"Phoenix?" Kai calls.

Ugh. Not sly enough.

"Don't want to interrupt," I say in Chinese, spinning back around. "Talk to you later."

He stands up, walking towards me. "Xiao Yan and I just finished." He gestures toward me. "This is Phoenix."

She extends her hand, her lips pursed together. "How do you do?" Her high-pitched voice matches the strong fragrance of vanilla. Taking her hand is like gripping a porcelain doll, even a gentle squeeze might break her.

"See you tonight, Kai?" she asks, ignoring me. She slides her hand down his arm.

"Not tonight," he says. "I'm busy."

She tries not to look disappointed. She makes him promise for a rain check then says goodbye. I try to exit behind her.

"Wait, Phoenix," Kai says, "I have something for you." He switches to speaking English the moment she's gone.

When I turn to face him, Chan's words replay in my mind, *stay away from that girl.* I'd hoped Chan wouldn't tell Kai my business, but I realize now that Kai will always know everything that passes between me and Chan and probably the other way around.

"What?" I ask, as if I don't already know.

He holds out a set of keys. "The factory. It's yours." His eyes are wide with excitement.

"Thanks." I grab the keys like it's not a big deal.

"You have done the impossible again," he says, jokingly. "How?"

Without meaning to, I frown. Too many mixed emotions are firing in me. I don't want him looking at me like that—like I'm supposed to celebrate with him. Like there's some camaraderie passing between us. Not after their argument I heard in the hall.

My shell, the one Red worked so hard to break, creeps up on me. I try to push it away because it reminds me of Celia. I don't want to be hard and cold like her, suspicious of each kind word. I want to be soft-hearted like a child who jumps at good news like it's a present; or to trust someone like I trusted Red. But Chan's opposition prevents me. The last person I should get friendly with is his son. I don't trust people very easily. I trust people with money even less.

"Didn't he tell you? I went down to thirty-five percent. Like I said, money talks." I start to leave. "See you later."

"Listen." An extension of the muscles in his arms predicts a thirty-percent chance his hand will touch me if I don't move. Three seconds to choose. His hand covers my shoulder. "Are you busy tonight?"

"No, but…" I draw it out, about to tag on an excuse except I go blank because my shoulder is tingling. Besides, even with all the practice I had at Madame's, I can't lie smoothly, nor do I really want more practice. I leave my response at that, curious about why he's asking.

"Want to get out of the city?" he asks. "You said you like old buildings."

The invitation surprises me. In China, parents' demands are to be respected. I explicitly heard Chan command him to stay away from me. But there's another reason he shouldn't invite me.

"You just told *your friend* you're busy tonight," I say.

"I am. I want to take you with me," he says, a boyish grin on his face.

"Where?"

"A place that can change the way you view a few things, I hope." He smiles.

I hesitate, but Red's voice is in my mind. *Growing requires trust.* I wouldn't mind upsetting Chan again, too.

Kai raises his eyebrows, waiting. Standing in his suit, he looks stern. I don't want to trust a boy who barks commands into his cell phone one moment and the next is kind, like that night in the pool house.

"Come on. Song Valley isn't that far away. We'll be back before bedtime."

I perk up, startled. Song Valley? If numbers could scream, they are doing just that in my head. *The exit sign I'd seen.*

Suddenly, Kai's offer sparks a much deeper interest in me.

"Are you going to wear that suit the whole time?" I joke, lightening the atmosphere.

"If I promise to change, will you come?" He smirks. "Leave after work?"

"All right," I agree. And why not? Everything should be fine.

Right?

TWENTY-TWO
PRESENT: PHOENIX

∞

SONG VALLEY, CHINA

After work Kai and I head out of town. We follow the river east, straight for the coast. The buildings shrink in size as we drive away from the smog-filled metropolis. It's nice to see green again and enter a slower pace of life, escaping the buzz of traffic and honking car horns.

After an hour, Kai veers off on an exit leading to Song Valley. I close my eyes, drilling into my mind of numbers, dragging up all I remember about that Song Valley sign but while Kai is talking, I can't concentrate.

"Phoenix?" Kai says. "Did you hear anything I just said? You kind of tuned out for a while."

A while. I sigh to myself. He means I ignored him for four minutes, twenty-three seconds. But it doesn't really matter how long it was, I should be listening. "Sorry. I was just admiring the countryside." Except my eyes were closed. *Oops.* Thankfully Kai doesn't mention anything.

The roads get smaller while details become more vivid—farmers dragging their oxen over rice fields, animals grazing, old tiled roof houses, corn drying on the pavement. Nothing is familiar. Internally, I would have mapped out the roads. But I haven't been here.

Kai stops at a small wooden house on the roadside. *Auntie Ma's BBQ Duck* is written on a plastic banner. "Wait here."

He returns eight minutes later with a large to-go box. "Two hot buns, brown sauce for dipping, walnut milk tea, and of course, duck. Barbequed to perfection." He starts the engine and drives down a small gravel road that looks like it's headed into the bushes. "We're early," he says, "so let's eat up here."

The smell of barbequed meat is intoxicating. With each breath, I can't wait to tear into a crispy piece of duck. After another three minutes, we drive out of the brush of trees and shrubs and into a small cove and my heart stops.

In front of us is a roaring body of water.

The ocean.

It's the East China Sea, but it's more than that. It's the Pacific.

My ocean.

It doesn't look like what I grew up with, but it's the same ocean. I'm just on the wrong side of the world.

I roll down my window to catch my breath. Any thought of duck vanishes in comparison to what I smell now. Crisp salt air rushes in, assaulting my senses. The roar of crashing waves and the sound of the tide coming in drown my mind in the past. Suddenly I'm at my 13th birthday at our beach house with red trim.

The ferry's horn whistles in the distance, signaling its departure. Fluttering seagulls circle overhead. I'm standing on the path that leads down to the water, to the dock with the swing on it. My dad is sitting there. He's trying to tell me something.

"Phoenix." Kai shakes my shoulder. "You okay?"

A hot streak runs down my left cheek. Tears? *Get a grip, Phoenix.* I scold myself and try to wipe my face without letting Kai notice.

"I just need some fresh air." I open the door and slide out, walking twenty-five feet from the car. I bend down and let my fingers trace the surface of the cold grains.

Sand used to comfort me. It was my treasure—one of those anomalies my mind didn't try to calculate. I was no Archimedes. It was just a part of nature, earth, rocks broken down into grains over time. I used to lie on it without a towel. I never cared if I had it all over my hair and clothes when I left. It was a reminder that there are hidden treasures out there for everyone, even me.

I take off my boots to feel the sand between my toes and walk towards the water. Each crashing wave roars a greeting as if it has missed me. Needs me. Will it take me home if I asked it?

This is all that separates me and my old life. This one ocean, the largest body of water in the world. I'm suddenly drunk on its sound and smell. Even after all these years, my ocean still has the same effect on me. It won't let me force it away like all the other triggers that remind me of home.

The Pacific-scented breeze massages my cheeks

and sends chills over my bare arms. For the first time in a long time my heart is quiet when I think of my family. Perhaps seeing the ocean is a gift from God, washing the Pratt off me for good, or cleansing me from Madame's hatred. Each breath feels like a new beginning. Each crashing wave, like hope. I can have a new beach. A new home. A new life.

A warm touch on the shoulder jolts me out of my trance. I look up and see Kai. He has come out to find me. He extends a hand to help me up. I take it. Once I'm on my feet, our eyes meet. I'm emotional and he can see it, but neither of us looks away. His hand, I realize, is still in mine and the warmth spreads over my body. Soon I'm wishing I could be wrapped up in his arms, or anyone's arms. I want to be held. It's been so long.

I drop his hand instead. My cheeks burn red. Our gaze breaks. We both stumble on words.

"The duck is getting cold," Kai finally says.

I smile weakly, daring one more peek at his face before we walk back to the Range Rover. Back in the car, he has set up the food. Dinner begins.

"Do you like it?" he asks tearing off another piece of duck.

Looking down, his half of the meal is nearly gone.

"The duck or the ocean?" I ask, realizing I haven't spoken much since we parked.

"You've hardly touched your duck." He hands me a piece. "I was talking about the view."

"It's beautiful," I manage to mutter. "I haven't seen the ocean in more than two years. I grew up 3000 miles that way, in West Seattle." My finger extends, pointing over the endless gray to the Pacific's horizon.

"Phoenix," he says, touching my arm, sending another quiver through me, "do you realize what you just did?"

"What?" I ask, suddenly nervous like I was caught speaking in my sleep.

"You just told me something about yourself."

He's right. It just slipped out. A moment of panic crosses over my face as if I've already told him my long dreadful story. But he takes another bite of duck and the weight passes. *Most fear is imagined,* Red used to say. *Laugh at it.*

"How do you know it wasn't a lie?" I say jokingly, opening the small plastic container of brown sauce.

"Because I trust you," he says. Trust me? He doesn't even know me. "Maybe if you'd trust me back, you'd tell me more about yourself. Can't be too terrible, can it?"

He has no idea. I'd shatter his peaceful nights if I told him his greatest fears were real and they existed in two people—Madame and King.

He passes me my hot tea. I grip it tightly with both hands, warming my fingers.

"So you haven't been home in two years? What have you been doing that whole time?"

"Don't press your luck," I say, shoving a piece of duck into my mouth. I can't get over how salty and tender and juicy it is. "Are you going to tell me why we're here?"

"We're going to the place I study Kung Fu. To meet my two masters." He throws the last piece of bread into his mouth.

"Why didn't you take Xiao Yan?" I ask, her image

still buzzing in my mind like a pesky fly.

"She can't appreciate the art behind Kung Fu," he says, starting the car.

"And you think I can?"

"Maybe. Or maybe you just need to see we're not training to be killing machines, but men who can protect what is good."

My face becomes stern. "Why are you doing this for me?"

"Doing what? I just want to be your friend."

I'm not sure of Kai's real motive for taking me here. He barely knows me and is already assuming what I need? It's annoying. On the other hand, he has sort of looked after me since I arrived. Maybe *being my friend* is all he wants. Maybe that's what I need. A friend. It doesn't sound too bad.

"Okay," I say. "Let's go."

We follow the small streets and enter an ancient village. Kai was right. The old buildings are stunning. Their old gray bricks, curved rooftops, and cobblestone streets play with my mind. I half-expect to see men with long queues stepping over doorway thresholds, women hiding behind hand-painted fans and draped in red silk, bowing to one another in greeting.

I keep my eyes open for any clues but see nothing.

We exit the village and arrive at a black tiled-roof farmer's home surrounded by fields of green vegetables. Kai explains that his two masters believe in living off the earth as well as helping the people who live nearby. "They are simple men with grand ideals," he says.

"How did you find them?" I ask.

"After my mother died, I became a monster." His

eyes fix on the green fields ahead. "I missed her. The older I got, the more restless I became. I got in a lot of trouble."

I think back to after my mother died. I dove into school and work with my dad, anything to cover the pain. Maybe Kai and I have more in common than I think. Suddenly I'm more interested in his story.

"I thought destruction of anything would help. I came to Song Valley out of disobedience to my father. These guys found me lurking outside. I told them I wanted to learn Kung Fu. To be powerful and forget pain. They told me to use their studio to destroy things, hit, punch and kick, and to come find them when the pain of losing my mother was gone. Then they would teach me."

"How long did that last?" I ask, noticing how big his forearms are and the tiny scars that follow his wrist to his elbow.

"Two months. When I finally realized anger and fighting didn't help the pain, they agreed to train me. That was my first lesson. They taught me that the opposite of losing someone is saving someone. We bring healing to ourselves and others if we concentrate on life instead of death."

I think about myself as he talks. What he's saying makes a lot of sense. Maybe it's why I'm still here in China, trying to heal my pain by saving trafficked girls and working for Chan to help the crash. Maybe the last year and a half can be healed. Maybe I can, too.

Kai parks the car. "The Sang Brothers changed my life. They're so different than my father. After my mom died, his fight was against the financial markets and he won. Good for him. Look where it got him. Now he wants me to follow his path even when he's not happy. He is not who he used to be." He shakes his head.

"My dad did the same, after my mom died." Kai looks shocked at my admission, but I'm strangely calm. I've never talked about my dad's grief with anyone. Somehow it feels right to say it out loud. Normal. It doesn't even bother me that I'm admitting this to Kai because he understands, and I don't think he'll share it with anyone.

Hearing this confession about my dad, however, does something weird. I loved my dad, but if I'm honest, he was headed down the same road as Chan. He never let me spend the money I made for him. He only wanted to make more. I wonder if he would have bounced back to his old self, if we all just had more time. I'll never know, though, so there's no point in speculating.

Kai holds the key in his hand and stares at me, as if he's deciding if he should ask another question or not.

I decide for him. "No more questions."

I jump out the car. Thankfully, Kai does too, without another word about my family.

Kai directs me down a small stone path through lush foliage. At the end we come to a covered area full of wooden dummies, bamboo poles stuck in the cement ground, large square stones, and hanging punching bags covered in rope.

Two men come out to meet us. They are dressed in the humble clothing of farmers. Dark blue jacket and pants, white tee-shirt, black woven shoes, no socks. They walk slowly. I'm not fooled by their outer appearance. In the span of ten seconds I've calculated enough about them to know I wouldn't want them to be my enemy.

They are just slightly taller than I am, but both have an upper body mass that is twice the build of an average man their height. Both also have acute balance, evidenced by the way they move lightly on their toes. Their hands, rough and callused, look like they spend their spare time pinching rocks in half. Physical appearance aside, the look on their faces hold a confidence that tells me they fear nothing. These men are lions.

Instantly, I step closer to Kai even though the numbers predict they are not a threat.

Surprisingly, they sense my fear, like great lions do, but instead of encroaching on me, they submit and back off. They become gentle, like lambs, like the gentleness of Red. I let down my guard. This combination of gentleness and power is rare in men. They know their own strength but can leave it in an instant to gain trust. I remember Kai's first lesson; *fighting won't heal the pain*. I decide to like them then and there.

"Phoenix *meimei*," one master says. His arms lift, and his left hand covers the fist he makes with his right hand in the traditional kung fu greeting. "I am Master Sang Tao, and my brother Master Sang Han. Welcome to our humble home."

I quicken at the dialect they use. It's the same as Red's. *Is Song Valley Red's home?*

I cup my fist, returning his greeting to show respect. "Thank you. I'm honored to be in the home of two true Kung Fu Masters."

"Xiao Kai flatters us. Unfortunately, the ancient tradition of kung fu is dying. There is no more place for us in the world. Now, we are just farmers."

"Why is it dying?"

"In ancient Kung Fu, to lower standards led to death. Kung fu stood for things that were righteous, pure, and just. When our services were not needed as before, there was nothing to cling to, like stumbling in the dark. In our hearts we wish for only one thing—purpose—but we cannot find it."

His speech saddens me, like it's me, hoping for purpose in my old life when it's gone. Starting over is the only answer for us.

"I hope you see the heart behind our tradition today," his brother says.

"I'm sure I will," I reply, my mind spinning with possibilities. I follow the men into an indoor courtyard made for sparring.

"For you." Master Sang Tao motions to a table set with hot tea, fresh-cut fruit, a variety of nuts, and dry meat. A firm round pillow is next to the table. I dip my head again in thanks before I sit, legs crossed in front of me.

Meanwhile Kai picks up a stone the size of a soccer ball and walks towards me. His expression is playful. Setting it down beside me, he says, "Keep this stone in mind when you watch us." He points to a small waterfall cascading over a mound of rocks in the garden behind the arena. "Also the water."

The two masters exit down a narrow hallway.

"Stones and water, huh?" I lift my eyebrows. "Are you going to get metaphoric on me?"

Kai laughs. "Listen, you can tell how strong someone is by their forearms." He taps his lower arm. "After bruising and callusing the bone, it hardens, making it strong enough to break through wood, brick, bone, and so on. Kung fu is not about muscle." Kai takes a deep breath and extends his arms. Then his arms cut through the air smoothly, like he's writing calligraphy. "It is about stone-like discipline, stone-like virtue, stone-like internal focus. It is also like water. Fluid, gentle, quick, ungraspable, unbreakable."

"What do you mean, *like water*?" I ask, playing along.

"Stand up and I'll show you," he says.

Jumping over the threshold that surrounds the sparring arena, Kai dips his fingers in the water. "In kung fu we call the two main defenses, *Water* and *Rock*. Water is implemented if someone has harder forearms than you—you avoid their moves by maneuvering around them." He shakes the water off. "Hold up your arm." As his punch comes towards me, he slides my arm along his to deflect it from the target on my body. "You should learn this technique, but if you are stronger, you implement the rock—blocking their moves. A simple block can transform into an attack."

"You said kung fu isn't about harming," I remind him.

"That's right. The fundamental teachings of kung fu is called *8 Hands* – essentially, it is 8 blocking techniques. Next, there's *36 Elbows*, another blocking technique. All defense. 36 Elbows is taught as a sequence. Learning to link the moves is key. Not many can do this. But if you can, the sequence enables you to fight a lot of people at once."

"Have you mastered it?" I ask, curious.

"Kung fu is also about being humble." Kai smiles largely. He doesn't need to respond for me to know the answer. "Now, for the different clothes I promised you." He turns and heads down the same hallway as his masters.

The three men come back dressed in black and white kung fu uniforms. Immediately they start warming up. With their forearms, they slam wooden dummies and glide speedily around the hanging punching bags.

Before I know it, they move into sparring. I watch carefully for the stone-like blocks and also the water-like deflections. Each of their movements is clearly executed, just as Kai said. When I watched men fight in the Pratt, what went on looked simply like brutality, the winner was whoever could swing the fastest punch. But kung fu was like a mathematical dance.

Kai moves gracefully. His footsteps are so light that if I closed my eyes, I'd hear nothing. All the muscles in his arms flex, defining themselves. His face is straight and focused as if there's only one goal in mind; but behind his focus, there's serenity.

Their sparring becomes more vigorous. Their actions remain smooth, choreographed, but their breathing becomes more exerted, like gusts of wind in autumn. I catch Kai's eye. Sweat beads his face, and he smiles at me just long enough for his two masters to double up on him. Is this the 36 Elbow technique he's employing now? It's clear that any average fighter would be no match for Kai, but his masters are too practiced, too strong. Kai keeps them at bay for seven minutes, three seconds, but then ends up on his back.

When they finish, all of them are wet with perspiration, but none look tired. They bow at my applause.

Kai comes over, a happy expression on his face.

"What did you think?"

"Impressive," I say. "I'll admit it changed my view, a little."

He beams proudly. "We are going to get cleaned up. Be out soon." They retreat down the hallway again.

My eyes move around the courtyard to the different plaques on the wall. A scroll with history of Song Valley draws my eye. Standing, I walk over to the article and study the map of the town. Chills travel down my spine.

My blindfold has been removed.

King. I'm in his hometown.

The map of Song Valley hypnotizes me from the wall. It's the ruins of the former dynasty, where the tunnels began. King and Red's hometown. Since I never drove through all of it, it's smaller than I had estimated, but the distances align perfectly with the map I already calculated internally—driving the back roads to the Pratt and to the port, the stint into Song Valley and... *the warehouse is just minutes from here.*

Is today my chance?

My stomach squirms with fear at the thought of being so near to King. A part of me wants to run far away. But nothing happens by chance. Or so Red believed.

A bowl of incense burns next to the small table. A box of matches is next to it. I grab it, slipping it into my pocket. Resolve sinks in.

I'm going to get those records. And if there's any *cargo,* I'm going to take it and light that place on fire.

It's dark by the time Kai appears. He's back in slacks and a dark gray button down. We spend ten minutes exchanging thanks, goodbyes, bows, and plans to meet again. It feels like an eternity.

Finally, we get to the car. Kai presses an automatic lock and I hop in.

Before he's seated, I blurt out, "Can we take a drive? What about the port?"

It's dark, but I put on my sunglasses and wrap a scarf around my head. Kai gives me a funny look.

"Sure," he says, gauging my expression. The car roars to life.

As we drive, Kai shares the local history. "It's an ancient town. Old legends from Song Dynasty. That's how the town got its name. Used to be the old port town, until the delta eroded most of the coast. Go west a bit and you can see a few stone structures at the old port." He's ignorantly describing the Pratt. If only the government knew the old barracks had underground catacombs and what they were being used for.

I nod in silence. I could tell him more, but I don't.

"The new port is as big as 500 hundred soccer fields," he spouts off. Then he surprises me with information I'm not expecting. "The old port is private property now. A man named Yu Chen owns it."

"Yu?" I say. "I thought a man named King owned it."

"Maybe. There was a land dispute after an incident in the town. Yu, the real owner disappeared, and the claim was withdrawn. If it was sold, the deed was never registered."

"How do you know so much about this place?" I ask, making a mental note to locate the real owner.

"My father. He followed everything that went on here."

"Why is he so interested in Song Valley?"

"Don't know. He hates it here. Claims gangsters live here." He shrugs it off with a laugh. "I am not sure where he gets that stuff."

It's official. Chan hasn't told him about the Pratt. That's a relief.

We arrive at the port gate. Kai rounds the corner slowly and stops the car.

"I know someone who works here." I point to the port, even though my eyes are on the small road leading to the warehouse. "Mind if I hop over to say hello?"

"What? Like a *friend*?" he says.

"Shocked?" I say playfully. *Friend* is definitely not the right word. But I don't want him involved.

Kai looks like he's about to object to me walking around in the dark, but his phone rings. By the way his voice changes and eyebrows raise, it's an important one.

"Give me fifteen minutes?" I say in a low voice. He nods reluctantly, pointing to the phone as if telling me it will be awhile. Perfect.

Besides, I'm just going to have a peek first. I'll rely on my calculations. Safe to go—low odds of danger—I'll proceed. Not safe—retreat.

I hop out of the car and walk around to the back hatch. There's a small puddle there, so with my boots I kick up a bit of mud and cover the license plate. Just like Guard San used to do.

I cut through a clearing in the trees to the warehouse's road. A large gray building appears. The warehouse. I take a minute to calculate dimensions and devise a strategy.

The doors of the warehouse are opened wide. Inside sits a container etched with big gold letters that read *Golden Shipping,* the company Madame uses for shipping cargo. Now I *must* enter.

I sneak over to the warehouse.

Industrial fluorescent lamps provide a harsh light inside the warehouse. Three people are visible. Two of them in guards' uniforms. They're occupied with a card game. One is smoking and overweight, the other guard fiddles with his phone. The guards were never very vigilant. The only one who worked hard was Bo Gong. Even back then, he tried to do something right.

The third man worries me. He wanders around the warehouse, searching intensely for something. I can't identify if I've seen him before. He's foreign, tall, dark hair. Could be a buyer. Or an associate. Which wouldn't necessarily be a threat.

All the dimensions of the warehouse are still logged in my brain. I have measured and planned my escape in this place before. Getting in and out should be no problem. In fact, every equation tells me it's safe to proceed.

I allow a span of eleven minutes for my purpose: get the records, schedules, and if the girls are there, I will have to recalculate. The distance between the guards and the front opening is 40 feet. The other man circles the back of the warehouse. I walk closer.

Passing the guards is a piece of cake. Even now, I feel no threat, because the guard who is 29-percent overweight is favoring his right leg and the other is still consumed with his phone. I can outrun both of them if I must. The last man, in the suit, is fit but seems lost in another world on the south side of the warehouse. I play to his distraction and go in the opposite direction.

I creep up to the first container. Its cargo door is open, and it's empty. Half of me is relieved, but I'm not satisfied. I check another container. Empty. There are steel boxes lying around. All of them are marked with an X but they are all screwed shut. Weapons, drugs, or textiles?

After searching the warehouse for three minutes and 45 seconds, there's no sign of any *cargo* or anything incriminating. I veer towards the office. I need those records and schedules.

My eleven minutes are almost up. I don't want Kai to worry. I have three minutes. One minute to retrieve the schedule and two to slip out unnoticed. I've got this. I sprint towards the office.

All of a sudden, a voice yells. "Private property!"

I jump, assuming they are referring to me. But how could they be? I sneak a peek and there's Kai, snooping around the corner, mumbling about looking for a friend.

"*Ugh*, did he follow me?" I groan under my breath. "I said fifteen minutes." Why do people always have to mess up a precise plan?

My equations recalculate. They're all negative. There's no way I can grab the schedule now. Worse, the two guards stalk the door. I won't get out that way—not if I don't want them to identify me. Through the shelves and boxes, I see Kai back off while still searching for me with his eyes until finally he walks back down the trail. I've lost sight of the third man in the suit.

"Close the gate," the one with the phone yells to the guard with the hurt leg. He hits the automatic door and the garage top descends downward. The back door is my only option.

I dash down the hall. An alarm sounds with a loud beep signaling an automatic lockdown. A loud click secures the office door. Another at the back door. No! I have to get out! I can't get trapped here!

The back door is not coded. It's an old school lock. I have to use an ID or a key. I drop around the corner, deeper inside the warehouse. *Think.* There's a bathroom to my left, ten feet. Factoring the number of footsteps and the distance of the voices, my numbers predict that the two guards are fifty feet from me and haven't seen me yet.

If I can make it to the bathroom, I can escape through the window. If I turn this corner, the odds of making it unseen are slim but I'll have enough time to escape. It's worth a try.

Before I put my right foot forward, another voice yells, "Stop!"

That voice. I recognize it. The man in the suit? I freeze and look around. *Run, you idiot.* But I can't. Numbers go crazy.

Slight accent. Low, just like his father's. Could it be? I hesitate, and that leads to—

The man catches me by the wrist. I struggle. My sunglasses fall to the ground. Obviously, he's not trained because it distracts him. I break free.

I should run, except the brown curls, green eyes, and dimples stop me.

It's him. Rafael. The only boy I thought I could trust.

TWENTY-THREE
PAST: MILA
∞

THE PRATT, SHANGHAI, CHINA

Workdays were the worst. The guilt that followed was so heavy, so dirty it took days to compartmentalize. My only compensation was the brief time above ground.

Tonight, the Shanghai sun set in a blemished sky of brown haze as a black Mercedes pulled up. A voice barked out behind a puff of smoke as a tinted window scrolled down. "Get inside." A face, dark and scarred, cracked a brown smile. He gave me a wink. I shuddered in disgust, as I did each time King winked at me.

The massive hand holding my arm belonged to Guard San. He looked down, a permanent scowl on his face. "Come on, you heard what King said." Inside the car I was enveloped in a cloud of cigarette smoke. I hopped onto the leather seat, instinctively looking for a seat belt that wasn't there. It was tucked under the seat like always. Why did I bother?

Two cars drove ahead of us and disappeared

around the corner. We were driving to the port for another delivery.

Sand and dust kicked up around us as we maneuvered out of the Pratt. We passed the collection of seven buildings. They huddled together like a kind of small Asian ghost town. Although they all appeared to be stripped of anything useful, within them a very complex operation hid in plain sight. Building three was for transactions. Building seven was the entrance to the Pratt. The rest were for storage, except the lighthouse.

Rubble of cement blocks, old Twenty-foot Equivalent Units, or *TEU's*, and broken beams lay weathered on the land. This junkyard was what King called his kingdom. At the main road, Guard San barked at me, "Blindfold."

"Who's coming today?" I asked, slipping it over my eyes. King brought me on days where two parties signed an agreement. He needed my eyes and my numbers to make sure he won in every deal. No one ever asked who I was. It was terrible and nice at the same time because I got to be out of the Pratt.

"Alexi and Cesare."

I perked up. Alexi was Madame's point man in Russia. He's dangerous, one of Madame's seven leaders. Lately, he'd been in China far too much.

Cesare Di Susa was a fat Italian man, reeking of cologne and steeped up to his black mustache in crimes of all sorts. Essentially, Cesare was a smuggler just like King, but he was ignorant party of Madame's empire, which made him expendable. He was here for fast cash, which King provided. Cesare exported Chinese goods to Italy and occasionally picked up payments for Madame via King. Out of all of King's associates, he was the most arrogant and *oblivious*. That was why it was so hard to believe he'd fathered Rafael, a boy whose smile brought out the sun.

"Oh?" I tried to act normal. "Is Cesare's son coming too?"

"Lai," Guard San replied, giving me his growl of a smile.

Rafael was seventeen, two years older than me. The first boy my age I'd seen in eleven months. When he first came into the Pratt, I couldn't take my eyes off him. Wispy brown curls. Eyes the color of evergreens. Big dimples. He was smart too, apart from not knowing what a thief his father really was. I didn't blame him. Love hides all kinds of things that were right in front of us.

Rafael never sat in on the meetings. From the two other times we'd spoken, it appeared he truly believed his dad was doing legitimate business with King. Who knows, maybe Cesare did too. Although, there were very low odds of that.

But if Cesare didn't know this much, Rafael knew even less. To them, I was King's associate.

As we reached the end of the road, past the warehouse and entered the main port, they removed my blindfold. The Port of Shanghai was a sea of its own— swimming with large container ships docked at every post, thousands of TEUs set in systematic rows, any number of cars, trucks, cranes, and equipment for unloading and loading the cargo. It was not surprising that things went unseen in this metal and iron realm that was the world's biggest port.

We pulled up to King's private dock. I stopped, suddenly dizzy. Numbers exploded in my mind. I squeezed Guard San's arm to steady myself. My mind sometimes calculated what was coming faster than I could comprehend. The numbers knew what would happen before I did.

I forced my eyes open. I promised Red I'd pay attention when this happened.

I concentrated on the port as numbers revealed my surroundings. Distances, heights, speeds, sounds—everything within a 100-foot radius. The numbers linked and assigned equations first to the ship, its dimensions, the men unloading the boat, the containers coming down the ramps; the ballast control; a flat calm sea, King's associates, the license plates of their cars; time of day, 12:45 am, Sunday; the numbers of workers on hand tonight, more than usual; most of them I didn't recognize. The list went on.

It was all wrong. And I wasn't referring to just another day with King, because frankly, everything he did was wrong.

In just a matter of seconds, my mind scrolled through variables, possibilities, predictions. I was soon nauseous, trying to calculate them all, until they narrowed their focus to the boat itself.

Negative.

The ship was dangerous, but I wasn't sure why yet.

While numbers spun mathematical equations inside my head, I looked around. I couldn't see anything out of the ordinary.

King got out first and walked on board. He motioned for us to follow. He'd sign the customs papers, receive cash for Madame, the guards would take the containers to the warehouse while King completed the deal on the boat, same as always.

King wasn't the sort of guy you disobey, so I knew I had to have a good reason for not getting on that boat. All I had was a negative number in my head telling me not to. That wasn't good enough.

Guard San opened my car door. I didn't move. He peered down at me as I shook my head. San, quick to pick up on hints, understood I was hesitating. He surveyed the premises, but nothing was out of the ordinary.

"Let's move," he said coldly. Then added in a softer tone, "I'll be here the whole time."

I inched my feet forward because I didn't have a choice. I did feel safer with Guard San at my side. Besides, I didn't know why the numbers highlighted what seemed to be a perfectly normal, totally illegal deal. But I'd learned that the numbers didn't lie.

Lights on the dock came on as the last of the sun sunk below the horizon. We walked on board and watched the unloading of the containers. I was immediately ushered into a small compartment with a wooden bench where I would sit and wait until I was needed to okay the deal. A different guard stood close by. King set his briefcase down beside me along with a bottle of *baijiu*.

I waited. I'd only come to the boat a few times, but I didn't remember seeing the barrels that sat by the other ballasts.

Exactly four minutes later Cesare and Rafael walked on board. King greeted them with handshakes. Cesare's oily black hair shone in the dock's spotlights and even from ten feet away I smelled alcohol on him.

In contrast, Rafael was a breath of fresh air. His head twisted, looking around. Probably for me. It's funny how people of the same age hone in on and migrate towards each other. Finally, he caught sight of me. We locked eyes.

The first time Rafael came to the Pratt, Cesare and King had something private to discuss before some deal. Cesare must have experienced a brief moment of morality because he wouldn't let his son sit in on the meeting. That day I was left alone (in a locked room in building three) with Rafael for a full 32 minutes I won't forget. I wasn't sure why King let it happen.

I stood frozen and blank-faced, as the cute Italian boy asked me my deepest, darkest secrets, like what my name was. Double-8? Josephine? Octavia? None of those would do. Then he asked a long string of other perfectly normal questions—*what I was doing in China, where I was from, what language I spoke*—all of which I couldn't answer either.

Finally, he asked one question I could answer. "You can speak, right?"

"Yes." I let out an embarrassed laugh.

Instead of my awkwardness turning him off, he just laughed.

"A girl with a thousand secrets," he said. "So, I will call you Mila. It means 1000 in Italian. *Va bene?*"

I smiled. Mila sounded pretty, much better than Double-8. "Okay."

The rest of the time we compared Roman history to Chinese history and talked about whether or not he should return home for university or stay in China to work with his father in his export business. I urged him to return home.

"China wouldn't be so bad," he said, gazing at me. "Especially since I've found things I wouldn't mind exploring."

My cheeks burned for eight minutes straight. A world record for blushing, I'm sure.

I thought about that night for 53 days—replaying how Rafael talked with his hands, the warmth of his kiss-greeting on both of my cheeks, his silly imitations of opera. Spending time with him felt normal. It filled me with hope, like he could save me somehow.

Today was our fourth face-to-face meeting.

Alexi boarded the ship next and my mood darkened. I'd never trusted Alexi. His body language betrayed his mind. If anything, he was King's equal, which meant we were never safe when he was around.

Alexi was with two Chinese men I didn't recognize. As I sized them up, their clothing looked peculiar. It had a weird shine to it. So did Alexi's. They were also wearing gloves and it was spring now. Were they planning to help with unloading the boat? Their back pockets were bulging. But what was in them? Alexi ordered his men to unload the containers. That explained the gloves. Negative numbers pulsed around them.

As one of them turned, I saw words tattooed on the side of his neck. The Chinese characters *cai* and *li*—money and power. I laughed bitterly for a moment. That summed up my whole world at the moment.

King walked over to my small compartment, leaning in through a paneless window. "Double-Eight." He slid a finger down my face. "Where are the documents for my client?"

"Here." My head dipped. I'd had a week to prepare them, even though I finished what he wanted in under an hour. I'd never tell him that, though.

"Good. Stay here. Guard San will call you before any decisions are made. You belong to me. I come out on top you hear me?" He watched my reaction. I nodded again, keeping my eyes on the ground, like a trained dog who had learned not to challenge its master. "Remember, *mei nu*. It's money time."

King walked back to Cesare and Alexi and headed below deck. My gaze returned to Rafael, who walked my way. The boat lurched slightly. Rafael lost his balance but caught it before he fell. He laughed it off and shrugged. "That was strange."

He was right. The water was not choppy enough to bring on that kind of lurch. I fixed my eyes on the containers being unloaded. King's men unloading the boat had that same shine on their clothing as Alexi's Chinese associates and they also reloaded new containers. More numbers spun.

I stretched my head out the compartment. Rafael thought it was to greet him, but really, I just felt nauseous and the small space made me feel worse.

"*Ciao,* Mila," Rafael said. "Can I join you?" The guard allowed him to enter the compartment.

His smile made me forget the nausea for two seconds until I noticed the man with the tattoo stabbing something in the corner with a knife. Alexi's other associate transported a barrel downstairs with the help of another man. I wanted to see it more clearly, but

Rafael planted a kiss on my left cheek in greeting. I tried to act natural, but I couldn't hide the mixed emotion I felt in this small sign of affection. I awkwardly turned my head for my right cheek to be kissed as well.

"*Come stai*?" he asked, three inches from my face.

"I'm okay, thanks. How are you?" I asked. His hair fell across his smooth face, and with each bat of his eyelashes I calculated the odds of him being adopted. It was impossible for him to be related to that sleazeball dressed in Armani, downing his first whiskey with King.

Rafael recounted his vacation in Sicily—climbing the volcano Etna, ferrying to Stromboli...I realized I was only half listening because I couldn't stop watching Alexi's men. Why were King's and Alexi's men leaving certain containers behind and bringing new ones on? If they all worked for Alexi, then King's men were greatly outnumbered. Why were the barrels being taken downstairs?

"So, after visiting Ginostra," Rafael explained, "I have been to both the smallest and the largest port in the world!"

"Fascinating," I said, completely distracted. Newton's second law of motion was playing out in my brain, suddenly configuring a function for balance. Dynamical systems graphed out the scene in front of me.

My mind charted and analyzed everything: the tanker's dimensions, the weights, the containers as they were carried out.

The tattooed man bumped his hip on a railing and the bulge in his back pocket dropped to the ground. It looked like a mask? More men went downstairs. Guard San moved into a new position by the stairs. I'd never been left unguarded so long before.

Another slight lurch of the boat edged me into Rafael's side. He was warm. Strong. Smelled of salt air and mint.

Embarrassed, I pushed myself to the side again, but I was pulled back towards Rafael, and it wasn't because he was cute. Was the boat listing? A string of negative equations shot across my mind concerning the barrels.

The boat. The barrels. The extra men. And I saw, no, *felt* the calculations unfold before my eyes.

My heart beat frantically now. We had to get off the boat.

My knee warmed. I looked down. Rafael's hand was on it.

"Mila," Rafael started, "I've been thinking about you since the last time, and I wanted to ask you something..." He searched for the right words.

The burning sensation in my knee raced up my body to my cheeks. What was he going to say? I really, really wanted to know. But not now. There was no time. I had to tell Guard San. But it dawned on me. King was below deck. Guard San was more than twenty feet from the compartment. I was less than ten feet from the ramp. *I could escape.*

But Rafael had to leave first, or Guard San would be suspicious.

"Rafael," I said, breathless and determining how much longer we had, "get out."

His face dropped into a frown. "Why?" he said, dejected.

I shook my head realizing how bad that sounded. "What I mean is, we can't talk right now. Something is wrong."

"Wrong with me?"

"No."

For a split second I thought about how to tell him something without saying too much. But it was too complicated.

"Go take a walk on the port," I blurted out.

His frown deepened.

"Sorry, that came out wrong again. I'll meet you on the port in five minutes, ok?"

"Why not talk here? We are not supposed to leave the tanker."

I tried another tactic. "Your dad's car, on shore, is more private. You go first."

"You don't want to talk with me, do you?"

I wanted to scream that there wasn't anyone I'd rather talk to right now, but if we stayed here, we may never be able to talk ever again. But I couldn't. It wouldn't come out because there were too many other things going through my mind.

"Just go. I'll meet you there."

But he didn't leave; he tried to interpret my hidden cues instead of just listening to what I was saying. Ugh, boys!

He looked disappointed. "Look, I can take a hint, Mila. Fine, I'll leave."

Relief. I'd explain everything later. Now that he was going, I'd be free to run.

But instead of leaving the ship, he went further in.

No! Not in there! I inwardly groaned. "Rafael –"

But he didn't answer. He headed to the stairs and into the mess I'd been trying to lead him away from.

My hand slapped down on the seat, stinging my palm. "Not *on* the ship! Not downstairs," I said under my breath. "This is an ambush!"

TWENTY-FOUR
PAST: MILA

∞

DOCKLANDS, SHANGHAI, CHINA

Run.

It was a horrible thought. But all the numbers said I could make it if I went now and left everyone behind, including Rafael.

After the last variable was put in place, I could discern everything clearly. This ship was going down.

Alexi had set a complex plan in motion to kill us and make it look like a container ship accident. But all the pieces weren't ready yet.

The containers were being unloaded and reloaded unsystematically for a reason. My dad owned a boat—not a large container ship, but all boats had something in place for balance. *Ballasts.* In this case, unloading the boat unsystematically could disrupt the balance of the boat, it would topple to one side and capsize unless the ballasts were transferred.

Alexi added another component. Fire. I first became

suspicious looking at their clothes. The *shiny-ness* looked like selafane, a synthetic fiber with an exceptionally high melting point. Fireproof clothes. The bulges in their back pockets were masks. Gloves on their hands for protection. The barrels, taken downstairs, must have been full of something explosive. An engine room fire. A perfect accident.

The extra men would overpower the sailors in the engine room downstairs.

The other containers blocked the exits. They planned to lock us in by fire and capsize the ship while they escaped free and clear. A double accident. No way to uncover the truth.

King didn't suspect anything because he often worked with Alexi. But Alexi had always wanted his prize. Unlike Cesare, he knew about what lay underground in the Pratt.

But they also wanted the merchandise and there were still two more containers to unload. Unloading took 2-5 minutes each.

If my calculations were correct, the boat could be rebalanced if the ballasts were transferred within three minutes. If not, we would be locked on a sinking boat by walls of fire.

The man with the tattoo nodded to the one in yellow, who nodded to the other sailors. The second to last container was being transported out.

No one was watching me. I had waited two years for an opportunity like this. I could run. Be free. King, my captor, Madame's seller of children, dealer of criminal secrets, would be dead, the world a better place because of it. All it would take was me slipping out of this compartment in the next 75 seconds. King would never expect me to run. Neither would Guard San.

But my second thought was harder to push away. *Rafael was here.* He was innocent. Then there was Guard San, who was my friend now, the men in the engine room, and the other guards. They were not innocent, but they didn't deserve death. Their lives too, had been ruined by King. Then there was Red. *Could I still rescue him if I left?*

"Aiya!" My fists tightened and my eyes closed so tight a headache forms. *Run.* Twenty seconds before they moved the next container. I could take the trail out past the warehouse, back to the Pratt. The guard in the watchtower would be distracted by the commotion at the port.

Even if Rafael left the boat with me, he was smart. He'd piece together that I knew about the ship burning and would never forgive me for letting his father die.

How could he not know his father was scum?

Because it's his father, stupid.

Numbers charged through my head. Another barrel went downstairs. The men moved the last container, getting into position, blocking the entrance of the ship. Still no one noticed me.

This meeting was about taking King for all he was worth and crowning Alexi as the next King. This had happened before, but King was always ready for it. That was the problem when you double-cross people. It eventually caught up to you. Today, everyone would die and another monster would replace King. Unless...

My mind raced back and forth. If I stayed and warned King, no one would die but I would remain a slave. If I ran, I abandoned Rafael, Guard San, and Red to their fates.

Ten seconds left to run. Four minutes until the last container was unloaded.

I grabbed the liquor at my feet. And even though my actions would keep me here in the Pratt, I jumped out of the compartment, and screamed, "King!"

The yell startled the men. Heads turned. They were surprised to see me, a young girl materializing out of thin air.

"King forgot his liquor," I said, loudly. I waved the bottle in my hand as naturally as I could. I wasn't really good at this lying stuff. Guard San was at my side in two strides. He cocked his head. My eyes rolled left, towards the men. "Just like he forgot with Sutherland."

I hoped the name was enough to convey my warning. Sutherland was a *laowai* who tried to double-cross King three months ago.

Guard San picked up on the cue immediately. "You'd better take it to him. Downstairs, first room on the right." He took out his phone. Back up would be here soon.

I took the bottle of baijiu and flew downstairs, bumping into Rafael on the way. "Find the boiler room and tell them the list is off. They have less than three minutes to transfer the ballasts. Warn them there is gas in the engine room. After that, get off the ship."

"What?" he asked.

"Go! Quick, please. And be quiet."

Rafael gave me a startled glance but ran back in search of the boiler room.

In the small office on the right, I found them all at

a table. They looked up at me, annoyed. King gave me a growl. I stretched out the bottle. "You forgot your liquor." I panicked with all their faces staring at me, especially Alexi's.

King didn't take orders from anyone, but he was no fool. His right eye was quivering. "Anything else?"

"Yes," I said, "I forgot to sign my name in the accountant section of your document. May I?" I leaned down, taking the pen, and found the bottom line of the document. It was not for an accountant. It was the date line. I hoped Alexi was not looking. Instead of signing my name, I wrote, *Sutherland, two minutes.*

King's eyes didn't flinch. "Gentlemen, the papers are ready. My assistant here says we have come into good fortune. Guard Feng, please take her out and get a more appropriate bottle of liquor so we can celebrate." He looked at me. We both know there was no other bottle. He believed me.

Guard Feng sensed King's words. King motioned to Cesare. "Go get their money." Even though King had it there, on him.

Cesare was clueless, but Guard Feng picked up on that too and motioned for Cesare to follow. We closed the door right as we heard a crack and a smash, and something like a window breaking.

What happened next was fast, and loud.

An alarm sounded through the whole boat.

Alexi's men raced downstairs, shouting to light the barrels. King's men followed.

Rafael ran out of the engine room followed by the ship's crew.

"Get off the boat! Quick!" the crew shouted.

But we couldn't. Upstairs there was more fighting. Guard San must have called in more men and blocking the ramp was the last container. One of the barrels burst into flames near the open container. Now we really couldn't get off the ship.

Cesare started fighting alongside Guard Feng as soon as we were upstairs. Someone shoved Rafael to the side. He gained his balance, grabbed me, and we dove into the compartment, staying low to the ground. Smoke filled the air.

I didn't see the rest of what happened, but the mayhem didn't last fourteen minutes before King's men subdued Alexi's men. When we popped our heads out, the engine crew was using extinguishers to put out the fire. I assumed the other barrels were never ignited.

Guard San approached the compartment again as King's men rounded up Alexi and the tattooed men and left the ship. I wondered if Alexi and his goons would be our next three Pratt-mates, or if they would suffer a more permanent doom.

"Out," Guard San barked. He had me by the arm now and led me around the container back to King's car. Rafael's eyes drilled into mine. There were no dimples because he was not smiling. Instead, those green eyes, the color of the evergreens accused me. He finally understood that whatever was going on wasn't innocent and somehow I was part of it.

Before I reached the car, one of the crew ran out to Rafael. "We had two minutes before this ship developed an irreversible roll. They were unloading the boat unsystematically. We'd all be underwater now if it wasn't for you."

Rafael found my eyes. He knew it wasn't him. Rafael wrestled his arm away from Cesare and ran over to me. "Mila, how did you know?"

"Good guess?"

"Impossible," he said. "You saw it while we were in the compartment. Didn't you? You saw everything, like a prodigy, or an angel, or something. You saved us."

For a moment I was dumbstruck. No one did that. No one looked that closely. He'd been paying attention. *He saw me.* All I wanted was to be known by someone and here this boy knew me. Maybe he could help. But would he after tonight?

"*Raffaele, vieni.*" Cesare grabbed his arm and led him away, trying to explain what had happened.

Rafael turned. "I won't forget this, Mila. If you ever need anything, I'll do it. Please, just tell me your real name."

If only my eyes could have talked, I would have told him everything. But his request was impossible to fulfill with Guard San holding my arm. Next time, I promised myself, I'd tell him everything.

But after days, weeks, and months of not seeing him went by, I didn't know if I'd ever get that chance.

TWENTY-FIVE
PRESENT: PHOENIX
∞

SONG VALLEY WAREHOUSE, CHINA

Rafael's frame is not thin like it used to be. His shoulders have filled out. His face is more defined. He looks older, more serious.

"Rafael?"

I want to smile but I frown instead. He's wearing a nice suit and he's in the warehouse, which can only mean one thing, *he's working.* So he learned who his father is and he joined him. To think I risked my life for him. I risked freedom because I believed he wasn't like his father. We even had *something*, small but real, didn't we? He was my only hope in the Pratt that my life could be normal. The only boy who saw me. The only innocent one. Or so I thought.

All kinds of emotions fill me. Disappointment. Rage. Pity. Disgust. *Hope* too, tries to surface. Things I wish I could tell him clog my throat. Telling him who I really am and what they have done to me. Pleading with him to leave this place, this life. But there's no time and if I wait any longer, the guards will be here. I can't get caught. My internal clock is ticking.

I'm breathless as I say, "Now's a good time to repay that favor."

Rafael wades through the dark hair, makeup, clothes. Thirteen seconds later he whispers, *"Mila,* is that you? "

I nod. His eyes widen as he recognizes me. Massive confusion follows. I can't imagine the stories he has heard or what he will tell the others. But there's no time to explain. He obviously knows I'm not dead but I will be if I stick around.

"Please, Rafael," I start, "you never saw me." It's all I can say. The guards run closer. They're shouting as their feet stomp through the warehouse.

"Rafael! Do you see them?"

He knows I shouldn't be here, that he shouldn't be either. His eyes read mine. He even looks ashamed. "Go." He motions to the bathroom.

I run, open the door. Above the sink is a small window—15 inches wide by 8 inches tall. At the right angle I'm small enough to fit through. I push it open.

Rafael shouts back. "I lost them. Quick, down aisle 9!"

My gratitude lasts just long enough to remember the security cameras. If they find out he helped me, I don't know what they'll do to him.

I'm almost out when a dark SUV tears around the corner, braking hard in a cloud of dust and spitting rocks. I have nowhere to run.

"Phoenix!" Kai's head pokes out of the window.

Thank God. "Phoenix, is that you?"

Jiche. He's watching me crawl out of a window on the side of the warehouse. I drop to the ground. "What were you thinking?" I yell, upset he ruined everything.

"Me?" he yells back as he swings open the door. "What are *you* doing?"

I make a mad dash for the car. The guards race around the side of the building as I dive into the front seat, my head low.

"Drive!" I scream. "Now!"

Kai doesn't ask questions but slams his foot against the pedal and speeds ahead.

My head stays low. Men are shouting behind us. "Take a picture of the Rover, you idiots."

Kai shoots me a concerned look.

"Don't worry," I say. "I put mud on the license plate."

"You did what?"

The car dips into a pothole at full speed, snapping us both forward. I bump my head on the dashboard. "*Aiya!*" I say, gripping my head. That'll leave a mark.

Rocks sputter from the wheels as we tear out of the port. A loud sharp noise, like a bullet goes off behind us. I stay low even long after the road becomes smooth concrete.

"You can come up now," Kai says drily, jaw clenched. We're on the freeway now. He's driving faster than usual. I don't blame him. I'm praying nobody follows us.

As I inch up and put on my seat belt, the car fills with heavy silence.

"Friends, huh?" Kai says, his eyes fixed on the road.

"If you had waited in the car everything would have been fine," I snap, thoroughly annoyed.

"Yeah. That's why you were sneaking out a window?" he says. "What if I hadn't come to your rescue? Huh? What would those men have done to you?"

I don't have the energy to explain that if he hadn't come to look for me in the first place, I would have made it back in less than eleven minutes and nothing would have happened at all. But I'm angry and I find myself arguing instead. "I don't need your help, Kai."

"Really? It looked like it," he shoots back. "Who are they?"

"Maybe they were the gangsters your father talked about," I say cynically. It's a part of the truth, and it sounds better than the whole truth—*Oh, just wanted to visit the men who ruined my life, yeah, they happen to run a clandestine criminal operation. By the way, did I mention the world's most wanted trafficker kidnapped me at age 15?*

Yeah, right.

"Okay fine. Don't tell me who they are. Tell me who you are instead and what you were thinking back there." His voice is controlled again, even calm, but it's obvious he's still worked up.

"I don't know what I was thinking," I say, mad at myself now. I was too impulsive. I should've never asked him to go to the port. He doesn't need to get mixed up in this business. I already took enough risks today and I didn't even get the schedule.

For forty-three seconds I visualize how Phoenix would play this out—a girl who stumbled upon something terrible and wants to forget it, who would be thankful for her rescue. Finally, I muster up the energy to say it.

"I was mistaken about that place," I start quietly. "And the people. They looked really upset. Thanks for coming after me."

Kai darts a disbelieving glance my way. Then huffs a large sigh. He doesn't believe me, but he doesn't ask any more questions. His face is focused on the road.

"Can you keep this between us?" I ask, meekly. "I wouldn't want your father to worry."

"Whatever you want, Phoenix." He drives the rest of the way back in silence.

That's it, I think. *It's over.* Just when I opened up to him at the beach and finally understood he wanted to be a friend I make it impossible to be one.

Over the weekend the smack from Kai's dashboard developed into a dark blueish-green bulge covering most of my forehead. It looked like my head got stuck in an elevator and smacked every floor on the way up. As if things couldn't get worse, Chan called me in for an urgent meeting on the day it looks its worst. I wonder what he'll think of my bruise. More importantly, I wonder what he wants to talk about.

The last time he called me in unexpectedly, he drily informed me that he'd hired a new accountant. He didn't need to spell out that I'd been right that first day in his office about the missing funds in the C-suite, or the chain store and insurance. He never said thank you, but he stopped questioning me. That day, I held a smile on my face for an hour and thirty-seven minutes.

I walk into his immaculate office. Chan is leaning down smelling one of the potted *moli* flowers on the ground, lost in thought. I clear my throat.

"Ah, Phoenix." His eyes lock onto the huge lump on my forehead immediately. Just what he needs to confirm his suspicions of me.

"Missed the game-fights, did you?" he asks, his finger unconsciously rising to touch the part of his nose I broke.

I shrug. "Just carelessness." Is he laughing at me?

He raises an eyebrow at me, not believing a word. Thankfully, Kai agreed to keep the secret between us. I won't be the one to explain our get away from King's warehouse.

"Well, are you okay?" he grunts, changing to a more serious tone. "Anything else hurt?"

My head snaps up. Did I hear that right? Is Chan looking out for me? Chan sees the shock on my face.

"I don't care how smart you are," he says, "you're still just a girl. No parents. No past. No one to look out for you."

So what he's really saying is, I'm one hell of a messed-up orphan. "I'm fine." Thankfully, he's in a hurry and drops the subject.

"Well, I can't complain," he says, jumping into business. "All of my accounts are rising as you promised, but..." He grabs a file from his desk. "Did you hear the news?"

I shake my head.

He rubs his forehead slightly. "Other companies are not doing so well." He clears his throat again.

Whatever he has to say is not coming easily. "I asked the Asia Bank Council to investigate the numbers. Their experts agree there's something wrong."

"What did they find?"

"I want you to ensure the future of my company," he says. "And there's a meeting tomorrow with the World Bank. I want you to come..."

"What did they identify, Chan?" I repeat.

Most people, after having been told they are crazy, or foolish for believing something, enjoy gloating when the facts come to light. This is not one of those times.

Please don't say it, I think, as I calculate what's next on his lips. But he does anyway.

"You were right, Phoenix," he says slowly. "About everything."

You'd think that after the Asia Bank Council agreed that a crash is coming, Chan would listen to my plan but he's more pig-headed than a mule. He still doesn't understand that governments or banks won't help China stay above water, and neither can I. Even if I manage to make a fourth of the money that Chan has, Asia Bank—the only operation large enough to handle distribution, won't just let me walk in and take over.

On top of that, the Expo is in less than three weeks and I still don't have the records or schedule or any buyer information. I don't even know if I'm brave enough to go through with the Expo. Each plan I devise to extract the girls doesn't check out mathematically.

Then there's the boy problem. Kai is spying on me for Chan. At least it feels like it. How else can I explain his odd behavior since the incident in Song Valley? He checks on me regularly—even though he doesn't really say a word. He's snoopy, but his gaze lingers on me longer than it should for a person he despises.

As if on cue, Kai pushes through the door—the second time today—with a cup of tea. He sets it down slowly, stealing glances around my office and at my computer. His cold kindness complies with cultural pressure to maintain harmony but he's up to something.

"Here's some hot bitterroot tea," he says, his voice not nearly as warm as the liquid steaming in the cup. "Try not to get in *trouble* in the next hour, huh? We've got a meeting soon."

After a week of this, I snap. "Look, Kai, I know your father told you that I'm 'trouble'. I proved that to you—so why bother coming around me at all? Unless you're trying to find more evidence for your father, I suggest you leave me alone."

He looks up at the ceiling, letting out a deep breath. I feel bad for snapping at him. Wasn't I the one who did something wrong?

"You're right," he says, jetting to the door. "You are trouble. I just thought maybe it was the good kind."

He leaves silently, his steps so swift he could be a ghost.

A gaping hole emerges in my chest. I wish that day on the beach never happened. That I never told him those things about me. Maybe that pestering feeling that I lost something would go away. Still, I can't deny admitting those things about my past felt good.

I push thoughts of Kai to another part of my brain, which is crowded, because they bump into Rafael, wearing that suit. Pushing away that thought is easier than thoughts of Kai. I've had practice forgetting Rafael.

So, in hopes Kai will forget the incident at the warehouse and forget me, I decline his offers of a ride into work. I hole up in my small office, with my eyes glued to the computer. Then after work I visit the factory. I've been slowly filling it with things I'll need—computers, surveillance, nerdy tech-tools like the ones we had at PSS, medical supplies, even blankets and clothes. I've also cleaned up inches of thick dust, but it only proves to me what an impossible task all of this really is.

I can't reasonably work for Chan and create a super bond—that may never see the light of day—and bring justice to King and Madame. Stress is adding up. I'm running out of time and here I am wasting time analyzing Kai's behavior!

Red would have retreated to his room already, commanding me to focus. Stress from a boy is the least of my worries.

Focus! I check off the next target on my list: Golden Global Shipping. I couldn't hack into it, so I decided to control it from within—Chan is now the main shareholder. With greater access, I should be able to reroute the shipments to a port of my choice. Not only will shipments arrive to King at the Port, but his payment will too—first into my pocket, then into the super bond.

Theoretically, if the bond works, in a few years, whoever controls it, could be the most powerful person on the planet, which is why I've come to another irrational decision. Apart from helping the girls, my cut will forever loop in the endless cycle I created until the economy evens out. I'll keep nothing.

The word *nothing* has a bad reputation, but actually it's not that bad. I've lived with nothing and lived with everything. One thing is for sure—money can't guarantee happiness.

Behind this action there's another motive. My vow to Red—to right all the wrong I've helped create. I want to beat the odds; to test it all and see if it comes back to me. If there's more out there, like that path with higher rules of which Red spoke, I want to walk on it. I believe, now, there is—so I have to try.

I take out a piece of paper and write one of Red's poems on it. I tape it to the wall. As I stare at it, I remember all he gave to me. If he were in my place, he'd do the same thing. The thought makes me smile.

I wonder what my dad would think of all this. Would he be like Chan or Red? I jump online and do something I promised myself I wouldn't do. Even as I'm opening a new window, I'm not sure what will happen if I bring him up from the dead. But my fingers can't help punching in the name J-J R-i-v-e-r-s.

An old picture of him at *i*Vision pops up. I scroll through articles about his investigation and the dissipation of *i*Vision shortly after my abduction. I locate our house in Seattle. The address is under new ownership. I shouldn't be surprised. There's nothing recent about my family. I can't even find the article about their death anymore. It's dead information. Like them.

I processed my anger with Red in the Pratt. *"I forgive your betrayal. Your love of money."* I let the past go, didn't I? But could I return home and start again? Seeing these pictures stings, not of bitterness or anger, but grief. I want to believe they would have loved me no matter who I was or what I did. I'll never get that chance. Death doesn't give us second chances. So I settle, closing the computer.

I catch Red's poem in my peripheral vision. I stop to recite it, like he used to make me do.

"White sun leans on the mountain then vanishes. Yellow river flows into the sea. If your eyes desire to see a thousand miles, go up one more floor."

Red referred to this poem 86 times when talking to me about my destiny. Basically, it means "aim high" and "if you want to reach your goal, you have to climb that extra floor. Work hard, persist."

Chinese always play games with words and their sounds. Many Chinese words sound the same but have different meanings. Red never wanted to play that game with this poem. I do it now, not sure why.

In the first line the word *jin*, meaning 'vanish', stands out. It sounds like the word for gold. I read the sentence again. "White sun reveals a mountain of *gold*." In the second line, the word *liu* for 'flow' sounds like the number 6 and the river could represent water, making it "*water of six*". Then in both the third and the fourth line I exchange more words that sound like numbers, namely, 1000 and 1. For the first time, I see this poem in a completely new light. I erupt in laughter.

White sun reveals a mountain of gold.
Across the river in six.
A thousand tunnels.
Go up one floor.

Red was a genius. All along, from day one, he was telling me where King hides his stash. It's in the old lighthouse, building six across the stream.

TWENTY-SIX
PRESENT: PHOENIX
∞

SHANGHAI TOWER, SHANGHAI, CHINA

No matter how I calculate it, there's no safe way to get into the Pratt and loot the lighthouse. That is why I have recorded the last instructions for the bond and other loans as simply as I can. Now, if something happens to me at the Pratt, the warehouse, or at the *Expo*, even a middle school student could follow my detailed plan for stabilizing the economy.

As I think about a name for the super bond, my father comes to mind. He always named his investment projects after their inspiration. I type out a name or two and delete them immediately. Nothing seems to fit.

To distract myself, I take out another sheet of paper with a small map of the Pratt. I trace the tunnels with delight. Taking King's treasure will be a stab to his very heart and a generous donation to China's economy. After all, someone has to keep him accountable.

After hours of work with my head down, my neck

begins to hurt. Chan's secretary buzzes me. "Someone on line one asking for you."

I perk up, alert. This is the first time I've received a call that's not Kai or Chan within the office. No one knows me. No one should be calling. My first week in the office, I told Chan to let people know I didn't want questions or visitors.

"Who is it, Secretary Lin?" I ask, looking out my window, shaking off a chill.

"The reception isn't clear. She didn't give a name. Just said it was urgent and that you'd be happy to hear from her."

She?

My mind does flips. That's impossible. Madame thinks I'm dead. King thinks I'm dead. *Jo is dead.* I'm Phoenix now, and no one knows her save three people. It's not her. The line beeps again.

I pick up and use a Sichuan dialect to disguise myself. "Who are you?" I ask sharply.

"It's better not to say now. We need to meet in person." The voice is soft, not Madame's. Still, I don't recognize it. "I have been meaning to contact you. I need to deliver something to you."

Trap. Lies. Do not fall for this again. "Not interested."

I'm about to hang up when she says, "Wait – it's very precious *cargo.*"

The word *cargo* traps me like a net. I can't hang up. Possibilities stream through my head. *It could mean anything. Don't trust her.*

"Make an appointment with China Generation," I say in Chinese. "Send details of the cargo to this address."

"I can't do that. I'm to deliver it to you alone, Phoenix, in person," the woman says. "The cargo is extremely exotic, expensive, *marked with an X.*"

Marked with an X? If it's what I think it is, that's impossible. But there's no other explanation.

"Tell me something that will make me trust you."

"*Ah,*" she says, "he said *trust* would be a problem."

"Who said that?"

"Your grandfather."

My heart leaps back into my cell. I'm Double-Eight again and Red's there, whispering, *"You can trust me."*

If she knows Red, there's an eighty percent chance she's telling the truth. But that's not what's moving me towards my decision. In this instance, *I feel* like it's going to be okay.

"All right," I say, taking an unaccustomed leap of faith. "Meet me at High Street, gate 34. Eight pm." If it is *cargo,* we need to take it there.

I hang up and relax my shoulders. Did I just trust a stranger? I hope my gut is right.

I slip out of work early because I don't want to be questioned or delayed. There are a few things I need to do before I meet the mysterious caller. In the lobby, I apply red lipstick, as dark as Madame's. Slide on a pair of sunglasses and a long dress coat that hides my frame.

I head for the main door. In my head I write a shopping list—food, medicine, pillows. If her cargo is what I think it is, I want to be ready.

Doorman Yu Tai swings open the door. He's not in his work clothes. I remember Mr. Yu's moonlighting offer and I jump on the chance to use his services as a driver.

"Have time to take me somewhere?" Again, I'm surprised. Seriously, trusting two strangers in under twenty-four hours?

"Sure."

We agree on a place and price. When Mr. Yu picks me up, we load everything into the car. The drive will be no more than twenty minutes. This is sufficient time to understand the man who opens the office door.

I start with his eyes. A mere glance, straight on, confirms my suspicions. He doesn't look away and is not afraid of what I might see. He's born with an extremely high aptitude of social skills and when he's around Kai and Chan or other businessmen, he acts like he belongs.

"What did you do before you worked as a door-man?" I ask. "You strike me as a white-collar man."

This surprises him. He acts as if there's something caught in his throat. He itches his nose and cracks his neck. He's taken off guard.

"What did *you* do before you worked here?" he responds. "You strike me as being too young and obscure to be Chan's assistant of finance."

Good point. We both stay silent. He has been noticing me, as I notice him. Interesting. The silence stretches. Another point in common—neither of us wants to confess first.

"Guess we're at a stalemate," he says.

"Guess so."

"Let's just say I had it all and all was lost," he says. "So here I am."

"Working at Shanghai Tower was your idea?" I ask.

"Actually, it was your boss's. He gave me the job,"

he says. "He knew my father."

Guanxi. I was right. Chan gave him the job.

"If you haven't noticed, Chan has a practice of hiring guys like me," he says. "Why do you think everyone loves him?"

People love Chan? It's so mind-blowing I want to ask more, but I only have a limited number of minutes for my already-planned questions.

"So, you're from Shanghai?"

"No."

The way he says it so absolutely, I know our conversation is over so I can't ask him where, but I have an idea on how to get my answer.

A minute later, we arrive at our destination, a small shop two blocks from the factory. Yu Tai hurries to open my door and unloads the boxes. As I pay him, I thank him in Red's home dialect.

He immediately returns the appropriate response in the same dialect, then hops in the van and drives off. Only someone who grew up there could respond so naturally. He's from Song Valley, just like Red. Just like King. Just like I suspected.

I hail a petty cab for the remaining two blocks. While calculating my backup plan in case things go wrong, I clean the upper rooms, set up the beds, and load food into the fridge.

An hour later, three females—one older and two younger—stand outside the gate. *Cargo—girls.* I knew it.

I approach the gate without opening it, calculating their movements. They have no tension in their bodies to suggest a trap. The two younger girls—with long black hair and beautifully symmetrical faces, drape their arms around their bellies, shaking. They look at me, terrified. I'm female, but that does not make me safe. I should know.

The two girls recoil after noticing me inspect them. Although they are dressed in thick jackets and baggy pants, they fold their arms across their chest to hide themselves, a sign of insecurity, yet their eyes remain empty. They have been broken. God knows how long it'll take to put them back together.

The 'X' is not hard to spot on their necks. No paper trail, but Madame loves to claim her work. Leaving a mark is the downfall of her pride. The scar on my neck will always be a reminder of that. I open the gate.

The older woman gathers the girls like a hen with her chicks. They stay very close to her as they approach.

When I come eye to eye with the older lady, I see a ghost.

"Phoenix. Nice to finally meet you," she says, sweeping in for an unexpected embrace. Her gentle touch on my back throws me off but helps me understand why the two girls huddle around her like chicks. I haven't felt a touch like that since my mother. I quickly back off and usher them through the gate.

"This way," I say, locking it.

"My brother told me much about you." She leads the girls through the front door of the factory.

"You're Red's sister," I say, comparing the map of her face to Red's.

"Yes, Dr. Ling." She observes the factory with obvious tension. "How did you know?"

"Same eyes."

"I am the youngest sister. Red got a note to me, telling me how to find you. I'm sorry it couldn't be sooner and without grave news," she says, a slight tremor in her voice. "I'm afraid we don't have much time."

At first, I think she knows about the economy, but she's far too frightened for that. "What is it?"

"King knows I helped the girls get out of the hospital. He has guards there now, daily, looking for me. I can't go back," she says, shakily. "He has informed Madame and she is on the hunt, too. We are not safe. We have nowhere to hide."

The safe house has begun. It's a good time to test the alarm.

It takes 56 minutes to convince the girls, *Hua Mei* and *An Ying,* that this old factory is safe. I even have to convince myself. Dr. Ling wanders back to prepare a meal for us while I do my best to direct the shaken girls to a hot shower. As I wait for them to get cleaned up, I listen to Dr. Ling humming in the kitchen. It's comforting that despite her fear, she can still find solace in the tune of an old Chinese folk song. Just like Red with his poetry.

After the girls are dressed in clean new clothes, I show them around their new quarters and tell them a bit about myself. I show them my neck and refer to myself as a Madame Girl, though I cannot bear to tell two scared, suspicious girls I was never trafficked.

My abuse may not be the same as theirs, but we all lived as captives of Madame's and King's hand. They begin to trust me.

While we eat a meal of noodles and green vegetables fried in soy sauce, Dr. Ling tells me she's familiar with King because of Red, but she does not go into the story of how Red was taken. Perhaps she thinks I know it already? I don't ask.

"After Red was taken for what he did," she says, "he stayed at King's to protect us. My family was threatened to stay away. Sadly, we did. We had lost so much already, but King kept threatening the residents. Slowly, we all moved or were pushed out. Before Red died, I got his letter from a man inside the Pratt. He told me about you and King and Madame. I wanted to help but was interrupted when I met them." She points to the girls.

"When the girls arrived at the hospital with forceful thugs pretending to be their boyfriends, I got suspicious," she said. "King has a history of taking girls to different hospitals, so they aren't recognized. These two had an X on their necks. I remembered my brother said something about X girls. I asked the girls if they needed help. Their escorts were out in the hall and the risk was great. The girls wouldn't talk. But after learning their diagnosis, I decided to get them out anyway.

"I had the nurse tell the men that the girls would have to stay overnight to watch for complications. The nurse reported back that the men were angry. The girls became scared. The nurse insisted they come in the morning to retrieve the girls. Finally, the men agreed and left the hospital. By then the girls had confessed everything. Next, I took them to my cousin in Suzhou. The hospital didn't know what I was doing. I just left. I wrote a doctor's note saying the girls were transferred to another hospital. But King's men learned who I was and trashed my house. They left a note that said, 'Red's cell is available.' We've been travelling from place to place for a month. I didn't know exactly when you'd be out. Red's letter was vague, but I knew it had something to do with Chan. Finally, I decided to call and ask for you."

"Why were they in the hospital in the first place?"

"Abortions gone wrong."

My stomach knots up. Madame's files scroll in my mind.

Dr. Ling is adamant now. "We have two girls willing to testify against King. And we have you. We have to call the police."

"No. We have to wait."

"Wait? Are you crazy?"

"Two girls aren't enough to put him behind bars for very long. I need to expose the Pratt and finish what Red started." I'm careful not to talk about my family or myself, but I briefly tell her about the economy and, although it's only a fraction, I explain my plan to take King and Madame's money first—then turn them over to the police.

Dr. Ling frowns. "It's too risky," she says. "You are just a girl. You need to turn them in now. Let the police deal with King and Madame."

"No," I say, hard. Dr. Ling and the authorities don't understand the economy like I do, and they certainly don't understand King and Madame like I do. I *am* the one to stop them. "This is the only way. I'm taking back every dirty penny I made for them. Red and I couldn't do anything before. Now I can. You can leave if you want, but I will stop them."

"No," she says. "I won't leave. Red trusted you. I want to help you."

Somehow, I knew she'd stay, because in a strange way, we were family. I turn to the girls. "What can you tell me? Names? Addresses? I need any details you can remember."

They tell me as much as they know, which is at best, vague. Dr. Ling and I map it out as they talk. Madame and King run seven major locations in Shanghai. Massage parlors. Hotels. Parties. The girls can only remember a few addresses and names of buyers.

"Golden Alley," Hua Mei says. "It's the worst, but most accessible, at least on Friday runs."

A surge of adrenaline spikes. Today is Friday. "What are Friday runs? What is Golden Alley?"

"Golden Alley is a drug den, a real rough spot. They run girls back and forth on Friday nights between locations."

"Golden Alley," I mutter. Why didn't I think of that street? Madame doesn't miss anything when it comes to gold. "I'm going there. Madame owns the whole street, I'm sure of it."

"It's private," An Ying says. "The doors are not even marked. But it's not guarded like the hotels."

"Phoenix, wait," Dr. Ling says. "It's too dangerous to go alone. Can't someone go with you?"

"No," I say. If I go alone, then no one can mess up my plans like Kai did at the warehouse. "It's on my way home. I'll just check it out. I'll be safe. I won't try anything heroic. I'll get info, numbers, then I'll make a plan. I promise."

Golden Alley is dark and empty, with "No Trespassing" signs galore. There is no sign of life, apart from a stray dog scrounging for food. This cannot be the right street. It looks like nothing has happened here in the last fifty years. It takes 87 minutes of hiding and watching before I decide to return home.

As I begin to walk away, a strange tapping starts. Perhaps it's hammering somewhere? There it is again. I stand, listening, but there's no rhythm between the taps that would distinguish a pattern. I look down the alley to my right. Nothing. I go left, even retrace my trail, but can't find anyone. I listen for six minutes longer, but no more taps.

A bad feeling comes over me. Perhaps my heart is warning me, or maybe I'm close to finding the destination. Red would say that feeling counts for something. But it's been 108 minutes and I'm exhausted. Work is going to be grueling the next day, and logically it makes sense to go home.

I resolve to come again next Friday. And every Friday until I find those girls.

TWENTY-SEVEN
PRESENT: PHOENIX
∞

SHANGHAI TOWER, SHANGHAI, CHINA

After work the next day, Kai stops me at the door. "Hey, *Trouble*. Let me drive you home." His voice is gentle, playful. "Don't want you stranded somewhere in the dark. Besides, I want to talk to you."

It's a bizarre comment, but I concede because I'm not going to the factory tonight. When we arrive, we cruise in through the gates and into the garage. Kai turns off the car. Usually he's very quick about jumping out but this time he waits. My door is already open. My right leg swings out, but Kai's arm stops me. It's a gentle touch, sending tingles down my arm.

"Wait," he says. His voice is low and serious. "I want to tell you something."

I pull my leg back in the car, close the door and turn towards him. His dark hair falls over his eyes. He takes a moment to comb it behind his ears. I've never noticed how naturally shiny and perfectly straight his hair is before. Not sure this is the moment to think about that. I straighten up.

"Yes?"

"I don't know what happened at the port and I don't care right now. Because it got me thinking about right and wrong, about who I want to be. I want to do things with my life, too. I don't know if I am thinking clearly or just being a complete idiot, but I want to do something bigger than myself. And that starts now."

"Like what?" I ask, stupefied.

"I'm in." The look in his eyes implies I know what he's referring to, only I don't. Is this about King? My past? Has he miraculously learned to read my thoughts?

He must enjoy the confused look on my face because he starts to laugh. "The crash," he offers. "My dad said you had some sort of plan. If he won't help, then I will. I do have a pretty big inheritance."

Butterflies take flight in my stomach. I can't deny I'm touched by his offer to help. It should be like this. People stepping up to the challenge. But our world isn't so black and white. Things are so muddled behind lies and scams, by greed and selfishness, by fear and failure that we have taught each other not to trust. Not to take the risks our hearts lead us to.

"Now I don't have nearly as much as my father," he says. "But I want you to use it—double it—I'm offering it to you. To us. To everyone. Whatever we can do to help prevent this crash."

He runs his fingers through his silky hair again. He's the boy I met at the pool. A strong, courageous boy—a boy I could trust. *Maybe.*

But it's hard for me to believe that when it comes

down to parting with the money, with no real guarantee of getting it back, that he'll agree. Then there's the problem with his almost fiancée. She certainly won't agree with this plan. Not with all her pearls...

He sets his hand on the steering wheel, looking straight ahead. "You don't believe me, do you?"

"This is not a game, Kai," I say quietly. "These are people's lives. I can't begin planning and investing then have you back out. Besides, what will your father say? Or fiancée? Did you tell her your plan? You should just save your money for your marriage and happy future."

"Fiancée?" He faces me. "What are you talking about?"

"Your father told me your marriage is already in the works. I think that if you're planning to gamble with your money, she should know about it."

Kai looks like he's about to start fuming but surprises me by laughing instead.

"Xiao Yan?"

I shrug.

"My father told you that, huh?" He shakes his head. "I should have known. Look, Phoenix, I'm not engaged. My father talks about this marriage like it's a done deal. Maybe she does too. But I haven't agreed to anything. Our fathers are in the same circle – they've tried for the last year to set us up. Chinese parents pressure their children to marry within the same social circle. It's the right match in their head, that's all."

"It makes sense. You're both Chinese elite."

"It doesn't make sense if you don't love someone. I have tried but I can't make myself like Xiao Yan. Sure, she's pretty, comes from a rich family, but she is not someone who could make me happy," Kai says.

"Your father knows this?"

He sighs deeply. "Chinese parents don't make these things easy to talk about. He'll be really upset. He's talked for years about marrying within the same social status. Good family. Career. Goals. My dad's traditional."

"Which means?"

"You find a girl who matches what you want, you propose, then you hold hands, get it?" He waves his hand. "Unless I find another girl in the same social status he'll freak out. But it makes me angry. My father didn't even follow his own advice."

"What do you mean?"

"He fell in love first, defied his parents and married someone they disagreed with. And now she's dead. Her love and death wrecked him forever. He's never gotten over it. That's why he is adamant about me following his advice. He says it will save me pain later on."

"Your mom wasn't high society?"

"Not at all. Of course, according to my dad she wasn't even human—she was an angel. But now he'd say that marrying angels isn't practical. They have different lives – and they follow their own ways no matter what you say. He told me once that if Mom had been from the same circle, she wouldn't have made the choices she did, and she'd probably be alive today. In the end, it's just my dad trying to save me from a broken heart. He's never loved a woman since."

The car goes silent. I can't imagine Chan doing something out of love. Layers. We are all a mess of complicated layers, some painful and some truly beautiful. The hard money-seeking Chan has more to him than I thought.

"I want the same," Kai continues. "To love someone the way my dad loved my mom."

His dark eyes lock on to mine. The car suddenly feels very warm. I'm glad Kai looks away first, because I'm not sure what to say. I have never loved anyone besides my family and Red. What Kai says makes sense because I know how my parents loved each other. *I get it*. If you love someone, you're not afraid of the pain. You're willing to take the risk.

One minute and thirteen seconds of stillness. Kai's breathing is the only sound I hear. It's so steady, so calm that I count his inhales and exhales. I don't want to leave his steady rhythm or the feeling I have in this car right now.

"So, you are sure about this then?" I ask, referring to the crash. "Because starting tomorrow we're going to have a lot to do."

"Let's do it." He puts his hand out for me to shake on it.

I take it in mine. He squeezes gently, two, three, four seconds longer than a regular handshake. My heart races like a rabbit's. He slides his hand slowly from mine before he hops out, opens my car door, and walks me to the guesthouse front porch.

"Goodnight, Phoenix."

"Goodnight, Kai," I say, closing the door behind me. Instead of walking back to my bedroom, I go to the front window and watch each of the thirty-eight steps he takes until he disappears into his house.

∞

The next morning, Kai nearly spits out his water. "You're serious? You're basing this whole plan on a theory? And we don't even have a tenth of what we need?"

I keep a straight face. "I know it seems impossible. No one has ever attempted anything like this. But hey, you showed up."

"So, let me get this straight," Kai says, "we just need to stabilize the economy for a year, is that right?"

I nod.

"Yes. Like I said, I'm giving up my part entirely. I'm not asking you to do that. If you want to back out, it's fine," I say. "Every investment has risk. This one more than anything."

Kai mulls it over. "You're crazy, you know that? I'm not promising to give up my part, but I'm still in. We have to try, right? Okay, what's next?"

"Then, we offer bonds. Those will last for longer than the first year. The bonds will inject cash into companies that are failing and keep them afloat until the economy gets back on track. Then we invest in areas that will be useful—energy, banks, transportation, food, land—all for funds to create more bonds and keep things stable. Theoretically, companies from all over China and the world will apply for the bond."

"What's this super bond called?"

I want to tell him the name I've finally chosen, but I hesitate. I don't know if I can trust him or not. Then again, he already knows a bit about my father, so I suppose it can't hurt. "It's called the J. J. Bond or *Jie Jiang* Bond."

"Why *Jie Jiang*?"

"Jie means heroic. Shanghai has a River—*Jiang*. That's it."

Kai cocks his head to the side again like he does when he picks up on my calculations. "Come on, Phoenix. You've never been that simple."

I breathe in suddenly, surprised. My eyes start to sting because here is someone in front of me who is looking at me, paying attention to me. I relent, a bit.

"Ok. I named it after my dad. He believed in using his money to help people realize their dreams. Essentially, it's what we're going to do. He named me after..." *Himself*– this is what I thought I could say but I can't finish. He can't know my real name. Neither can I tell Kai that my father's name in Chinese is translated with *Jie* or that *Jiang*, which means River, was my last name. Or that J.J. could also stand for Jeffery Joseph, the person I was named after.

I brush off my emotion and quote Red instead. "Uh, I was named Phoenix so I could rise from the ashes and do something worthwhile. In a way, if we pull off this plan, my name will finally have meaning."

"Brilliant," he says. "So how do we buy Asia Bank?"

"That will be tricky." I bite my lip. To carry out my plan we actually need his father. He's the only one who has enough money to sustain it. "We need a lot more money. Donors. Benefactors. Who does your father know in politics who can leak information about the economy crash?"

"I'll get the word out."

"Good. I have some donors, too," I say. "I just need a bit more time to secure their funds."

"Great." He smiles. But I frown. My stomach lurches

to my feet thinking about the Pratt and the Expo.

Because when I use the term *donors*, what I mean is I have to succeed at stealing it, and by succeed, I mean, I have to survive facing Madame and King.

Kai proves to be a faithful partner investing what he can into my two-part plan. While working at his internship, he contacts banks and companies and potential donors. This frees me up to focus on Madame and King. I buy my ticket for the Shanghai Expo and try to learn as much as I can about Maxima Moreau's new summer line. Come July 10th, I have no idea what will happen.

At some point I'll need to involve the police. Should I tip them off to the shipments? The hotels? The Pratt? But tip off who? I need someone on the inside of the police, someone who can be trusted.

As for the shipments arriving in China in a few weeks, they're part of my plan. They'll contain both money and girls. King will also be present. I'll need to successfully steal all of the money and catch King red-handed first. Then I will get the police involved. After running through eighteen failed scenarios, I haven't figured out how to pull it off without getting caught. My brain needs a rest. I pull out the article about myself I printed a few weeks ago.

I stare at the little girl's eyes in the picture and read it for the 16th time. I set it down just as Kai enters and sets a cup of coffee on my desk.

"Coffee, cream, but no sugar, right?" He heads for the door, but not before he sees the article. "What's that?" he asks. My heart races. He reads the title in two seconds, meanwhile I have already come up with seventeen reasons to explain why I am reading it. "Child prodigy, huh?" Then like a lifesaver he shrugs it off. "I thought it'd be news about the economy. See you for lunch?"

I nod and sigh in relief. "Thanks, Kai." He leaves.

After catching my breath, I take a drink. Dark roast. No more tea for me. Even the smell of coffee energizes me. What are the odds that a Chinese boy would teach me, a girl born in the land of Starbucks, to like coffee? Kai reminds me of my father. I'm ready to savor every sip while going over the details of Chan's latest deal when the secretary buzzes and asks me to report to Chan's office immediately.

I tuck the article about Josephine Rivers away in my desk and head for the door.

I wonder if Chan changed his mind about Asia Bank? It's torture to sit one office away from the only person on the planet with the resources to pull this off. Again, I marvel at the circumstances that brought us to the same city. No coincidences. Pondering this thought lasts only 53 seconds—the time it takes to walk into Chan's office. His eyes burn like fire the moment I enter.

"You have decided to show up for work."

Instead of answering, I pass him a file so he can be impressed with the money my investments have made, and we can finish on a good note, for once. "Good morning to you too."

He opens it, glances over the contents, and sets it aside. "Why are you investing in Maxima Moreau's Textiles? My new accountant says you're following her businesses like a hawk."

"Her investments are profitable for us all," I say, cutting it short. I need to invest for her to believe I'm a real buyer or the Expo will be a bust. He picks up a new paper.

"And why is China Generation investing in global shipping transportation, hotel chains, and a farm over 1 million acres? What are you up to?"

They're following my every move? "Your numbers are rising," I say. "I make the calls in what to invest in. That was the deal."

"Six more months—"

"What?"

"Six months. Then I want you gone."

Months dissolve into fractions of days and minutes. King and Madame will be done. I'll be free to go home. Start over. Maybe even visit my family's graves. I should be happy, but the thought stings me.

"Fine," I say.

"There's more." He examines my hair, which has changed again, this time to an even darker brown. My lipstick is lighter though. A soft pink. Maybe he's looking for another bruise. "Why are you and Kai spending so much time together?"

"I'm seducing him to the dark side," I say drily, enjoying the expression of horror on his face. I sigh and shake my head. "It's just business, Chan. You know that." Kai told his father about his decision to help me. But as I stand here, I wonder if Chan is more bothered by Kai bringing me coffee this morning. Even I don't know what to think of it.

Chan holds his finger to his lips. He puts up with me because his investments are doubling. He knows

I'm working on my own investments, but he doesn't even ask. He still doesn't trust me, and I guess I don't trust him either.

"That had better be all, Phoenix," he says quietly. "My son has a future. I don't want you holding him back. We are Chinese. I don't care how well you speak our language. You will never be one of us. If I learn of anything else between you two, the deal is off immediately. I want you to back off."

This is why he called me in. Because of Kai. It had become routine for me to eat lunch with Kai—on the company, of course. It was a chance to bounce ideas off him about solving the crash. Although he took me to high-end restaurants downtown where I'd calculate the price of a shrimp into days and years and people, I still enjoyed just listening to him tell stories. But lately, every time Kai invited me for lunch, Chan would schedule a meeting, or send me a new list of companies to investigate. I get it now. It's his way of keeping me away from Kai. And for the sake of preventing the crash, I must obey his wishes.

"Sure. Whatever." A lump gathers in my stomach. "Is that all?"

He looks up. Worry spreads across his face. "You said before that you had a plan. I want to hear it."

My eyes snap up to meet his. "You're willing to help?"

"No. I want to know what my son has gotten himself into. That's all."

"All right." While I explain my two-part plan and how the J.J. Bond will work he doesn't say a word. His eyes are locked onto something small in the corner of the room. On a shelf sits the old pawn from Red.

TWENTY-EIGHT
PRESENT: PHOENIX
∞

SHANGHAI TOWER, SHANGHAI, CHINA

Chan watches me like a hawk for the next three days, especially when I'm with Kai. He also works me like a dog.

Thoughts of home distract me. Seattle will be affected by the crash too. During the Great Depression, President Hoover's initiative built affordable housing for the poor in Seattle called "Hoovervilles". The idea failed. Nice neighborhoods, like my old one, became shantytowns like the Pratt where gambling, prostitution, and crime of all sorts rose drastically. If Chan doesn't contribute to the super bond, it could happen again. Madame and King will grow richer while the good guys suffer.

A picture flashes in my mind of my sister Lily living in a place like the Pratt. I shudder. Lily may be gone, but her spirit is not. I can't let that happen—regardless of who it is happening to.

Once, during one of the smaller recessions when I was growing up, I asked my dad for a new computer, pointing out he could pay for it with the money I had helped make, but he refused to give it to me. In hindsight, he never gave me any control over the money.

I'm suddenly very sad. Madame explained five times how she'd contacted my dad, but he refused her ransoms because he only wanted me for the money and that wasn't possible anymore. She said my dad would never try to get me back. After months of waiting...it made sense. I guess I never saw it before. After all, when my mom died, he dove into business headfirst, telling me it was his cure. My dad had a good heart once. He wasn't always driven by money. Once he had paid our neighbors' insurance bill when they didn't have enough. Mara even made them chocolate chip cookies. They used to be so caring. What happened? When did his vision of helping people dissolve? I slump back in my chair. These questions are useless. I'll never get an answer to them, so I should stop asking.

Everything is gone. My family. My father's company, iVision. My home. Even the concept of home is a murky puddle. Right now, the only thing I'm clinging to is that feeling on the beach with Kai. My ocean and a new beginning.

A knock on the door breaks my thoughts apart. Kai sneaks in. I'm thankful for his distraction.

"The menu for today is Italian." Kai lifts my jacket from my office chair.

"Sorry, Kai." I pull the jacket back. "I can't." Beside the fact that it'll upset Chan, I have to give Kai space to find the right girl—the one he described in the car.

I'll never be that girl. The thought both surprises and grieves me. *Did I ever want to be that girl?*

"What's wrong?" Kai says, plopping down in the chair in front of me.

"Everything's fine," I say, twirling a pen in my fingers.

A twinge of guilt pinches when I look at his eyes full of concern. For once I wish I could just talk about what happened to me. Red understood the shame, the weakness, the pain. But Kai's from a world where his family loves him. If I admitted to him how I was betrayed and kidnapped and forced to do horrible things, he'll know how weak I am, and worst of all, he'll understand it was because I wasn't loved. He'll wonder what's wrong with me. Kind of like I do sometimes.

I press the thought from my mind "Any progress?"

"We're plugged into a few banks, some of the stocks you advised, tech companies. We have also invested so much into the largest dairy, maize, and potato farms in the world, we're practically owners," he reports.

Suddenly Kai amazes me, investing his money, time, and faith into my ideas. Sometimes, when I'm talking about the math side of things, he asks me to explain the equation. He's no fool. He knows there's more to me than a good math student.

"Well done," I say,

"I saw the Sang Brothers last night," he says, smiling. For three minutes he tells me about his practice session, making me laugh.

He's quite unlike his father, so sociable and creative. Hard to imagine he'll follow in his father's footsteps. And that face, too...I catch myself staring. His smooth brown skin. The way his eyes smile when he talks. It's like they're the only thing I see...

Wait.

His eyes *are* the only thing I see—*there are no numbers*—just two dark eyes staring back at me.

The numbers are gone!

My world goes black, like I'm blind without my faithful numbers defining everything. I'm about to panic when one by one the numbers turn on like a switch. A full screen of graphs, dimensions, and measurements, everything normal. I exhale.

What just happened?

It was only for a moment, but my brain begins panicking as to *why*. I add up the reasons around me, examining everything in the room to add to the equation of possibilities. The lighting, the coffee, an allergy, Kai? Nothing accounts for it.

"I need to get back to work, Kai," I say, obviously uneasy.

"Ok. Do you need a ride home today?" he asks. "Or are you going to dart off after work like the last several weeks?"

Kai is becoming very suspicious. For the past week he has offered to drive me home every night, but I've refused. I've been searching everywhere for more X girls—the squares downtown, I hang around the hotels and Golden Alley. But I've come up with very little. Frustration is building. I can't enter the hotels alone, and I can't risk buying them yet.

"No ride, thanks. I'm busy tonight," I answer.

"A boyfriend?" he asks.

At this, I can't help but laugh. "You're kidding,

right? With all that we have going on? I'm far too busy for that—"

"Well, that's a relief. We wouldn't want the second Great Depression to happen because of a secret affair." He laughs. "Seriously, where do you go at night?"

"I hang out with prostitutes," I say, in a deadpan voice. His face goes flat, eyes wide. "I'm joking. I just like being alone. Time to think, you know." I shrug.

"Time to think, huh?" he repeats, his head bobbing. "I'll just have to find a way into your thoughts then."

My cheeks flush with warmth. Kai holds my gaze before he walks out. He's on to me, determined to find out what I'm doing. If I know Kai, it won't take him much longer.

Today I play the part of Chan's nameless, personal assistant. We sit at a table with twenty-five experts in finance and government and watch their faces pale as Chan explains the pattern behind the mega-recession.

An economist with a round face speaks up. "Already the price of gas has gone up. The stock market has dropped dramatically," he says. "Airlines, too, are reporting major losses. How bad are things going to get?"

"The worst is yet to come," Chan tells them, not mentioning it would've been much worse if Kai and I had not picked up some of those stocks. "As we know, if China falls, then it will have serious implications on other countries. We'd like to offer a possible solution to cushion some of the damage…"

Chan gives me the floor to pitch my solution for the bailout plan and the J.J. Bond. I keep my eyes on the charts as I speak. I use a pure dialect of Beijing Mandarin, throwing in local northern words to disguise my origin. I don't mention my name—it doesn't matter. They have to believe this plan is Chan's if it is ever going to be approved.

"Thanks, but our government has its own protocols," one official replies in response to the proposed plan. "We will, however, publicly support your super-bond program for private individuals and corporations after you initiate it."

"Thank you." Chan catches my eye, as if to say. *I tried.* It's wasted breath to explain again that those protocols won't save the economy nor that my solution is impossible without Chan's money. I leave frustrated, hanging on to a fool's wish that Chan will change his mind or that King's and Madame's gold will be enough.

After work, I'm at the factory. With an allotment of money, Dr. Ling remodeled. It's fully operational and comfortable. There is a medical room, gym, food storage, and even my 'hacking room' full of tech stuff is equipped with plush rugs and cozy chairs.

"Wow," I say, walking around the factory. "Everything looks great. No trails?"

"No," she replies. "I used my cousins' accounts to buy everything. Then they deliver in sets to the factory next door. We do everything according to protocol."

I sigh. Dr. Ling has agreed to stay here full-time until King and Madame are behind bars. But it's like these women are the ones behind bars. The factory is on complete lockdown, with working surveillance cameras, alarms, and rules.

Dr. Ling has become quite savvy when it comes to security. The girls rotate local vegetable markets each week, so no one notices them. They go outside only a couple hours a day. They rarely leave the compound. But they can't live like this forever. The pressure to end this is increasing.

I take out more cash than she can count. "Here's more for you and the girls. Give whatever you like to your family. I'm sorry."

She gives me a motherly squeeze on the arm. "Don't worry about us. It'll be over soon. The girls are safe. That's what matters."

Revenge is not the reason she is here. Restoration is. The fulfillment of what Red wanted long ago. I can't let them down.

I admit, without her, I'm not sure what I'd do with the girls. She's older, wiser, and calmer. She has experienced loss and trauma and remained a stable, hopeful person with her values intact, which means she doesn't lose it when listening to the girls' stories. She's helping them heal in a way I never could.

As part of her therapy, Dr. Ling gives them freedom to do very normal things, like reading, cooking, painting, and decorating. They're healing, slowly. As I watch, I wonder if parts of me are healing too.

If only I could free more girls. My Friday trips to Golden Alley have been fruitless. But the numbers tell me I'll hit the mark one day if I don't give up. So I won't. Because something tells me if I can find one, I can find them all—save them all. Then perhaps, I can save myself.

Shanghai summer sunsets are a blend of oranges, grapefruits, and strawberries. The rich colors are enhanced by the pollution, but it's also too pretty not to appreciate.

Today the World Bank issued a warning about the recession—to be frugal in the coming several months, to conserve supplies and resources. It was very level-headed, assuring everyone that experts were developing fast solutions.

My office is humid and stuffy. The rest of the building is air-conditioned, but I refuse to use it. I have been cold too often to enjoy it. Besides, paying to be cold doesn't make sense to me.

There's a knock on the door.

"I already emailed you the electronic copy, Mr. Chan," I say without turning around.

"Wrong Chan," says a friendly voice that makes my stomach flip.

I turn. Kai walks slowly inside. He's in his suit as usual. "Have you eaten?"

"No, I haven't left the office for twelve hours and eight minutes."

"Well, maybe 48 minutes of rest and food will do you some good," Kai jokes. "Come on, the night has really cleared up. I'll take you to dinner. I refuse to take no for an answer."

I look at his pinstriped tie. "Not in the mood for fancy."

"Me neither. Now that we trust each other, I want to take you to a secret place, one of my favorite restaurants. A place not even my father knows about," he says, smirking.

"We trust each other?" I laugh, making a joke. Well, half a joke.

"Just you and me, *hao bu hao*?" The way he looks at me—so sure of who he is and what he wants—makes me forget about Chan's warnings.

I close my computer. "*Hao.*"

"Meet me in exactly ten minutes, thirty-seven seconds downstairs," he says with a grin, shaking his head.

Little does he understand that showing up on the dot is not hard for me to accomplish.

TWENTY-NINE
PRESENT: PHOENIX
∞

PUDONG, SHANGHAI, CHINA

I tug gently at my dress, which is sticking to my thighs, hoping he doesn't notice. Then I wonder when I started caring about what Kai thinks.

On any other night, I'd be searching individual faces in the square. I'd notice the smell of spicy pork barbequing across the street and the kids buying bubble tea at the brightly colored street vendors. I'd comment on the red glow polluting the Shanghai skyline and how we should do something about it, but tonight I don't do any of those things. Instead I inwardly curse the humid night and my choice of attire.

"Where are you taking me?" I ask him. "And why are you dressed like that?" When I met him downstairs, he had changed clothes. His shiny black hair is now tucked under a New York Yankees baseball cap. He's wearing jeans and a white v-neck tee-shirt. It's a far cry from his usual slacks and tie.

"I told you," he says playfully, "a place my father won't find us." His dark eyes narrow as he smiles. "And tonight, I am American, just for you."

"Thanks. The clothes change everything. Really, I can't tell you're Chinese anymore."

"Good, because I can't tell you're American anymore," he says lightly and takes my hand. What he says has truth to it and it hits me hard, but I'm too distracted by him taking my hand to think about it clearly. I don't know who I am anymore.

What I do know is his hand is hot and sticky from the heat but strong, making me feel secure. I don't let go.

We stroll down the Waitan, staring across the water. Advertisements light up the sky, replacing the stars. The icon for China Generation blinks along with the rest of them. With each blink, I remember how different our worlds are.

"This way," he says as we cross the street. He redirects my gaze towards a small alley, dark and dirty. The kind of street that haunts my dreams.

We stop in front of two young boys squatting on a curb. A pile of sunflower seed shells and cigarette butts litter the ground in front of them. I notice a small sliding glass door tucked down a few steps into a cement wall. A pungent smell of smoke, oil, and red chili peppers slips from the cracked door, causing me to cough.

"We made it," Kai says, looking at the glass door. "Lucky Noodles." He points to the Chinese characters stuck on the window in red.

The misspelled English sign is next to the Chinese.

"You mean Luoky Nocdles?" I say, laughing. "You're right. Your father wouldn't be caught dead here."

The restaurant is nearly empty. An assortment of multi-colored plastic patio furniture decorates the small room. Three men with red faces are smoking cigarettes in the back corner. They have finished eating but their bottle of *baijiu* is still half full. They are talking so loudly that they don't seem to notice us at all.

"How did you find this place?" I ask him. Nothing about this hole-in-the-wall joint bothers me after being in the Pratt, but a city boy like Kai?

"Shanghai's best kept secret," he answers. "Best fried noodles in town."

"So you weren't forced to come here?" I ask sarcastically, thinking of the exclusive restaurants where Kai usually dines. There, multiple people stand at attention near his table, awaiting his every need as they serve a banquet fit for a prince. Here, we'll be lucky to walk away without E. coli.

"I am not my father, Phoenix," he says, his face becoming serious. "There are more important things to me than money. I thought I proved that to you already." His hand grips mine harder. The look in his eye is the same one I saw the day I watched him and his martial arts masters sparring. Calculated, determined, confident.

A small Chinese lady with a red apron who is wiping down tables looks up. A man in white kitchen clothes comes out with a mop. They are closing, but after looking us over they wave us in anyway.

The golden statue of the Money Cat sits blankly on the counter, its paw mechanically swinging up and down welcoming the spirits of wealth to enter. I wonder if it can sense who is beside me.

We walk across the slick white tile, choose a table, and sit down. The walls are empty except for four signs of the Chinese character *fu* for 'blessing', one hanging on each wall.

"It's too hot tonight," I complain, fanning my neck to stop my hair from sticking to it.

"I don't know a lot about girls," Kai says, "but that handy hairband has been around your wrist for as long as I've known you, and you've never used it. If you did, it'd make you a lot cooler by getting all that hair off your neck."

How is it that Kai notices things that other people don't, like un-used hairband? But if he saw my scar, he'd be sure to ask questions. "Nah," I say, shrugging. "I like my hair down."

Our menu is located under the plastic table covering. "Convenient," I say, taking a napkin to wipe away the smudges so I can read it. I choose *qing tang mian* with tofu. Kai decides on *chao mian* with beef. We call the waitress over.

At the table beside us, a child and his mother slurp noodles but stop long enough to stare at us for a good minute. *"Laowai,"* his mother says to him, assuming I can't understand her. *"White people can't use chopsticks well."*

There's a visible change in the mother's face as she hears me order my noodles in Shanghai slang. Later when our food arrives, she continues to critique my use of chopsticks and my choice of the Chinese traditional dress.

"See, Kai," I say, finishing my soup, "your baseball hat and my dress don't change anything. We are who we are."

"We are who *we* say we are. Not them." He takes off his baseball hat, running his fingers through his black hair.

"I don't know anymore."

"The sun and moon are different, but they both bring light to the world, right? Listen," he says quietly, "I know something else is going on with you. I can sense it. You're planning something besides the Asia Bank stuff. I want to help you, but first there is something you need to do."

"What's that? Learn to fight like you?" I ask. "I don't need weapons to win this one. I have all I need."

"No, not fight. You have already learned to survive. I can see that much." His eyes become gentle, and he takes my hand again. "It's time to learn a new lesson."

"Oh yeah?" I slip my hand from his.

"Yeah. Open up. Let people in. Trust me." He tries to take my hand again. I pull it back. Kai stares at me. "If you don't talk, how else can I know you? Help you?"

My throat tightens. What he's saying makes sense. Even Red told me I must do this. But I can't let go. My own grip on my heart is too tight. I fear if I let go, I'll completely unravel. I can't let that happen now.

"You are helping me," I say.

"I'm not talking about the economy. I'm talking about you."

"You know enough," I answer weakly.

"What's that? One day you show up out of nowhere. Good with math, directing my dad's company? Then somehow you discover the next Great Depression before anyone. And you like old buildings, so you buy my dad's factory and don't forget that night at the port—it was just a fluke." He shakes his head. "After all this, I still don't know who you are or where you came from...or how long you'll stay after you finish whatever you say you're not planning. Can't you tell me these things?"

"Why should I?" I ask.

"I've been trying to be a friend to you. Don't you see that? As far as I can see, you have no one else to tell. You have no other friends."

A hard knock lurches in my stomach like I've been punched in the gut. Sadly, it's true. I don't have any other friends. But is he really my friend? A part of me wants to believe he is, and the other part warns me to protect myself from more pain. My dad said he loved me, but I couldn't trust him. So why give Kai a chance? Normal people won't understand.

I wish there were numbers when it came to feelings but there aren't. Red told me to follow where my heart would lead me, instead of my mind. *The numbers,* he said, *would teach me.* But they aren't helping now.

Red said I'd have to take the next step towards a new beginning, which requires trust. But my calculations are making me dizzy and when I look at Kai the numbers fade somewhere around his eyes. I blink several times and they return, but this scares me more. It must be the stress, and Kai is making it worse.

Maybe I'll tell him later, but not now. Now I need to escape. "Thanks for dinner," I say, standing. "I'll walk home."

Kai reaches for my arm, but I jerk it away.

"Listen, I didn't mean to upset you. I only want to be your friend," he says. "Please let me take you home."

"No. I'd rather be alone," I say, against my gut. "See you tomorrow. *Ze Wei.*"

Outside, I accidentally kick over a bowl of cigarette butts. The stale smoky air catches in my nose.

I leave Lucky Noodles feeling flustered. *I know he's right.*

Stupid! Why is my mouth locked up so tight? I'm helping others when I can't even help myself. I would have given up by now, seeing all the brokenness around me, if it weren't for that small chance of beating the odds.

A simple equation tells me that risk, even if it is small, is behind every great change, a big part of beating the odds. If I take that step, I really can change, and the world can too. Opening up to Kai was that small risk and I just missed it.

Emotion swirls inside like a tornado. I walk faster. I don't want to go home. I need to clear my mind. I want to make the wrongs right. At the next intersection, I realize where I am. It dawns on me that it's Friday.

Maybe I'll make something of my night yet.

I head in the direction of Golden Alley.

THIRTY
PRESENT: PHOENIX
∞

GOLDEN ALLEY, SHANGHAI, CHINA

The equation running through my head is negative as soon as I arrive. Golden Alley has a vehicle parked on it for the first time. A van, blue and shiny. The license plate is not from Shanghai. I walk next to it slowly.

Just as I get behind the van, another van pulls up in the alley, same kind of license plate. A girl stumbles out, landing on her knees. Her face is bleeding. A man follows—the one who shoved her out? This could be the ticket in, the door into Golden Alley.

I watch them as he drags her across the street until he reaches a grey door. He taps on it three times. The girl is pleading. The repetitive word, *please,* slips past her bloody lips, past the man who is hovering over her, directly to me. He waits for her to lift her head and when she does, he slams a fist into the side of it.

As her body collapses on the cement sidewalk, a splash of dirty water sprays the man's pants. With a vulgar curse, he kicks her in the ribs. Another *please,* this time nothing but a whisper. The man seems upset that no one is answering his knocks, but I'm glad. I know where the door is and there is only one man to deal with regardless of the ominous equation telling me to run.

I have gotten myself into a real mess this time. It's clear this will not work out to my advantage. The man is twice my size and by the look of it, he has had lots of practice. He is scarred on his left cheek, his fists are large, and even in the dark I can tell his eyes are soulless.

But can I just walk away? The word coincidence is a childish thought in my mind. No. I chose to walk down this street. The girl doesn't know it, but she is talking to me when she pleads—the only witness to this brutality on what they thought was an empty street.

But the numbers in my head tell me there is absolutely no way I can help her. All equations are negative for us both. We can't out-run him or out-fight him.

If I proceed, I will be hurt, or killed, or worse, captured. I can't go back to Madame. I won't. I'm trembling now.

Leave, Phoenix.

I should call the police.

No, there's no time. I tap my leg, calculations hailing like a dark storm. I need to make a choice.

It's clear I can't help this girl. If I walk away now, I could help more girls in the future and stop Madame from poisoning this world. This is the better option and yet…there's something stirring in my gut.

Cocking my head forward, I scan the doorways. A

little light comes from the streetlamps. The smell of garbage and urine fills the street. *Leave.*

I step backwards and the girl's small voice calls out again. *Another step back.* I'm against the wall in the shadows. They cannot see me. I can escape unseen. Around the corner is a main road. I'll call the police. Solicit someone's help. This stupid dress! I left my phone because it has no pockets. *I'm walking away.* Possibly the first smart thing I have done in a while.

"Please."

It's the only word that comes out of the girl. Each time she says it, the man hits her. Why won't she stay quiet? I know why. She won't give in.

I can't shake the equation in my head. *If you walk away, she dies.*

Although the numbers are negative, I focus on the 1% chance that a small risk can change the odds, and my heart begins the leap forward.

An empty beer bottle is in the gutter. A new variable. Still low odds, high stakes. But it's all I need to turn back.

I move in with all my force and speed, sweeping up the bottle on the side of the road. The man turns, sees me coming, but doesn't have enough time to defend himself. I smash the bottle against his head with all my strength. It hits hard but bounces back in my hand, unbroken.

He gropes for his head and gives me a look of surprise. I'm surprised too. I expected the bottle to break, but it didn't.

With a surge of adrenaline, I choose my next move. I'm not a fighter, but I know where to kick a man. And

I do, hard. He drops to his knees. As the bottle is still in my hand, I smack him again, this time harder. He finally collapses down onto the pavement. I toss the bottle aside, hearing it smash into pieces.

He is down, at least for a moment. I go to the girl. She has bruised legs and arms. Cheap jewelry. Her shirt is ripped open and her skirt barely covers her underwear. But then I see it—a small X on her neck and a red diamond birthmark below it.

A Madame girl! Her eyes are swollen, and her lip is still bleeding. *Hurry, Phoenix, you can't help her if she's dead.*

"Can you hear me? You need to get up," I say. We only have seconds before the man recovers.

She looks up, afraid of me too. She's already slipping into unconsciousness. Wrapping my arms around her, I try to get her to her feet. Her body goes limp. She can't be more than a hundred pounds, but I can't lift her.

The man rouses, grunting like a rabid dog.

"Wake up!" I yell to the girl and frantically look around for anyone to help me. There's no one else around. I should have listened to Kai when he told me not to go out alone.

The man stands, still gripping his head. A blank stare veils his face. He is injured but not incapacitated. He reaches in his pocket, pulls out a cell phone.

I can run away, be safe within minutes, but my feet won't move.

"Help!" The word slips out instinctively. Slipping my hands under the girl's armpits, I drag her slowly away. If I can just make it to the end of the street, I can find help. Forty more feet.

The man is talking to someone, but I'm too focused to listen. She's heavy and slipping. I don't want to hurt her more by dropping her. I adjust my arms. I move faster. Twenty more feet.

The man hobbles down the road. Slowly, but on his way.

I won't leave her.

I'm almost to the end of the road. I think I can make it when the door he knocked on earlier opens. Two men in shabby black suits race out.

"There!" one of them shouts, pointing in our direction.

I drag her faster, but the men close in around us. The girl is ripped from my fingers. What Kai taught me about self-defense runs through my mind, but it's too late for me to act. One of them is already on top of me. Something harder than bone rips across my forehead. A metal ring? The side of my face burns. I taste blood in my mouth.

I join the girl on the cold wet cement. A boot goes into my gut. My lungs grasp for air. My stomach surges with pain but what's worse is that they are misting her. I hold my breath and turn away, but I smell that unmistakable scent of oranges and bleach. The mist they used to drug me on Madame's boat.

I can't pass out. I frantically spit it out onto the ground but it's too late. A bit of it is in my mouth. I'm not hallucinating, but there's enough that the numbers fade.

The man I hit is cursing but my ears ring too loudly to follow it. They pick up the X girl and walk her to the alley door. I'm next. He'll mist me. I'll be out and it'll all be over.

I get to my knees and crawl away. If only I could calculate, I could buy myself some time. A hand shoves me to the ground. I flop on my back and extend my foot, kicking at his face as hard as I can. He raises his hands and I cringe at what's about to happen next.

Then a figure, fast and lean, runs up towards the man. In one fell swoop, the newcomer takes the guy down. The other two men run to help but the stranger is too quick. With swift strikes of arms and legs, the man from the door moans loudly and falls on top of the first guy, and soon the one I hit with the bottle joins them.

A face leans over me, and I smile.

Kai. But he isn't smiling back.

"What are you doing?" he yells, angry. "This street is not on your way home!"

All I can get out is a moan.

"What was all that talk before about you being able to *take care of yourself?* You are lucky someone is watching over you." He checks the girl's vitals and body for any major damage.

He helps me up. The pain is unbearable, but I have been here before. I'll survive. I'm more worried about the girl. I hobble over to her, drop to my knees, and check her pulse. She is alive.

Kai doesn't say anything but he's already lifting and carrying her to the main street in his arms, in silence. I'm close behind him. He hails a cab. "We need to get her to the hospital."

"No. Take us to the factory," I say, holding my head, which spins and fizzles like a coming migraine. There's mist in my system. The numbers are gone, just like last time, but it's not enough to knock me out. Kai looks at me, ready to protest, as if I have a concussion too. "Trust me," I say.

He relents. "High Street, gate 34," he tells the driver, holding the girl's head close to his chest, concealing her bloody face and gently protecting her neck from further injury. She's out cold, which is better than feeling the pain I do right now. The driver doesn't ask any questions.

I'm gripping my head, waiting for streams of numbers to reemerge, when Kai starts to go off on me.

"Why were you walking around this area alone? At this time of night? Are you crazy? You could have gotten yourself killed! Then what?" He is steaming mad. "Never do this again! Do you hear me?"

"Since when do you tell me what to do?" I snap, even though I know he is right.

He doesn't say anything. He just lets out an incredibly long sigh, shakes his head. I have really upset him, the second time tonight.

Finally, he rubs his fingers up over his forehead, slowly working them through his hair. "Look, I can't see you get hurt like that, okay?" he says, his eyes firmly fixed on mine.

"Okay, I'll be more careful," I say.

"That's not good enough, Phoenix. Promise me you will never go back to that street again." He takes my chin and lifts it so I can see him through my left eye, which isn't swelling. "Promise me." His voice is sharp, emotional.

"I promise," I say. Then I notice his hand, which is still touching my chin. I don't know why it's shaking.

THIRTY-ONE
PRESENT: PHOENIX

∞

THE FACTORY, SHANGHAI, CHINA

We have been in the car for seven minutes. The numbers have returned. Now if only my head would stop pounding.

Kai sees me wince as I touch my head. "Are you okay?" There is still tension in his voice.

"I'm fine," I say, wiping away blood.

We pull up to the gate at High Street.

"Phoenix, we need to get her to a doctor," Kai says as he lifts her still body out of the car.

"There's one inside."

He looks at me as if I'm crazy, but regardless he heads for the garage entrance of the former China Generation warehouse. After we get inside, the changes astonish him. An Ying rushes out, stopping abruptly when she sees Kai.

"Who's that?"

"Go wake Dr. Ling," I tell the girl in Shanghai dialect.

We take the elevator to the top floor. Kai carries the girl to the back room.

Once she's safe in Dr. Ling's hands, Kai accompanies me to the small restroom in the lobby where I clean my wounds.

Kai takes the washcloth from my hands and washes the blood from my face. He's upset and confused, but he cares—that much is obvious. Maybe it's just adrenaline but his eyes lock on to mine as if I might disappear if he looks away. I must have really scared him tonight. Is it possible he's afraid of losing me?

"Thanks for coming after me tonight." I try to make amends. "It could have been a lot worse."

"Why does the factory look like a hotel for the FBI?" he says, cutting to the chase. "Who are they? And while you're at it, why don't you give me one reason why I should trust you?"

I'm silent. Contemplating. Analyzing. How can I tell him something without telling him everything? That same lump in my throat rises.

"Fine. Don't tell me. Don't tell anyone anything!" Kai says.

I expect him to walk away, but instead he takes some antiseptic pads and disinfects the cut on my face.

"I knew what I was doing," I start to defend myself, but how can I when Kai came to my rescue? He's with me now again—I have a second chance to tell him. Calculations never factor in second chances, but here I get one.

"Yes, just like at the warehouse, huh?"

"You don't understand," I say looking at my bandaged hand. My eye stings when I open it.

He sits on the chair beside the counter. "Then why don't you explain it to me?"

"If I don't talk about it, they can't get anything else out of me," I say.

"Talk about what?"

"My gift with numbers."

"You being good with numbers isn't a secret, but I am too, and I can't do what you do for my father's company. You're going to have to give me more than that if you want me to understand what's going on. I want to understand you."

Kai is right.

Red's dead. My family's dead. There's no one left who knows who I am. But who cares? Why does it matter? No. That's not true. My mind is playing tricks on me. My insides cry out to be known, helped, loved. If I don't open up, I'll be swallowed by death like an ocean, covering over me silently, wave by wave. If I can't open up now, with Kai, I'll never open up with anyone.

Kai leaves the room, frustrated. Through the doorway I see him rubbing his temples. After five minutes and thirty-six seconds, I move slightly and groan. I ache all over—my face, back, leg—so I linger in the antiseptic white bathroom a moment longer.

The room is void of color and reeks of things meant to be discarded. This will be my life if I don't choose to walk out of here and share my life with someone. But how can he understand my circumstances? The odds are so improbable, he might think I'm lying. And if he believes me, then he might feel sorry for me, or think he has to try to heal me.

My mind drifts to our conversation at the beach. There he created a natural segue for me to talk too. Brief as that moment was the feeling was...*healing.* I once thought healing would come after I buried the pain and it slowly decomposed. But maybe healing will come when I dig it back up? Expose it and let it go.

I push off the countertop and leave the bathroom. Kai is on the couch in the lounge. Ankles crossed and arms folded across his chest. He looks up, his stare compelling me to sit. So. Kai is the lucky guy who gets the heavy burden of my past.

I'm nervous.

"I admit, tonight back in the alley, the calculations were not in my favor, but the fact is, numbers are why I'm still alive."

"What does that mean?" he says, still slightly annoyed.

"You're familiar with differential equations, right?" The question is more of a statement. He should know with all of his studies in math and finance. He nods.

"Well, imagine that concept in a person."

Kai's brow wrinkles. He doesn't understand, so I explain how numbers stream through my head at speeds faster than a computer, calculating everything around me.

"I'm a mental calculator. That's why I work for your father. I can calculate anything—money is the easiest of all."

He's silent, like he's working hard to solve a problem. That problem being me.

"Back up—if that's true, what did these numbers predict back in the alley?" he finally asks, speaking calmly this time.

"Negative outcome. For me at least."

"But you moved forward anyway?" he says, leaning forward.

I nod.

"You knew you'd get hurt?"

I nod again. "It was a risk. I was willing to take it to save her life. There's always a slight possibility that a risk can beat the odds, and it did. We saved her."

"I don't understand. Why would you risk your life for a prostitute?"

"She's not a prostitute," I say back, sharply. "Not by choice anyway. That's why I have to stop Madame."

"Who is Madame? What are you talking about?"

"Madame is a millionaire. A murderer. A liar. An international trafficker and my...former captor." If my head is spinning, his is too. What will he think when I tell him more? "She's known by other names, too, like *Maxima Moreau*."

"Wait a minute. Maxima Moreau is Madame?"

"One and the same."

"Start from the beginning," he says. "Tell me what happened when you got to China. How did your family die? How did you get here? Why do you have those articles about that little girl in your office?"

So, he saw more than he let on that day. If Kai were a detective, he'd already have a thick file on me. But there's no hiding anymore.

"I *am* that little girl," I say, swallowing hard. "I'm the prodigy."

His eyes widen. To my surprise, my mouth opens, and I begin to talk.

At first, it's a trickle—a word here about my family, there about Seattle, another about my mom. As I let go, the gates are broken down, and words rush out like a flood.

Kai's jaw tightens as I relive the details. His eyes don't flinch. They are solidly locked onto mine.

I get to the part about how my Dad never came to find me and how Mara gave Madame the details of my PSS job. Years of heaviness crumble away, but it still hurts. Can I ever truly let them go? I don't know.

"Did Mara know who Madame was?"

"Very unlikely. But PSS was a secret, and she talked anyway. Mara certainly didn't know Madame planned to kill them. It was always Madame's plan though. She didn't want me to have anything to go back to."

He may want to stop listening now, but he nods for me to keep going.

"Octavia means 'the eighth'. Having me was her obsession…" I still hear her voice in my head. *We're the same, Octavia. Powerful. And I'll make you more powerful yet.*

"Why you? What's her obsession if not for the money?" he asks.

"I don't know," I say. "I wasn't there long enough to figure it out. As odd as it sounds, she wanted to love me. She didn't want me to suffer what the other girls did. It grew hard to remember who I really was and what was real or right or wrong. If it weren't for Red, I'd have been a goner."

Kai rubs his temples. If he knows who Red is or how his father knows him, he doesn't say. I want to respect Red, who said to wait for Chan to tell me. Which means I may never know.

I explain the guilt, which plagued me nightly, for obeying her. "I—I had no choice," I explain. I pull my hair to the side. "This is why I always keep my hair down." When he sees the scar, he cringes. "Then came Lev..."

I tell him everything from how Lev attacked me to the Pratt. From meeting Red, to Chan, even what really happened that night at the warehouse. Kai's fist balls up as I talk. I think he may hit something. But he doesn't, he only urges me to continue.

In certain places—I get choked up, but something keeps me talking, pressing this story out once and for all. Three slow, silent tears sting my eyes and roll down my chin.

Kai shakes his head. He has no idea what to say. He's very quiet, processing my story, until he jumps to his feet.

"We need to call the police immediately. Madame, King. They need to be arrested—now."

"We can't. Not yet."

He's confused. I pull him back down to the couch. "At dinner you asked what I was planning. Well, I'm going to make their lives of crime mean something."

"What are you talking about?"

A slight smile rises on my lips. "A generous donation to the super bond."

"How do you propose to do this?" he asks.

I bite my lip. "Your dad."

"You aren't doing anything illegal, are you?"

"Not exactly." I breathe in deep. "Let me explain."

"A heist? That's your plan?" Kai exhales loudly, his hand going through his hair.

I grab more files from the factory office to show him. "It's the only way," I conclude, "your dad is the only one who can support this super bond, but we still need a lot more money. Madame and King have it. It's only fair that what they took for evil should be used for good."

He flips through all the notes. "That's a big plan. You're going to steal all their money—plug it into our bond—then rescue the girls while shutting down their criminal ring...*alone?*"

He sees right through me. "It will work," I say, my gaze snapping away. It sounded easier on paper, but in reality, I haven't figured it all out, but inside, I feel it will work. So how can I give up? This is my chance to fulfill my vow to Red. To make his death count.

Kai rubs the scruff on his chin, thinking. I wonder what he sees in me now. Determination? Hopelessness? Insanity?

"So what about Song Valley?" he asks, moving on.

I pull out the map I drew by memory, of the tunnels, the buildings, and the roads from the Pratt to the warehouse and the port. "Loads of money and stolen valuables are in the Pratt." I indicate the lighthouse. "Donation number one."

I spill everything on King, ending with tonight. The girl's face smeared with makeup fresh in my mind. A sharp pain invades my stomach. A human who was once labeled *cargo.*

"Donation number two: If I can get King's schedule

for the Golden Global Shipments, I can reroute Madame's delivery to King's private dock at the Shanghai Port." I explain we have less than three weeks for this to work. "If I can intercept them, it'll be a flock of birds with one stone. The girls. A half billion in cash. Dirty customs agents. King. Madame's right hand will be cut off. I just need the schedule and the list of buyers. That's why it was so important that we weren't caught at the warehouse." We talk over the shipments before I hit the last point. "Donation number three: The Expo." I explain that all I need is the routing number with the spin code to gain access to Madame's hidden accounts. I don't tell him that I plan to be the buyer.

He listens intently. Never taking his eyes off me. "When do the police get involved?"

"After I get the money and the girls." *And justice.* "If we are going to prevent the collapse of the economy, I need to plug that money into the system without any interference from the authorities. After that, anything goes."

"What if you gave the police leads for all the international routes Madame uses with the other ring leaders? That way, you can keep the Chinese shipments but gain the police's trust."

I calculate the possibilities. "That could work."

Kai grins. "Josephine Rivers, child genius. We should show that article to my dad—graduated at 15 with a PhD. He'll finally be impressed."

"Not likely." I smirk. "Your dad knows money and degrees can't bring back the dead. I care nothing for those. All I want is my life back. To start over. Only I can't yet. I was meant to be here to help stop the economic crisis, or at least try."

For a moment, I forget I'm talking to Kai and see my story like an outsider. I didn't choose Shanghai, but here I am. I was thrust into dark corners, but I was protected, and who would have guessed I'd have learned to operate on a global scale from criminals like King and Madame? Puzzle pieces. Everything fits together, nothing wasted.

If I can pull it off, this will be my part in history. The fulfillment of Red's vow—to fight evil with good. I see now what Red meant by choice. I could have walked away. Made my own money and floated on by as the world drowned. I could have left angry and bitter, forgotten everything, and started over. I could have let King and Madame roam the streets with no one to stop them. But I didn't. *I chose to stay.* I don't know if I can help the crisis or save the girls, but I choose to try. Choose to risk. Believe the odds can be beaten—this is who I am. It's my destiny, with or without math.

"You know, the way you are going about this," Kai breaks in, "no one will even know it's you who prevented the crash."

"It's not about that," I say. "I don't need to be in the history books. I just need to do my part."

Kai is silent. One, two, three minutes tick by. Maybe he thinks my plan is stupid or dangerous. Maybe he's confused about the J.J. Bond or overwhelmed by my depressing life story. What can he say? Sorry about your life? That won't change anything. My secrets are out like jewels thrown on the ground. It's up to him whether he picks them up and treasures them.

His big dark eyes peer into mine. I shiver. Eyes communicate much deeper than what numbers calculate, or words express. Right now, words aren't necessary, and numbers can't tell me how I feel as I stare into his eyes. Thrill mixes with fear. The unknown collides with hope and desire. With each quarter of a second his stare intensifies, as if he's climbing another wall into my heart. I feel bare. What is he thinking? Will he treat me differently now? Can I trust him?

The numbers fade again—an after effect of the mist? I don't care right now because my belly is doing backflips. His hand stretches out and his fingers run through my hair, and down to my cheek. It's warm. "If I could multiply anything, it'd be you." His hand moves to find mine. "There should be more of you all over the world. At the same time, I'm glad there is only one of you. And that you're here with me. No coincidence, right?"

"What?" I say meekly, cheeks burning.

"What I mean is, it's not a coincidence that…"—he draws closer—"that our paths crossed." He leans in. "That you are two inches from me." Our knees are touching. His eyes flash to my lips and my heart pounds out of control. "That you are beautiful." Both of his hands cup my cheeks. "That we need each other." Our lips touch. The warmth of his breath is on my mouth. "My father warned me about this. But it's too late. *Josephine.*"

He softly brushes his lips over mine before pulling me into him. My first kiss is softer than I thought it would be, more perfect than what I'd imagined as a girl of thirteen, but that's not what produces electricity in my heart. *Kai called me Josephine.* The first time someone has said my real name in more than 700 days. It's like music, magic. He knows what I'm thinking because in between his lips kissing different parts of my face, he keeps whispering my name in my ear. Each time I hear it, Josephine comes back to life a little more.

Finally, he wraps his arms around me and holds me tight. I sink into his arms and nuzzle my face against his chest. The sensation is warmer than any blanket and safer than any locked door.

THIRTY-TWO
PRESENT: PHOENIX

∞

THE FACTORY, SHANGHAI, CHINA

It's two in the morning. We're both too tired to move, much less go outside to get a taxi home. My eye is swollen and my body aches. I suggest we sleep at the factory and make a move in the morning. Kai agrees.

I lead him up the staircase to the vacant third floor. It's furnished modestly but it's warm and comfortable. Kai takes one room. I take the other.

As I lie in the small bed, my body is lifeless, but my mind wanders restlessly. Scenes from the night flash in and out like blinking lights—the girl, the fight, Kai, and Chan's words about Kai marrying a proper, traditional girl. At one point I agreed with that, but now it combats the memory of Kai's lips on mine.

He *has* been a good friend to me these last few months. I feel something for him, but is it love? When I was young, I always envisioned something like my mom and dad. Meeting casually, falling in love, and marrying until "death do you part". A promise they kept.

Love. That dreaded subject that math can't explain. Statistics show that international relationships cause more stress than same-culture marriages, predicting low odds of success. Add my lack of experience. Lack of trust. Disbelief in love. I'm not sure how to proceed, or if he's serious…and yet…Red dared me to hope that love could be real.

My eyes sting. I'm too tired to keep calculating. I'm too tired to be afraid. If I've learned one thing, it's that some things just need to be risked.

Love is one of those things.

I wake with a start. Kai sits on my bed, staring at me. One eyelid won't move. The other blinks until his familiar smile comes into view. I slept so heavily I didn't hear him come in. It's past 10:00 o'clock in the morning.

A burst of energy shoots up within me. I spring into a sitting position. He draws me into his arms. They are strong, like his hands. For a moment I want to fall back asleep inside them. The same smell of mountains, forests, and rain radiates off him, whisking me away to a green place. How can a city boy smell like this?

"How long have you been up?" I ask. He is bouncing off the walls, and I know we don't have coffee downstairs.

"Hours."

"Really?" I yawn. "Wow."

"What do I call you now that I know your real name?" Kai whispers.

"Uh…" I hadn't thought that far. I can't answer. The consequences of unveiling my identity could completely destroy my plan if he calls me Jo. The answer is on my face.

"Your secrets are safe with me, *Phoenix*," he says into my ear. I buzz with the same electricity as last night. Without saying it, I know he will not call me Jo until the time is right. He holds me. For three seconds it doesn't matter if I ever get out of bed.

"Three weeks, right?"

My eyes shoot open. "We have to get to the office! We have work to do." I nearly knock him over getting out of bed.

"We will later," he says, "but first, get dressed. Meet me downstairs in the back room in ten minutes. I have a surprise for you."

In the bathroom I wash my face, feeling all the bruises that line the left side of my face. My left eye is puffy and purple, but not totally shut anymore. Makeup can't cover this up.

There's a closet of spare clothes on the second floor. I wander down to find something comfortable. I choose a long, loose-fitting blouse, and black leggings. Hua Mei enters the room and shrieks.

"Jie!" she exclaims in her Shanghai dialect. "What happened to your face?"

"Don't worry about me." I slip the shirt over my head. "Did you hear about the new girl?" I explain everything. She fusses over me until I convince her I'm ok.

This all takes seven minutes.

Outside, Dr. Ling is by the door where the girl is sleeping.

"How is she?" I ask.

"Stable. She'll sleep for a couple days, but she'll live."

I peek inside. The girl sleeps peacefully on the bed bathed in the morning light. Her face is clean of make-up, making the bruises much more visible. I shudder to think of what she has lived through.

My hand fingers my own bruise. From the door I whisper to her. "You're worth it."

My three minutes are over.

"Kai and the others are waiting for you in the conference room," Dr. Ling says.

"Others?" I turn around so fast I nearly trip on my own shoes.

Kai just learned about this place last night and he's already bringing others into it?

I race downstairs, kicking myself the whole way down. How stupid I was to think I could actually trust him.

The door bounces against the wall as I open it. "What is this all about?"

There's a group of people around the table in the conference room. It takes me a minute before I recognize faces. The regular street clothes throw me off, but after I picture long white pants and a black belt, I see the Sang Brothers. They dip their heads at me. Besides them Yu Tai sits with his cocky grin.

Three people I don't know also sit at the table. One white boy and one black girl, both wearing glasses. The boy looks university age, smart, nerdy but the black girl is as young as Kai and I, which makes me nervous. The last stranger is a Chinese guy with broad shoulders and a face so stern I fear he's here to arrest me.

I walk past the stacked boxes of medicine and stored food in the corners to Kai, who's pulling out an empty chair for me.

"That eye looks better if you smile," Kai says. He pushes the chair in as I sit down. Everyone says a brief good morning.

"Thanks," I grumble, casting a suspicious eye around the room. "What are the Sang brothers doing here?" I dip my head to them. "And who are those three?"

"Patience." Kai addresses the room. "Thank you all for coming. Let's begin." His tone is the same one he uses in a business meeting. "Phoenix, you have rescued one girl in three weeks."

"Three," I correct him.

"Dr. Ling found the other two by chance."

"I don't believe in chance." There's an edge in my voice.

"Please let me finish," he says calmly. "Your plan isn't bad, but I think you can do better—"

"I'm doing the best I can," I reply, a bit disheartened. Kai's the only one here who knows what I'm juggling—the bond, King, Madame, the girls. It's not fair, but I refrain from bringing up any of those things. "I don't see anyone else trying."

"Phoenix, hear me out," he says.

Red says it's foolish to talk without listening first. I sit back in my chair, cross my arms. "Okay, I'm listening."

"According to you, there are seven major ring leaders connected to Madame. You want to shut them down and take back what they took from you. More importantly, you want to save the girls. You can't do that alone. Last night's injuries prove that."

I touch my puffy eye as Kai talks. It hurts but not as much as Kai's case against me. He told me I did the right thing last night and now he doesn't think so? I want to argue. But he looks up at me as if to signal our agreement of *hearing him out*. I bite my tongue.

"What you need is manpower. More evidence, spies, strength, enforcement. Perhaps a team?" he says.

I sit up straighter. Did I hear him right? My good eye strains to get a good look at everyone.

"After you mentioned Yu Tai, I asked my father about him. An interesting fact came to light. Yu Tai, care to share?"

Yu Tai nods to Kai, stands to address me. "You asked me what I did before I worked for Chan. I studied business, like my father, before King took everything from my family, including our father."

Instantly a camaraderie forms with Yu Tai that I don't have with other people. "What else did he take from you?" I ask.

"The Pratt," he says. "My father was the rightful owner. It was passed to me when he was killed. I'm the one who ran away." That day at the beach, Kai explained that the Pratt's real owner had disappeared. Now I know why. "I'm not unique. Song Valley's people have suffered greatly at King's hand, but no one had the courage to stop him. They are too afraid. But I'm not anymore. I'll do anything to end his terror and take back what King has stolen."

A chill spreads over my body from the resolve in his

voice. King will finally get everything coming to him. Yu Tai sits back down.

"Master Sang," Kai says, "the floor is yours."

"Phoenix *Meimei*." Master Li bows. His fist covers his other hand.

"Master Sang," I return his greeting and dip my head.

The master sits in his chair like a rock, still and solid, unbreakable in spirit and body.

"You know why we are here." Master Sang stands. He is not tall, but I shrink in his presence.

He doesn't have to say it out loud—I remember our talk in Song Valley. *Purpose.* His words strike me hard in the chest. I know what it feels like to be without vision, without purpose. Wondering who I am and why I'm here.

"Kai has told us what we need to hear. We are at your service. We and our brothers." My heart is knocked over by his offer.

After Master Sang sits, Kai introduces the three people I don't know. "These two are brainiacs from my department. Jessica and Phillip from Oxford. They're here short-term, doing research in Shanghai, who happen to be interning at Asia Bank. They want to help you with the Bond."

"Interesting."

"And the big guy," he says, "is my cousin, Agent Bai."

"Police?" I ask, nervous.

"Better than police." Kai smiles. "He works for PGF, Private Global Forces, the largest global security company in the world. He's connected to every security and law force on the planet, but we can *hire* him. He'll do whatever we ask, within reason of the law. Resources beyond your reckoning."

My mind reels with possibilities. Twenty-one days are left until the Expo and the delivery. Numbers connect the dots until a clear picture forms. We could take down the Pratt, bust hotels, custom agents, get Madame and Kings' money for the bond. What I never had was manpower. With this team working alongside me it's all possible.

I scan each of their faces. Strong, fast, quiet, wise. They're perfect for what needs to be done.

I didn't allow myself to think others could—or would—help me. And now, like a gift, they are giving me what I want. The same things Red wanted.

I tap my knee like I do when a new calculation is forming. Kai clears his throat. He's smiling at me, waiting for my approval.

A small laugh escapes. "So, should we have a secret handshake or something?"

THIRTY-THREE
PRESENT: PHOENIX
∞

THE FACTORY, SHANGHAI, CHINA

My dreams are becoming real. We spend the next week hammering out details and come up with a plan. King and Madame's worlds will crumble like a 10-point quake on the Richter scale, and they won't know what hit them until it's too late.

My new team is more resourceful than I calculated, and they are following my plan to a tee. Master Sang and his brother have recruited the last twenty true disciples of kung fu and are positioned to escort girls from the Golden Angel Hotels as we speak. Yu Tai has rounded up two-dozen Song Valley residents who have been wronged by King. They have filed official complaints and claims for everything that has been lost, including the Pratt. This is more than enough to bury King in a legal hole from which he could never climb out.

Kai's cousin, Agent Bai, is indeed resourceful. Not only has he discreetly obtained a new passport for me with my real name, he has added more manpower and surveillance tools, while indirectly cooperating with his Interpol connection, Dutch Detective Hansen.

Turns out, Interpol intercepted the files I sent out with Arrow Mail. The files helped Detective Hansen build a case and he's been tracking Madame in five countries ever since. They tell me that Celia's real name is Maryam Maatar, born to a Turkish mother in France.

"Okay, we have thirteen days," I say to the group with a strong voice I didn't really even know I had. I marvel, for a moment. In a way, I'm their leader. This plan I worked out so long ago now has arms and legs that I designed. "There are three shipments, sixteen hotels, and the remaining 'lower five'." I hand them a detailed map with names, directions, and dates. Each person reads over it even though they have spent the last week memorizing the information and planning their moves. "Thanks to Chan's investments, we now own four of the largest hotels where Madame operates. Madame knows nothing, and we'll make our move at the right time. All we need now is the schedule for shipments, which has the names of the dirty customs agents, the names of buyers, and the men scheduled to do pick-ups and drop-offs then I'll reroute Madame's cargo to arrive to King's dock at the port and we can replace Madame's custom agents with our men. Then we clean out the Pratt and the warehouse."

"How do we get the schedule? It's not like we can just walk into the Pratt and ask for it," asks Master Sang.

"Ah," I say. "That's where you come in. Do your

kung fu ideals say anything against kidnapping?" I explain in detail what, or rather *who* I need. The brothers set out right away.

Our meeting continues. "The final piece is the Shanghai Expo," I explain. "Interpol will replace Celia's buyers with their men. They'll be wearing cameras. I will confirm Madame's identity, isolate the routing number that gains her a chain entry into her main accounts and then they'll arrest her." Everyone nods. "All in all, an estimated 3 billion in cash, cargo, and girls."

"Is it dangerous for Phoenix to be that close to Madame?" Kai asks Agent Bai.

"She won't be," he assures. "We've secured a ground office for her across the street with agents nearby. Her job will be done via satellite."

A small part of me knows I should be closer. I'm the one with the math. They can't see the possible outcomes that I can. But Agent Bai won't risk me being seen by Madame. For once, I give in.

The meeting adjourns. Kai stays to help me work on the bonds. I smile as I watch him. He has taken things very slowly with me; listening as I open up; a gentle touch here, a hug there, a kiss perhaps. He's patiently waiting for me to trust him more. It's not hard to do.

Later, my mind drifts to the Sang brothers. Our plan won't work if we don't get the list of customs agents or buyers. *Where are they?*

It's dark now. We pack up our stuff and are about to turn off the lights when the brothers bust through the door with a blindfolded man beside them. *They have him.*

I walk up and peel back the mask. Two green eyes flit wildly around the room until they land on me. His eyes widen with disbelief.

I smile. "Hello, Rafael."

"Mila." Rafael bends down to kiss both of my cheeks. "The girl with a thousand secrets."

We linger, taking each other in from head to toe as old acquaintances often do. He grins. His dimples still give him a look of innocence. I smile back too, but when Kai steps closer and wraps an arm around my waist, I break it off.

"Call me Phoenix," I say over my shoulder, pointing him towards a table with small stools. "Let's talk."

Tea is poured. The brothers sit on each side of Rafael. Rafael eyes Kai's arm around me, then meets my eyes.

"You never worked for King, *vero?*"

I shake my head. "Put two and two together, did you?" To my surprise, I spout off a brief explanation of my kidnapping down to what really happens at the Pratt.

It's different than when I told Kai. I stick to the facts, like an unemotional book report. Even still, Rafael's face pales.

"I see you joined the family business. Making the world a better place?" I don't mean to be snide, but I can't pretend I'm happy about it. "Why? I really don't want to see you in prison, too, you know. I thought you were different."

"*Senti,* I didn't know what I was getting into," he says, shaking his hands in the air. "It's my father. I trusted him. He told me it was imports. He explained away that night with the fire as a fluke. I am not even sure my dad knows what he's doing."

That part I believe. His dad is a dunce. King never felt threatened by Cesare because he's too easy to control.

"It was supposed to be my first deal that day. Then you appeared, like an angel, shaking me to reality. The pieces started coming together. Even now, my dad suspects me. I can't support what he's doing. I was looking for a way out when your guys found me."

I turn to the brothers. I gave them strict orders to interrogate him before bringing him here. "He doesn't know much, Phoenix," Master Sang says. "He cooperated from the beginning."

"If you want to prove what you just said, you can help us. We don't have a lot of time, so I'm going to be blunt. We are shutting King's operation down—his blackmails, his brothels, his gambling, his embezzling at the ports. The summer transactions will be his last. I need the entire schedule for domestic and international deliveries, and who's on the list for pick-up and drop-off—guards, associates, and customs. I also need the Shanghai Expo buyer list. You will get it for us."

"*Si. Ho capito.* It will take a while."

"We don't have a while."

"*Va bene.* I can tell you who's on pick-up for Shanghai." His eyes fall to the floor. I understand why.

"How much is Madame paying your father?" I ask.

"300,000 Euros."

"Okay. Don't change that. King needs to think everything is business as usual," I say. "Tell King to come too, that Madame has a new buyer he'll be interested in."

"Anything else?" Rafael asks.

"Yes. Access to building seven, three, and one—and the warehouse."

"This will never work. I'll have to get passwords, codes, keys! The guards will be suspicious of me right away if I ask for all of this."

"Find a way," I say, "because if you don't help us, you will go down on that ship."

He sighs. "I'll find a way."

"These men will assist you." I motion to Kai and the brothers. "Once we snag King, I want everything he knows about Madame. If King doesn't cooperate as nicely as Rafael, you know what to do."

"What about my father?" Rafael says.

"I can't help the bad choices he's made." I empathize with the pain in Rafael's eyes. "He can still make good ones too. He can give us all the networks and contacts for Italy—customs, buyers, and anything he knows. If he agrees, we'll request trial in Italy rather than China. I'm sorry, Rafael. That's the most I can do for him."

"*D'accordo.* I'll tell him, but I will not force him to do anything." Our eyes meet. The pain, disappointment, and confusion swirling inside him aren't hard to miss.

"What about you?" he asks. "After all this is done, where will you go? What will you do?"

Kai slips his fingers between mine and locks down on my hand.

"That's a good question."

∞

Numbers forecast that even perfect plans have bumps in the road. And my plan is no exception. The whole week has been chaos.

The economy is shaking more each day. America is starting to feel the effects as well. News is stirring up panic. The World Bank publicly supported the J.J. Super Bond, and the initial application process opened. Over a thousand companies have already applied for interviews. Everything depends on what happens this next week.

There's tension throughout the whole city. But the real tension is in me—the J.J. Super Bond is not nearly at the magnitude of cash flow that we need. Even if we are able to successfully storm the Pratt, and obtain Madame and King's stash, it's still not enough for the economic bailout and the super bond.

In the meantime, Agent Bai tipped info over to the police about two of Madame's massage parlors. They were infiltrated and the police rescued twenty-six girls in one night. Madame will suspect a routine bust and think nothing of it.

There's a knock on my office door and Yu Tai walks in holding a paper in his hands.

"You got the deed?"

Yu Tai nods. "King destroyed the original, but through Agent Bai's security clearance, we got into city records and got a copy."

"Once this is over, Yu Tai, you can begin a new life with what rightfully belongs to you," I say.

"My honor will be restored but the property is worthless because of the erosion. No chance of developing new ports there ever again," he says.

"Wait," I laugh, "you don't know?"

"Know what?"

"King wanted your dad's property for what's beneath it. The ancient catacombs from the Song Dynasty."

"The legend? It's real?"

I nod. "History's going to get a new chapter. Every major archeologist, geologist, historian—not to mention tourist—will beg you, *with gold*, to get access there. Just watch."

Yu Tai looks stunned, then walks out, blissfully happy.

After two minutes and eighteen seconds, Rafael walks in with a briefcase.

"*Buon giorno*," he says, his Italian kiss-greeting warms my cheeks.

"Morning," I reply.

"You know, you are more beautiful than I remember."

"*Grazie*," I say, blushing. We stare at each other. Something passes between us. I know what he's thinking, because I'm thinking it too. Perhaps in another life, we could have had something. But that chance has passed. That spark I felt when he came to the Pratt was real, for that time. He was a gift of hope during my captivity. A sign I could feel something normal for a boy. I needed him then. But Rafael is not what I need now.

Just like that, I let go of those memories and questions regarding Rafael. They've been answered. I don't need to think about them anymore. A picture of Kai in his jeans and tee-shirt floats in my mind and business takes over.

"So, what do you have for me here?"

"Take a look." He opens the briefcase. Inside are keys, codes, USB drives, paper copies of schedules, lists of names. Even a bottle of mist.

The mist—a last-minute request. I feared the girls would react like prisoners of war when the kung fu brothers come for them. Like POWs, the girls are sometimes disillusioned by the time help arrives, so they fight against them, believing it's another trap. I told the brothers that if it came to that, the mist might be the gentlest way of getting them out.

I nod approvingly at Rafael. He was faithful to his word. To get everything we asked of him.

"Your father?" I ask.

"He gave up the contacts very willingly, left a lump of money for you and returned to Italy on the first plane," Rafael says, handing me a plump envelope. "King still thinks he's meeting my father on Friday. I visited Agent Bai and recorded a confession of what I know. I'll stay 'til Friday to help, but then I'm heading back too. To take a chance in Rome or London."

"Thank you, Rafael."

"I told you I'd return the favor, *Mila*."

"My real name is Josephine," I say. "I'm seventeen. From Seattle, and you were right, I am a prodigy."

He cups my hand in his, a satisfied look in his eyes. We say goodbye and good luck, even though we'll see each other in a week. But for us, it's closure, something we didn't have until now.

It's done. We have the names, the schedules. Later, the team comes to the office. We get to work finalizing the last details—rerouting the shipments, investigating buyers and custom agents, replacing them. My nerves are an ocean of restless waves.

We go over the plan one last time. Golden Alley tomorrow, the Pratt in three days, and the Expo in five.

I hope we can hold it together for five more days without getting caught.

THIRTY-FOUR
PRESENT: PHOENIX
∞

GOLDEN ALLEY, SHANGHAI, CHINA

We are two blocks from Golden Alley. Agent Bai adjusts a small Bluetooth device in my ear, making sure it's connected to his and Kai's.

"It's working," I say, hearing everything like a three-way conversation. "I want a play by play update."

"Got it." The Sang Brothers, Agent Bai, Yu Tai, and Kai move in toward Golden Alley, while I hang back on a busy, lighted corner. I wanted to go in with them, for the girls' sake. But after they convinced me I wouldn't be helpful until after they subdued the thugs running the place, I agreed to wait for their signal.

It's Friday. Hua Mei says that there are always more buyers on Friday, mostly street scum.

As I wait, I think of this morning. It was the first day of hotel infiltration for the kung fu brothers. Four hotels down, and everything went as planned. They 'replaced' Madame's men with Master Sang's men.

Kept up appearances, payment runners, business as usual. No one suspected anything.

According to Kai, buyers got quite a shock when they entered the hotel room expecting a girl and found a beefy kung fu master instead. I imagine the look on their faces and smile.

We've recorded 35 confessions. Eighty-six girls have been safely rescued, 52 that needed medical attention. I still hear Kai's voice...*I had no idea horrors like this existed.*

I expect tonight to be quick and effective like yesterday—a piece of cake since it's all lower level operations. They can't be as sophisticated as the hotels.

Kai's voice pops up in my ear now.

"Going in." There's a loud crack. "Door's open."

For 78 seconds there's nothing but light breathing in my ear until an angry male voice starts cursing and Agent Bai starts yelling, "Get back!"

"What's going on?" I ask.

No response. Another loud crack, voices are raised. In the background girls are screaming hysterically and there's a lot of loud smashing sounds. A fight has broken out.

"Master Sang! I need back up!" Agent Bai yells.

"Over there, more buyers!" Kai's voice.

"They're struggling too much. Yu Tai, mist them!"

"To the vans, quick!"

"What's happening?" I ask. My mind races through a series of calculations, but I need more variables. Despite not hearing the signal, I run toward the alley, heart pounding.

When I arrive, all hell has broken loose and flooded

into the street. I count, stunned. How is it possible there are so many girls here? So many buyers?

In the chaos, I look for Kai just as a noise tears through the streets. *Sirens.* I snap up to see Kai's eyes, worried and serious.

"Get out of here, Phoenix!" Kai shouts. "Now!"

I don't question his command. I find a taxi on the main road and retreat to the factory as fast as I can, processing the scene I've just witnessed: dozens of girls bolting from the door, screaming, struggling, fainting. Buyers attacking Master Sang. Agent Bai slamming another man to the road, handcuffing him.

Red's poem crashes like waves over my mind trying to calm me. *Sun glows gold...*

My thought is cut short by Agent Bai's static-masked voice breaking up in my ear, "A crowd...gathering! ... Police! ... Disappear!"

Numbers shatter like glass in my mind as another siren is added to the noise. Our plan's odds of success lower each second. If this goes public, Madame might follow the trail to the hotels, then to the boats, and then to us—and basically, we're screwed.

Last night's fiasco makes the morning news. Interpol's representative covers it up for us, explaining it as a routine bust but I can't shake the bad feeling in my gut that Madame will have seen through it.

At lunch, more bad news follows. Inflation has risen steeply over the past two months. Small shops have begun to close, and schools are cutting budgets.

A normal cycle that should correct itself, they say on the news.

People have no real idea of what's really coming.

I raise the white bowl to my lips, shoveling the remaining rice into my mouth with my chopsticks. Today this bowl of rice costs less than a dollar, but if we can't secure the money we need for the super bond and correct the economic free fall, soon it could cost more than twenty dollars. So many mouths will go hungry. I can't let that happen.

I hurry back to my office. As I prepare for the bond and loan interviews, Kai roams in unexpectedly.

"Hi. How are you?" he asks. The bruise on his face from last night is a real shiner. I wonder how he explained it to his dad.

"What's wrong now?" I ask. He's supposed to be finalizing details for the Pratt take down with Agent Bai. "Do you need me?"

"I do." He plants a kiss on my cheek, pulls back, and finds my eyes.

"I was referring to the plan," I say, my body pulsing with electricity. I'm still getting used to him touching me.

"Everything's in order. I just missed you." He turns to rummage the papers on my desk. "Last night shook you pretty hard. How are you?"

"Not as optimistic as you."

"Want to talk about it?"

"Just tell me where to find nearly $1.2 trillion to plug into the Chinese economy and I'll be fine." I feel an eruption coming on. "We're robbing two notorious criminals of everything they have—without telling the police—and I'm still not sure we'll have enough. And now, Madame might run before the Expo! And without Asia Bank we can't implement the final bond installments."

My head collapses onto the desk. "I wish these mountains of papers would fall and bury me and I'd never have to get up again. Then the responsibility would fall on someone else to find a solution. I could donate my brain to science. They could open it up and maybe the solution would be inside."

My back warms in the center. Kai's hand is circling softly. "Remember why you are doing this. You are meant for this. Stay here. Take all the time you need. One application at a time. We'll get enough, you'll see."

I sigh. "I shouldn't complain. I have help." I point across the hall where the two other brainiacs, Sheri and Phillip, are solving problems and working out new systems for smaller banks according to my J.J. Bond instructions. "Any more news on Madame?"

"No. We are working on the last Golden Angel Hotel, the one where you stayed. It's tricky because Celia will stay there during the Expo."

Kai feels me shudder when her name is spoken and pulls me in for a hug.

"It's okay. She's not your concern anymore," he says. "That's why we are here."

"Thanks," I say, even though I know that's not true. The Expo is around the corner.

Kai pulls my head to his chest. The minute I hear his heartbeat in my ear, my fear dissipates. My thoughts drift to pleasant things I haven't allowed my heart to access—ice cream on the beach, winter nights reading books in front of the fireplace, *love.* I can't get over how hearing the thump of his beating heart never grows old. It beats over and over again, strong and steady—

—Something's wrong. Usually I'd have an exact number of heartbeats logged right now, but I don't— which means I'm not counting them—which means...

My eyes snap open, darting around the room. The distance between me and the door. The window size. The desk and the chair. There's nothing assigning numerical definition to my office. The numbers are gone. Just like when I'm in a dream, only now I'm awake. I stay motionless, the *thump thump* of Kai's heart still in my ear, wondering what to do next.

I squeeze my eyes shut several times and like a switch the numbers turn on. I can calculate again. Kai has a normal heart rate of eighty-eight beats per minute.

Hmm, I think, *that's strange.* It must be a coincidence. But then again, I don't really believe in those.

THIRTY-FIVE
PRESENT: PHOENIX
∞

THE FACTORY, SHANGHAI, CHINA

The highest melting point in the world for a pure metal is 6,192° Fahrenheit. This fact alone blows scientists away, but not me, because on some days I feel like that metal. My computer-like brain has a high aptitude for what it can handle. But these days, my brain must be getting fried. Numbers jumble up or fade in and out like a radio signal.

It happens when I stare at the J.J. Super Bond for too long, or when I look at Kai, or right when I wake up. I've never experienced this before. It worries me.

In front of me sits a stack of papers I should be working on, but I can't focus with my numbers distracting me like this. The coffee's not helping. I massage my temples with my fingertips, but it's useless. I grab my purse. Maybe a walk will clear my mind.

On foot, I head toward the factory in auto mode thinking of Lulu, the new girl, who's walking and even laughing again. Dr. Ling will be there too. Maybe she'll know what's happening to me.

I enter through the back gate. A shuffling noise startles me to the left, twenty feet away. I push back into the doorframe. There's a small flowerpot at my feet. It's not much, but I take it into my hands. I crouch down, peer around the corner. My defenses drop when a tall, thin man comes towards me.

"What are you doing here, Chan?"

"I came to visit the factory," he says.

"How did you get in?" I ask, angrily. Now that Kai knows, it seems all kinds of new things are happening. "I changed the locks."

"I have a right to know if you are doing something illegal," he says, evading my first question. "Especially since my son is involved and bruises are appearing on his face."

"So you're spying on me," I say, a bit hurt. "I can't believe that you would accuse me of doing something illegal!"

"Consider where I found y—" He stops abruptly. Chan is not looking at me anymore but behind me, his eyes wide with disbelief, as if he sees a ghost.

"Good afternoon, Chan Da Ge."

My head whips around. Dr. Ling stares at Chan. A smile, slow and comforting, rises on her lips.

Da Ge? Am I hearing things, or did she just call him "big brother?" If she wasn't acquainted with him intimately, she would never use that expression.

"Ling Xia Hui." Chan clears his throat, trying to remove whatever it is that's making it hard for him to speak. He examines her slowly from head to toe.

"How the years have passed."

"More than ten," she responds in her usual calm manner, but tears gather in her eyes. She steps closer. He, too, moves forward. I, however, back up. To them, I might as well be invisible anyway.

"When I saw you last, you were still a girl," he says, stumbling for the right words. "You have changed a lot."

My anger dissipates as I watch Chan melt into a boy, unsure of himself. Who is Dr. Ling that he is transformed into someone I can't recognize? Will I ever know who Red is to him?

"You've not changed a bit," she says, "except sterner in the face."

"I'm sorry about your brother, your family...for how things worked out..." He breaks eye contact. He's choking up. Pain zigzags across his face marking an ache I know well—it's the expression of a man whose life was stolen from him. But how?

"The past is the past. Red did not dwell there. I don't either. You know my family, Chan Ge. It wasn't your fault," she says, lips trembling. "I've missed you. We all have."

Chan lowers his eyes, tears slipping down his cheeks. He clears his throat, one, two, three times. "I'm sorry, Ling Ling."

"It's all forgiven. Except now, there's more bad news..."

His stupor flees. He returns to the present place and time where I'm in the picture.

"How do you know her?" He points to me. "What are you doing here?" he asks, suddenly very confused.

Her eyes ask me for direction on what to say.

Awkward silence settles. I jump in.

"Chan," I say, "it's time you learned what we're doing. But I need to have your word that what we tell you stays here. People's lives are at stake."

He tenses into his usual stiffness. He steps backwards, like he has been put in this position before and won't be cornered again.

Dr. Ling goes to him. Her round eyes peer up at him, like a gentle supplicant, praying him through hell. That's when I notice what a beautiful woman she is. Her passion for life and helping people radiates like Red's.

Chan crumbles underneath her kind eyes. He bows his head in submission to her, and steps forward.

"Do I want to know?" he whispers.

"Red would say yes." Her voice is barely audible but steady and calm, like a faithful stream trickling down a dry mountain.

Thirteen questions string through my mind regarding Red and Chan's relationship. About their past. But I don't ask. There's no time. We take the Pratt tomorrow night. While I don't understand what's passing between them, I do understand I'm not the one to explain the factory's operations.

"Dr. Ling will show you around. I have other things I must attend to." Facing Dr. Ling, I say, "Leave the girls upstairs. Just show him the facility and explain our vision."

"Girls? What girls?" Chan says, suspicion growing. "What kind of an operation are you running here?"

"Trust me, like you once trusted my family," Dr.

Ling says, "I will tell you everything."

I slip out the back door unnoticed, weighing the risk I just took. Depending on what Dr. Ling tells him, Chan can make or break tomorrow night.

Tonight, King will face justice.

So far Chan hasn't interfered. In fact, he made an unprecedented move. He took the day off—canceled all of his meetings. He left early, without telling Kai where he was going or when he would be back.

On one hand, it worries me; on the other hand, it's a blessing. He's been out of our hair all day, and I hope for the rest of the night.

As I stand just behind the tree line surrounding the Pratt, familiar numbers define the old abandoned buildings and old TEU containers. My body vibrates with adrenaline. The Pratt is dark and appears abandoned, but I know better. Down below it is alive as ever.

I turn to Rafael. "You're sure only the underground guards are on duty?" I ask. Rafael did far more than I required, too much maybe, because my calculations pulse negative equations.

"Yes. I reassigned the guards to the warehouse. I dismantled cameras. The buildings are unlocked. We should have no problem subduing the remaining guards downstairs in 7. We take what is ours and go."

It's too easy, I think. A rat wouldn't take cheese from a dismantled trap without suspicion. Still I need to trust Rafael. Not only is he trusted at the Pratt, our plan will not work without him.

"The perimeter is clear," Agent Bai confirms, then assigns his men, each to a building.

"All right, let's go."

The small cellar door beside the lighthouse is already unlocked. Only Red knew about its entrance into the Pratt. I'm sure this is where King stashes his goods. I'm counting on it.

We have three hours to execute my plan and we can't afford any major delays. Step one is loot the lighthouse. Step two secure the shipments at the port. Finally, empty the Pratt.

Yu Tai stands above ground waiting for the signal to move in and load up the loot.

Kai and I open the hatch and jump in the cellar. We step over old boxes and stacks of useless boat equipment until we come to another hatch. Inside, stairs wind down, directly below the lighthouse.

The familiar scent of mildew, latrine, and incense sting my nose. These catacombs are less frequented. Centipedes and spiders crawl for cover as we shine our flashlights.

Ten meters later, we reach a door. Behind it, there's another door with a lock. "Found it."

The lock on the door takes me less than two minutes to crack. I expect a storage room filled with cash alone, but as we shine our lights, I discover I was wrong. It's a pirate's treasure chest, a true dragon lair if I ever saw one. The room, which is actually a small tunnel, is lined with shelves that are stacked as high as the ceiling with currencies from all over the world, mainly America, Europe and China. Gems and jewelry and gold rings, surely stripped from former patrons, are secured in metal boxes. King's retirement fund is much more than I imagined, and much of this is because of me.

"Move in," Kai calls over to Yu Tai. But there's no answer.

"Agent Bai?" I say.

Kai's eyes dart up. "It's disconnected. Something's wrong." Kai pulls me towards the way we came.

"No," I say. "Follow me."

We fly through another tunnel heading toward the part of the Pratt I'm familiar with. I close my eyes, seeing the map in my head.

"Go left." We come to building 3 and sneak up another exit where I catch a view of what's happening outside. The Pratt is surrounded with a whole troop of King's guards, fully armed. It's dark, but I count at least 48 men. Agent Bai and his team, 25 men, not including Yu Tai and Kai, are at a near face off with them. There are never this many men on duty. They should be at the warehouse unless...they knew we were coming.

A motion near the driveway grabs my attention. It's Yu Tai! He slides past all the others unnoticed, jumps in his van and speeds away! *He's leaving us?*

Golden Alley flashes in my mind. Not another failure! My brain filters through possibilities. Mathematically, we can win this. We are more trained and organized, but not without a lot of bloodshed and risk of King finding out. *What if he knows already?* The delay alone might cost us the port and we can't risk anyone getting hurt, especially Rafael. We need him to finish our plan.

I panic. Where's Rafael? He's nowhere to be seen. Did he leave too, like Yu Tai?

Just then, a large guard throws a man down on the ground and holds him down shoving his knife against his throat.

I gasp, grabbing Kai's arm. No! Not Rafael!

Another guard aiming his gun at Agent Bai yells over to the guard holding Rafael. "We should call King."

"I can handle this myself. King's got bigger things to worry about." The old familiar, gravelly voice rings in my ears, completely changing the odds. I recalculate my chances factoring in the owner of that voice and the fact that tonight really is the biggest shipment, or else King would have stormed over here by now. Tonight, needs to succeed. But all my calculations hang on a risk, who's more loyal to whom.

"I knew you were up to something, kid." The guard growls, the scowl deep. "Tell me who you are working for—or daddy's going to be sore you've gone missing."

There's no more time to wait. I need to risk this, or Rafael might die; our plan might fail. It's now that I find out if the favor I fought so hard to earn in the Pratt was worth it.

I bolt from the door. "Let him go, Guard San," I shout and run into the circle. "He's working for me."

The guard's head snaps up to meet my gaze. He's so startled by what he sees he drops his knife. "Double-Eight? You're alive?"

THIRTY-SIX
PRESENT: PHOENIX
∞

THE PRATT, SHANGHAI, CHINA

"It can't be. You're dead." San looks at me like he's seen a ghost.

"It's me, old friend," I say to my old jailor. "I'll explain my resurrection later, but for now I need your help." I peer into the crowd of guards. Many I've assisted in some way. They knew me—respected me—they watched me become one of them.

There's a murmur amongst the other guards. "Double-Eight." One by one, they lower their weapons.

"Yes. You know who I am, and I know who you are. King's taken something from all of us—money, family, our livelihoods, our freedom. It's time to take it back. I'm offering you a second chance…" As I speak, Guard San becomes the broken man I met in the hallway all those years ago, at a crossroads—will he risk King's wrath for a chance at new life? Not everyone will agree to this plan—some fear change, even good change. I know this, but for Red, I must try. What he taught me so long ago, I'm urged to say now. "Brothers, this is not who you were created to be. Let's end this tonight."

Silence blankets the Pratt for 11 seconds as King's men look at each other, then at me.

The hush is interrupted. Yu Tai's van tears into the Pratt followed by a stream of other vehicles. So he didn't abandon us. Loads of people, dressed in common clothes, speaking Red's dialect come streaming out. Song Valley's townsmen who have also been wronged by King. They've come at last to stand up to King.

"King's done enough damage in our town." An older man challenges King's men. He is obviously familiar with some of them. Most likely, they are former neighbors and relatives of the criminals. Warily, the rest of the Song Valley folk stand next to the old man.

Guard San walks over to me. "I'm in." He is the first of many to extend his hand to me. My heart lightens. Night is coming to an end. Day is finally dawning, and many more than I will get justice tonight.

The three ships I rerouted are already in the harbor when we arrive. I should be celebrating what's about to happen and I am, but it doesn't make me forget the hundreds of girls that were lost.

I grab Kai's hand and gather my courage.

"Be strong," Kai whispers in my ear. "They'll need you."

Agent Bai and Yu Tai prepare the vehicles to transport all the goods and *cargo* once I do my part.

The first boat's holding compartments are opened, and I step in. Wild-eyes flicker and figures recoil into corners. The room is putrid. As the light brightens, I count: 151, 152, 153 girls, dirty and terrified. One can't stand, another is in very bad condition. They are sick, some lying in their own excrement. Some of them are just so young it hurts.

I choke up. My own kidnapping flashes in my mind. A hundred little Josephines stare at me in terror.

I shove the door as wide as it can go. Light pours into the darkness.

"My name is Phoenix," I say, reaching down to hold one of the littlest girls to my chest. "I'm here to help you."

Three hundred and eighteen girls are now miles away from Madame's wicked plans. The depth of gratitude in their eyes will stay with me forever.

"You okay?" Kai asks, wrapping an arm around me.

I nod, certain I'll cry if I speak. "We saved some, Kai." Tears escape my control and roll down my cheeks. "They can go home."

Kai holds me tightly. "Maybe someday you can too."

The thought falls like a guillotine. I have nothing to go back to at home.

I check my watch. King will arrive soon. As they finish unloading, I prepare my *gifts* for King.

It's half past midnight when King pulls up to the port. Rafael parks next to King in Cesare's car. Kai moves into position to back up Rafael if necessary.

My skin tingles. I've waited a long time for this moment. But now that I'm here, I realize that this night isn't really about me anymore. Others have waited far longer than I. Tonight is for Song Valley, and I will deliver.

Agent Bai has already tipped off the police for tonight's aftermath. We'll hand everything over to Interpol and let the law enforce the proper penalties after we're done. Agent Bai gave King's guards a chance to come clean: those who didn't, we locked up for the police. Guard San gave me his total support, as did many others. I think of Red and thank him silently.

King arrives. He gets out of his car with his typical swagger and lights a cigarette. I listen in on the mics that were planted on Rafael and Guard San. "What the hell are three ships doing here?" King rants. He glances around the harbor. "Where's the crew? Where's Cesare?"

"I thought he was with you." Rafael feigns ignorance and phones his father twice with no answer.

"Check the warehouse," King says as if upon cue. Rafael drives back toward the Pratt.

King and Guard San walk onboard the first ship. When King sees the containers are unloaded and empty, he pulls out a gun. "What's going on?" he shouts. "Secure the perimeters."

A small box sits on the table where he usually negotiates his deals. He opens it. He takes out a piece of paper. The deed to the Pratt. Below it, there's a stack of court orders showing hundreds of debts and legal claims against him.

"What is this?" King looks around nervously and rips up the documents. He's confused. "Where's my money?"

Guard San shrugs. They check the second ship. Again, the cargo is gone, and the usual customs agent and money runner are not there. Instead there's a small briefcase. King opens it and finds two *hongbao*, small red envelopes that are given to children during holidays. Inside the first one, he finds 44 RMB, the unluckiest number he could ever find, representing death and despair. The second envelope has another 44 RMB. Eighty-eight in total. A gift from me.

King twitches but he doesn't freak out. He curses all the way to the third boat. My heart skips a beat when he arrives. Within the third ship is my favorite gift. King's not a fool and doesn't bother searching the cargo containers. He goes straight for the envelope on the table. The envelope has no *hongbao*, just 88 RMB, and a note that says:

Dear King,
Thanks for the lighthouse. It's money time.
Your ghost, 88

"Back to the Pratt! Now!" His face contorts. He's a cornered bear, a king in battle, outnumbered with his castle besieged. He goes berserk, swearing all the way to the car.

They speed down the road toward the Pratt like it's a matter of life and death. We follow behind them, my heart pounding.

King checks the lighthouse first, which allows us time to slip into the main operating tunnels of the Pratt and into the prison area he is sure to check. He has no idea what's waiting for him. The lighthouse was cleared out two hours ago.

In the dim light, Kai smacks away cobwebs just as we hear a mad man burst into the main prison area of the Pratt, tipping over chairs and shelves, and roaring. "Where's my money?"

The prisoners are not in their cells. No one is around. King searches for his guards. "Where is everyone?" Lastly, he slams open the door to the tunnel behind his office, another long and wide space, which is now emptied of goods. Even though the light is dim, he sees what's happening.

King's face fills with shock. He bolts for the door, but it slams before he can get there.

A light brightens as someone lights a lantern. Yu Tai walks out first, followed by the Sang brothers. "Remember me? I'm Yu Feng's son."

Dr. Ling comes forward next. "Red's sister."

One by one, Song Valley residents, although still afraid, step out stating their claims. From another tunnel emerge multiple Pratt prisoners, Rafael, Guard San, Guard Feng, and other guards whom King blackmailed.

"Do something!" King yells to Guard San and Guard Feng.

Agent Bai steps forward, flashing a badge.

No one moves. They step to the side, making way for someone in the back to come forward.

Me.

"Hello, King," I say. "Your taxes are due."

The smell of fear and sweat oozes from him, adding to the dank air in the vault. King's expression changes into that of a wild dog, twitching.

Before Agent Bai can handcuff him, King maneuvers

around him, slams his fist hard into Agent Bai's temple. I'm not even sure how he managed it, but he didn't become King of the Pratt for no reason.

King dives through the door, taking his chances through one of the Pratt tunnels. The masters race after him. Song Valley residents follow after him too, screaming all hell. King won't escape them, nor will he get far. Every exit is blocked with more Pratt prisoners who are eagerly waiting for their chance to say goodbye to King.

If I know King, he won't go down without a fight. But this time he won't win, because the King of the Pratt is not on his throne anymore.

THIRTY-SEVEN
PRESENT: PHOENIX

THE PRATT, SHANGHAI, CHINA

After interrogating King, we get more information on operations all over the world but nothing new about Madame.

"Dead, huh?" King's face is bloody and he's seething, mostly at me. "The only reason I believed that stupid lie is because Guard San couldn't hide his grief." His smoky voice laughs but it sounds more like a cough. "You bought my guards, too. Impressive."

"I didn't need to. They're my friends. I'm only giving back what you took away. You ruined yourself, King."

He's not the slightest bit fazed. "Are we done now?"

"You haven't finished. I want Madame's secrets."

"She's a freak. Won't eat on Tuesdays. Obsessed with gold. Refuses buyers from Australia. Probably a hundred more neurotic compulsions I don't know about. You'd know more than me."

It's possible he's telling the truth. Although I suspected he'd have bought more information about her.

"You're a fool to think you can catch her, Double-Eight. She's everywhere."

Involuntarily, I shudder because I know what she's capable of. She's always one step ahead.

Kai enters. "The police are here."

"He's all yours," I say to Agent Bai. I look over to King. "If you cooperate, they may go easier on you."

King glares smugly, growling curses at me as he leaves.

I inhale one last breath of stagnant, suffocating air trapped in the Pratt before I walk upstairs and out of those unforgettable doors.

Up top, I take in a mouthful of fresh air and a sense of freedom like never before.

Kai grabs my hand. "You never have to return here again, unless you come as a tourist," he says. Yu Tai has plans to make the newly discovered Emperor of Song Dynasty's Legendary Catacombs a grand exhibition.

I get into the car without looking back. "Nah. I've already seen everything."

I wake to the sun shining and birds singing. They must know, like I do, that the Pratt is cleared out. That the prisoners are set free. That King's rule has ended. Rightfully all creatures should rejoice.

I rest my elbows on the windowsill, staring into the garden. Flowers bloom and the grass seems greener than usual. But the sun won't last long, I think, especially if I can't find an alternative to Asia Bank.

The crash is closing in on us. People are losing their jobs. No matter how I invest our money, we will not have enough. I won't panic until after I account for Madame's generous donation, which hopefully will be today at the Expo.

After a shower, I dress in a business suit, wrapping a dark red shawl over my shoulders. I swipe my lips with a soft pink gloss and walk down the path that connects to Kai's house.

Agent Bai is already at the table in front of his computer, sipping at his tea flask, and compiling all the evidence from King, hotel busts, the kidnapped girls, and confessions. He was able to work out a deal for Guard San and the others. There will be some penalties, but they'll be able to start again. "Thirty minutes," Agent Bai informs me, rubbing the purple shiner on his cheek from King.

I grab a cup of the coffee brewing on Kai's counter and join him on the couch.

J.J. Bond figures are strewn across the coffee table. I pick up a projection sheet and start to mumble something about Madame but drift off mid-sentence as I look at Kai.

He's dressed in a black V-neck tee-shirt and gray jeans, both of which are fitting enough for me to see how strong he is. I follow his biceps down to his hands then up again to the open tip of the V-neck. His chest alone looks so inviting I could lay my head down and forget about the economic crash and the Expo forever.

"Phoenix?" he says, pleased with where my eyes have wandered and made fools of themselves. "You were saying?" Kai flexes his right bicep. "Coffee's not *strong* enough? The bond needs something *stronger*?"

I shake my head as heat burns in my face. "Oh Atlas,

please save the world with your muscles."

He tackles me in a hug. We laugh.

"I was saying that if everything goes smoothly today, I'll have reached my quota for payback. Everything I made for her will finally go to a good cause and she'll be behind bars. Justice."

His arms secure around my waist. We stay wrapped up together and silent like this for three minutes. Chan's disapproval lurks. He warned me against this relationship. I sigh. We untangle to sift through applications and tally up more numbers.

"Are you ready?" Kai asks me softly. "To see her again?"

"I won't really see her," I assure him. "My role is one hundred percent virtual, from across the street, in a secured office, guarded by six men. But yes, I'm ready for this to be finished."

Kai leans in for a kiss. It's long, and soft. My hands slide down his shoulders to his arms.

I pull back, open my eyes. The calculator inside me has stopped. Just like before. The room around me is just walls and chairs and carpet and Kai.

Kai notices my confusion. "What's wrong?" He puts a hand on my knee.

My head snaps down to my knee then up at him. It's just a small touch but it's so much more, because I didn't know he'd touch me *until he touched me.* More precisely, I didn't calculate his movements. I'm about to panic when, slowly, one equation marks the width of the door, then the ceiling to floor, then a stream of numbers graphs out my world, back to normal. I shake my head.

It's happening more frequently.

He's waiting for a response.

"I'm fine," I lie. Thirty minutes are up. "Let's do this."

Interpol and Agent Bai's men have the massive Expo Center surrounded. Not a single door, window, or crack in the wall is unguarded.

I watch from across the street with Agent Bai's colleague, Agent Yin, beside me. Six more agents guard the door outside.

After fourteen minutes of watching the doors swing open 429 times and 931 men and women in suits and high heels enter the Expo Center, Agent Bai sounds in my ear and my computer screen lights up. Hundreds of stalls and booths display goods from companies around the world. It's like a mini fashion show inside. "I've got visual," I say.

My screen divides into three parts. Agent Bai's view with the main team on floor three where Madame is located and two with the undercover buyers.

The plan is simple. Agent Bai's men will impersonate the four illegal buyers attending the expo. We should be able to trace the spin code from one of them, but as extra insurance, we'll trace every other buyer too. After the buyer makes the purchase, and the spin code scrambles, I'll get the chain entry into all of her accounts. I'll trace it and transfer the money into an account I created at Chan's corporation for the super bond. Once that is done, we pass on our proof of buyers and international smuggling. Then Interpol will take over.

"First buyer is going in," Agent Bai says.

I follow on the screen as the buyer moves in. M's Textiles logo comes into view first. Then Celia steps around a corner, accompanied by two men. Shivers shoot down my back.

"That's her."

"Locked on target."

Celia shakes the buyers' hands, then steps back into the shadows, head scanning the room. She's searching for something, *or someone.* Can she sense the number of eyes on her? Is she turning into King, always anticipating the knife aimed at his back? Only, she's not acting nervous, but almost excited. Whatever it is, her mind is clearly not on the Expo.

Celia's assistant, a young man, walks the buyer through the purchasing process. What the buyer sees is on my screen. As he makes his payment transfer, there is no spin code at all. It's a regular routing number. Huh.

After a few more legal buyers, another illegal buyer makes his move. This time the spin code scrambles, I memorize and plug it in to test it right away. But the chain entry is denied.

"Not it," I confirm.

"Patience. We'll get it." Agent Bai promised he won't make a move until that magical payment with the routing number is found.

The next illegal buyer is given the same number. Denied. I begin to worry. What if I'm wrong? It is just a theory.

Three hours pass. We trace every routing number that buyers use to make their transfer—one by one. Each, a dead end.

The more I watch Celia, the more memories return. *I chose you, Octavia...*

The second-to-last buyer transfers his payment and the computer lights up. The routing scrambles and a spin code appears. I enter it and this time the chain entry is granted.

This is it!

Dollars multiply before my eyes as the spin code links me into a massive web of accounts. I dive in. All of her accounts are an open meadow before me. I transfer everything into the bond account at China Generation. It's working!

I'm so busy calculating I forget to tell Agent Bai the good news until he's in my ear first.

"Phoenix?

"We've got it—"

"Don't move. We lost her. Coming to you." The screen goes black and random dates circle in my head. *Mara's fifth birthday. My parent's 10th anniversary. Lily's last piano recital. First day with King. Red's death.*

I slap the desk as I understand our mistake. We had to wait until the second to last buyer. That burned a lot of time...

"Agent Yin?" He doesn't answer. That's when I notice his head is down on the desk.

The lights cut out. An icy finger runs over my cheek. Once again, I'm fifteen years old and alone with a nightmare.

THIRTY-EIGHT
PRESENT: PHOENIX

∞

EXPO CENTER, SHANGHAI, CHINA

I'm shoved into the adjacent office just thirteen feet away where the six guards are passed out on the floor. Celia stands beside two men with guns trained on me. I calculate my odds of escape. Not looking good.

"You've come back to me, Octavia." Her eyes crawl into mine, like a demon looking for a host body, but I hold her stare, pushing her out.

"That's not my name."

She laughs eerily, chilling me to the bone. I pull my jacket tighter. "I'm not the little girl you took at the pier anymore. I won't let you control me no matter what you do next."

"You're alive," she says, ignoring me, her shiny, red lips spreading into a smile. "I'm free now. We both are."

I cock my head, confused. Instead of blistering mad that I'm not at the bottom of the Pacific, she sounds happy. "I don't understand."

"You've haunted me, Octavia, for the last year." She laughs louder, a victorious, mad laugh. "Until I saw you again, alive."

I'm shocked. I took all the proper precautions never to be seen. "When? Where?"

"In the perfectly prepared papers for the Expo. No one else could have prepared them but you."

"But they are just…"

"Numbers? I'd recognize you, your work anywhere. We're connected, can't you see that?" She inches closer to me. "Come away with me, Octavia. You and I will start a new life together."

"No." I shake my head. The very idea is repulsive.

"Octavia, I can give you everything. Even what you hold most dear."

"You've taken everything from me, Celia."

"Not everything, darling. I still have secrets. Come with me, and I'll tell you everything."

"The police are everywhere, Celia. You won't escape this time." Four minutes since Agent Bai warned me to stay put. Where is he? Does he think I'm safe?

"Octavia, you know me better than that. I'm always one step ahead." She leans closer, whispering, like I'm supposed to read between the lines. "Secrets, darling. If they catch me today, I'll be free tomorrow. Didn't I know they'd be there, and you'd be here? I came anyway. To see you. And you're alive. Please, come. I've only ever wanted to love and protect you."

Love me? I cringe. During the time I lived with her she tried to love me like a mother. She gave me gifts and money, but she never gave me a choice—and without freedom, love can't prosper. This time, she has no power over me.

More men shuffle in. "Maxima, time's up."

She stares at me. "Your choice, Octavia."

"You'll have to kill me, Celia. I won't come with you." The resolve in my voice shocks her. It shocks me, too. Deep inside I know that even if I die, she hasn't won. She couldn't change who I am.

"I didn't want to do this." She frowns and takes the gun from the man. "Turn around and face the wall."

My forehead leans on the cold cement. I squeeze my eyes shut and wait for the end. Perhaps Red will meet me there, on the other side.

"Let me hear you count to ten, darling. For old time's sake."

"One...Two..." I count slowly, praying with each number that my death will count—that the file sent, that the numbers check out, that the police will catch her, that her trafficking will end.

"Eight...Nine...Ten." When I stop nothing happens. No bullet goes off. Thirteen...Fourteen...

At fifteen seconds I open my eyes and turn around. Celia's gone without a trace.

At fifty-six seconds the police burst into the room. They find me in a corner, mumbling the same words over and over.

"She let me go."

I pace my living room for the third hour waiting for news and reflecting on what just happened. How did she know we were there? Why did she let me go? The longer I wait, Celia's words eat away at me like a parasite. *I'm always one step ahead.*

After the police found me, they escorted me through the radius of six city blocks that were on lockdown. Every authority in Shanghai is out searching.

There's a knock on the door. Kai jumps off the couch. Agent Bai and the Sang brothers walk in. The defeat on their faces tells me what I don't want to hear a second before they do.

"Madame has escaped."

"How could you let her go?" My chest tightens. I'm nauseous now. *Angry.* Everyone is silent. My fist slams down on the desk.

"The place was surrounded, Phoenix. Her escape was impossible," Master Sang says.

"Obviously not." I'm pacing again. I'm caged, trapped in a box with no oxygen. It grows smaller and tighter by the second. *Didn't I know they'd be there, and you'd be here?* "If we lose her, I lose everything I've worked to achieve."

"You have access to all of her accounts."

"Who cares about the money? She'll just remake her identity and start again," I say.

"We need your gift to find her, Phoenix," Agent Bai says. "Trace her location. If we pinpoint a source she's using, we can bring her out in the open and find her."

My mind juggles ninety-eight destinations and names. I spout off a list.

"Hold that thought," Agent Bai interrupts me. "Detective Hansen is an expert at tracing anything."

"What can we do, Phoenix?" Master Sang asks.

Everyone waits on me to weed out improbable variables and come up with a logical starting point.

After all, I'm the one who knows her best. I'm the one with the gift.

But as I set to calculating a new plan, there's a break in the numbers. The calculations predicting where she'll go and what she'll do fade away until I'm a blank page.

Dread ripples to the shore of completely new territory. There's only one plausible reason for my sudden halt in numbers and that cannot be a possibility. Not now. Not ever.

Kai reads my face and draws away their attention. "The hotels."

"Interpol has combed every possible hotel in Shanghai. Nothing," Agent Bai replies. "PGF came up empty, too. Interpol wants Phoenix to point us in the right direction."

I push my thumbs into my throbbing temples. *Think, Phoenix. They are counting on you.* What do you know about her? But I'm still blank! Blank! Blank!

Brother Sang makes a phone call. Doors open and close. Cars start and drive away. I hear it all but without numerical definition it means nothing.

I'm letting everyone down, letting Celia escape.

How could this happen now? *Why* is this happening? I didn't believe this could happen. But it is. I feel it.

My gift. I'm losing it.

I don't say a word about my gift. I simply promise to call when I think of something. Thankfully, they are in a hurry, so they agree.

Kai tells his cousin he'll catch up with him. The minute the door closes, I forget about everything— the girls, the bond, King's trial. Not even Celia letting me go or her escape is on my mind. I'm frozen, consumed by one thing that threatens my whole being, my entire identity.

My gift.

What if it never comes back? The thought sickens me with grief. The clock says more than an hour has passed, the longest lapse yet, and I can't make the numbers come back any more than I can fly like a seagull. What caused this? Stress? Trauma? Tears roll down my face.

Kai's hands find my face. "What is it?"

"Kai, it's bad." I sound more desperate than he has ever heard me. It startles him.

"You can tell me."

"My gift. The numbers. They're gone."

He shakes his head. "You're sure?"

I nod.

My hands shake. He reaches out his hands as if in very slow motion. Now I must guess. Will he hold my chin again? Grab my hands? Neither. He pulls me close to his chest. My numbers don't predict his movements. I used to think I'd like this, like in my dreams. But now I'm not sure if I can function without calculating. It's been part of me for so long, I don't know who I am without it.

"I can't lose my gift now." I whisper. The stacks of applications on the coffee table need my unique skill, not to mention Madame on the loose. "How can we find Madame without my gift? Or multiply our funds for the bond?"

"You said it yourself, everything is in place for the J.J. Bond," he says, trying to comfort me. "All we need is to feed the funds into it."

"Kai. Madame's money isn't enough. I could have multiplied it. But now…"

"It'll be okay," Kai says. "I don't know how, but I promise. We'll find a way."

Red's voice echoes behind Kai's. *Destiny is not what you're meant to do, it's who you're meant to be—all else pours out from there.* How can I be me without my gift?

"I'm sorry, I've got to go. Detective Hansen is waiting for me." Before Kai leaves, he kisses my cheek. "I'll text you as soon as we know something."

THIRTY-NINE
PRESENT: PHOENIX
∞

FRENCH CONCESSION, SHANGHAI, CHINA

I stay home all day, sifting through J.J. Bond applications. This I can do. Thank God I wrote out the requirements for bonds beforehand. It's dark when I pick up my phone and check in with the team.

Agent Bai: *No Madame yet. Found another trail.*

Master Sang: *Another hotel was closed. 30 girls rescued.*

Yu Tai: *The tunnels are cleared, archeology team arrives on Sunday.*

I should be happy. The places of my nightmares are all disappearing, but I can't rejoice. I'm terrified as I ponder a life without numbers to guide me. What will I do? Who will I be?

Sleep is the last thing on my mind, so I keep working. I change into sweat shorts and a tee-shirt. In the kitchen I pour a hot cup of jasmine tea. Heading to the couch, I grab my computer and settle in for a night of checking applications when there's a knock at the door.

There are only a few people who would knock on my door and they're all busy now. Even fewer who would come this late at night. Flipping the hall light on, I go to the front door. It's probably Kai or one of the girls from the factory on High Street. Through the peephole I see someone else.

Unbolting the door, I swing it open. A man stares back at me. In his hands there's a chess pawn.

"Mr. Chan, what a surprise."

He's dressed in casual slacks and a polo shirt but has house slippers on. He must have come over here from the main house on a whim. I invite him in for tea because it's the polite thing to do even if I'm tired and it's late. He refuses, as custom, until I urge him several times to accept.

"Fine, just one cup." His voice is different. Not the usual commanding voice I know from the office. "I have something to say to you."

"Welcome," I say, swinging the door open, "it is your house."

"Why is it so hard for you to accept something from me? I told you this house is yours." He looks at me. It's the first time I see Kai's face in his. He's not wearing his glasses and the lines around his face seem softer.

He walks through the living room, surveying all his former belongings. "You have not done anything with the place."

"I'm not much for entertaining." After last week, he's familiar with my after-work activities. Is this about the factory?

Walking into the kitchen, he immediately pulls up

a chair and gives me that look that says *let's start the meeting, time is money.* I assume something is wrong. Picking up the canister of green tea leaves on the counter, I open it, pinching a few leaves and dropping them into a small teacup. Pushing a button on the automatic hot water dispenser, I fill his cup and set it in front of him.

His face is serious as he thumbs the pawn in his hand. He sets it on the table for both of us to look at as I settle into a chair.

"I guess you are wondering how I know Dr. Ling."

"The thought crossed my mind," I say. "Along with Red, Kai's mother, and King."

"Red was my best friend," he says.

"Best friends? Impossible." They're opposite ends of the stick in every way.

"Blame fate. It can get around anything," he says. "Our social status and families are completely different. I'm high society. He's from the countryside. His family is spiritual, mine are superstitious. His favorite color is orange, mine is black. I'm tall, he is short. The list goes on. We're a disaster of a match. But we had one thing in common." He picks up the chess piece. "We played everything—xiangqi, weiqi. But our favorite was chess. I was the chess champion in my district, and Red was champion in his. One summer, fate had us compete."

Red. Even without a math gift he could beat me. But he never mentioned anything about championships. He was too humble for that.

"Before meeting Red, I believed that all countryside people aspired to not much more than raising chickens. That is, if I ever thought about them. So after I met my challenger, I'd planned to beat him and celebrate my title before lunch. But Red beat me. Fair and square. I couldn't accept it. I ranted and raved."

"That last part is hard to believe," I say with a smirk. Chan grimaces.

"Because of my family's status I believed I was better than him. I accused him of cheating." Chan twirled the little pawn. "Red held this up and said, "*Every pawn has a different strength, and every king and queen, a weakness.* You are upset because a pawn beat a king. But not everything is what it seems. Some pawns are actually kings and queens, and some kings and queens are just pawns.""

A lump emerges in my throat as I remember my first meeting with Red. A little misty eyed, I glance up at Chan. We are thinking the same thing.

"Red and his sayings!" Chan mused. "What made it worse was that he wasn't boastful like most champions. After the tournament he slapped a pawn in my hand and said, *I'll teach you, if you want.* I refused. I'd lost so much face that I challenged him outside the tournament. He agreed. But secretly I tucked the pawn away, along with his offer to teach me." Chan paused, a solemn expression on his face.

"We played best out of five. First two matches, he won. He was obviously better than me, but then he did something I wasn't ready for. He let me win the next three matches. He made stupid mistakes, gave me the game. I called him on it, and challenged him again, but he said he had a better idea.

""Come to my house,"" he had said. ""I will teach you my secrets. Next year, you will be champion.""

Chan shakes his head in wonder. "A champion never shares his secrets. You keep those to yourself because they profit you. But Red wasn't like that. Not concerned with winning or losing. He was concerned with friends, people. With doing what was right."

As Chan talks, all the things I love about Red return. He won people. His whole purpose was for others. To show them who they could be. That was his prize. I'm proof of that, and my heart aches for him.

"The next day, without my parents knowing, I went out to his hometown. Song Valley. His parents were farmers, polite, simple people. Wood and dirt floor. Hardly a curtain on the window. But they were clever. A wisdom and harmony rested there that I didn't have in my own home. Everyone loved each other.

"Red did exactly what he said he would do. He taught me everything he knew. I didn't know why, but I just kept coming back. I improved at chess, but I also began to laugh in that house. His mother cooked up the best wild roots and vegetables I'd ever tasted. I'd bring her meat as a gift. Their family was poor, but even then, they helped families much poorer than themselves. I learned what it meant to be family. My own parents never laughed at my jokes. But Red's family did. I'd soon preferred them to the circles I ran with back home." Chan sips his tea. "Red, although he was the best, never entered another competition. The following year, I was the champion, just as he predicted. I'd also gained a best friend."

"What went wrong?" I ask.

"After the competition I gained something else. Red's sister."

"Dr. Ling?"

"No, the first born. Moli," he says. "She was my wife."

"Your wife?" The moli flowers in his lapel, in his office, all sentiment. Pieces of a puzzle come together. "Red is Kai's uncle? Red never told me. Kai doesn't know?"

"In China, if there's a tragedy, we often do not talk about it," he says. "Moli was as kind as Red and just as clever. She didn't have a formal education, but she was an expert of the human heart. Red was who he was because of her. When I was near her, I could take over the world. I loved her. And despite my flaws, she loved me too.

"Her parents were delighted. But as expected, mine disapproved. I fought them, telling them I loved her, I'd pay for her to go to school, that she'd make something of herself. They warned me it wouldn't work out, eventually something would go wrong. But they agreed that if I enrolled her into university classes to become a teacher before our wedding, we could marry."

"At the wedding Red gave a speech." He held out two pawns. "'This is the symbol of our friendship, love and unity. As pawns and kings, we vow nothing is impossible. Chess is a game, but life is not. In us, we have seen a brotherhood from two worlds, a marriage brought together by fate alone. Love, more powerful than honor. May this pawn remind us to live as kingly pawns and humble kings, not for ourselves but for each other.' Then he blessed our marriage."

For a moment, I wish he would stop talking so I can let it all soak in, to feel it. But he doesn't.

"My parents never accepted her. But we were too happy to notice. Meanwhile, Red kept hassling me about his former high school student that he considered to be very dangerous. King. Red predicted he'd ruin many lives if there wasn't intervention. At first, it was just money, materials, cars. Later, anything he wanted. King usurped property. Brothels were set up. Then girls, daughters went missing. King threatened Song Valley residents into silence." He rubs his forehead. "Red hassled me for six years for help. My business was growing. Kai had been born. I was busy. I didn't want to get mixed up in criminal business. Finally, I stopped visiting Song Valley. I refused to let my son go there. But Moli wanted to help Red and Song Valley."

"When Kai was six, King discovered the Pratt tunnels and tried to seize the property from Yu Chen. The land had been in the Yu family for many years and they were close friends. A group who'd been wronged by King gathered at Red's, finally brave enough to stand up to him. That weekend, Moli went, too. I felt sick and begged her not to go. It'd be her only time, she promised. She was right."

Red was convinced that he could persuade King to change, but as fate would have it, Red interrupted some kind of deal. King's buyers, believed to be betrayed, fled with King's money. King blamed Red, and the chase was on. Red hurried to his house where everyone was gathered. But King was close behind. As everyone fled, King opened fire. Yu Chen and Moli were hit. When King caught Red, he threatened to kill the rest of his family if Red didn't pay back every penny of what he'd lost in the deal. Red asked me for help. He promised to make all things right. He'd find a way to convince King to change, to restore everything that was taken from Song Valley. But I was angry. I blamed him for Moli's death. I responded a year later to Red through Bo Gong, that I'd pay the ransom, but Red never contacted me until he did it for you. I always regretted not helping Red back when King was just a boy." He frowns.

Now I know why he locks himself in the office all day. He has held this inside for more than twelve years.

"After Moli's funeral, I was too ashamed to visit her family. I never spoke to Kai about Red or his mother's family. My parents blamed my disobedience, and soon I believed it too. My poor son would never have his mother again. My sweet angel, gone. All I had left was my career and my son. I vowed to protect him from the pain I suffered. But he is too much like Moli. Too much like Red."

He pauses. "When I met you, it scared me. Red was in you. If you got too close, you'd hurt us. You'd hurt Kai. I realize now I have to give that up. I can't protect him anymore."

"So, what are you going to do?"

"Humble kings and kingly pawns, right?" He scratches his head. "Oh, I don't know! I'm no good at this idealistic stuff! Maybe I came for Moli. Or Kai. Or Red. I couldn't save myself from pain, but maybe I can save others. I was wrong not to forgive Red. To let him stay there. I can't change that, but I can do something now. I want to make Kai and Moli proud. For Red to live on." He lifts the pawn. "I won't back down anymore. I'll lead your J.J. Bond. I've made an offer on Asia Bank."

I blink, incredulous. Did I just hear him right?

His eyes widen and light up like a fire. A caged man has been set free. A lost man returned to his destiny. Am I looking at the man Moli and Red knew? If so, I can see why they loved him.

"Red would be proud. I am too." A single tear rolls down my cheek.

He grunts and looks away, embarrassed at our emotional moment. I blink back my tears and get down to business.

"You're sure you want to invest in just a *theory*?"

"I read over your plan again. Discussed it with Kai, too."

Before he goes any further, I stop him. "I need to tell you something. About my gift."

Chan pales as I explain how it worked and now how it's gone. I picture him standing up, walking out, and denying we ever had this conversation. But he doesn't. Instead, he pensively rubs at the stubble on his chin.

"What's the damage?"

"None yet. All we needed was you. I've already implemented the J.J. Bond. Now, we test it. Potentially, you'll be the most powerful man in China for the next century. It's worth the risk, huh?"

"This old pawn is in for the long haul," he says. "Do you think we stand a chance?"

He extends his hand. Chan and me. A team, as it was meant to be. We shake on it.

"The odds," I say, "have just gotten better."

FORTY
PRESENT: PHOENIX
∞

FRENCH CONCESSION, SHANGHAI, CHINA

Chan's story is fresh in my head. I'm pulsing with energy. I rule out sleep—I don't want the details to fade just yet, or for my mind to drift towards Celia, or losing my gift. I'm feeling brave. So, I take a step I wasn't willing to before. Swimming.

I change into my bathing suit and slip into my robe. I take my phone in case Kai calls and meander out to the pool. It's a warm night. The pool is ready to go. I slip into the room, recalling my first night here. The same steamy, sticky feeling drenches me as I drink in the scent of flowers. I chuckle at how I thought Kai was the pool boy.

I take off my robe and stare at the water. I don't want this to be a big deal, to waste time reliving all the reasons I steered clear of water. So instead of a ceremony, I jump straight in.

The water is warm and smooth. It's my first time

swimming without numbers. It's freeing. If there's any place I can forget about my gift, it's here under the surface.

I dive until my belly and fingertips inch across the bottom of the pool. I push up and breach the surface. I float on my back, spin around like a dolphin, and I swim, swim, swim.

My ocean.

Why did it take me so long? How could I forget how much I love water? I'll never let Madame or King or Lev take this from me ever again.

That's it. I crawl stroke over to the edge as fast as I can. I push up with my arms.

Without numbers I know exactly how to get Madame. Why didn't I think about this earlier?

My body drips water over everything as I frantically reach for my phone. I hope Kai is still with Agent Bai.

He answers on the first ring. "Kai? I know how to find Madame."

He puts me on speakerphone. Agent Bai shouts in the background. "Well?"

The three syllables on the tip of my tongue taste bitter and rotten. I'm eager to spit them out. "Lev D'Ambre."

A text message buzzes me awake. It takes me a minute to pull away from dreams of chess, Red and Chan, laughter, and the occasional flash of Lev.

My hand flaps over to the bedside table, grasping for my phone. Once it's in my hand, I squint, working hard to peel back my weary, chlorinated eyes. Maybe swimming until two am wasn't such a good idea.

The message is from Kai: *They found Lev. Meet outside in 20?*

I respond, then throw on a mauve dress, black flats, and sunglasses. Outside, Kai waits in his car.

"Morning." I lean over to kiss his cheek.

"Nice dress." His face is pale. Probably just tired. He pulls into traffic.

"So, I, um—" Kai tries three times to tell me something on the way but gives up and changes the subject. "Your gift return?"

I shake my head.

He inhales and exhales, controlled. There's definitely something on his mind.

"Why are you acting so strangely?" I ask. "Is this because of your dad?"

"I need to tell you something," he says. "But you have a lot on your plate right now. After Lev, okay?"

I shrug. "OK."

Kai's jaw muscles tighten. Is this about my gift? Celia? Rafael?

At the PGF office, we sit with Detective Hansen and Agent Bai in front of a one-way window. A man sits inside. Lev D'Ambre.

I grip down on Kai's hand. "Where did you find him?"

"Right where you told us he'd be. Golden Angel Hotel."

I stare in at Lev. He slides a hand over his perfect hair. The creep is always betraying Celia. My stomach feels tight and nauseous. A flash of fear draws me back to that day. I quiver, and Kai pulls me closer. "It's okay," he whispers twice in my ear. "I won't let anyone touch you again."

I settle down. "What's your plan?" I say to Detective Hansen.

"Madame has completely gone off the map," he says. "To find her, we need to get her back online. As you suggested, we'll entice her with a video clip or a message from Lev. If she watches for approximately 40 seconds, we can pinpoint her location."

The recording begins. His confession is cold and factual. Lev does not need persuading to expose all of Madame's deeds in order to save himself. He's scared. Anyone who knows Madame should be. He bargains to tell everything for a deal, especially for protection. It proves he never felt an ounce of true affection for Celia. Now, in a way, he's free.

Lev pleads innocence. He claims he is Celia's biggest victim—only involved through association. All he wants is to go home to Europe. I'm not sure what the police will offer him, but I can't imagine he'll get off free and clear.

"When I first met Celia in Spain, she was Silvia. That was before I knew she had seven false names..." Lev goes on for two hours, retelling how he learned about her "business", and her true character. He had tried to run, but she wouldn't let him. That was the beginning of his self-medication, cheating, and living in terror.

He gives detailed information, locations, even intimate secrets. "We have a house in Oro, Spain," he says. "It's a small chalet in the middle of nowhere, paid in full under my name, but with Celia's money. It has necessary supplies if we ever needed to run. Our plan has always been to meet there if things go wrong. Two days ago, she told me to meet her 'there'. I assume Oro is where she meant."

After this, Detective Hansen records two messages for Celia. In the first, Lev explains that he has bought the tickets but won't leave until she lets him know she's safe. If the first doesn't work, they will play the second: Lev's confession to the police. Anything to make her watch for 40 seconds.

At one point, they ask about me and tell him I'm alive. Guilt plasters his face, and he starts twitching like King.

The recording finishes.

"How are you doing with all of this?" Kai asks me. I shrug. "I just hope this works."

"Will you stay here, with them?" he asks. "If she takes the bait, you'll get to see her reaction via satellite."

My mind drifts off. At first, I wanted to see the look on her face when she learned Lev has been with other women. But after thinking about it, I decide I don't. Betrayal hurts. Even now, the stab of my own betrayal from Mara twists in my stomach. Madame is wicked, but the pain of betrayal is so deep, so damaging, I don't care who it is, I can't bear to watch it on anyone's face, even if they deserve it.

What digs at me most is that she believed Lev truly loved her. This will be her final breaking point. Their relationship was always doomed to destruction, just like anything built on a lie. But according to Red, after lies are rooted out, new life can sprout. Maybe it's a good thing.

Finally, I stand up, grab my purse. "No. I won't stay. I don't ever want to see her face again."

After spending all morning at PGF, a taxi drops me off at China Generation so I can focus on the J.J. Bond for the afternoon. When I enter the office, Chan is talking to Phillip but waves at me. I smile and walk to my office. Other employees greet me, too. Warmth rises in me from that unnoticeable blessing called *normalcy*.

I don't feel completely at ease. Losing my gift has been heavy and Madame on the loose makes me nervous, but back in my office I notice how lighthearted and hopeful I am, how comfortable I feel here.

At six in the evening a driver takes me to the cottage. The same lighthearted feeling stirs as I head through the gate and into my house. The sun is setting through my living room windows, bathing the art on the walls with golden light. The colors are magnified. I even have a skip in my step as I head to the kitchen for a cup of tea. As I walk over the marble floors, I pause to examine everything around me.

For the past several months, this house in the Shanghai French Concession has been my *home*. Though I don't really spend much time here, it has made me feel safe and comfortable. Good memories are planted here.

On the dining room table are more flowers from Kai in full bloom. Next to them are financial reports for his father and finally the keys to the factory on High Street—Kai, work, girls. Those three things have regulated my life since my last "death". They brought purpose back into my life. It hits me that things haven't been so bad lately, like fate is finally smiling on me.

Kai should be here soon to eat dinner and help me work. The interviews from abroad for the J.J. Bond have started and we have a lot to do now that

Chan's on board.

There's a knock on the door.

"Come in."

Kai walks in holding a box from our favorite Beijing duck restaurant. He sets it down and comes over to me. I'm about to reach up and kiss him when I notice he's frowning. My stomach knots up. He had wanted to tell me something.

"What is it?"

He holds out a piece of paper. "A police report. Read it."

"Did they find her?"

"No. But—"

"I don't want to read anything right now." I sigh. "You and the others are taking care of Madame. The Pratt is gone. I have to focus on the J.J. Bond. Can it wait until tomorrow?" I grab the box, breathe in. "Yum. I'm hungry."

"It's not about Madame." He takes the box from me. "You'll want to read this."

"Why?"

Kai won't back down. "Read it."

I sigh my submission, take up the paper, and read the headline out loud, "*Benjamin Jones Survives Boating Accident.*"

"Who's Benjamin Jones?"

"He's the man who supposedly died in the Seattle Sea-Fair boating accident two years ago along with his two brothers," he says, his face straight, waiting for me to react. "The boat that crashed didn't belong to Jeff Rivers."

Did all oxygen just get sucked out of the room?

"Is this a joke?"

"I did some investigating on my own. Jeffery Joseph Rivers is not dead."

"Kai. Stop. I saw the article. My family is dead. Madame planned their death. And she carried through."

"Did you actually read that article?"

My brain races backwards, not through numbers but *memories*. That day, Madame had just learned about Lev and the swimming pool incident. She was steaming with anger, holding a crushed piece of newspaper in hand, about to throw me to King. I glimpsed only the headline—*Family of Three dies in Fatal Boating Accident*—but I didn't actually read it. My mouth dries up.

"The article she showed you was real. There was an accident, but it was a family of three brothers. It wasn't *your* family. She used it against you. Your father lives. *Your family* lives."

"Impossible." Questions, emotions rip through me. *Pure gold doesn't fear...*

"I've looked, too. There's no sign of their business in Seattle. The house is gone. There's no address for them. Not even a bill in their name for the last two years."

"I followed the same trail you did, and..." He takes my hand. "I want you to be very calm as I say this. After your death they moved...to China."

My knees give out. All the screams I've ever heard now ring in my ears like a rock concert. Dizziness sets in. I'm going to pass out. Kai takes hold of me.

"Where?" I remind myself to breathe.

"Not sure yet, but we're going to find them. We're going to get you home."

FORTY-ONE
PRESENT: PHOENIX

∞

FRENCH CONCESSION, SHANGHAI, CHINA

Home. Family. The words fall off my lips in a whisper, like I'm not permitted to say them out loud. Like if I do, that girl of fifteen, curled in a corner, crying for *home* in her sleep will come back.

So...I'll see my family again and then what? What would I say to them? How can we ever go back to normal?

I kick the couch and throw my purse on the floor. If only we were visiting the Sang brothers, I'd take my feelings out on the burlap punching bags.

"Stupid!" I scold myself. That day with Madame, there was a chance she was lying about my family. I always knew that—she lied to everyone—but I saw the headline and heard her tell me. I was scared to die and a complete fool to believe her.

Why now? I don't know what to feel. Seeing them again was never a possibility.

My hands hold my head. Kai is silent, but his hand rubs the center of my back. I've just gotten used to living here. To being without them. To starting over.

Why couldn't the news have been delivered slowly, like drips from an IV needle instead of a harsh injection? Why on the same week do I have to lose my gift and watch Madame escape? And now this?

I'm used to pain like this, I remind myself—immediate and sharp, like ripping a splinter out of a wound. I can bounce back. The fire only makes me stronger, right?

I look up. Kai's confused. He doesn't understand what I'm feeling. He thinks I should be happy. Am I? No answer surfaces. I should be preparing for our week, but I can't wrap my mind around seeing my family alive or going home. What if I do go home? What about Kai? Do I just leave him?

All over again, another kind of death knocks on my door. Death to my expectations, ideas, and plans. Once again, I must modify and adapt. It's the kind of death Red talked about.

"Seeds only bloom into a new plant after they've died," he'd say, "you've *died* twice. You get to bloom more often than the rest of us." He knew, like I did, that we all face these things, as we enter new seasons. Red would say losing my gift is a seed that will blossom into something new.

There I go thinking about my gift again. Or lack thereof.

What will my dad think about that?

I'm still good at math, but I can't see the numbers any more clearly than the next guy. My father will be disappointed for sure, but Mara? Elated. And Lily, who knows? Does she even think about me anymore?

The clock ticking is the only sound in the room. "It's getting late," I say. "We have work to do. Chan will meet with more Asia Bank managers tomorrow. People will be lined up at China Generation's door. Don't forget our meeting with Officer Bai about Celia tomorrow."

I tear open the box of take-out. Grab chopsticks. "Let's eat."

We don't mention my family for the rest of the night.

Interviews last all morning. At lunch Kai does all the talking, about everything, except my family. I refuse to bring up the subject.

He tells me that the Pratt inmates are willing to testify and Rafael agreed to testify after Interpol gave his father a plea-deal.

"What about Yu Tai?" I ask.

"His family sold the Pratt to the government for a huge sum and are moving to Hong Kong." Finally, Kai puts a hand on my shoulder. I know what's coming. "No luck with finding your family yet," he says. "I'm looking everywhere, but China's a big—"

"Country?" I interrupt. "3.705 million square miles. Yeah, I know."

He takes the hint that I'm not ready to talk about it. We head back to the office. We work until after dinner when we get a call from Detective Hansen.

"Get here quick. The video worked."

We drop everything and race out the door.

As soon as I see Agent's Bai's face I blurt out,

"Where is she?"

"At Pudong Airport."

"Quick!" I say, an idea rising. "Give me a list of all the airlines leaving Shanghai tonight. I know what to look for."

A search is done. They give me a list. I know Madame better than anyone. My brain may not be "calculating" but I feel neurons firing, connecting to different parts of my brain, not like a prodigy but like any person figuring out a new game. There are eight airlines with gold in their names like *Golden Japanese Airlines. Golden Lotus.*

With Agent Bai and Detective Hansen, a list of all the passengers is made available. She's tricky. She's bought tickets on eighty-eight flights all with and without gold in their names. On the eight airlines with gold in their names we identify seven of Celia's pseudonyms. Celia Marsovich to Miami. Dora Sanchez headed to Barcelona. Silvia to Venezuela. Maxima Moreau headed to Johannesburg, South Africa.

One catches my eye. Maryam Maatar on the Golden Myanmar flight to Brisbane, Australia. *Madame doesn't do business in Australia,* King had said. That number I saw in her files long ago. Brisbane's not connected to anything gold, is it? Yet my gut is churning. Red would tell me to trust that, even if it doesn't make sense.

"She's going to Australia," I say. Kai, Rafael, and Agent Bai look at me with wide eyes.

"Australia?" Agent Bai looks doubtful. "With her real name? What does she think we are, fools? No evidence points to that. Lev said Spain. And this morning she made a call to Venezuela."

"Yeah, I know. But using her real name is like hiding out in the open. She's done it before." I remember her permutation locks on the keypad on my door in the Golden Angel Hotel. "Besides, there are only seven fake passports and eight real choices. The eighth is her real name. She won't go anywhere else. She's too smart."

"Why Brisbane?"

"I don't know, but she knows Lev confessed, that we're on her trail. What if she kept her real passport hidden from Lev. She's leading us on a goose chase."

"Celia's desperate," Detective Hansen says. "Desperate people don't think clearly. They always go where they have help. It's probable that in Spain she has more passports, money, and an escape plan. Like Lev said. Besides, you and King said she never works in Australia."

"Exactly. It's a place we don't expect."

"King described her as obsessive and maniacal. She avoids Australia for a reason. Using her real name is a ploy to throw us off in a direction she'd never go. Lunatics don't suddenly embrace their fears. Now, we have eighty-eight flights with all her names to choose from, and seven viable options. We have bank transfers, calls, and leads for Spain and Venezuela," Agent Bai argues. "We only have two teams available to move into those locations immediately."

"Sorry, Phoenix," Detective Hansen says, "The other teams can't be redirected that quickly, especially without solid proof. We have to stick with the most likely leads on this one."

"A year ago, there was a number written in her notes with an area code for Australia. That's something," I blurt out.

"Are you referring to the nursing home again?" Agent Bai asks.

"Yes."

"We have checked it out. There's nothing there. No gold names in Brisbane. She's called tons of other cities in the last year but Australia only once."

"But –" My stomach tightens even more. Even without numbers I sense something is wrong. "I know her. She's going to Australia."

"Look, Phoenix, you've been a huge help. But Australia's too far of a stretch. All the evidence points to Spain or Venezuela."

"All right." There's nothing I can do to convince them, so I let it go. But that number in Australia haunts me.

Agent Bai calls in the directions to his team.

I excuse myself, telling Kai I'll meet him later.

I check the clock. The time difference is six hours between China and Australia. The sun just came up. Before I think twice, I taxi over to my office, dig up that number, and pick up the phone.

"Summer Centers. How can I help you?"

"Can I talk to one of the nurses there?"

"Actually, ma'am, there are no nurses here. Brisbane is the main office. We handle the finances and registry. To talk to one of the nurses you have to call directly to our facilities on the Gold Coast. Can I give you the number?"

"Gold Coast?" I choke.

"Yes, ma'am," she says. "Want the number?"

"No, thanks." I hang up.

Gold Coast. The eighth location. The eighth name.

If Interpol won't stop her, I guess I'll have to do it myself.

But how? I don't know anyone in Australia.

*Oh wait...*I do.

I rummage through Chan's accounting files as I did the very first day and locate the random wire transfer.

A man answers. Bad Australian accent, smoky voice.

"Bob Lee?" I say. "It's Double-Eight. How'd you like to be on the good guys' side? I need your help to take down a queen."

FORTY-TWO
PRESENT: PHOENIX

SHANGHAI TOWER, SHANGHAI, CHINA

The next day is painful as I wait for news. Thankfully, I'm busy. People from all over China are standing outside our gate, hoping to have a chance to be enrolled in our bond and loan program.

The secretary comes into my office and sets the book of appointments on the desk. "There is another construction company online asking for an appointment for an interview. Foreign owned. Their file is on top."

"We've filled the quota for construction already. Tell them we're sorry and to try World Bank."

"Yes, ma'am."

I pull the pile of applications towards me, ready to discard the construction file, when the name leaps off the page. I nearly tear the paper as I pull it up to my eyes.

It can't be.

My hands fumble as I reach for the phone. They're

shaking so strongly I can barely grab the line and punch *lobby*.

"Secretary Lin?" I gasp into the line. "Get that construction company back on the line and inform Ms. Mara Rivers that I can see her tonight."

I slam the phone down before I change my mind. My shaking fingers manage to dial Kai's number.

After I listen to him explain that Interpol raided Venezuela with no success and are waiting for news from Oro, Spain, I tell him about Mara.

"Phoenix, I'll leave now if you need me," he says, concerned.

"No, it's okay."

"What are you going to do?" he asks.

"I don't know yet."

"Be strong," he says. "No coincidence. You'll have the right words. I'll wait with PGF until they have news, but I'll come directly afterwards. Okay?"

"Okay."

Ms. Mara Rivers arrives at five o'clock as requested, but I delay our meeting until seven, forcing her to wait awkwardly in the executive cafeteria. My personal secretary serves her dinner, assuring that nothing is wrong only that I'm a very busy woman.

After sunset, they escort her to the boardroom. I want it poorly lit when I meet her. An interpreter arrives promptly, as usual for all my meetings.

My hair is down, dark-chocolate and straight. I touch up my make up with darker shades and lines than usual, and even wear a dark pair of glasses. The tall heels and a long dress hide my frame. By the time I look in the mirror, even I don't recognize myself.

I don't have a plan, or calculations to help me.

I let her go, buried her in peace back in the Pratt. Did she do the same? Did she bury me? But now we're raised from the dead. And in this life, her fate is in my hands.

As I walk in, the office secretary announces, "Ms. Phoenix, ma'am." The room has a soft glow from a standing lamp. Da Li, my interpreter, follows me and translates everything from Chinese to English.

"How do you do?" Mara stands to greet me. I nearly lose my balance as I take her in. A perfectly delicate woman stands before me with a striking resemblance to my mother, only years younger and less joy in her gaze. "I'm Ms. Rivers." She extends a hand.

My Phoenix persona immediately takes over. I bow my head at her and acknowledge her hand but walk towards my desk without grabbing it.

"Please sit." The interpreter translates. Mara takes her place on the leather couch across from me. Her hands fold nervously in front of her. The interpreter sits beside her.

"Thank you," she says. There's no sign she recognizes me but her eyes flick to every part of my face. If I'm not mistaken, she shivers a bit and rubs her arms. "We are very thankful you granted us a meeting so quickly. I understand applications are backed up. They're calling it the *miracle bond*. How can China Generation have the assets and generosity for this?"

I tilt my head into the shadow. Mara's voice is sweet. Is she flattering me, or has she softened? I can't tell because I'm not listening very attentively. I'm watching her eyes. Watching for something—truth, lies, justice, repentance, anything. Whatever it is, I need to see it before I take any action. The equations I crave never arrive.

"It's our destiny, perhaps." I reply in a low voice.

"My proposal." Mara offers another file.

But I don't pick it up. I have read it twice. No, three times. But I'm not interested in her application. I'm interested in her family. *My family.*

"Yes," I say flatly, staring. She squirms. My eyes have not shifted. It's making her nervous.

She leans over to the interpreter and whispers, "Please don't translate this, but if I'm making any cultural mistakes, please let me know." The interpreter assures her nothing is wrong.

"In your own words, tell me your current situation," I say. "Then I'll need to ask you some very personal questions. It's all part of the program."

Mara nods. "We moved to China about two years ago. At first, we did quite well, but now we've exhausted our resources, and our projects are on hold. As you know, construction is one of the industries that halts completely during recessions. Your bond assures we remain part owners until we are able to pay you back."

After my phone call with Kai, I devoured all the information on the company they started that I could find. Dad had bought land in China years ago. It hadn't occurred to me that he would try construction with Mr. Bao, his old partner. Xi He Construction did well the first year, however, according to Phillip, they'll lose everything by the end of this year because of debt. This does not interest me.

"You refer to 'we' but you're not the head of the company."

"My father, Jeff Rivers, is the CEO."

He is alive.

Electric shock. Stabbing. Tingling all over my body. My eyes close at the sound of his name. It rushes over me like the wind. I'm the one rubbing my arms now.

"Why is he not here with you today?" I ask, sharply.

"He is sick, ma'am."

"What kind of sick?" The concern on my face and in my voice must show because Mara perks up. Her back straightens.

"He has not been well for more than a year, almost two. Doctors cannot account for it."

Did she just say almost two years? That's about when I was taken...

"What other family members do you have?"

"Excuse me?" Mara holds the papers for the bond application. "I have filled out the application entirely."

"We have this interview for such questions," I lie. "We need lots of information to verify truth. With the crash all kinds of scams are coming in."

"Of course," she says, reluctantly. "I have a younger sister."

"No one else in your family?"

"No, ma'am," she replies to the interpreter.

"I do not mean to pry, but I need to know of any other deceased members. You see, it will turn up on our search after the application is approved, if you do not verify it, I'm afraid there may be an automatic refusal of the bond."

Mara pales. A frown appears on her lips. Perhaps the subject stings? I don't care. I need to hear her say it; to see the look on her face.

I also need to remember to speak Chinese. English is on the tip of my tongue, like a flood pushing against the dam. If I am not careful, the dam will break, and I'll yell at her like when we were kids.

Mara fiddles with her pen, slowly forming words. Her brow tightens, and she swallows hard. "My mother died in a car crash," she says, "and my other sister… died as well."

"Your deceased sister, what was her name?" Will there be remorse? Has she carried pain as heavy as mine? My face is hot, yet the cold of the Pratt seeps into me, Madame's darkness fills my eyes. It's all I can do not to shout, pour out my suffering, show her the marks on my body.

"Her name was Josephine." It's a whisper, barely audible.

"Excuse me?" I need to hear her say it. I lost everything when I was taken, even my name. I want it back. The sound of my own name haunted me for two years, mocking me of the life I lost. Perhaps hearing her say it will satisfy my desire for justice and my nightmares will stop.

"Josephine," she says louder.

My name on her lips has an opposite effect. Instead of feelings of justice, a deep chord is struck. Floods of childhood memories erupt of two little girls playing dolls, eating pizza, opening Christmas presents. I have to look away.

"How did she die?" I choke out, face down at the files on my desk.

"Sorry, Ms. Phoenix, we don't know. She disappeared."

"Disappeared? But you said she is dead."

"We assume so. She was abducted. Unfortunately, her body was never found." Mara looks sick. Or guilty? Sad?

"So, she could be alive? Wouldn't that be a miracle."

"A miracle that just may make my father's heart stop. He all but died when he lost her," Mara says.

"He—uh," I say in English but catch myself and speak in Chinese. I scoot to the edge of my chair. "What else happened to him?"

"After my sister's abduction, he suffered severe PTSD and months later was hospitalized for a while. Last year, he developed a type of muscle deterioration."

"I see." A lump lodges in my throat. *Dad.* Are those tears forming in my eyes too? I blink them away. *Get through the interview Phoenix.* "What about your other sister?" I ask.

"I'm sorry. Is this necessary for the interview?"

"Forgive me. We need a lot of details. Each company is evaluated by their history." I stop and swallow hard. The amount of effort it takes to resist prying every single detail I want is sky high. "Well, just tell me about her, so I can fill in the details. What does she do? Can she play any instruments?"

"Uh, um...yes. She can play piano." There's confusion on Mara's face. My questions throw her for a loop. She's wondering how this is relevant. What she doesn't understand is that to me Lily was dead not long ago and now she's alive. Living. Breathing. Materializing before me as she speaks. "Please just tell me what I can do for the loan."

"Yes, Ms. Rivers," I reply. My interpreter is also a

bit confused. He has sat in on other meetings and nothing of this sort has occurred. "One last question—" It's over the top but I can't help myself— "Have you ever been involved in criminal activity?"

Anger rises in my cheeks. She's the girl who dropped me off at the pier. Who handed details to Madame. Can the forgiveness I gave to her in the Pratt last?

"Last question"—it's over the top but I can't help myself—"Have you ever been involved in criminal activity?"

Mara cocks her head.

My eyes drill into her. The questions I long to ask her but can't twist like a tornado inside me—*Have you ever been an accomplice of sorts? Ever been bribed? Received illegal money? Tortured? Starved? Held against your will?*

I have, I want to tell her.

She's nervous, scooting away from me deeper into the sofa.

"No," she says. "I have never been convicted of a crime, if that is what you are asking."

Liar.

She's trembling now. I am too. The interpreter looks from me to her, eyes wide. My heart thumps wildly. Fire spreads to every limb because she is lying. We would not be in this meeting if she were telling the truth.

"Let me explain something. We are very thorough at China Generation. I see the need to assess your case a bit more. You will need to bring the whole family in for interviews. If this is possible, I'll approve the bond for the first year. You have three days."

Mara jumps to her feet. She thanks me quietly and leaves the room. When the doors closes behind her and the interpreter, I crumble onto the floor, tears spilling onto the ground. I rock there, my head on my knees.

I am a phoenix, flying.

I won't let go of my sanity now. I just regained it.

I have risen from the ashes.

My family will come here in three days.

I will not crash but soar.

I stand. My body obeys the command, but numbness overtakes me. My hands reach for the phone. I dial the secretary.

"Yes?"

"Tell Ms. Rivers they have to be here by Thursday or no bond," I say without emotion. "And Lin? Deposit a hundred grand into their accounts and pay for their transportation."

"Yes, ma'am."

I move my chair next to the window. The Shanghai skyline is lit up. I can't count the lights like I used to be able to do, so I lose myself in them as I would in a campfire.

After only five minutes Secretary Lin rings again. "Sorry to disturb you again. It's the police."

"Put them through," I sigh, tired but ready for this to be over.

"Phoenix? Agent Bai, here," his low voice says. "We've got her."

"Spain, then?"

"No." There's a brief pause. "Australia. Bob Lee— apparently a friend of yours—contacted us after we arrived in Venezuela. He is one heck of an ox. Last night, he was able to hold her even in her state of rage until the Australian authorities arrived. We could use a guy like that on the inside."

They got her. Bo Gong. I knew he could do it. For a moment I forget Mara and celebration appears on my face.

"Hate to admit it, but you were right. Thanks, Phoenix."

"Where is she now?" I ask.

"On her way back to China, to prison."

I breathe a deep sigh of relief. Everything is done. Closed. I can put her behind me now.

I thank Agent Bai. I'm about to hang up when he stops me.

"Phoenix?" He hesitates like what he is going to say next is difficult. "One last thing."

"Yes?" Whatever he has to say can't be any more emotional than what I have already experienced meeting Mara. I can handle it. "Go ahead."

"Celia has only one request before her trial."

As he speaks, I realize I'm wrong. Very, very, wrong. I don't think I can handle this.

"Her request," he says, "is to see you."

FORTY-THREE
PRESENT: PHOENIX

HONGKOU CORRECTIONAL DISTRICT, SHANGHAI, CHINA

The next night my dreams are invaded by Celia Marso-vich's icy eyes and red lips. To deny the last request of a person is a big deal. I don't know what will happen to her and I couldn't care less—but there's more to it than that—she has something I want. Numbers can't advise me. My heart deceives me and the battle rages on. I toss, turn, sweat, scream. I battle. I analyze.

Why did she choose me? Why did she let me go? These are questions only she can answer.

By morning I make a decision—to face her one last time. If I get my answers, perhaps I can bury her forever.

When Kai and I arrive at the prison, the policeman holds out a report to me. "Take it. You'll want to read it." The woman in the picture—Celia—looks years older. Pale, freckled, no makeup, strung-out hair, a frightening creature to behold.

"Celia's connection to the Australian nursing home was a woman, a mother figure, who at one point cared for her, who knows nothing of her crimes. She was in stage-five dementia when Celia transported her to Australia. Since then, hands off Australia."

Another officer comes out from behind a thick metal door. "It's time." I shove the report in my pocket for later.

I find Kai's hand and squeeze. He takes hold of my shoulder. "I can come with you."

"No. I have to face her alone."

My feet drag down another hallway. The empty corridors are eerily quiet, only silent questions seems to echo and bounce off the walls. She knew I'd be at the Expo. She wanted me to escape with her. What will she want this time?

My heart quickens.

I am safe. She can't hurt me anymore. This time I took everything from her—her life, money, Lev, *her crimes.* She has nothing left except pain.

If I could take that away too, would I?

The thought strikes me hard. It's a "Red" question. It leaves me breathless and squirming. Do I want to see her die?

No.

I don't want to see any more death.

As I make my way through the final hallway, I silently pray I'll see remorse in her. Change is possible. Perhaps with a second chance Celia can change too.

At the end of the hall, there's a large white door with a sign that says, *Maximum Security: Solitary*

Confinement. The officer escorts me in. Even though Celia has been here for several days, the faintest trace of her perfume wafts in the air.

There's a plastic stool, the kind a child would use, beside her cell. I sit. At first, she doesn't notice me. I watch her pick at her nails. Her face is deathly pale. Her hair is tangled into a red knot on her head pulled back so tight that her skin stretches in an unnatural way. Without makeup, wrinkles and freckles show on her face like never before. How old is she really? Her cheeks are wet—from crying? That would be a stretch.

The guard rings the bell beside her door. In long slow movements, she looks up at me. "Octavia?" she stutters, her eyes, black and watery. "I knew you'd come."

Celia crawls up to the bars, gripping them like a caged beast. She looks childlike. Not like the powerful woman I knew, draped in gold and jewels, the snap of her fingers holding so much power. But then again, she doesn't look frightened either. Her words tickle my ears, *if they catch me today...*

"Come here," she says, touching the glass with her hand, "I want to be sure I'm not hallucinating."

Logic can't explain why I touch her hand on the glass. Even though there is glass separating us, I can tell her hand is ice cold. I recoil before she can do anything else.

"Why me, Celia? Why did you choose me? When all those other girls..." A thick lump blocks my throat. I don't have the heart to say the rest. "Why did you let me go at the Expo?"

She traces, what looks like numbers, in the air

with her finger. I don't know how long I wait before she speaks.

"You are *me.*" She peers up through the bars. "You have my gift, the one that was stolen from me."

Is she saying what I think she is? My eyes widen as it dawns on me. It's as if I've known it all along—Celia had something that matched me, equaled me. All her obsession, her hatred, her genius, was always there.

"Yes, Octavia. You can see it now. I was a prodigy, just like you." Her eyes light up. "But unlike you, my opportunities were scarce. When I was nine, I was orphaned. No one cared about me or my gift. No one cared that numbers invaded my world. I survived by my gift alone for two years before a neighbor took me in. A woman who was kind and gentle, unlike her abusive husband...Men are dangerous, Octavia. That's when I realized I needed to use my gift to be faster, wiser. But the man was stronger. My gift waned with every time he touched me. By the time I was 17, I outsmarted him. I learned how to escape danger, to make money, to take revenge. I learned how to be great. Thinking about getting my numbers back was the only thing that kept me sane. Wickedness, goodness, meant nothing."

The energy shifts in the room. "I despised everything and everyone...until you. I recognized it immediately. Your gift. What you were doing in your father's company. *You had my numbers.* But you were pure. At first, I wanted to end you, but I couldn't. It would be like ending my own life. I vowed to protect you – so that nothing bad would ever happen to you. No one would ever hurt you the way they hurt me. I chose you, Octavia. You would inherit my empire.

You'd be my one success."

Celia smiles. I can't be sure if what I'm looking at is kindness or pure insanity. Does she not grasp that her twisted idea of protecting me was ripping me away from my family?

"We are the same, Octavia. Can't you see it? I let you into my home, to give you everything. I loved you the way I was never loved." She twitches like an earthquake victim reliving the moment the walls began to tumble. "When I sent you to King's, it was the first time in years I felt *regret, guilt.* I hurt the one thing I promised to save. Your blood was on my hands. After you 'died' you were everywhere. In the computer, in the streets, in my dreams. I died a little more each day, but then light sparked again. You were alive. The Expo was my last chance. If I let you live, I'd live too."

Even as she is speaking, I can't believe my ears. I have become really good at detecting lies, and nothing rings false. She's a victim, like me. She suffered for years. She's like a knot, twisted and pulled tight, suffocating, but somewhere in that mess, goodness is fighting for redemption.

"You said you'd give me what I most cared for?" I ask, even though I'm not sure I can handle much more.

"Your family is alive." She says it like it hurts.

"I figured that out already."

Her eyes are still frozen in place like it's not really her talking. "I lied about..." she picks at her short bitten back nails—"your father."

"Which part?" My chest beats so hard I'm afraid it'll open up right here.

"He never stopped loving you," she says. "He spent

all he had trying to find you, but I couldn't trust him, Octavia. He's a *man*." She said the word like it had a bad taste.

"My sister?"

"She knew she was doing something to you. She just didn't know what. She blamed herself, entirely. I enjoyed watching her suffer."

My heart beats fire. For almost two years I believed my father had dismissed me like loose change. That Mara hated me and never regretted what she did. It's as if a veil has been removed, the clouds swept away. What was so foggy before is coming into focus.

Our time is almost up, and my emotions are a hot mess.

Celia blinks. Her eyes are wild again. "Do you still have your gift?"

"Not really," I answer.

"Who was it? When I get out, I swear I'll—" she growls, suddenly defensive.

"Nothing like that. It just left." For the first time since losing my gift, I don't feel hollow, but warmth stirs in my chest. Of all the people with whom I could share my thoughts, I do it now with Madame.

"It's strange not seeing numbers everywhere," I start. "I realize now, though, I don't need them. They taught me what's in my heart. I know my own limits. I know who I am. I see the risks and I'm not afraid to take them anymore. I don't need to be a prodigy to be great. And I never needed to be a prodigy to make the right choice."

Weight lifts off my chest. "That goes for you too. Our gifts change, but we never really lose them. You were born with a gift and you became powerful even after you lost it. When you were Madame, you chose to use your gift for evil instead of good. But you've been given a second chance, Maryam. You can choose to change. That little girl can come back."

Red believed anyone could change if they wanted to. Right now, in this moment, I believe it too.

"Maryam has been dead for so long," she says. "Celia has taken over. Madame controls them both."

"No. I don't believe it," I say pointedly. "Maryam has a chance. Like Josephine does." The next words escape my mouth, surprising even myself. "I can testify in court that you're remorseful, that you want to change. It may help your sentence."

"You would do that for me?" she says, a hint of the girl comes out.

"I will."

For a moment, her eyes glisten. That glimmer I used to see is there—a little girl, longing to be cradled, loved, and redeemed. My heart breaks into a hundred pieces. Without much thought I hold out my hand to the window again. The little girl smiles.

As I watch my own fingers, I can't believe it. My captor, the root of my suffering, the woman who scarred me forever. How can I extend a hand to her? How can I forgive her? But I am. I can. I choose to.

Just when I think Maryam will touch my hand, the little girl in her eyes slips away. A woman, mature and hard-hearted, snaps up and groans. She refuses my hand. Her eyes become cold. This woman doesn't listen to reason.

"I didn't ask you to save me," she snaps. "I have

plenty of people for that, Octavia. You can go now."

The guard arrives. The moment for truth passes. Her one act of kindness, done.

"Maryam, wait—"

"No. I've let you live. But you will never be rid of me, Octavia. We will always be connected. We'll find each other again."

"You have the strength in you to change," I say in vain, but she is already yelling at the guard to get rid of me.

I walk away, dizzily.

Before we reach the last hall, I ask the officer for a moment. I sink into a cold metal chair and pull out the report the policeman gave me about Maryam. Inside there's an article about Celia as a young prodigy winning an award in Istanbul. When I look at it chills ripple over me. The girl in the picture could have been me. A big smile on her face, bright eyes hoping for the future ahead. I stop—*it is me. I was taken, too.* Because of her.

"Maryam Mataar," it reads, "Gifted child who was orphaned, abused, and trafficked from the age of 9. At 17 she killed her captor. Lived in Europe for several years before moving to the United States and nine other countries. Speaks nine languages and has trafficked girls for nearly 29 years."

I stare at the white wall. Terrible images of Celia as a small girl, helpless and abused, tear at my mind. That pained expression she had learned to hide. That sorrow embedded deep within her. Her twisted idea to protect me. Her awkward attempt at loving me. I can't hold back the urge to cry.

Finally, I stand, and leave silently, full of mixed emotions. I hope she'll make the choice to change. And somehow, even though the odds are slim, I hope there is a Red down there in that prison, ready to do for her what he did for me.

FORTY-FOUR
PRESENT: PHOENIX

FRENCH CONCESSION, SHANGHAI, CHINA

Celia's and King's money have finally been funneled into the J.J. Bond system. Chan's purchase of Asia Bank was successful, and the final installment of the blanket amount was set in place last night. Now starts the real test. Will the bond work?

Theoretically, there will be dips and losses, but nothing too uncontrollable will happen. Life should go on, mostly as usual. Countries will not divide. Wars will not come. At least, the numbers say they won't.

Since Yu Tai sold the Pratt, the tunnels have been crawling with scientists, historians, archeologists, and journalists. The Pratt is on every TV in China and abroad. Prisoners share their stories and the police are solving crimes from years past. They are even thinking of making a film about it.

New doors have opened for Kai throughout this process. Interpol was so impressed with his help and planning that they offered him an internship next year. He's ecstatic.

There's only one thing left to do: meet my family, who arrive tomorrow.

Tonight, I'll have dinner with Kai at his father's house. But first, I need to finish getting ready.

I stand in front of a mirror. I wear a black cocktail dress, short and straight. My make-up is light, but noticeable. My hair drapes down in front, covering my chest like always.

The hairband is not around my wrist. It's in my fingers. Slowly, I pull my hair back, grabbing it all in one hand. I twist it and spin it into a small roll on top of my head, securing it with the band. My neck feels bare, exposed. I'm tempted to release my hair or put on a necklace. But I don't. Instead I'm captivated by the lines of my jaw and the definition of my ears. I'm seeing myself clearly for the first time in years. My face has become so oval, like mom's. I look older. I add an additional few bobby pins to my hair and walk out. My back is straight, and my chin is up.

Chan is laughing, staring at Dr. Ling as I step into their house. They have, not surprisingly, announced their relationship. He looks like a different person. She, too, is beaming. I'm happy for them. They wave me in. They don't notice my hair, but Kai does.

He jumps to his feet, immediately rushing over to me, whisking me around the corner.

"You look amazing. You should wear your hair up more often," he says, reaching up to touch my hair, then sliding his fingers down my ear and jaw to my chin, then neck. "Turn." He twirls his finger.

He acts like he wants to see my dress, but I know better. I obey his request and spin slowly. "You're beautiful," he says. And suddenly warm fingers trace my scar, then his lips trace it. Shivers blast down my spine. "And strong."

We take our seats and enjoy an exquisite meal. At the end, Chan raises a glass for a toast. "To theories and risks. To kings and pawns!" Our glasses clink together.

"So what are you going to do now that your gift is gone?" Kai asks, as we turn inward towards each other, ignoring the public display of affection from across the table.

"Who knows? Maybe I'll try something ridiculously hard, like writing a book or acting. We all know what the odds of success are in the arts." I give him a wink.

"Knowing your luck—uh—destiny," he says, "you'll do great."

Kai sets his chopsticks down, swallows his last bit of sparkling water, and holds out a hand to me. "Walk in the garden? I need to discuss a big decision with you. You are still a great advisor."

"Love to." We leave Dr. Ling and Chan and stroll through the garden to the patio by the pool house. The night is warm. The lights are turned on. It reminds me of the first time I saw Kai fixing the pool. We stand next to each other, admiring the garden.

I'm still getting used to my new life, my new brain. For example, I'm keenly aware that the flowers hanging over the fence are just pretty petals falling open, bursting with reds and blues and yellows, smelling of jasmine and honeysuckle and rose. They are not numbers anymore.

I haven't forgotten what I know. All the facts I've learned are still there. I still have the capacity to calculate numbers, but only one possibility at a time. And without intense work, I can't offhandedly spout off the intricacies of Newton's laws in whatever is working around me. Numbers don't invade my days or nights anymore. Star gazing doesn't give me a headache. Sunsets don't launch me into the workday in Iran or South Africa. I'm not concerned about the earth's rotations. I'm just here, in the present, where Kai is beside me. But I still feel my gift. I feel it changing. Into what, I'll have to wait and see.

Kai leans into me and kisses me lightly at first, then stronger. Finally, he pulls back, serious.

"So, what's this big decision you wanted to discuss before my family comes tomorrow?" I ask.

"A future investment. A long term one." He holds out an envelope.

Business? At this hour? I try to hide my disappointment. I thought he'd want to talk about something more personal. At least it could have waited until after meeting my family tomorrow. I bend down, pretending to smell a potted jasmine.

"Oh yeah?" I say. "What will you invest in that you haven't already?"

"You." He motions to the envelope. "Open it."

I slide my finger under the envelope and pull out what is inside. Two airplane tickets to Seattle—one with my name, the other one with his.

I don't say anything because if I do, I will cry.

"I promised I'd get you home. But you can't get rid of me that easily." He grabs my hand. "I know the odds are against us, as you pointed out earlier. We are young. Impulsive. Different. But haven't we learned that some odds can be beaten? If your family whisks you back to America, I will be forced to come after you." He pulls my chin up so we meet eye to eye. "Tell me we can beat the odds and I will never let you out of my sight."

"What about your father?"

"He almost kind of likes you now."

"He'd never agree to this relationship." Chan and I have come to terms. I'll admit that he has changed, but... "I drive him crazy. He found me in the Pratt. I broke his nose the first time I met him. I also almost singlehandedly ruined his empire."

"All true. But you compelled him to start a new life—a better one," Kai laughs. "He knows how I feel. He's given me permission."

"You asked permission?"

"Of course," he says, smiling, "I am traditional. Like father, like son."

His arms wrap around me. That feeling of warmth, safety, of *destiny* comes with it. I'm not sure when, or how it all began, but what I feel for Kai has grown into a wreath, all the different pieces woven together, creating a circle with no beginning and no end, like it was always meant to be. I cannot see the future, but one thing is clear: I don't want one without him.

I pull him closer, breathing in his familiar scent, holding him tighter than I have ever held anyone before.

"I love you, Phoenix," he whispers against my ear.

"I'm not Phoenix anymore," I say. "I'm Josephine."

FORTY-FIVE
PRESENT: PHOENIX

SHANGHAI TOWER, SHANGHAI, CHINA

There are moments in everyone's life when they stop and wonder - *how* did I get here? That moment for me is now. They call me Phoenix, but that is not my real name. I live in China, though I was not born here. I am rich and powerful, but I care nothing for expensive things. The people behind that door were supposed to be dead, but that is not true either. If truth really can set us free, then after two years, my chains will finally fall off.

Last night I had nightmares that everything in nature tried to stop our reunion. A tornado, an earthquake, a flood. All kinds of disasters that would separate me and my family forever. But I woke up alive. Nothing has happened, except a dip in the stocks. My family has touched down in Pudong and they are on their way here right now.

My hands and feet tap incessantly. I check the clock

every two seconds. I can barely hold a cup of tea in my hands without spilling it.

What will I say when I see them? How will I tell them who I am? How can I tell them about the last two years? Will they embrace me or treat me like a stranger? Will they be disgusted when they learn what I've been through? Did they enjoy not having me around? Did they miss me?

Dad's and Lily's faces bounce in my head. They won't look like I remember them. People change. If I don't look the same, how can they?

I check my hair in the mirror. Long and dark. I take out my brown-colored contacts. My eyes have darkened. They're not the ocean gray with the hint of faded beach wood they used to be, but the color of a forest after the rain. They've softened, too. Instead of seeing fire burning, purifying me, there's hope in my eyes. Hope for a new beginning.

A knock on the door sends my thoughts flying.

Kai comes up behind me. "Jo." That voice melts my fears and cradles my questions. Peace floods me. My hands stop shaking. "They're here."

I turn to face him. His high cheekbones, smooth and brown. His calming voice. I lean into his arms. He's my safe place now. He makes me stronger. Now I can go into that room without falling over.

"Do you want me to come with you?" he whispers, his lips on my ear.

"No, you've done enough," I say. He found my family. He did it all for me, for my healing. "Thank you, Kai."

His lips press down on my forehead and he drops

his arms. I walk out of my office over to the conference room.

The door in front of me is like an invisible, impenetrable brick wall. It's been closed for more than two years. First by borders, then lies, then prisons, then death. But it's open now and I'm supposed to walk through it to find what once was lost.

Impossible odds separated us. Impossible odds bring us back together. I guess the impossible isn't always what it seems.

I push open the door.

Three strangers sit at the table. My father has aged beyond his years. His hair has a lot more gray, his face tired and worn. Beside Mara sits a girl—a young lady actually, and more beautiful than I imagined she would be, Lily. And Mara. Her face has slimmed down, accenting her high cheekbones—she's the spitting image of our mother. *They've changed so much.*

Despite the urgency simmering in my stomach, I enter the room slowly and bow courteously. All three stand to return my bow. When my head tilts up, I stand before them in silence with nothing—no contacts or makeup—to veil my appearance.

My father pales, like he has just seen a ghost. He doesn't take his eyes off me. He reaches into his pocket, pulls out a handkerchief, and wipes his brow. Lily and Mara exchange a look. I'm not sure how to read it. Maybe Mara told them Phoenix resembles Jo?

I smile weakly, my hands trembling, waiting for them to recognize me, to say something. But they don't.

An impulse to run to them shoots through my veins, but my feet do not obey. For three days I thought about what I would say in this moment, but now it flies completely out the window. They don't know who I am.

Mara speaks first. "The interpreter?"

"We won't need one," I say to her directly in English, hoping my voice rings a bell. I walk closer, into the light. They still don't recognize my face or voice? Instead of just telling them everything that I planned, I move in as Phoenix. "Your loan has been granted," I say sharply. "You will have full funding for a year."

Mara gives me an uneasy look.

My father stands, though it's visibly difficult for him to do. His limbs shake. Once on his feet, his eyes meet mine. "Ms. Phoenix, I'm honored that you would grant us a super bond that takes weeks to get. Thank you for your generosity." His low rumbling voice causes me to turn away before an explosion of tears climbs up my throat into my eyes.

Mara cuts in. "There's been some mistake. A substantial amount was deposited into our account designated for iVision. I'm not sure how it got there or why. iVision disintegrated long ago. We applied with Xi He Construction. We have the money with us, to return it."

I don't answer. I'm not focused on Mara anymore but Lily. The innocence in her eyes breaks apart my façade. "You've grown up so much," I say to her. Is my voice shaking? I don't care if it is. Lily shifts in her chair uncomfortably, not knowing what to say. "Do you still play piano?"

"Yes." A cautious expression crosses her face. She sits up straighter, then adds, "Actually, I was recently accepted into a very prestigious high school for the arts."

"I always knew you'd be great. What about you, Mara?" I ask, turning to her. "Still sailing?"

My staring makes Mara uncomfortable and she stiffens. Our conversation three days ago no doubt set her on edge. As well as the mysterious money deposited in their account and the fact that I didn't answer her question. She clears her throat. "From time to time."

My father interrupts. "Excuse me. How do you know about *i*Vision?"

"I know a lot of things," I say. "You started it because you believed in people. You believed in fixing things. Even the creaking stairs in your beach house. They drove you crazy until you fixed them." I step closer. "You'd watch Professor Q with your daughters every Sunday. Your wife was named Candace. When she died, you could barely keep it together. You'd stay in your office late at night and weep." I turn to my sisters. "Tails, your cat, was gray. Is he still alive? He loved to sleep in the bay window facing west. Lily, you loved sleeping with him until your mother died. You said the nightmares scared him. I actually hoped you'd kept sailing, Mara. You said you'd sail around the world to forget your pain…"

Their faces widen with confusion, surprise, and pain. Fear, too?

"I know a lot about you," I continue, "like what happened to your missing sister." I think back to my time in the Pratt when I buried them, the words I spoke then to my father, to Mara. "She forgives you, Mara. She doesn't blame any of you. It had to happen."

My hands feel heavy as they fall, like bricks, at my sides. The blood in my head and limbs drain into my stomach. My heart beats violently in my chest. Dizziness sets in. I steady myself on the wall.

Lily covers her mouth. Mara gasps out loud.

"How?" my dad asks, tears filling his eyes. He's moving towards me so fast he knocks his chair aside.

"It's me," I say, barely a whisper. "It's Josephine."

After three hours of tears, and a couple more hours filling in the blanks of the missing two years, I still haven't mentioned the loss of my math gift.

My blubbering about Madame, King, and the Pratt, and the crash and how much I missed them, how I never thought I'd see them again, how I thought they were dead, how Red changed me, and how Kai saved me, seem to be one long string, only interrupted with bursts of tears, tissues, and more crying.

My dad has not stopped hugging and kissing me, as if to make up for all the years he couldn't.

Mara hugs me too, so tightly I think she might have broken a rib. "I thought I'd lost you forever," she says. She tells me she loves me about a hundred times. "Can you ever forgive me?"

"I forgive you, Mara. I never stopped loving you."

"Can you ever trust me again?"

I grip her tightly as another sobbing fit threatens to start. I know rebuilding a relationship with my family won't happen overnight, but it will happen, and for my part, I won't hold anything back. "I'll start today."

Another hour passes and no one says it, but we're all thinking the same thing. We wish Mom were here. To have her arms entangled in ours. To hear her laugh and see her smile. I miss her so badly. It burns in places only time can heal. I know I'll always miss her, but I have my family back. I know she'd be happy we are all together again. She'd want me to treasure this time.

Lily touches my face and plays with my hair telling me how beautiful I am. It's good to have little sister adoration again. She fills me in about the high school and her new boyfriend, Mason. Then she pulls something out of her purse. It's a piece of old lined paper.

"Your speech," she says. "I've carried it with me everywhere."

I blink, unbelievingly. "Really?" I remember giving it to her that night at graduation. I take it from her hands, unfold it, and read the lines I wrote over two years ago.

SPEECH for graduation:

(Tell a joke first) I guess we've all been "counting" the days to graduation, huh? (laugh)

My name is Josephine Rivers and I'm up here because I count (laugh) …In the grander scheme of life, you count too. We all count.

(Serious pause)

A respected friend asked me once what I wanted to be remembered as when I died. A prodigy? A mathematician? I didn't know. So I thought about it. I remembered the old story of Alfred Nobel, known for the Nobel Peace Prize. He wasn't always known for that. It was a choice.

Before he became an ambassador for peace, he was the genius chemist who invented weapons, like dynamite, that eventually brought horror and pain into the world. As the story goes, his hometown accidentally printed his pre-written obituary, and he woke one morning to read about his own death in the newspaper. It went something like this, "Alfred Nobel, the merchant of death, has died." Alfred, who was clearly still alive, sat shocked in his chair, asking himself an important question. Did he want to leave a legacy of death and destruction?

Thankfully, he had a second chance to change the course of his life. To change his destiny, and the world, to be known for peace instead.

We all have this chance.

I don't believe in accidents. In my world of numbers there is no such thing as coincidence. We are all here at this time and this place for a purpose. Each day really does count. I have my gift and you have yours, and we, like Alfred Nobel, can choose how we use it. If I can use math, great, but whatever I do, I'm going to make every day count.

Let's count on each other to do the same.

Thank you.

I fold it into my pocket, smiling to myself. Somewhere, inside of me, my heart had been speaking all along.

FORTY-SIX
PRESENT: PHOENIX

SHANGHAI TOWER, SHANGHAI, CHINA

The Rivers family—it feels so good to say that—is starving. We are done crying for the moment and we want to eat.

I make arrangements to meet Chan and Kai and Dr. Ling for dinner. They have become my other family here. I want my real family to know them.

As I hail a taxi outside, my dad smiles as he watches me speaking Chinese to the driver. He always wanted me to learn Chinese. I usher them into the car.

Before he gets in, he looks up at the Oriental Pearl Tower. "Jo, my daughter the prodigy, ends up in China, working for the richest man in Asia and dating his son!" He lets out a big sigh and continues. "You'll never have another worry again."

Oh yeah. I forgot to mention the part about the J.J. Bond in which I have surrendered my share and losing my gift. We are in the car now, all squeezed together.

Not the best time to make this rather large confession. I decide to enjoy dinner and tell him when we get back to my villa in the French Quarter.

The evening is joyous. My sisters love Kai right away and by dessert he is teaching them kung fu holds. My dad and Chan talk business, scheming ideas for new companies together. Chan offers his family's country-side house for them to stay. Dr. Ling's kindness radiates, making them feel important, loved, and at home.

Someone else is here. Maybe in our conversation, or in Kai's face or Ling's soft voice, or just in my heart, but Red is with us, too. And he's rejoicing.

The night ends and we arrive home. With a cup of warm tea in our hands, I muster up the courage to talk to my dad.

"Um, Dad? There's a chance all of the money we're recycling into the economy will be drained."

"Yes, you mentioned something. And so?"

"So," I start, nervous. "After this recession is over, there's no telling if I'll even have a penny to my name."

"You've never had to worry about making money, Josephine," he says with a wink.

My father—more than Chan, more than anyone— knows what I'm able to do with money. *Was* able to do. But I can't do that anymore. I don't want him thinking I can. I want our new life to be built on something entirely new. I want Mara to know she has a normal sister now. That means I have no way of securing my family's future anymore. If I don't come clean now, it may be harder later. Will he be disappointed? Here is the real test. Where I learn how much they love me for who I am and not what I can do.

"I'm not a prodigy anymore," I blurt out.

Dad's and Mara's expressions go blank. "What do you mean?" Dad asks urgently.

"The numbers are gone. I can't calculate equations like before. I need a calculator, like a regular person," I say, looking at Mara. "Sorry, Dad, I wish I could work for your company again. Make your money back. Secure our future, but I can't. Not with math, anyway. But I promise to take care of you. After this year passes, we'll make an honest living. We will gain back everything we lost."

My dad just sits back and laughs.

"Dad, I'm serious," I say, wondering why he is laughing so hard. Maybe he's in shock? "I'll find a job. I'm still young. I've got to be good at something else."

He laughs harder. Maybe he thinks I can't do anything else? "Dad, why are you laughing? You always said I was worth more than a hundred and fifty million, right?"

"Jo, you are good at a lot of other things. And I can't wait to see you do them."

"So you're not upset that I can't make all that you lost back?"

"I have everything back. I have you back."

He's not making sense. Perhaps I'm a bit slower now that I don't have equations streaming through my mind in nanoseconds.

He tilts my chin up to meet his eyes. "Josephine, every dollar that you made for *i*Vision went into an account that only you can open. Your salary—or share if you will—never went into my pocket." This is the first I've heard of this. I search his face for more answers.

My father takes my hand. "The first time I watched you calculate investments that made millions, I made an important decision," he says. "I never wanted to look at you, my daughter, as a source of money and exploit your gift. I kept what we needed for the business and our family, but I put everything else into a private account under your name. I thought about telling you. But I never thought you were ready until..." He pauses, a sad expression on his face. That's what he was trying to tell me that day on the beach. "When I was investigated, they shut down *i*Vision but they couldn't touch your money."

"Didn't you claim the money when you thought I was dead?" I ask. He shakes his head.

"I never believed you were dead." He reaches for me. I bury my face into his chest. That same scent I knew long ago, that same embrace when I used to climb on his knee. "It's all yours. I never cared about the money, Jo. I cared about you. I spent everything I had trying to find you. I hoped against all odds you were still out there. And you were. I love you, Jo. You are all I ever wanted."

His words hit me like tidal wave, crashing over and over and over me. *I never cared about the money. I only cared about you. I love you.* My head feels heavy and light at the same time. I'm running on the waves and tide. I'm dancing on the moon. I'm flying between the stars.

Everything I did for him. Everything he did for me. It was all out of love.

Red was right. Love can't be counted or calculated. The more you give, the more it comes back to you. It increases where things like money can't and will remain even when the world doesn't. It has to be trusted, given freely, risked. I understand now. It's in love that we find our infinity.

Everything I thought I lost has been gained once again. Doubled even. I have *two* families now, *two* countries I call home.

My dad pulls me closer. I feel him tighten his grip. We stay like this for...actually I'm not sure. *A really long time.*

FORTY-SEVEN
PRESENT: JOSEPHINE

ALKI BEACH, SEATTLE, WASHINGTON

Misty salt air fills my lungs. Seagulls cry. Ferry whistles blow. I bend down to run my fingers through my ocean's cold grains. *I'm home.*

Kai and I meander along the beach, dodging the waves. My family waits for us up ahead at a small coffee shop for breakfast. Things couldn't be better. So why am I thinking of Celia?

Maybe because her trial is today in Beijing.

Since we arrived a few weeks ago, I've taken Kai to see my old house, my school, even the harbor where I was abducted. It's been painful and joyful, but most of all, healing.

Celia's threats still haunt me, but the ghosts of my past are fading. Maybe I'll never entirely be free of her, but I won't fear her anymore. I'll choose not to. Red taught me to focus on the light. *There's still good to be done*, he'd say. *You're not dead yet.* And he'd be right, as usual. I just don't know what or where or how to do it yet.

Kai leads me to a part of the beach where there are fewer rocks and gently pulls me to the ground. I scoot closer to him because he makes me feel safe, and today thoughts of Celia are particularly strong and there's a surging feeling in my gut. I've learned not to ignore that. I'm building up to tell him when I stop.

A boat sails around the bend. Suddenly I'm breathless and dizzy. I tap my knee, heart beating frantically.

"Kai," I whisper, hearing the tremble in my voice. "Madame will to try to escape after the trial. I know how she'll do it. We need to call Detective Hansen right now."

"How do you know?" he asks.

I don't move. I certainly don't blink. Silently, I lift my finger and point straight ahead.

The sailboat. It's not just a white vessel cruising the Puget Sound anymore. It is a blueprint of numbers and dimensions and angles and distance. Like riding a bike, my brain instinctively jumps into action—recording, connecting, predicting, theorizing. The vessel has a different name and it's a newer model, but I'll never forget its twin. The dimensions match that of Madame's schooner, *Secrets,* the boat that stole me away.

At the Expo, Celia told me twice she had "secrets". She'd wanted me to understand what she was planning. Now I do. In one complex string of equations all the possibilities and variables are knit together. I even see Detective Hansen's telephone number, which I'm going to call.

I can prevent this. This time, I am one step ahead.

"Jo?" Kai touches me on the shoulder.

When I blink the numbers vanish like a gust of wind. The white vessel sails out of view and the distance so clearly marked between us is merely waves now. I wait a moment, but the numbers don't return. I take out my cell phone and dial Detective Hansen.

As the phone rings, I ponder the brief reappearance of my gift. It could be a coincidence, but then again, I don't really believe in those.

EPILOGUE

Two months later
PRODIGY STEALTH SOLUTIONS,
SEATTLE, WASHINGTON

It's Monday—the most exciting day of the week now that my father has turned crazy protective on me. I'm on the University of Washington campus where I teach gifted high schoolers quantitative analysis—the only job that doesn't seem life threatening to my dad. I have just finished when my phone lights up with a number I recognize—not because of my gift. For this number I used my ordinary human brain to memorize it by simply rehearsing it over and over. It's Prodigy Stealth Solutions.

PSS started calling me months ago. And despite my father's strong objection to having anything to do with them, I haven't been able to stop thinking about their offers.

"Jo?" It was her again, Ms. Taylor, the short, plump, and extremely stubborn founder of PSS.

"You shouldn't be calling me anymore," I say with a tone that doesn't even convince myself. It was I who gave her my personal, unlisted number that only a few people have. "My father would kill me if he knew I was talking to you. You know I can't take the jobs you are offering me." A lump sticks in my throat like I've just swallowed a bowl full of sand.

Unlike the public, PSS knows my gift is unstable. It flickers in and out ever since China. But even without its unique twist, I'm still considered a math genius who now has business experience. The minute the news was released that I was alive, job offers started rolling in like restless ocean waves.

Most jobs don't interest me, but when PSS calls, it's like the chemical reaction when two substances bond. I believe I could do the job, believe I could help. But my father is intent on me rebuilding my life—*a normal life.* He's intent on keeping me safe. Forever. But *normal* is not what I want. *Purpose* is what I crave—safe or not.

"I'm not calling about a job," Ms. Taylor continues in her firm but gentle voice. "The kids in our tech department discovered something."

I'm silent but a spark of hope shoots through my chest as if I know what she'll say next.

"Can you walk over here?" she asks.

Ms. Taylor knows it's Monday, just like she knows I'll stop by. The PSS office is conveniently located in the Guggenheim Hall, the same hall where I teach math. Unbeknownst to my dad, I've gotten into the habit of visiting after I finish teaching since a few of my prodigy friends work there.

Even before I answer, my feet head that direction. "I'll be right over."

I glance down at my wrist. A watch—something I never needed before—replaces my old hairband. Before

I walk, I set the timer and map out the way to the PSS office in my mind—down three flights of stairs, at the end of the hall on the right. Each day, I try to simulate what my brain once did naturally.

I reach the last staircase when my phone rings again—not a number I recognize. I register the country code, +216, is for Tunis, Tunisia, but immediately afterwards it blinks, and the country code changes to +44—London, England. I don't know if I should pick it up when it morphs once again to New York. *What the heck?*

"Hello?" I say, with a boldness I forgot I had.

A robotically altered voice crackles through a line full of static. "Josephine Rivers?" a young male voice asks. The accent is unmistakably British with a hint of something else. Arab? Iranian? Swedish?

"Who is this? How did you get this number?" My body tenses, on guard.

"I got it the same way you would have before you lost your gift, *Double-Eight*."

My breath catches. It can't be possible. Is this stranger claiming to have the same gift as I did? Madame is the only other person on the planet who made that claim.

"You miss it, don't you? The way it defines the universe into beautiful, intricate paths." His voice is low. I can't decide if he is taunting me or not.

I should hang up, give the number to Detective Hansen to trace. But I don't because his statement pricks a sensitive place in me, and now I'm angry. He's dangling a carrot on a string before a starving horse. My mouth longs to take a bite.

"Whoever you are, I think you know the answer to that," I snap. Truth is, I've somewhat adjusted to living without my gift, but that doesn't mean I like it.

"Keep walking, Josephine. They're waiting for you. You still have 129 feet, which will roughly take you 1 minute and 32 seconds to arrive according to my calculations. Believe me, you'll want to hear what they have to say…"

"What do you want?"

"To warn you about your *boyfriend*. I'll be in touch." The line goes dead.

The room spins slightly, mimicking my thoughts. What does he know about Kai? How does he know about *Double-Eight*? I need to call Kai, Agent Bai, and Detective Hansen—certainly not my father. I'm about to dial Kai when the stranger's words return. *You'll want to hear what they have to say.* Ms. Taylor. She's waiting.

I run the remaining 129 feet arriving in the exact amount of time the boy predicted. I'm slightly shaking when I open the door to PSS.

Ms. Taylor's tiny 5'2" frame rushes from the back office. Her dark curly hair gives her another few inches. Behind her wide rim glasses, her eyes beam with excitement until she sees my pale face.

"Jo? Are you ok?" she asks. I redirect my focus to the wrinkles around her eyes. Surely, they represent years of scientific breakthrough. It's comforting.

I contemplate telling her but decide against it. "I'm fine," I say. "What was it you wanted to tell me?"

"We think we've found it." Her smile feels wider than my ocean.

"Found what?" I say.

She leans in close, taking off her glasses. "A way to get your numbers back."

DISCUSSION QUESTIONS

1. What names were given to Josephine throughout the book? What was the significance of each one?
2. What does the ocean represent to Jo? What important moments in the book take place on a beach?
3. Jo speaks multiple languages and changes her appearance frequently throughout the book. How does this reflect what is going on inside of her? Consider what Red tells her: "Destiny is not what you do. Destiny is who you are. Everything flows from who you are, then folds into everything you do."
4. Red tells Josephine, "Orphans dream of vindication. Sons and daughters dream of destiny." How do the changes Jo experiences throughout the novel reflect this?
5. How does Jo's gift with numbers shape the course of her life? What causes her to lose her gift? What will it mean for Jo to no longer have it?
6. Madame is a villain but also has a tragic past. What do Jo and Madame have in common, and how are their paths different? How does knowing Madame's past shape Jo's feelings toward her?

ACKNOWLEDGEMENTS

Publishing your first book is a big deal and if I were to thank every person who impacted Calculated, this section would be impossibly long...but here's my best shot.

First, I'd like to thank my agent, Amy Jameson, who didn't just sign me for my books, but believes in me as an author and person. Thank you for all the hard work behind the scenes, taking my calls and letting me process with you, and going ALL IN whenever I needed you. You're amazing.

Second, many, many thanks to Wise Wolf Books and the Wolfpack team—Rachel Del Grosso, my publisher, Mike Bray and Paul Bishop, Lauren Bridges, and my cover designer, Cherie Chapman. This team is a force to be reckoned with—your confidence, enthusiasm, hard work, and innovation is inspiring and has pushed me to the next level. Thank you for taking a risk on me and my books, for believing in the Calculated series–and championing it as your lead title for the imprint. I'm honored and blessed.

Thanks to the Chengdu Crew. This book would not have been written without your encouragement and support. Katie Wong, my first writing partner in Chengdu, thank you for spending hours brainstorming things like how many gold cities we could find on the world map, lol. Garrett Jones, you spoke life to this book and my writing dream every time I saw you for years—your encouragement was priceless. Thanks to Sarah Zhang, Erin Humphrey, and Rebecca Woo-Krauss who read and edited, sometimes the whole book in a day because I needed feedback asap, then read it again—I'm overwhelmed by your devotion and kindness. To all of my favorite Ladies in Chengdu & around the world—you know who you are. You never stopped believing in this moment. This is a team victory. To the Bowens—you supported me in countless ways and loved on my kids so I could finish this book.

Bethany Zhu, I never forgot that day you told me I should write a book about China—we never thought it would be fiction. Surprise! Your words meant more than you can imagine. Shuai Huan Huan, Annette Hu, Giulia Zhu, and Jacob Chen, Vivian Wen, Lisa Zeng, Aygul, Guzal J. and Zorigul Y. —my best Chinese friends who loved me, and took me into their homes, lives, and hearts forever. You changed my life by giving me your friendship. This book wouldn't have been written without you.

To my countless Chinese friends and students. I can't possibly name you all. You taught me about your language and culture, taught me poems, how to cook chuan cai, and took me places that I could have never found on my own. You gave me the riches of China, along with friendship and belonging.

Thank you to Master Li Quan—your dedication and passion for training the next generation in the true art of traditional Kung Fu is inspiring.

Thank you to my Chinese reader & writer friends—Jenny Xu, Dan Ge, Annette Hu. Your insight was invaluable.

Thank you to my PitchWars community—you changed my writing life. To Pintip Dunn, who chose this book, nurtured it, and gave it a chance to succeed in the world. To my 2016 Pitchwars clan who encouraged me for years, and to those of you who read Calculated, critiqued & endorsed it —Tara Creel, Amaris Glass, Rachel Griffin, Ernie Chiara, Adalyn Grace. Special thanks to Brenda Drake—I've been so blessed by your support.

Thanks to Ellen McGinty and Lorie Langdon—your support, wisdom, laughter, encouragement, and feedback are gold. I adore you both.

Thanks to the KidLitNet community— Elizabeth Van Tassel, Kara Swanson, Chelsea Bobulski, Shannon Dittemore, Mary Weber—you've been a great support during Calculated's launch.

Thanks to the Spinning Pen gang, my dear friends and early readers—Kim Vandel, Kathleen Freeman, Jenni Claar, Rebecca Henry, Jessica Jade, Doris Fleming, Michelle Tsang, and Hilary Bowen-Magnuson. Thank you for loving this book! To Dana Brown, Candace Mieding, Abigial O'Bryan, Katie Wong, Caleb Robinson, thank you for pursuing this writing dream with me. (Now I'm waiting for your books.)

Big thanks to everyone on my Street Team for the Calculated launch! You are the best!

Thank you to the Cyborons, Lundquists, our Calvary community in Kenai, and the entire Westgate family— you've been SO supportive as this book was birthed. Thanks to the Decker family, who let us live in their guesthouse where Calculated was conceived and outlined!

Thanks to the London-Pakistan Crew, Uncle Zafer, Saira Peter and Stephen Smith, who spoke confidence to my writing dream. To James and Dolly, your faith and generosity inspire others to achieve the impossible.

Thanks to my wonderful in-laws, Diane and Terry, (and the whole McBee clan.) You go above and beyond for your kids and their dreams, even flying to multiple countries!

A huge thanks to my parents, Richard and Hellen, you gave your kids every chance to explore, create, or make a mess—no matter what we did, you always believed in us. Dad, you were the first reader, storyteller, and writer in my life—you gave me the gift of creativity and showed me how to work hard. Mom, you taught me not to fear and if I had a dream to pursue it. Thanks to my big brother, Isaac, for always dreaming big with me. To my sister Olivia & brother in law, Ishmael—true team players—you fought for this book as if it was yours and your support was deeply heart felt. To my sister, Leanne, an amazing creative force running at my side, thanks for always believing in me.

Thanks to my three little wild things—for loving my stories, for patience as I wrote, and for believing in this moment before it happened.

Biggest thanks to Ira, my husband and best friend. You read Calculated a hundred times because I asked you to, you listened to every new plot twist and idea, gave amazing feedback, but most of all you gave me your unfailing love and support. You never doubted this book and when I did, you got me back on track and did everything possible for me to get it done. The backbone of this book belongs to you.

And to the one who inspires my greatest adventures and wildest dreams, the one who gives me the strength, creativity, and faith to do them. Jesus, you are my infinity.

ABOUT THE AUTHOR

Nova McBee is a hopeless nomad and culture nerd who has lived and worked in Europe, the Middle East and Asia. She speaks multiple languages, including Mandarin, and lived in China for more than a decade writing books and teaching English and Creative Writing to teens and adults. She thrives on complex plots, adventure, making cross-cultural connections and coffee. She currently resides in the beautiful Pacific Northwest with her husband and three children.